T0191433

The
CUP

THE MADIGAN CHRONICLES
BOOK FOUR

Marieke Lexmond

ACKNOWLEDGMENT

Thank you, readers, for going on this magical ride with the Madigan Family and me. In this book, the world is expanding. I enjoyed working on Luna and Freya's relationship. To delve into their shared history and develop their characters was fun! This book will take you all the way to Greenland. I had the pleasure of shooting a documentary, "A Greenland Story," there in 2019. It made such an impression on me. It has been delightful to integrate that special place into my world.

Much gratitude to my friend and artist Nicole Ruijgrok for designing these stunning tarot cards! The series wouldn't be the same without you. A special thanks to Yvonne Borgogni and Charlotte Crocker for your support and help! Grateful to my test readers, April Kelley, Annemieke Klarenbeek, Annette Beil, and Karen Karlovich, for their honest assessments. A hearty thanks to my mother, Ria Lexmond-Wooning, for enabling me to publish this book. And my publicist Tracy Lamourie for her enthusiasm and help, you rock!

Once again, BookBaby did an amazing job designing and publishing the book!

And my husband, Jeroen Hendriks, for his unwavering belief in my skills and for always pushing me to my limits! That is where the magic happens.

Happy reading!!

Marieke

TABLE OF CONTENTS

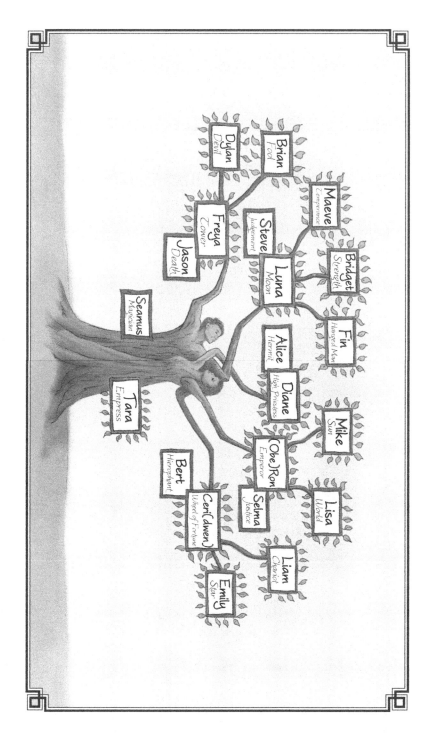

FAMILY TREE

PROLOGUE

A FORGOTTEN TIME AGES AGO

Colel's bronze skin shimmers in the sun. She's in her early twenties, her short frame is stocky, and her long dark hair hangs like a curtain down her back. A big sigh escapes her while she absentmindedly pets her friend who brought her here. The big Griffon snuggles up to her to give her comfort. They're on top of one of the highest mountains on the planet. Even though it's the middle of the summer, being so high up gives her goose bumps. The cold wind is blowing and her feet, planted in the snow, start to numb. The Griffon's body heat gives her enough protection but it looks like she won't be staying long anyway. This was her last option. To reach this portal, you must have wings, which had kept alive the tiniest sliver of hope that maybe this one was still open. Because of its difficult location, this portal was mainly used by creatures. Since the Fates had closed the ways between the worlds during the great divide to save the species from themselves, Colel has been searching for her sister Eztli. For over a year, she has visited every portal she could remember. As the witches of their village, it was part of their responsibility to travel regularly to the different dimensions to learn and to gather supplies to help the village survive the battles and fierce rivalry with the other settlements. When the Fates threatened to intervene in the societies in order to maintain the integrity of the species and the uniqueness of each world—nobody believed them. The dimensions and creatures were destroying each other. Not that anybody could even remember how it all started… they lived in balance and harmony for a very long time. Hours before the Fates in fact closed the portals between the dimensions, they sent out a warning. Colel and Eztli had split up, hoping to save time as they tried to take care of some urgent needs. Colel made it back in time, but Eztli never came home. Colel couldn't even reach her through their twin bond. They always had—and that means always—been able to do that. Now it was an empty void. In her heart, Colel knows Eztli is stuck in Fairy.

Tears escape her as her last hope of finding a working portal is dashed. She takes one last look over the land below. The mountain range with its snowy and granite peaks, the slopes are disappearing into a thick forest for as far as the eye can see. The world has calmed down, and parts of the forest are regenerating. Humans are recovering, and the few creatures that still live among them will not be able to go home either. The Griffon licks the tears from her face.

"I know. We should go." In one last desperate attempt to reach her sister, she throws out her witch sense. It rushes down the hills and ripples through the forest like a stone thrown in a pond. But her sister doesn't answer.

CENTURIES LATER

Colel has reached extreme old age, and she now feels her time has come. She had outlived many generations due to her mixed blood. Her parents were part-fairy, mermaid, and had a touch of something demonic. With her last breaths, she moves deeper and deeper into the forest. Readying herself to return to the earth. Every now and then, she stops to catch her breath and to smell the musky scent of the moss and ferns. It is calling her home. Gosh, she can't wait. All those years, she never gave up trying to find a portal that still worked in the attempt to reach her sister. Unable to have children, her existence had been incredibly lonely. Her many gifts had always set her apart from the others, even though she kept them safe and healthy. The hole left by her twin was never filled, and it had become a dark place.

Unable to go any further, she decides that this is the spot. Carefully, she lowers herself to the ground and sits with her back against a giant tree. Opening her witch-self to her surroundings and letting her life force seep into the ground. Her mind wanders, fading into the deep when she senses something pulling her back. Something she hadn't felt in a very long time. Colel wants to pass over, but the pull is too strong; she struggles to open her eyes. A shock runs through her. Only a foot away is her twin Eztli, not a day older than when they got separated. It must be a dream.

"Oh my Goddess, it is you!" Eztli's melodious voice pulls her further back from the brink.

"Is that really you?" Colel rasps.

"What happened? I was not even gone one moon cycle!" It's a rhetorical question as they both know what happened. Something that had always been one of the dangers of going to Fairy. Time could run differently there.

"How? I tried everything." Colel's voice is barely a whisper.

"We were able to repair one portal. I came as soon as I could." Eztli's eyes are brimming over. This can't be happening to them. Of course, she noticed immediately that earth had changed a lot since she got stuck on the other side, but never ever had it occurred to her that centuries might have passed.

Colel feels her life slipping away. There's no time to waste. Her elven ring, given to her by her father on his deathbed, taught her a lot. Family history is embedded in it. The ring separated from her hand, a definite sign of her transition. Gently she takes it off and reaches for her sister's hand. No longer able to speak, Colel uses her mind to connect to her twin. Now Eztli is right there; it is as if they have never been apart. Eztli looks at the wrinkled hands that are trying to put the ring on her finger. Her father's ring. Right, her parents must be long gone if Colel is this old.

"Quiet and listen," Colel orders her.

"I can give you energy," Eztli starts an incantation.

"It's too late for that. You have to let me go."

"Noooooo. Don't leave me."

"I have only minutes left. Listen. This ring holds our family legacy, history, and knowledge. It's a combination of fairy and demon magic. It is up to you now to keep the family alive and strong. Remember us. I couldn't have any children. There is no

one for you here. The human race is dwindling. Go back to where you came from. Survive. And remember, our abilities blossom when we mingle with others."

With fascination and horror, Eztli watches as the ring becomes one with her hand. When she looks up, her sister is gone. She screams, and a wave of grief escapes her. Colel's old and frail body is already being absorbed by the earth, the power that has fortified them for so long. Sobbing loudly, Eztli throws herself on the ground and lets this tremendous loss take hold of her. For hours, maybe even days, she just lays there until her thoughts make sense again. The ring is urging her on. She must keep their legacy alive—their bloodline. 'Blood'; that's what her name means. Had her parents foreseen this?

Two of Wands

PART 1

TWO OF WANDS "DOORWAY"

"There are things known and there are things unknown,
and in between are the doors of perception."

—ALDOUS HUXLEY

GREENLAND, THE NORTHERN TIP CAPE MORRIS JESUP

A whistling wind races over the white landscape. The snow pushed forward by the wind forms a thin layer racing over the ice sheet, which covers some of the oldest rocks on the face of the earth. This far North, temperatures are already way below freezing in late September, and there's only a limited amount of daylight. The fall equinox has passed, and soon enough, this place will enter the four months of darkness. It's hard to imagine that anything can live here.

An arctic stoat sticks his head out of a little hole. With his white coat, he blends in with his surroundings. He quickly scans the surface and takes stock of potential food and predators. After a second glance, he jumps out and turns some somersaults, his black-tipped tail whipping back and forth. His tiny frame is agile, as his weight is slightly over a pound. Salik is overjoyed to be back in Greenland. He had missed it a lot, the ability to shapeshift into his other self as often as he wants to. To go hunting, running, the feel of the snow and ice between his paws. This is his home; it's where he belongs. His family had settled here several generations ago, witches from America who had fled with a powerful elemental object 'The Cup of Plenty' in the hope of keeping it safe. They eventually found their way to this remote island, Greenland, which, in those days was very hard to reach. Eager to fit in and make a life for themselves, they immediately began trading with the local people. In time, his great-great-great-grandmother fell in love and married an Inuit shaman. It's always surprising what can happen if you mix magical talents. Their family developed shapeshifting. Many generations later, it had become as natural to them as walking—the ability to change at will, as often as they wanted. As always, being different makes you stand out, and so, to keep the Cup and themselves safe, they moved further and further up North until they reached the most Northern tip of Greenland, where people rarely venture.

Salik is sent out to sniff the air; the family has been buzzing with unrest. Something is going on with the other elements, putting his mother Snowflake, and Granny Laakki on high alert.

He doesn't see any reason to worry. This place is far away from everything! Extremely hard to get to, let alone find, and the Cup is in the safest place imaginable. Their magical safety net is strong with a mix of witch wards and modern technology. Nothing gets past that! They should relax.

Salik is in the middle of another somersault when a loud crack draws his attention. He lands on all fours and tries to determine where the noise came from. Quickly, he puts his ear to the ground—the ice beneath it is rumbling. Something is making its way straight toward him. The air is charged with electricity, and his fur stands straight up. Shit!

Another loud crackling noise, closer this time. Is the ice breaking? That's not possible; they're not on an ice shelf. Something hits their magical barrier right then, and the perimeter lights up with a flash. Discharging some of that built-up energy into the air.

For a split second, Salik can't think. He's in full panic mode; all he wants to do is run. Then his years of magical training burst through his mind-numbing fear. It takes only a second to transform into his human self, and now he is standing upright, fully naked, with his dark hair flapping wildly behind him. He thrusts his hands forward and pulls up an additional shield while simultaneously sending out a probe to the danger ahead. He needs to know what he's dealing with. The cold doesn't seem to bother him, and he runs toward the edge of their parameter. Something is chipping away at their shield. It won't be long before it creates a magical hole to come through. He can't let it reach their home. With one hand touching the ice and the other reaching for the sky, he starts an incantation in the hope of capturing the spell sent here. The wind begins to form a feeding funnel while the cold adds power from the ice cap below. Just as the spell finds a way in, he drops his shield. The spell is attracted to the magic in front of it.

"SALIK, NO!" he vaguely hears when the spell hits him with such force that he gets thrown tens of feet back, the spell and his protection shattering in a million pieces of ice glass, which pummels his face and body. His hair turns from solid black to pure white from the sheer force.

His mother, Snowflake, reaches him first, followed by the rest of the family. They are alarmed by the parameter wards. Salik is lying unconscious on his back, blood dripping into the snow from many tiny wounds, the red in stark contrast with the white. The ice is cracked in the form of a lightning bolt as far as they can see. However, Salik did manage to negate the spell.

LONDON

A loud laugh escapes Lucy Lockwood, a prim-looking elderly woman in her seventies, while she admires the result of her spell. Finally, a breakthrough! Too much had gone wrong lately in her pursuit of the elemental power objects.

There are four magical objects in the world that rule the elements. Several centuries ago, four sisters had separated the Cup of Plenty, which governs the power of Water. The Wand of Wisdom—Fire, the Dagger of Consciousness—Air, and the Pentacle of Growth—Earth. The temptation and combination of powers had grown too strong for the group of witches guarding it. Running out of options, the sisters pledged to keep it safe and hidden, and each of them went their own way. While their families grew, they passed on the duty to their eldest daughters. Lucy's family guarded the Wand of Wisdom, representing the power of Fire. When her mother decided that the responsibility of the Wand should go to Tara, Lucy's twin, Lucy tried to grab the power for herself. She was young and foolish and got banned from the Madigan family.

It had taken her till recently to locate one of the other families and to steal the Dagger of Consciousness, the power of Air. But her do-gooder sister and her brood got involved! Lucy can still sense the loss of the Dagger. The crater of absent power it left behind when Maeve, one of Tara's granddaughters, managed to sever her link to the Dagger and attune herself to it.

Even her son Set abandoned her and threw her out of his home; she traveled to London. It has always been one of her favorite places. With the witch history here, it's undoubtedly the place to find some answers.

Luckily, one of her friends is out of town and has offered her the use of his home. A dark witch with a sound library and an inspirational workspace down in the basement. A witch circle is embedded in the century-old stone floor; candles illuminate the dungeon, and Lucy's eyes are still adjusting after the flash of light from negating the spell. She created a spell that targeted the elemental power of Water in the hope it will point her in the direction of the Cup, and it had hit home. Not necessarily THE place where the Cup is but an area with an exceptional amount of Water energy. A perfect starting point. Slowly, a form etched into the floor comes into focus. A lightning bolt points roughly to the northern part of what looks to be an island. She can't wait to discover which island it is as it doesn't look familiar to her.

Stiffly, she gets up and walks the circle backward to release the protection before she can grab her phone and take a picture of the form on the floor. No doubt Mara has no trouble finding out where this is. She's so savvy on a computer. Lucy stops; how could she have forgotten! Mara and Cal, her grandchildren, are still in Fairy. Most likely captives of Mab, the Queen of Fairy. In all these years, she had been a master at compartmentalizing. That she abandoned her grandchildren to save herself is something she had resolutely stuffed away. Not that she cared much about her grandson Cal, but Mara was a talented young witch and had been great company the last couple of years. Not willing to admit that she missed her and might even feel bad about it, she moves on to the problem at hand. Hmmm, should she ask Set? That idea is dismissed as quickly as it came up. With a big sigh and a flick of the wrist, she extinguishes the flames as she exits the room. She must figure this out herself; it can't be that hard! The island looks pretty big.

NEW ORLEANS

Tara Madigan, the family's matriarch, a much relaxer-looking version of Lucy but unmistakably her twin, sits behind her desk in her bedroom, staring into the garden. Her happy place. After Seamus disappeared again out of his magical portrait, she couldn't bear to face it all the time and decided to rearrange her room. The picture gave her much comfort since his passing. Defying the Fates, refusing to pass through to the afterlife, he had inhabited one of his magical paintings and kept her company. Not able to talk, but at least they could see each other; to see his smile every day, his compassionate eyes…. Seamus had disappeared for a long time when Cal, Lucy's grandson, used Seamus' card from the Magical Tarot Deck. The young man must have used it again since the portrait remains empty. When these magical cards are used, you get pulled from your current life, which for Seamus is his painting.

Currently, the garden manages to distract her from the loss of the power of the Wand. Just a little bit, though. It never occurred to her that passing on the Wand of Wisdom to her granddaughter Bridget would have such an impact on her. The empty feeling is almost unbearable. Her mother died very soon after she had transferred the power to Tara. Will this happen to her now? The emptiness sucking the life out of her?

Too many gloomy thoughts for this early in the morning. Maybe she should see what this day brings. She shuffles her favorite tarot deck with practiced hands and pulls a new card of the day. The Two of Wands, two wolves are carrying a stick toward a smoldering fire in the foreground. Working together, a doorway. A good card, wands are cards of action and movement.

She can see this card working in Bridget and Maeve, her granddaughters and fraternal twins. It was a surprise to find out that Maeve is a Siren. That she could keep that hidden for such a long time is unbelievable. The real shock came when the girls tried to move the Dagger of Consciousness to keep it safe from her own twin Lucy, and it had transferred its powers to Maeve. After eight generations, two of the elemental objects are back in one house, and the energy is palpable for everyone. Their twin bond amplifies the powers even more, and they have become scarily powerful. Bridget and Maeve are working with the ancestors for a month now, gaining more control. But Tara finally understands why so many moons ago, the four sisters, on that fateful night, had decided to separate the elemental objects and sworn never to bring the four elements together again.

Doubt starts to creep in about the wisdom of her choice of Bridget. Wouldn't it have been better if she had kept it a little longer? And what if—what if she would have let Lucy keep the Dagger? All this fighting would not have happened, and the family would still have lived in peace. A dangerous train of thought, as Tara knows all too well that her twin Lucy had no honorable intentions with the power of the Dagger and probably wouldn't have been satisfied with one element. Lucy has always been ambitious and has an insatiable hunger for power. This was simply the only way, but where is this all going? Her vision of the future is clouded. She's never been a great seer, but a hint or a glimpse of the future would always be there. Now there's only fog. Her brain is mush; she's just a useless older woman. Here she goes again, down the road of dark thoughts. Time to make breakfast. If she's lucky, Maeve will have made something, but the days that her granddaughter would bake and cook all day are over. She's now occupied with her studies about Air. How to wield and control its power, learn more about the family history, and make plans to try to anticipate what comes next. Because this is all far from over.

Stiffly, she gets up and makes her way down to the kitchen, the heart of the house. The welcoming smell of baked goods reaching her before opening the door is promising. Maybe Maeve did decide to bake today.

When Tara steps in, it's not Maeve, but Emily, offering Wes a muffin.

"Well, what do you think?" Emily looks at Wes full of anticipation while he takes his first bite. A big smile grows on his face, and with his mouth still half full, he manages to say, "It's delicious!"

"As good as Maeve's?"

"Absolutely!" he reassures her.

Seeing the happiness on Emily's face warms Tara's heart and snaps her out of her dark mood. Wes, Bridget's boyfriend, has been such a gift to the family. His playful nature reminds her of Seamus, and his bright spirit is a great help in making the house a home for the family again. Somehow that had slipped away after Seamus died, but that changed ever since Wes came here with Bridget and her dogs. He's an artist and is painting away in Seamus' atelier.

Wes is also the only one who has been able to comfort Emily. The young girl has been through so much in the last couple of months. They all have been. But it has been particularly hard on her.

When Ceridwen, Emily's mother's fairy powers were awakened, they transformed her. The wild magic changed Ceri so much that she and her human husband separated. Ceri and Liam, her son, now live in Fairy. Emily, however, turned out to be more witch than fairy and, much to her dismay, must live with her father. However, Emily spends most of her time here at the Madigan Family home. When witches are in puberty, their gifts emerge, and it's necessary to learn how to handle those. As her father is merely human, the family is where she needs to be.

A loud popping sound snaps Tara out of her reverie. Only now does she become aware of the octopus creature quietly sitting at the end of the table. Perfectly still, if it weren't for the weird sound of his synapses being pulled off the table's surface. Cephalop is a fairy and came back from Fairy as Emily's bodyguard. He gives Tara the creeps. His strange appearance and an octopus-like form give him a deceptively friendly vibe, but behind those watery eyes is a sharp mind and nothing escapes his notice. He seems to possess a vast knowledge of Fairy and this world. He makes her uncomfortable.

"Cephalop, how are you doing? Any news from Fairy?" Tara tries to sound casual.

"Nothing, Mistress Tara," is his smooth reply.

Unable to come up with more conversation, Tara reaches for a muffin. When she bites down, the taste explosion brings an instant smile to her face.

"Wow, Emily. Maybe even better than Maeve's! Where did you learn to bake like that?"

Emily beams, "Maeve has been teaching me; she told me that I'm now in charge of the kitchen."

Well, well, that might turn out to be an excellent idea. This girl got a knack for baking!

Far back in the garden, inside the family tomb, Bridget and Maeve sit in a protective circle, each at the corner of their element. Since they acquired the elemental powers, they have spent half of their day in the tomb honing their skills as witches. At first, Bridget was sorely behind, but no longer. The sisters have both grown into their power and studied the lore and the family history in depth. The other part of the day they try to spend apart. To keep from mingling the elements.

The tomb is larger on the inside than you would expect upon entering it. Magic has extended the room, and this is the Madigans' ritual space. Their safe haven. Tombs of their ancestors, all of whom have held the Wand, form a circle around the middle. A well-worn altar is placed at its center. The wax dripped down from many years of burning candles, forming obscure shapes on the floor. Stone hands hold torches that light the area, and their shadows flicker eerily on the walls. Not as unnerving as the three skeletons sitting on one of the tombs. Their bodies have withered away, but they stay present to help the next generations of the Wand. It's a scary sight at first, but the Madigans have grown up with them and are no longer bothered by this morbid sight. Agnes, Molly, and Megan are cheering Bridget and Maeve on. However, these old ladies can go from cheeky onlookers to scary teachers in a split second.

The girls have sprinkled the boundary of their protective ritual circle with salt this time. Bridget sits on the south side of the circle. The home of the power of Fire. Sitting cross-legged with her arms spread to the side, she looks straight at Maeve while flames steadily flow up above each hand. Maeve sits in the same position on the east side of the circle, the home of Air. Above her hands, little tornados have formed. The girls stare at each other, which is unnecessary as their twin bond is fully restored and stronger than ever. Their capability to reach each other through mind communication is uncannily easy these days. The possession of the elemental powers has heightened their magical skills and solidified their special connection as twins. They always know where the other one is, even if they are shielding. This is one of the things they have been working on the hardest. They understand the importance of keeping the elements separated. The draw of power is ever tempting. Even though they have made significant progress, there's still much to learn. In today's exercise, the ancestors want them to combine and separate the powers again. If they can do that, they are indeed in control.

"NOW," shout the ancestors in union.

Bridget flicks her wrists, and the two flames merge, suspended in the center of the protective circle. A split second later, Maeve does the same; her tornados also join and flow as one around the flame.

"Well done!" Agnes croaks.

The girls relax, just a little—which lets the tornado fan the flame and quickly grows out of control.

"No, no, NO! Rail it back in!" shouts Molly.

Bridget scrambles up and furiously waves her arms while reciting something in an ancient language. Maeve is lying on her back doing more or less the same thing. Their efforts do nothing for the growing flame; their powers complement each other and, once combined, are not easily separated. The perimeter of the protective circle is the only thing stopping the roaring flame. But this presents a new problem. Their circle is quickly filling up with Fire and Air; they must take control, or they will be consumed.

"Do something!" echo the desperate voices of the ancestors from the tomb.

"*We have to suck it in!*" Maeve urges inside Bridget's head.

"*What?!*"

"*You know. Draw it in and let it flow through us.*"

For a moment, Bridget flashes back to a memory of the first day she came back to the Madigan home, and she had seen Tara do that with all the anger directed at her during that family gathering.

"Right!" confirms Maeve.

When in the middle of performing magic, Bridget is still not capable of keeping a shield up.

"Whatever you're doing, HURRY!" pierces the voice of Agnes through their thoughts.

"Now," Bridget literally starts to pull on the power of Fire and tries to swallow it while Maeve drinks in the Air.

"Yes. YES!" Agnes seems to approve.

"Don't hold it in. Let it flow through!" adds Molly.

The Fire and Air are being absorbed into the Earth—dissipating. Exhausted, Bridget and Maeve fall back. "Wow! That was intense," Bridget says out loud.

"Control! Control at all times. We need to do it again," Agnes sternly tells them.

"I'm empty," Maeve says.

"Yes, let's try again tomorrow," Bridget agrees. "I need a shower." She's soaked in sweat from all that heat.

The ancestors sputter indignantly but let the girls go their way.

ICELAND, REYKJAVIK

It's already afternoon in Reykjavik, and Luna, Bridget and Maeve's mother, sits quietly on a bench overlooking the water. Iceland has been an experience so far. Reykjavik, a small modern city with its Scandinavian-style houses, manages to be both inviting and welcoming despite its somewhat cool exterior. There's a deep-rooted traditional way of living. Contact with fairies is normal here, which probably explains the number of portals on the island. Maybe her fairy sister Ceri knows more about that. Luna is still not used to Ceri's transformation, her wild powers, and otherworldly looks. Those emerald eyes shine with a knowledge alien to humans. It happened so quickly, together with all the stress about the Dagger of Consciousness and Tara's horrible twin Lucy. They haven't in fact had a chance to process it all yet, and Luna is dealing with plenty of problems of her own.

The gentle lapping of the waves against the rocks calms her down. Inside her, though, is a whirlwind. Not something she's used to. The last several months have been challenging. Good and bad things have happened. As Tara's most powerful daughter, she was always secure and confident in her abilities. But after the backlash from an unkept promise, her magical powers have weakened. She should have never promised Lucy safe passage in Fairy. Of course, she could have known that Mab would intervene. When a witch makes a promise, there are consequences when you break it. She's experiencing those consequences right now! Even though it wasn't her fault, she had made the promise, and when things didn't work out as planned, Luna got hit with the backlash. Her punishment, or that's how she sees it, is that her magic comes and goes, like the ebb and flow of water, and it has become unreliable. This scares her shitless. A witch relies on her magic, which has always been there for her, and now…involuntarily, she shivers. Thinking about her magic brings tears to her eyes. These days, she's uncommonly emotional too. Is that her insecurity or a byproduct of the magical shell that is embedded in her forehead? Immediately, her hand reaches up to caress the ribbed shell. It has been a month since her vision of the mermaid that put it there, but it still feels alien to her. The vision sent her here searching for the Berthelsen family, who guards the Cup of Plenty.

Luna is sure the Cup is not in Iceland. There are plenty of witches here, seemingly friendly and welcoming. Until you try to get information, they turn terribly tight-lipped. For several weeks she has been painstakingly making her way into the witch community, while Tom, her boyfriend, and Bridget's police partner, has been using his deductive skills to research.

The Berthelsen family had landed here from America but must have moved on. Moved on to where? That's the million-dollar question. They could be anywhere in the world.

The community is small, and it's clear she and Tom are not getting anywhere; they should have gone home. However, Luna can't face her family now.

Her fading magic makes her unstable. Desperate, she bursts into tears. The water seems to reach out to her. Tears flow freely; crying is all she's doing these days. She doesn't know how long she has been sitting there with her head in her hands when she feels a comforting arm slip around her, pulling her close. This only makes the tears flow even more.

Tom doesn't say anything. He just holds her until the tears dry up.

"I'm so sorry," Luna utters while she tries to wipe her face, her eyes still swollen. "I can't seem to stop anymore."

Tom gives her an encouraging smile. What more is there to say? They've talked endlessly about her problem. Tom is powerless to help her. He's a police officer and as far removed from magic as you can imagine. But he loves her so deeply; it pains his heart to see her so distraught. And now he has to tell her the bad news. "I need to go home."

"To New Orleans? Is it something with the girls?" Luna jumps up, ready for action.

Gently he pulls her back onto the bench. "No, my home, Boston. They want me to come back to work."

"Oh." Her face falls, and tears start to come again. "Oh, God." The tears spill over. "What am I going to do without you? Can't you stay?"

Tom gently pushes her away from him. "Luna. Luna! Look at me."

Finally, she looks him in the eye.

"This is not like you. You are strong and confident. Stop."

Luna wants to say something—

"No. You have to stop giving into this. Yes, your magic is wonky. Yes, it makes life harder. But you're not only about your magic. Maybe it's good for you to be on your own for a while. You need to figure this out. And I'm not helping. Maybe it is better that I leave."

Luna sits up straight. His words are like a cold shower. "You don't mean that."

Tom holds her face, "I love you. All of you! Witch or not. But you need to find your way back to you. This new you." His eyes dart to the shell on her forehead.

"Right." A big sigh escapes her. "I don't want you to go."

"I know…."

Luna centers herself—for a moment, she looks like the old Luna. "Are you ready to go back? Are you sure you're fully recovered?"

This makes Tom smile. "I think it's time. You figure this out," he waves his arm around. "All this magic mumbo jumbo, and then we will figure out how we can be together."

The genuine smile on Luna's face warms his heart. "I think I could get used to Boston," is all she says. Now, they are both smiling at each other like teenagers in love.

"Come, let's walk back. I've made reservations at our favorite restaurant." Tom pulls her up, and she hooks her arm in his while they walk back into town.

LONDON

Frustrated, Lucy snaps her laptop shut. Mara always makes it look so easy. Time for a glass of wine or something. She flips on the lights while she makes her way to the kitchen—the days are noticeably getting shorter. She turns on the light switch in the drawing-room and freezes when her eye falls on a globe—one of those old-fashioned ones on a wooden stand. Low tech might work better for her. Eagerly, she looks for the picture on her phone and slowly spins the globe, scanning for large islands. In the photo, it looks substantial. There's Iceland, totally the wrong shape! She rotates it some more, and when it comes to America, she turns it slightly back. Greenland! That can't be it? Is that even an island? She thought that it was part of Canada. On closer inspection, it is an island; more importantly, it's the island she's looking for. Her glass of wine long forgotten, she opens her laptop again and googles Greenland. She doesn't know the first thing about it.

FAIRY

Ceri Madigan, Tara's daughter, Keeper of the Land of Fairy, a responsibility inherited from her fairy father, sits in her study in her fairy home. Her emerald eyes are glimmering while she tries to follow what's happening right in front of her. It might be the fifth time she's replaying this specific memory. Fairies have a unique way of storing them. They encapsulate them in a globe form, which you can replay at any time. It's a three-dimensional experience, like you're in the memory yourself, with images, sound, and smells swirling around you.

This is the oldest globe she has found in the house—fairies of old are fighting with terrifying creatures. These fairies do not have the polished look they seem to possess now but are monstrous. The sky is bright orange, and the sun is purple. Not a place Ceri recognizes.

"Where is this?" she murmurs out loud, knowing that Sparkle, her fairy guide attached to her ear like an ear ornament, will understand the question is for him. By now, she's so used to him being there that it's hard to imagine not having his vast knowledge at her fingertips. It had taken a while before they found a comfortable way to work together. At first, it upset her to have a fairy attached to her all the time. But in the end, she hates to admit it, Felaern, her biological fairy father as she decided to call him, had made the right choice in providing her with a guide. Otherwise, she would have never survived this far.

"I don't know, My Lady," replies Sparkle in his ever-seductive voice. "This must be the dawn of time. Long before my or even Felaern's time."

"Fairies are known for keeping immaculate records. Do you think Mab has them?" suggests Ceri.

"Look at them! Those were barbaric times. I don't think there's much left from those eons."

"I want to know more about it," Ceri insists.

"Why?! There's so much more urgent stuff that you need to learn," Sparkle tries to pull her back to the matters at hand.

"My instincts, my dreams, my whole being lights up with this memory. I don't know why or how, but I haven't gotten this far by ignoring my gut."

"You're too impulsive," Sparkle counters.

"This has nothing to do with impulse. I want to know more. More about where fairies come from and what and how the portals work. Seamus would understand; he had an infinite curiosity about these kinds of things."

Sparkle keeps quiet. Ceri doesn't need to see him to know he's pouting. He's like that when he doesn't get his way.

Seamus, the thought of him sparks an idea in the back of her mind. It had been such a shock to see him at Mab's a couple of weeks ago during that horrible fight. She got over her initial irritation with him and worked through some of her issues. Seamus is the man who raised her. He encouraged her and helped her develop all her gifts. They had a special bond. He is her father in all things that matter. If only there was a way in which she could solicit his help with this. He would love this challenge.

Mab, Queen of Fairy and an all-around scary woman, is lounging on a couch in one of the smaller chambers in her palace. The air is buzzing with giant butterfly creatures that form endless patterns to amuse the fairies below. The light is dimly filtered through vines that form a dome overhead. It's slightly claustrophobic to be in a vined dome with others, but the room is just big enough, and there is a hint of a summer breeze that keeps the room cool. There are no regular seasons in Fairy, as there are on Earth. Here, the weather is more governed by the Queen's moods. Groups of Mab's subjects are scattered around the room having hushed conversations. None of them is near their Queen. Most of the time, it's best to leave her alone.

Today, Mab is wearing a tight body suit in her signature red and looking reasonably normal. Her wings are folded away, and her actual features are hidden behind her smooth, almost human look. Calculating her options, she takes stock of her inner circle in the room. There's only a tiny group in here, sporting red in their clothing, a sign that they're loyal. Her most trusted subjects.

Being the Queen of Fairy means you are constantly on your toes for others who would gladly knock you off your throne. That, however, is not currently her most significant predicament. Those Madigans have been a thorn in her side for long enough. Those girls are both attuned to an elemental power now. So, it might not be a good idea to go for a full-frontal attack. Their abilities must have grown and gained in strength. Mab had got a taste of that herself.

Not something she will forget anytime soon. Nobody attacks her in her home and gets away with it. Mab doesn't like to lose. For several weeks, she has been plotting what her next move should be. It's complicated now that Ceri, Tara's oldest daughter, is the Keeper of the Land of Fairy. Luckily, she still has much to learn about Fairy, and it's relatively easy to keep an eye on her. The one thing she has gotten out of all this is Lucy's granddaughter Mara. A highly gifted magical creature with a most exciting heritage of a witch and a voodoo queen, and she's positive she has a whiff of something demonic as well. Not as much as that young man, but it's there. That lady has potential. Time to put her to the test. After that, she will concentrate on the young man, Cal. He's uncooperative, undoubtedly because he has somehow attached that annoying witch Seamus to him. Mab wants to unravel that bond and then see if that young man truly has a backbone, and in the process, it would be nice to be able to punish that old man. Fairies' memories are worse than elephants; she remembers that he is the one who stole Ceri from her when she was still a baby. Never mind that Mab had stolen her from Tara first.

This is a problem for later; now, she needs to focus on Mara. The logical thing to do is look for the other two elements, Water and Earth. No doubt that's precisely what Lucy and Tara are doing. Let them do the work. After all, she has someone she can send on an errand for that. Time to test Mara's and Lucy's bond.

"Mara, my dear," Mab's melodious voice rings through the room. Instantly, everybody falls silent and turns toward the person this is directed at. Mara is seated quietly in a corner reading a book about fairy magic, the one thing that gives her any joy here. Ten years she had promised to Mab, ten very long years, an endless time, but if she can at least use it to expand her knowledge and abilities, not all is lost. Mab has a fantastic library, and she has free access to it. Until now, she has been devouring book after book and learning so many new things.

"Mara," Mab's voices urge her, a little more insistent since the young woman doesn't respond instantly.

Mara untangles her legs and gracefully makes her way to Mab, curtseying, "My Lady. Your wish is my command." Mara had been given strict instructions on addressing the Queen of Fairy.

Satisfied, Mab leans back, "It's time for your first assignment, dear."

Mara plasters a fake smile on her face to hide the uncomfortable feeling that is creeping up on her after this not-so-subtle insincere endearment.

"I'm ready…my Queen." This almost makes her throw up. Never in her life has she bowed down to anyone. Not even her Grandmother Lucy, a harsh teacher, who didn't tolerate disobedience, but Mara was her favorite, and Lucy always encouraged her to be confident and strong in her gifts.

"Am I right to presume you're up to speed on the Elemental Power Objects?" Mab cocks her head.

"Yes, Ma'am."

"Is Lucy looking for the Cup or the Pentacle?"

Mara hides her shock—shit, she obviously didn't think this through when she made this deal. She doesn't want to betray her grandmother.

"Well?" Mab slowly sits up straight.

"I don't know," Mara quickly answers.

Mab's catlike eyes become little slits. "Really? You think I believe that?"

Mara runs her options through her head. There's no good one. But she will not betray Lucy. "Yes."

"May I remind you that your grandmother didn't hesitate to abandon you here in Fairy to save herself? I didn't even experience an inkling of a rescue attempt. You and your brother were expendable in her eyes."

The butterfly creatures stop flying around and form a halo above Mab. "To save your sister, you swore to serve me for ten human years. Do you remember?" The smile on Mab's face sends shivers down Mara's spine. Nobody can instill fear in your heart like Mab. She starts to perspire.

"Do you need a reminder of whom you serve now?"

Mara swallows but still doesn't answer.

Mab casually glances at her wrist and the different tattoo-like bands around them. She locates the one she wants, looking Mara straight in the eye and licks her lips while touching the band. Instantly, Mara screams, a shock runs through her, and she falls to her knees.

"Right," Mab says as if this all didn't happen. "The Cup or the Pentacle?"

"The Cup," whispered Mara.

"That wasn't so hard now, was it?"

Mara shakes her head.

"I want you to go back to Earth and find Lucy. Let her lead you to the Cup. I'm sure she has done her homework. She's always been very resourceful, that one."

Mara looks around her, but the others conveniently keep their distance from her. "I'm not sure if Gran will let me join her."

Mab focuses on the tattoo again.

"But of course, I can persuade her," Mara quickly adds.

"My thoughts exactly. And don't forget. I can hear everything you say or do and then some." Mab winks.

Mara is unsure what to do next, but Mab has already turned away, dismissing her.

In another part of Mab's extensive palace, Cal sits in his prison. It's like he's inside a giant tree. It could be worse. He has a comfortable bed and decent meals three times a day. The only downside is that he can't go out. However hard he tries, it's like they have cut his magic off. It's there, but it's not there at the same time. Frustrating. The tree doesn't have a door. The fairies seem to enter through a different part every time they bring him something. Light comes in through the crown from between the branches, and the temperature is always constant. He has tried to build some makeshift stairs to climb out at the top, but whatever he put against the bark, the tree just grows taller. He used utensils to carve a hole through the tree's bark, also to no avail. And all the time, Seamus can easily fly in and out as far as his card parameter lets him float. The Magician card, depicting Seamus, from the Magical Tarot Deck, secure in his pocket. It's what keeps the ghostly witch attached to him. Until he has fulfilled his purpose, he will not be able to return to his normal life. Seamus had explained to Cal that he had refused to pass over after he died and instead was living inside an enchanted painting he had made himself when he was still alive, keeping his wife company. His upbeat and curious nature helps him making the best of any situation, so he's having a wonderful time. He loves Fairy and chatters on about it constantly.

"Can't you explain how I can reach my magic?" Cal asks him for the thousand times.

"Dear boy, if you can't sense your magic, how do you expect me to explain it to you?" Seamus twirls around above his head.

"You know me. You learned more about me than anybody after you possessed me. There must be something you can do?" Cal pleads with him.

"You could let me possess you again. I can get you out of here for sure."

"No. Never."

"That's what you said last time," Seamus teases him.

"Oh, come on. If you know how to get out, just tell me."

Now Seamus floats down and hovers right in front of Cal's face as if his ghost hands are trying to hold Cal's head between his hands. "Magic is in the heart. To get out of here, you need to want to be able to go home or to your loved ones more than anything."

Seamus doesn't need to say it out loud. Cal doesn't have anything like that to hold on to. His Grandmother has abandoned him in Fairy. His father doesn't care for him, and he has no home.

"I have that, though, so if we combine our skills, we can make it. It's the only way. We've been here now for how long, a month? You've tried, boy, you've tried." Seamus drifts up again, higher and higher, till he's gone. "You know my condition," his words floating down to Cal, leaving him all alone again with his thoughts. Seamus wants the impossible from him—to turn his back on his family.

Hopelessness is a familiar feeling for him. He had gotten acquainted with it very well while growing up in Lucy's home. She was never affectionate to him and, as it turns out, never taught him much either. Not about himself or magic. These last couple of months has been an eye-opener. Why does he still feel loyalty toward her while she has shown him none? Cal needs to take control of his own life. It turns out he's a talented witch after all. With the fire demon in him, he needs to learn stuff. And irritating as he can be, Seamus has been the only one ever to help him; that's what it means to have a friend. As he did save his life once already, he should trust him. Trust him enough to get him out of here? Like when he saved him from Vhumut, the fire demon, his grandfather…. Cal trusted his grandmother and look where he ended up. Abandoned in a heartbeat. All his life, he had done everything in his power to help her. It was never enough. Seamus is not his grandmother…. His instincts tell him to decide soon. Maybe, as a start, he should rely on his gut.

"That's a terrible idea. You will only piss Mab off even more!" Maeron sounds exasperated. He's Ceri's second in command, and she depends on his infinite Fairy knowledge and guidance.

Ceri lets her hand brush through the beautiful flowers in her garden, releasing some intoxicating fragrances while she turns toward him.

They've been walking in her garden behind her house. Felaern had made this sacred space thousands of years ago when he became the Keeper of the Land. The caretaker of everything considered Land and the creatures connected to it. Now, this role has been passed on to Ceri. It's a symbiotic situation; she nurtures the Land, and the Land feeds her. It made her fairy and witch powers grow exponentially. The garden surrounds the tree through which she can always connect to the land of Fairy.

Ceri is not ready to give in to Maeron just yet. His intimidating physique does not affect her. He's a fairy of the old days and pledged loyalty to her house.

He has become an invaluable friend, and she relies on him for navigating the Fairy court. Without him, she doesn't know what she would have done. She's known to be a risk-taker, and this plan could end up in her family's favor. The Madigan family, in this case, as she has two families now. The witches and the fairies. Ceri has never been a strategic planner; a more impulsive approach is her modus operandi. And more importantly, this could be a chance to work on that question of their origin. Her new obsession. "Mab will never be my friend, so why bother?"

"There's a difference between being her friend and pissing her off. There are still big holes in your knowledge. You can't afford to be challenged by her."

"Thank you for pointing that out," Ceri can't hide her irritation.

"You're welcome; always a pleasure," Maeron looks at her eagerly. "This is the right response, right?"

This makes Ceri laugh out loud. "Yes, perfect." The earlier irritation is forgotten. She has been trying to teach her fairy family irony or a bit of sarcasm, but it has been challenging. They're masters at evading and skirting the truth— in that sense; they tend to miss out on playfulness.

"Still, I might do it. I know it's dangerous, but I can't let this opportunity pass me by."

A sigh escapes the handsome fairy, "You will do what you want anyway."

"There's that." Winks Ceri.

"Did you ever consider that this young man, Cal, might not want to be rescued by you at all? He has held off your father's offers so far." Now Maeron comes straight to the point.

"I know. But Seamus wants to possess him. My method might be slightly less invasive for him."

ICELAND, REYKJAVIK

Luna hugs Tom tightly for the last time. He's about to check in for his flight to Boston. People are bustling around them, and even though it's a small airport compared to most American ones, it's a lively place, full of the upbeat feeling of people heading to places.

"I can't believe you're leaving me here all alone. I'm going to miss you," Luna says and immediately softens the accusation.

Tom laughs and kisses her again. "You'll be fine. Sort out that magic and get those local witches talking."

"Thanks, Sherlock. Easier said than done."

Tom looks around, "I've been meaning to say this, but I don't think you'll like it."

Luna stands up straight. Tom hesitates.

"Enough with the suspense. Just say it!" She simply needs to know now.

"Why don't you ask one of your sisters to come out and help you? It might be beneficial with both problems."

Luna about faces, "And whom am I going to ask? Diane is still a mess, Ceri is lost to us somehow, and the girls are busy learning to control their powers."

"You have another sister...," Tom quietly offers.

"Freya?!" disbelief shows on Luna's face, "you can't be serious."

"Everybody always gives her a hard time because she's so blunt. Maybe you didn't notice, but she's the one you can always count on in the end," Tom offers. His sharp observation skills have had everybody in the family pretty much figured out.

"We've never gotten along," Luna counters.

"You don't have to get along to work together. I work with people I don't like regularly," Tom shrugs.

Luna doesn't reply. Tom can see, though, that he has planted a seed. "She's a good person. Think about it." He gives her one thorough kiss and heads toward security. Once through, he turns around and sees Luna is still staring at him. With a final wave, he disappears into the crowd.

NEW ORLEANS

Eyes like two dark coals bear into Diane's, Tara's middle daughter. She is seated opposite Set in a protective witch circle. Around them, the world seems to be on fire. They have only eyes for each other while they build up the magic inside the circle between them. The red glow plays on her face; Diane has never looked so confident and in control. Little bolts of lightning start to discharge—

A moan escapes Diane; someone has touched her, pulling her away from her vision. She usually hates having visions, but the experience with Set has left her so confused. She doesn't ever want to see him again, but every vision she has these days are about them together, and somehow, she can't get enough of them. Again, someone shakes her lightly, and instead of waking up, she is pulled under into another premonition.

Freya, her eldest sister, is arguing. She stands in the kitchen of her own home. It's dark out, and moonlight shines on her. It's not a full moon yet, but it brightens the kitchen. "I'm not going to do it." A bell tolls between space and time. A signal that something significant is decided. Immediately, the vision changes to a bright summer day in the Madigan garden, but that's the only bright thing. The entire family is gathered around a pile of woven dried sticks. On top of it lays a body; Diane strains to see who had died, but it's blurred, and the vision doesn't let her see it. At the head of the pile stands Freya, in all black, her hair twisting in the wind. Tears stream down her face while she sings a haunting burial tune.

Diane is hurtled back to the beginning of the vision. Freya is on the phone again—

"Wake up! Diane, wake up!" Freya is shaking her. Diane has been screaming during the vision, worrying her. Over the last month, she had spent much time with her strange seer sister. Diane's ethereal looks and otherworldly glow make most people uncomfortable; she's the opposite of Freya's down-to-earth and straightforward disposition. They never had much in common or did things together. Diane's wife Alice still refuses to see her after a love potion has thrown Diane in the arms of Lucy's son, Set. That's why Diane is back at the Madigan home. Being the only one left, Freya has been taking care of her. At first, her sister had been too weak to do anything, and it took several weeks of magical and human remedies to get her back to normal. Whatever is normal for Diane. Her constant visions make it hard to keep her in the real world. Freya is all too aware of the danger of this number of visions. Diane should resist more; if she keeps going down this path, she will go insane.

Diane's eyes snap open, and her hands shoot forward and grab Freya's head between them. "Freya, I beg you to make the right choice when you get that phone call. If you refuse to do as asked, the consequences will be grave."

Diane lets go, but Freya stands frozen in place. This is freaking her out, big time! Diane rarely tells anybody about her visions; in all her years, she had never said anything to Freya.

"What…what do you mean?"

Sadness creeps into Diane's eyes. "When you touched me, the vision changed, and it was about you. I saw you in your kitchen. It's night, and the moonlight is shining on you. I don't know who, but someone will ask you something, and if you refuse, there will be a death. I was back at your house again when you pulled me out. But when it's a loop like this—"

"You have to tell me more!"

Diane sighs, "That's so frustrating about all this—I never get the whole picture. But the loop signifies an important moment in your life—a crucial turning point. Think before you answer. Make the right choice, or we all suffer."

The heavy air twirls around and settles like a weight around Freya's neck. Great…. Just what she needs. Something else to keep her down. For as long as she can remember, she has felt this unexplainable anger inside, a sense of incompleteness. It fuels her irritable character. This is not how she wants to be, but despite everything she tried, she could never shake it.

FAIRY

Cal is trying to relax on his bed with not much else to do in his confinement. Seamus barely comes to visit, too busy chatting it up with fairies. The urgency to act is building inside him. It makes him anxious as he doesn't know what to do or even what he wants. He has nowhere to go. His family has abandoned him—twice. He can try to escape if he only knew how; to have Seamus possess him again frightens him even more. He doesn't want to go back to Lucy, but despite everything, she had given his life some purpose, distorted as it might be. Never before had Cal to choose for himself. It's something he has always desired. Now the moment is here; it's overwhelming. He has no idea who he truly is and what he could or should do. Maybe staying here a little longer isn't such a bad idea.

A scream escapes him when the world around him suddenly dissolves completely. His scream is followed by Seamus' as he too is pulled along. The ground is coming closer fast, and to his surprise, he lands softly on his feet.

"Well, well, well. Welcome, young man. It has been a while, and I feel we've gotten off on the wrong foot." Cal would recognize that voice anywhere; slowly he turns around and faces Mab, Queen of Fairy. She looks lovely today. Her hair hangs all the way down, almost touching the ground. It sways pleasantly on a gentle breeze. She is dressed in a pure white flowing dress with specks of red poppies, which at first glance gives Cal the impression she's blood-spattered. He blinks while the dress shimmers as it flows in the light. Everything about this setting is friendly and welcoming down to the pleasant jasmine-like smell and the soft noises of a calming brook.

"Don't let her fool you," whispers Seamus in his ear. Cal didn't need the warning. He has seen her other side, not something easily forgotten. And even though everybody treats him like he's stupid, he's indeed not. If he has learned anything from the events of the past months, it is that things are often deceptive, and it's wise to be on your guard—always.

"I can't seem to be able to get rid of you," Mab turns her attention for a second to Seamus. "How are you attached to this gentleman?" She leans forward and quickly smells the air around Cal.

"He called me," Seamus smoothly answers, just as skilled in skirting the truth as any fairy.

"I thought you were dead."

"That I am."

"And yet you're here. That must irritate the Fates. Tut tut," Mab's eyes twinkle. She knows all too well what happens to creatures that upset the Fates.

Turning back to Cal, she caresses his face. "What shall I do with you? You know, we used to have games with humans in the old days."

Cal stiffens.

Mab laughs, "Some found it too barbaric. Do you have any gifts like your sister?"

Cal wisely keeps his mouth shut.

This time, Mab caresses his aura, "You have talents; maybe you can be my servant."

"I don't want to serve anybody anymore." There, the words left Cal's mouth before he could hold them in. Never again, he repeats to himself. Not even to save his skin. He wants to be free. He should thank Mab for making at least that much evident in his mind.

"I'm not going to keep you in that prison, you know. I don't like having just another mouth to feed. Everybody has to do something useful here," she says and with a wave, she indicates her realm.

Before Cal gets a chance to step back, Mab steps forward and grabs his shirt, pulling him only inches from her face. "I will ask you once nicely." She kisses Cal on the lips and wiggles them open with a playful tongue. Cal is overwhelmed with the taste of rosebuds and desire, quickly forgetting his horror. When she pulls back, his eyes betray him, he would like some more. "Do you want to be my servant?"

Cal opens his mouth to agree, but Mab playfully puts her finger on his lips. Eagerly, he leans against it. "I know I can be a bit intoxicating. Think about it. But remember, the next time, I won't ask so nicely." Mab releases her finger, and Cal moves in for another kiss, right when Mab's face turns to her true self. A creature of nightmares.

The next second, Cal is on his back in his cell, screaming and screaming, unable to get that face out of his mind.

Seamus tries to slap him in the face to snap him out of it, which of course, doesn't work. His ghost hand passes right through him as always. "Cal. CAL! Come on, man; you've seen worse than that. Snap out of it!"

Cal stops screaming, but his breathing is still very labored. "I can't! OH NO!" That is all he repeats, over and over again.

"You could just let me possess you…." is all Seamus whispers in his ear.

Cal hates to admit that that is rapidly becoming the only option.

NEW ORLEANS

Freya is exhausted when she finally makes it back home. Trying to be quiet, she walks into the dark kitchen. Jason, her husband, must be sleeping. He always gets up so early in the morning. Now that Luna is overseas, with Diane so fragile and the girls too busy, Freya's workload has tripled at Under the Witches Hat, their family business. After finishing her reading sessions, she stayed there till late, making spells. Time for a glass of wine to wind down. She couldn't possibly sleep yet. Too many things are whirling around in her head. When she opens the fridge, it brings a smile to her face. Jason left her a plate with all sorts of little goodies to eat and a nice bottle of white wine with a note on it, "Drink me!"

Shortly after, she is sitting at the little bar in their kitchen, enjoying a piece of savory pie. Just what she needs. The moon is almost full, and it illuminates the kitchen. Freya feels herself finally settling down when her cellphone rings. Who on earth could be calling at this time of night?

Luna, her caller ID shows, right….

"What do you want? DO you know what time it is?" Freya can't help herself. She and Luna have been at it for as long as she can remember—never agreeing on anything. That dynamic seemed to have improved recently as they agreed on several things where Tara messed up, but irritation is still the first emotion that boils to the surface when she talks to her sister.

Freya senses Luna's hesitation and the pronounced swallow before she replies, "I called the Hat, and they told me you had just gone home."

"What do you want?" Freya never learned the skill of chit-chat, especially not with this sister. Best to get to the point, and then she can return to her glass of wine.

"I need your help," Luna squeezes out.

"Wow! That must have hurt."

"You're the only one I can ask."

Great, the only one. Of course, she's Luna's last choice. Well, she can take her business elsewhere. "I'm kinda busy here. Taking care of Diane. Doing three jobs at the Hat. I hardly have a chance to see my husband. I can't add your problem to the pile." There, take that! Satisfied, she takes another sip of her wine.

"I didn't mean it like that," Luna tries to soften her poor choice of words.

"How did you mean it?"

"This is very hard for me," Luna's strained voice is at the point of breaking.

That doesn't go unnoticed by her older sister, but she has no sympathy for Luna. She's such a know-it-all—the most powerful witch of the family.

Luna breaks down on the other end of the phone and starts crying. "I am having problems with my magic. The backlash—my magic is failing."

For a moment, Freya does feel sorry for her. The backlash isn't Luna's fault. Your magic failing is unthinkable. Freya can't imagine life without it. "I'm sorry, but I already have too much on my plate," She replies, softening a little. "Try one of your daughters."

More hiccups and tears are flowing on the other end of the line. She's not the right person for Luna.

"I need help looking for the Cup. And 'I' need help." Luna is now practically begging. That she had called her is worrying; it showed that the problem must be devastating. Still, Freya is not the right person. "I can't leave here; they need me now. I'm sorry—"

She's about to hang up when another shimmer of the moonlight reflects off her glass. Startled, Freya looks up and sees the moon. Diane's premonition rushes back to the front of her mind. How could she have missed this? What had Diane said? Make the right choice, or we will all suffer. For Goddess' sake! Freya takes a deep breath in and out.

"Freya? Please…," comes another plea from Luna.

Another deep breath. This is going to be interesting. "I'll come."

"Thank you!" Luna's words are heartfelt; Freya can literally taste her relief.

A bell tolls in space and time. Freya feels the air shifting. An important choice has been made. Let's hope it's the right one.

BETWEEN SPACE AND TIME

The Fates, Mother–Maiden–Crone, sit at their scrying pond when the bell resonates through their realm. "I can't wait to see what happens next," crows the Crone. The Madigans have been entertaining them for some time.

"We'd better get back to work," Mother urges the others, always the responsible one. Or at least that is what she likes to think. Ever since the Maiden has been obsessing with Diane, they have been pulled more and more into the drama unfolding on Earth. For the Fates, who are supposed to be neutral, interfering in earthly matters generally doesn't end well. But if you live forever, endlessly deciding who lives or dies, you need something to take your mind off things now and again.

ICELAND, JÖKULSÁRLON BEACH

Lucy stands with her bare feet buried in the black sand of this exceptional beach in Iceland. The ever-changing landscape of masses of ice deposited from the glacial lagoon. They look like diamonds scattered on the beach, which gives it its name—Diamond Beach. She had flown from London to Reykjavik to catch a plane to Greenland when she decided to take a couple of days here. Iceland is exceptional, with its connection to nature and magic still very prevalent. It will give her some much-needed time to recharge her energy. No longer able to rely on the Dagger energy, she's feeling her age. As a witch grows older, her knowledge and her powers grow—yet dissipate at the same time. It's a strange contradiction. When you're young, your gifts flow like a wild brook, with lots of energy jumps and unexpected turns. As you age, you develop much better control, but the power becomes a slow-moving river. Each has its pros and cons, but she wishes she still possessed some of that wild brook. Any which way, if she's going to confront the family who holds the Cup, she must be in the best possible shape. Whatever or whoever deviated her spell has significant power. This will not be as easy as when she took the Dagger from that young witch.

This beach covered in all those pieces of glacial ice is an excellent source of old solid energy. Water with age and knowledge. Besides that, it's also a joy to look at. Lucy throws her arms wide and invites in the potential that is released by the melting ice. This cold flow of energy whirls inside her body and fills her with satisfaction as she senses her magical reservoir being replenished. An unexpected tickle at the back of her neck snaps her out of her trance. Immediately, she whips around toward the source of her disturbance. In the distance, a person is walking toward her over the black sand. Lucy squints; it's hard to determine who this is. Quickly, she mumbles a protection spell. You never know; always be prepared. Hmm, that looks like a woman. Again, Lucy squints against the sun. Is she waving? My Goddess—that looks like Mara! She experiences a feeling of instant joy quickly followed by caution. This can't be real; it must be a trick. Mab took her granddaughter, there's no chance she had let her go. Surely Mara hadn't managed to escape by herself?

Lucy doesn't move and patiently waits till Mara stops about six feet away from her.

"Grandmother!" a smile breaks through on Mara's face. Over the years, Lucy's grandchildren had learned never to hug her uninvited.

Lucy opens her arms and Mara steps into her embrace. The women hug tightly. Lucy sniffs Mara and carefully lets a probe of magic run around her aura and then along her skin. It is Mara; her little magical investigation didn't find anything unusual. No spells attached or unknown traces. Mara wears a dark one-piece with long sleeves and a red sash. It gives her a confident and mysterious look.

Mara steps back and takes a closer look at her grandmother. "You are a hard woman to find."

"How did you escape?" This is unexpected, and although she could surely use some extra help, this makes Lucy wary.

"Even Mab needs to focus on other things, so I bided my time. Luckily, when I returned, not that much time had passed. Set made it clear we're not welcome there, so I followed your trail to London, and now…," Mara gestures toward the beach.

"You didn't make a deal with her or something?"

"You taught me better than that."

"And your brother?" Lucy doesn't care about Cal, but so far, Mara's answers are not particularly satisfying. It's best to keep her talking.

"He's on his own. I haven't seen him since we were captured."

This rings true to Lucy. Maybe Mara is telling the truth.

"I'm here to help. What's the plan?"

"I don't need any help; why don't you go home?" hints Lucy.

"Which home? Boston burned down. Utah is compromised, and we over-stayed our welcome with Set. I can't stay with my mother. We're homeless." Mara's eyes fill up with tears, and she turns away from Lucy as tears infuriate her.

Irritated by the lack of alternatives, Lucy mentally runs through her options. Mara can't go home as they don't have one. She could use the help but Mara's emotional state is worrying or annoying at least. The holes in her story are the biggest concern. Way more cons than pros. She scans along the beach for a moment in the hope of a sign. A seagull swoops down and poops, hitting Mara right on her shoulder.

Well, that's a positive sign. "Okay, you can come along."

Mara turns back toward her and can't hide her relief. "Where are we going?"

"I'm in Iceland to recharge my energy. Know any good spots?" Lucy evades the question.

FAIRY

Mab sits back with a satisfied grin on her face. She had followed Mara's conversation and had anticipated Lucy's request for a sign. The seagull was brilliant; she pats herself on the back. Soon, very soon, she will hold an elemental power. She can feel it in her bones.

One of the things Ceri has been working on lately is experimenting with her witch and fairy sides. So far, she treated them separately, but there must be an advantage to having both gifts. Since she pissed off Mab, it felt like a perfect time to work on that.

For that purpose alone, she grew a room in her house with a witch circle in it—her magical work-room. A pentacle is etched into the floor with a fairy precious stone on each point. A forest green one for Earth, turquoise for Water, bright blue for Air, red for Fire, and white for Spirit. The elemental quarters of the circle are a sight to be seen; she had outdone herself there. Each quarter's image starts around the round form of the circle and flows all the way up the walls and across the ceiling. For North, the element of Earth, tree roots define their quarter of the circle and form a small forest that seems to grow upwards from the floor. Using her fairy magic, she has added movement, and it feels like the forest is alive, with deer peeking between the trees, birds, and other fairy-like creatures. For the West, Water and ocean surf teases the edge of the circle while a kelp forest grows up from there, full of fish and other life. The lines between earth and water seem to flow into each other organically. For the South, Fire, flames are licking at the edge of the circle, and a hot sun blazes in the bright blue sky above, which blends very nicely with the East, a sky full of clouds and birds. An average human would probably be overwhelmed by all the movement and senses, but Ceri is used to things constantly moving in her house. She starts to find it very soothing. The circle's center is serene and focused; the rest is like a giant living bubble.

At the moment, Ceri focuses all her attention on an amulet lying in front of her on the small altar. The circle is active and vibrating, and energy swirls all around her. For hours, she has been summoning different energies and weaving them all together. Starting with the traditional witchcraft method of weaving the four elements together for protection, she later added the fairy elements. She finished it with a dose of her connection to the land, providing an extra layer with which she hopes the wearer of this spell will be shielded from Mab.

The amulet is pure silver, and the weaving she attached to a dome is made of golden threads, which are aglow with her intention. A rush of anticipation flows through her, as she arrives at the finishing touch—the energy build-up is massive. This is the most complicated spell she has ever attempted to make. Sweat is pouring down her face and back as she throws her arms up in the air and starts to pull the energy together. The tension is almost unbearable; it reminds her of the first time Mab had forcefully pulled her Fairy side to the surface. She can do this. In an almost alien voice, she recites, "elements, forces, Goddesses, and Gods, protect the wearer of this spell against all enemies; humans, fairies, and creatures alike. Keep him hidden, keep him safe. So mote it be!"

With her last strength, she pulls it all into the amulet. The golden dome flattens itself against the silver and melts together.

The sudden dip in energy makes her stagger back. Her hand reaches for the altar to steady herself. Totally spent, she barely manages to release the protective circle before she collapses, her hand tightly wrapped around the amulet.

That's how Liam finds his mother. He felt the buildup and release of a great deal of energy and come to check on her. Quietly he lifts her, careful not to wake her, and lays her at the foot of the tree that connects her to the Land of Fairy. That will be the quickest way to recharge her energies. For a moment, he's tempted to look at whatever she is holding in her hand, but when his hand reaches for it, his mother's eyes fly open. "It's not for you."

Startled, he steps back, and Ceri dissolves into the Land of Fairy. The amulet is now half embedded into the tree's bark, where it will be kept safe for her.

Right, his Mom is scary sometimes.

Hours later, Ceri has materializes refreshed. She's so lucky; what a gift she has received. At first, it felt like an unbearable burden, but the longer she stayed in Fairy and learned to fine-tune their relationship, the more joyous it became. With quick strides, she returns to the house where Alvina is ready with refreshments. Some food will do her good as well.

With a sigh, she settles behind her desk in the study and finally takes the time to examine the spell she has wrought. "What do you think? Will it work?" she asks out loud.

"I hope so," is the doubtful remark coming from Sparkle in her ear.

"Hope so?! You said this would work!"

"Who knows? It has never been done. You wanted to push the boundaries," he bounces it back to her.

Ceri turns the amulet around and around in her hand. The gold glitters every time the light hits it.

"My compliments, My Lady. It looks and feels strong. It radiates power. Shall we put it to the test? Mab has talked to the young man and given him an ultimatum. We need to move fast."

"I know. I know," Ceri stalls. "It's just—"

"Scary," Sparkle finishes her sentence. He has started doing that lately. A sign he knows her well. "You wanted to experiment. You like to take risks, remember…."

"Thanks, friend," Ceri doesn't try to hide her sarcastic tone. She takes a breath and looks at the connection with Cal on her hand. Another of her impulse actions. To follow Cal and Mara when they first came to Fairy, she had managed to attach a communication device to Cal. It had turned out useful, and now it is downright brilliant. The only way to talk to him without Mab knowing.

"No sense in waiting," she adds. She wants to get it over with. Gently, she rubs the leaf connection with Cal; so far, she has only listened in, and although this was not a strong psychic connection like the one with Bridget, it will do the job. Still risky—the payoff could be worth it, though.

This connection looks like a watery mirror, and when it takes form, she has to bite her lip not to laugh. Cal's confused face is staring at her in disbelief. He moves in and out of frame as if trying to look behind it, unsure what this is about.

"Cal, please, this is a secret connection. Mab can't listen in on us."

Cal is back in front of the mirror and looks skeptical.

"I know you know who I am, so I will come straight to the point. Is my father there as well?"

"Seamus?! I need you," Cal shouts up, and for several seconds nothing happens. Cal motions him over. Seamus's face appears in the mirror and brightens instantly when he sees Ceri. He blows her a kiss. This brings a smile to her face and evidently relaxes the old man. Seamus must also remember the tension between them the last time they met.

"I have a proposition. I can spring you out of prison without possessing you or whatever Mab has in store for you. However, I do expect a favor in return."

"No kidding," Cal's suspicious tone is not lost on her.

"You can always let my father possess you, but I'm sure that has to be unpleasant, and Mab is likely to find you, wherever you are." Ceri knows which buttons to push.

"Can you protect me?" Mab scares him the most.

"Yes, I can," Ceri vouches with complete confidence that she's not feeling.

Cal perks up. "You can promise?"

"I can."

"What's that favor? There must be a catch."

Seamus follows this eagerly, fully trusting that she has something interesting up her sleeve.

"I want you to research our origin here in Fairy and on Earth."

This is not what he expected, "What does that mean?" Cal frowns. Seamus is jumping up and down with excitement behind him. Ceri knew Seamus would love this. Her father has always had an endless curiosity about the past.

"Where do witches' gifts come from? Have the worlds always been separated? Those kinds of things. We will talk about it, and I can show you what I have found so far," Ceri offers.

"Why don't you do it yourself?" Cal finds it an odd request.

"It will involve much traveling and I simply don't have the time. It is crucial to me, though."

Cal leans in, knowing he has hit on something, "Why?"

"That, young man, is none of your business. Do we have a deal?" Her commanding side is showing.

Seamus is urging Cal to do it. She doesn't need to hear him to understand his body language. Cal hesitates. "Can I think about it?"

"The longer you wait, the more likely it is that Mab will grab and enslave you. Do you want to take that chance?" Ceri knows his weak point.

Nervously, Cal scans his room. At the same time, Seamus keeps urging him on.

"We must act now. Nobody suspects anything…yet," Ceri adds.

Cal looks from her to Seamus and back. "You promise to protect me."

Ceri nods.

"How is this going to work?" He repositions himself before the mirror. "Do I jump through?"

"Wait. First, we bind our promise. Cal Lockwood, do you promise to research for me our origin until I'm satisfied? In return, I promise to keep you safe from harm."

Cal mulls this over in his head. Sounds good to him. "One thing: when I have fulfilled my promise, will I be free to do whatever I want?"

"Yes," Ceri agrees. That's a long way down the road, and she can always tip off Mab if he becomes a pain afterward.

"I promise."

A promise made; the leaf around Ceri's and Cal's fingers tightens as the universe reacts to bind them.

"Now, get me out of here," Cal demands.

"I will pull you through the Land of Fairy, as a normal portal would attract Mab. Be ready; it might be a little unpleasant for a human," Ceri wryly adds.

"What?!" Cal shouts as the connection snaps shut.

Three of Cups

PART 2

THREE OF CUPS "JOY"

"Happiness comes in waves. It'll find you again."

—UNKNOWN

FAIRY

Cal sits fuming in his cell. Where did that Ceri woman go?! She was supposed to rescue him. He made his promise, and now she has disappeared.

"I would lie down if I were you," Seamus suggests. "Ceri said this could be unpleasant."

"What if Mab shows up before she gets me out of here?" Cal is panicking.

"Calm down—several minutes ago, you didn't even know you would be saved. If Ceri promises something, she will do it."

"You only say that because she's family."

"Young man! You should know me better than that by now." Seamus chastises him.

Cal looks at the ground and plops onto his bed.

"That's better; relax. I'm sure she'll be here soon enough." Seamus has no idea what it meant when she said she would pull him through the Land of Fairy. He leans back and stares at Cal.

For the next half hour, nothing happens except the occasional splutter from Cal.

A loud groan from his prison tree makes him bolt upright.

"It must be happening now," says Seamus needlessly.

The cell is shrinking, and the tree trunk is moving in; while the space becomes smaller and smaller, everything in it is being absorbed into the tree's bark.

"What the hell!" Cal is getting seriously worried, turning around and around, and unable to escape. Panic starts to mount.

"Relax and lean against the bark," a whisper floats by.

"Hell, no!" Cal is having second thoughts.

"Do it!" Seamus tries to push him against the side. They're now crammed together in the small center of the tree. Before long, there will be no choice left. Cal sees Seamus slowly being consumed by the tree. The space is so small that the edges touch him from every side, claustrophobia hits him, and he screams loud as he slowly gets drawn in by the tree. He is forcefully dematerializing. Ceri is taking a considerable risk, as humans generally can't dematerialize, but she hopes this will be possible with him being part demon. Sparkle had sounded pretty sure of himself. It's excruciating and scary; Cal's consciousness is aware that he's being pulled along the Land of Fairy's lifelines. After the initial pain and shock, it becomes such a wondrous and alien experience that his human mind has difficulty processing everything. Colors, feelings, and thoughts all move through him, or is he moving through them? Losing track of time, he's suddenly forced back into his body and aches all over. He stands, whole again, against the tree's bark inside Ceri's Garden. She slips the amulet around his neck as soon as he's whole. Its protection zings in place.

"Welcome, Cal Lockwood, to my home," Ceri says formally.

"Good Goddess Lady, never do that again," Cal pants.

"You're welcome. I put an amulet around your neck. Never take that off. It will keep you safe from everybody here and on earth."

Gently he touches it, using his witch sense to study the complexity of the weave. Wow. It's a work of art. It has some magic woven into it, which he doesn't recognize; it must be Fairy.

"Come, young man."

"Cal, my name is Cal," he automatically says.

"Right, follow me, Cal. I will feed you and, in the meantime, tell you what I'm looking for," Ceri waves for him.

Intrigued by the beauty of her garden, he walks behind her while trying to take in as much of his surroundings as possible. As soon as there's some distance between him and the tree, he slowly pulls Seamus out of there; his ghost hands feel over his ghost body as if he too had been dematerialized.

"That was incredible. Can we go back?" he asks Ceri.

"Hi, Dad. No, we can't. It was the only way to get him out, and it's not advisable for humans. But as you taught me, sometimes you must bend the rules," she answers.

Seamus shines. He's so happy Ceri is on speaking terms with him again. This is so special that she can see him as well; hopefully, he will be able to make things right between them.

As soon as they walk into the house, Alvina is there to welcome them.

"Alvina, Cal needs a bath and some new clothes." Ceri doesn't need to explain that they need to get rid of the red. "Also, something to eat and drink, and if you could show him to the study afterward, I'll be waiting."

"My Lady," Alvina is about to courtesy, but just in time, she catches herself. This is rewarded with a big smile from Ceri. Finally, she's learning!

Mab is fuming in front of Cal's cell, which now looks like a typical tree again. The Master of Containment is doing his best to blend into the background. Nobody wants to get in the way of the Queen when she's upset. And especially not if you were the one that was supposed to prevent this. He notified her as soon as he noticed Cal was missing. Mab has been dealing with some complicated Fairy politics. Otherwise, she might have sensed something herself. But if you're the ruler of a realm, there's only so much that you can focus on at a time. This human was not on her priority list. Now that he's gone, it's a whole different story.

"How could this happen?!" Mab shrieks, not expecting an answer. She opens herself up to let Fairy flow through her, hoping to sense a trace of Cal somewhere. Nothing. Does that mean he's on Earth? Nobody has opened a portal unless…. Swiftly, she puts her hand on the tree's bark, but it doesn't reveal any of its secrets. It's unmistakable to Mab who must be behind this. There's only one other person interested in humans. Ceri. But why? How? This man was her enemy. What is her gain? Her powers must be growing if she can rescue him without leaving any evidence. Hmmm, time to keep a closer eye on her Keeper of the Land.

"You!" her head snaps towards the Master of Containment. "Get me Spymaster."

NEW ORLEANS

Wes is frantically painting in Seamus' old atelier. The witches cleaned it up after Maeve was attuned to the Dagger in this room, but Wes can't unsee the ritual. It haunts him. His dreams are filled with the sight of the twins soaked in blood. Bridget has been very caring, not something that comes naturally to her. She only recently experienced her own trauma when Lucy tortured her. That probably helps her understand what he's going through. Not that he experienced pain himself, but the horror of the images is something he would have preferred to have missed. In the beginning, the whole witch thing was so cute, and he found it the most exciting thing ever. Very sexy. The first time he laid eyes on Bridget at the art show's opening back in Boston, her confident, mysterious, yet vulnerable aura had drawn him to her. It didn't surprise him that she had unique gifts. It only made him fall in love with her even more. Her family had been such a trip, and the whole experience fueled his artistic side. He had never been so productive. He has already painted three paintings in this room. Typically, that would take him at least half a year.

The attachment to Bridget's sister is a whole other thing. Maeve's extraordinary beauty and cooking skills are hard to resist. It felt safe to welcome her as a friend and sister, as his heart already belonged to Bridget. But he can no longer deny that he loves Maeve as well since he had drawn the extra card in the Magical Tarot Deck—Unity, which depicts the three of them intertwined. Can you love two women at the same time? Sisters—twins?!

After the ritual, he had doubted for several weeks if he could still love them at all. Bridget was so sweet and caring. Maeve had done her part to take care of him, but every time she touches him, he can't help but see her bloodied state. He has withdrawn from seeing them as much as possible, claiming Emily needed his support. A perfect shield from the real problem. The house is increasingly filled with troubled souls. The sisters are so busy trying to control their new powers that he could easily slip under the radar.

At first, Bridget suggested he move from the atelier to another room as she could no longer enjoy the porch where she was tortured, but Wes felt he needed to paint. Here. Right here. Process it—get it all out. He has been painting furiously, five canvasses at the same time. They're full of the twins, magic, and blood. He doesn't dare show them to anyone; they're pretty intense as if they are telling a story. Each painting is only partly finished. Something is different this time. Is it possible to acquire magic? His paintings seem to be alive. It's both disturbing and fascinating. He knows the paintings of Seamus, Bridget's grandpa, are alive. But the first paintings he did in this room were not moving or anything. At first, the family was concerned that Seamus' supplies were enchanted, but although his paintings were extremely lifelike, they didn't move. These new paintings, however—MOVE. Unsure what to do with this, he keeps working on them, and every time he leaves the room, he makes sure they're hidden from sight. A knock on the door makes him jump.

"Breakfast is ready," says Emily cheerfully from the other side.

A breath of relief escapes him. Geesh! He needs to chill a bit. "Perfect! I'll be down soon." Quickly, he wraps things up. He has been painting since Bridget left his bed that morning to go to the tomb to study with the ancestors.

Tara stands with her eyes closed and her bare feet planted in her favorite herb garden. She woke up early this morning and drew her card of the day—the Three of Cups. Three anemone fishes are swimming above three cups, surrounded by sparkly bubbles. Joy—such a positive card. Friendship, relationship, mutual respect. It suddenly improved her mood. She felt better for the first time since she passed on the Wand.

More like her old self. She decided to enforce that with some Earth energy, her dominant element. Now that Fire has diminished, her natural affinity is blossoming again—standing with her feet in the soil nourishes her soul. It has been forever since she was this grounded. The plants, all things growing from the earth, share energy, filling her with magic again. Her aura is glowing, and somehow, she's getting better. Stronger, not so much in power, but her personality is more robust. She no longer wants to crawl under a rock and disappear. She understands why her mother faded away so quickly, but she can still be of value. The girls must feel abandoned by her. Like the ancestors, Tara could be a sounding board, and her knowledge could be invaluable to them. As if thinking about the twins conjured them up. When she opens her eyes, they're making their way to the house. They pause for a moment when noticing Tara in her garden. The girls want to walk on, but Tara waves them over.

It's a little unnerving that they don't even have to look at each other and almost move as one toward her. "How are you doing? Are you making headway with your studies? Are the ancestors helpful?" The questions burst out of her. What a difference a bit of energy makes.

"How are you, Gran?" Bridget asks without answering any of Tara's questions.

Tara wants to make a snippy comment, which she manages to swallow. After all, she just stopped doing anything and had let Maeve and Bridget sort everything out by themselves and even let them deal with all the family dramas.

"I'm sorry I wasn't there for you." A breeze through the garden enforces the truth of her words.

"It's okay, Gran," Maeve says, "the ancestors told us it is quite an adjustment—"

"—that you needed time," Bridget finishes her sentence.

"When I woke up this morning, I felt different—more myself. I wanted to let you know I'm still here. I still have a lifetime of knowledge. I'm here to support you." Tara looks down, embarrassed by her absence.

Maeve kisses her on the cheek and throws an arm around her. "Come, breakfast is ready."

"How do you know?" Tara can't hide her surprise.

Maeve's eyes gleam with a bit of mischief while her hair seems to flow around as if she's permanently underwater.

When they enter the kitchen, Emily has a small feast waiting for them. Fresh muffins are coming out of the oven, while a delicious breakfast casserole is already on the table. Cephalop is happily spooning from the dish. He evidently has no problems with human food. His appetite would border on enormous for human standards, but he doesn't gain weight at all. His metabolism must be different. Who knows? He's a strange-looking creature. "This is so good!" he says to Tara, Bridget, and Maeve as soon as they step through the door. That makes Emily laugh, and her happiness spreads to the others.

It is tempered a little when Wes enters, and Bridget instantly worries when she sees the lines of fatigue and stress etched on his face. Guilt for not being there enough for him bubbles to the surface. Wes has been keeping her and Maeve at arm's length. It was such a shock for him, the whole ritual. Then, they have spent so much time with the ancestors to get a handle on all of this that poor Wes has been neglected. She mentally notes that she needs to push through his defenses and find a way to help him.

Wes grabs a muffin, his vice, and plops in a chair next to Bridget, who reaches for him and gives him a gentle kiss. Even now, he still stiffens a bit. What is she going to do?

Spontaneously, she asks, "Do you maybe want to go for lunch at Commander's Palace? It will be a nice change; I realize I haven't shown you much of New Orleans yet, and it's such a staple."

Wes shrugs.

"You should go," Tara chimes in.

"For sure. You can get dressed up. It will be good for you to get out of the house," Maeve adds.

"Sure," Wes replies with little enthusiasm.

Even though Wes's reply is lukewarm, Bridget is happy to have him to herself for a little while. It has been quite some time since it was just the two of them. Maybe it will help.

"Liam is picking me up!" Emily is so excited about that. "He's going to take me to the Fairy equivalent of an amusement park!"

"Wow, that sounds fabulous," Maeve is happy for her. She also needs something positive.

"Are you going too?" Maeve asks Cephalop. She has taken a liking to the octopus fairy. His watery presence speaks to her.

"No, she will be well guarded in Fairy, and I will have some time for myself here. Maybe do some sightseeing. Do you want to join me?"

Maeve blushes slightly—Bridget notices.

"I would love to. If you're okay on your own, Gran," Maeve looks at Tara.

"I'm thrilled you're all going to do something enjoyable for a change. We all need a good pick-me-up. I'm feeling so much better today. I will hold the fort. Don't worry." Satisfied, she leans back, nibbling on one of Emily's scones. It seems forever since she felt this positive. It warms her heart to see everybody doing better. Almost everybody. Suddenly she's aware that Diane is not there. "Where's Diane?"

"She left before the sun was up and told me to let you know not to worry," Wes softly answers, "Sorry. I forgot…."

Diane sits on the steps of her home in the Marigny. The cute home is still quiet. She has been sitting here since daybreak. This morning she woke before dawn and decided she needed to start mending her life if she didn't want to go down the road of insanity—one of the pitfalls of being a gifted seer. Many years ago, she tried to end her life, and Alice saved her. How could she repay that by going down that road again? She has already hurt Alice so badly. It has taken a while before she even dared to face her shame over everything that happened. Poor Alice. After being Diane's rock for all these years, she deserves an explanation. Much more than that, actually. A simple apology will not be enough. But Diane must start somewhere if she wants to repair their relationship. That begins with facing up to what she has done and talking to Alice.

Alice changed the locks and doesn't respond to any of her messages, so this is about the only way to catch her. Diane uses her witch sense and brushes past Alice inside the house. Right. Patience.

Soon enough, the front door opens. "It's you." That is all Alice says before turning back into the house, leaving the door open. An invitation of sorts. Diane gets up and follows her into their kitchen.

The kettle is boiling, and without a word, Alice makes a pot of tea while Diane slides onto one of the kitchen chairs. "You didn't return any of my calls."

"I wonder why?" Sarcasm is dripping from Alice's words and makes Diane cringe.

"I'm sorry." It slips from Diane's lips, and she knows it was the wrong thing to say the moment it comes out.

"REALLY?! That's what you come here to say? I'm so angry with you!" Alice starts crying. "I gave you everything. I l—l—loved you?! I want to punch you in the face." Angry, she forcefully puts the teapot down, and the water splashes over her hands. "OW!"

Quickly Diane jumps up, grabs Alice's hands, and whispers a healing spell. Instantly, the angry red spots recede. Alice's tear-stained face is now so close to hers. The anguish, the anger, the hurt, and love swirl around them. Diane drinks it all in. Yes, even after all this, there's still love. Otherwise, Alice wouldn't feel so strongly about what happened. The love still resonates with Diane. Not in the way that Set's dark soul-touching love affected her. But a love built on years of trust and togetherness. Gentle love. "Can I ever make it up to you?" whispers Diane.

Being a witch makes you open to others' emotions. It can be a curse or a blessing. In this case, it's clearer than words. Truer. It's hard to hide those intense feelings. Alice must in return be getting a dose of Diane's sentiments. For several minutes, they just stand there, holding each other's hands.

"Thank you for healing my hands," Alice finally says. It deflates the emotionally charged air around them. "I don't know. I honestly don't know if or when we will be okay again. It's a lot."

"I know. I will tell you everything," Diane offers.

Alice flinches, "I'm not sure if I want to know. It also drives me crazy that I don't know. Hell, I don't know what I want." Desperation is taking hold again.

Diane is crumbling inside; will she have the strength to see this through? If she wants this to work, she has to be able to watch Alice go through this and absorb the pain that she has caused. It's the least she can do. Determined to go forward, she looks Alice straight in the eye, acknowledging the harm she has caused. Again, several minutes pass with much unspoken spoken.

"I'll do whatever I can to mend us. I miss you. I love you…," Diane pleadingly says.

Alice takes a moment and then gives a big sigh. "Damn. I've never been able to resist you." The tiniest of smiles on her lips.

GREENLAND

Down in the deep cold water off the coast of Greenland, Sedna is relaxing while her hair gets combed by two mermen. A sea mammal escapes every time their combs brush through her lush long dark hair. Now, two giddy seals wiggle free, twirling around her before they take off into the void. For as long as she can remember, she's been down here as the Goddess of the Sea. Or maybe that's not entirely true. She can still feel and see the sun on her skin in her memory. Something she has never stopped missing, living in this place where hardly daylight filters through. After eons, she finally forgot why she angered her father Anguta, a creator-God, who helped shape the world, and why he threw her overboard. Sedna has been one with the ocean for so long now, there's no place she would rather be.

Although the people of Greenland still remember and honor her memory, times are changing. She can feel it in the water, however slightly. Even here in the deep, it's warming up. Her minions tell her of the ice melting. For several decades, she has noticed the noise level in the ocean change. Power boats and big trawlers drown out the whales' songs and the dolphins' clicking. It irritates her. Every year, it gets busier and busier. For a while, she had stopped combing her hair, and shamans started to show up to appease her. As long as they show her respect, she will support them with life. Give them plenty of fish in the sea.

Absentmindedly, her foot rubs the Cup lying in the sand at her feet. Right, she had forgotten about that. Time to call the witches; they need to come and get it. Sedna has felt the eyes on her, peeping through the kelp. Someone is coming, and it's not hers to protect. The Berthelsens have been keeping her company for some time. They're an entertaining bunch—gifted and fun, maybe a bit emotional. But who's she to point fingers. After all, her emotions had landed her down here all that time ago. As she has no hands, she rubs her foot around the edge, creating a sound that vibrates up and up.

The hair in the back of Aputsiaq 'Snowflake' Berthelsen's neck resonates with a song from the Cup. The mother of Salik, and the guardian of the Cup of Plenty, is down in their icy home in the most Northern part of Greenland. Sedna wants to see her, and she has no doubt what that is about. Salik has been slowly recovering from the locator spell that had hit him. His hair will probably stay white for the rest of his life. Like most young people, he thinks it's cool. For his mother, it's a reminder and a warning that things could have turned out way worse. They need to be on high alert. Someone is coming for the Cup. They have felt Air and Fire stirring for a couple of months now. That had never happened before, and they can only presume the other families are not in control anymore.

Swiftly, she makes her way through the cold hallways, formed like domed ceilings as in the old churches. Their home is a work of art. Many generations have used their creative magic on it, and the ice sculptures throughout are mesmerizing. Such a shame they can't show them to anyone. The whales moving in and out of the ceiling in this part of the house never fail to make her smile. The Berthelsens are a tight-knit family and fortunate to be surrounded by so much beauty.

Their home is extensive, and she has no trouble avoiding the others while she finds her way outside. The cold wind hits her, but her puffy keeps her warm. She manages to move quickly over the snow toward the coast with a simple spell. It's never wise to keep Sedna waiting when she wants to see you.

Snowflake scans the landscape once she reaches the bare granite rocks along the water edge. Except for the lone polar bear climbing onto the ice, there's nothing around. Better to be careful with all that's going on. She quickly undresses, playfully changing into her dolphin form while jumping in. As the holder of the Cup, her additional powers enable her to transform into creatures related to Water. Their shapeshifter gift amplified. She jumps and wiggles for a couple of seconds, settling into her new shape before diving into the deep and quickly getting into the rhythm of her powerful tail strokes.

It never takes long down here before some company shows up. There's a relatively large community of merpeople here. Conveniently away from busier parts of the ocean. It might seem busy here, but it's nothing compared to some places down south where they used to live.

Two mermaids flank her and have no trouble keeping up with her strong strokes.

"Snowflake! Just the person we need to talk to," says Aquata on her left.

"Sedna wants me. Can I come back to you?" Snowflake doesn't need to explain that you don't keep the Goddess of the Sea waiting.

"We will come with you. It might concern her as well."

Another piece falls into place; a heavy feeling settles in Snowflake's gut. Things are going to collide. Are they up to the challenge? Their lives far away from everything have given them a false sense of security. And as they developed as witches, no doubt the others did as well. Even though they occasionally venture into the outside world, there must be advantages actually to be living in it. Anyway, they will find out soon enough. Letting her witch sense run ahead of her, she can sense the Goddess not too far away. They wind their way through a thick kelp forest that gives way to her throne, lodged in dense coral; her hair is like one with a school of Atlantic herring escaping from it. They swarm around before disappearing.

"Aputsiaq, my dear, we need to talk," Sedna motions to her with her stump to take a seat. "I see you brought some friends. Aquata. Sinann," she says, acknowledging them.

"What grants me the honor of your call?" Snowflake doesn't beat around the bush. Her nerves are on edge.

"I can no longer look after your precious item. I am being spied on. Eyes are watching through the kelp. I fear it's no longer safe here. I'm sure I don't have to remind you of your responsibilities."

"Of course not, Goddess, Mother of the Sea. My gratitude knows no bounds for your generosity of watching it for so long." Snowflake has enjoyed the additional power of the Cup, and at last, she finally understands its true weight. Her son attacked, the Goddess has been watched. Her duty is calling; it scares her. For generations, it has been a powerful boost for her family. Why oh why does she need to be the one to defend it?

Aquata pulls her back to the present when she adds, "I ran into a water witch when I was recently down South. It alarmed me as she was searching for you. The witch claimed she wanted to warn you. Others are coming for the Cup."

The water around them ripples—truth is spoken.

"Three times now I have been warned. Bad tidings. We will soon find out if our family is worthy." Snowflake accepts her fate.

"I gave the witch the Scallop. Here is the other half. You will know who she is. It might be a friend."

"Thank you! We'll see. I know you're my friend." She gives the mermaid a nudge with her beak.

"Enough with the smooching. I have work to do." Sedna has no time for trivial things like being nice to each other. "Take the thing and be gone."

Dismissed, Snowflake grabs the Cup in her beak and heads back home.

ICELAND, REYKJAVIK

Freya steps into the arrival hall of Reykjavik Airport. It's small like the one in New Orleans. She's never been a traveler and has always preferred to stay home. Jason travels a lot for his job, he had encouraged her years ago to get a passport in the hope of exploring some exotic destinations, but Hawaii is the furthest they got. Pretty exotic by her standards. This trip makes her uncomfortable on so many levels that she doesn't know where to begin. For the hundredth time, she rubs the calming amulet around her neck. It had kept her sane on the flight. That people choose to sit in a plane out of free will is beyond her. Like her mother, she prefers her broom. But to take that as far as Reykjavik was a little impractical. So here she is, coming to the rescue of her least favorite sister, Luna. Another one on the list of uncomfortable things. She would have never agreed to this if it wasn't for Diane's premonition.

"Over here!" Luna's clear voice comes from across the hall. Freya would have sensed her sister if she hadn't been so distracted. It is something she has always been able to do. Luna shines bright. However, her light seems to be flickering when she turns toward her now. Hmm, something is going on after all. No doubt as Luna must have been desperate to ask her for help.

"You came," Luna sounds relieved. "Thank you. It means a lot."

Freya closes her mouth, swallowing her snippy remark. Okay, universe. Got the message. If this is going to work, she needs to control this automatic irritated reaction that Luna brings out in her.

"We're family," she simply replies. That should be safe enough. Freya is, above all, loyal to her family. Even to the less favorite ones. Like her twin nieces. How dare they grab the elemental powers for themselves? But even if they desperately needed her support, she would be there for them—no need to tell them, though.

"Come. I'll take you to the hotel; you must be tired from the trip." Luna grabs her suitcase and motions her to follow.

When Freya walks out and the fresh air—right from the ocean—blows in her face, something inside her connects. It's like coming home. A shiver runs up her spine, and the hairs on her arms stand up straight. This land resonates with her; no place has ever done that. It stops her in her tracks. What is this? She closes her eyes and lets her witch sense flow out for a moment. It rushes over the land that is beckoning her. It's thrilling and makes her smile. Never, ever, has she felt this way before. She laughs out loud.

This makes Luna stop and turn around. The sight of her oldest sister genuinely laughing out loud is something she has not seen before. It's as if she radiates happiness. It makes her pause. How come she can't remember seeing Freya happy? "Are you okay?" Luna doesn't know what else to say.

Freya's eyes snap open. "I love it here." Her mood has been lifted, and she couldn't be happier that she came. "Let's drop off our bags, and you can show me around while you tell me what's going on." Freya strides forward.

Startled by the sudden change, Luna must hurry to catch up with her sister.

FAIRY

Ceri draws her fingers together, pulling the image of the ancient fairies fighting back into the memory globe. Seamus has been swirling around it, absorbed by the astonishing realistic enactment. Cal sits on the sofa in Ceri's study, and she is leaning against her desk.

"This is the oldest fairy memory I have. Whoever I ask here can't tell me when or where this was. Fairies are meticulous record keepers; this makes me curious." Ceri walks around her desk and gracefully slides into her chair behind it.

"It's so real," Seamus says as he admires the globes on the shelves. "Are they all like this?"

"Yes. Why is this memory here? Why did Felaern collect it? Where did he get it?" she muses out loud.

"Do all fairies possess these memories?" wonders Cal, joining the conversation for the first time. He has been reticent since Ceri pulled him through the Land of Fairy. It must have been a bit distressing.

"Most families do, I've been told. Felaern, like you," Ceri says looking at Seamus, "had a passion for history, so I have a larger collection than most."

"What are you after? What do I need to do to fulfill my promise?" Cal goes right to the point. "I can't very well go from door to door and ask if I can see memories." He almost sounds sulky.

Seamus hovers in front of him, "Boy, where is your sense of adventure?! Research starts somewhere, and one thing leads to another. I love this. History is full of knowledge, and you wanted me to educate you. Well, this is an extraordinary opportunity for you!"

"Really?!"

"Yes! Do you think knowledge is just there in your head? It requires study and practice. Study means reading books and stuff."

Ceri smiles, Seamus might be a ghost, but he hasn't changed one bit. Cal is lucky and unfortunate at the same time. Seamus is a fabulous teacher and simultaneously the most annoying one. "I want to know more about the dawn of time. Where do all creatures come from? Are Fairy and Earth the only dimensions? Where do witches get their gifts from? I know you've done some research on that already," Ceri bounces these questions toward Seamus.

Seamus leans back, looking almost comically as if he's relaxing in a comfortable chair, taking his time to answer this question. "I got intrigued when I met Tara. She was such a gifted witch. Over the last centuries, many witch families' powers have been fading. Most of the time because they married regular folk. It's important to follow your heart, but maybe not when it's about our witch gifts."

Pointedly, he looks at Cal. "What?!" The young man shifts uncomfortably in his chair.

"Look at this fine specimen of a witch," Seamus points at Cal. "His father is half-demon. That makes him a quarter demon or however the genes play out. And he has more demon fire in him than his half-sister. So much potential."

Cal makes a face.

"Yeah, you don't believe me. Look at Ceri; who knows what she's capable of?" Seamus points out. "So somewhere along the eons, we got discouraged about mingling with others. But by whom or what, I don't know," he adds.

"Time to find out!" Ceri encourages them. "You're welcome to all the books and memories here. It's a place to start. I'm sure there must be some sort of thing equivalent to libraries here in Fairy. You can ask Maeron. He's been around the longest and can help you get into places. I think your protection will hold unless you truly meet face to face with Mab. So be careful. If you need to go to Earth, let me know as I need to make a special portal for you. Again, we don't want to put the Queen on alert."

"Copy that," Cal answers; he has zero intention of running into Mab anytime soon.

NEW ORLEANS

Maeve is fidgeting with her brightly patterned summer dress. Although fall is here, it's still warm in New Orleans. She's checking herself in the mirror in the hallway. Quickly, she licks her fingers, trying to mold one of her unruly curls into submission.

"You look lovely," the watery voice of Cephalop makes her jump and turn around. He looks just the same. All of a sudden, very aware of her appearance and trying to look her best for him, her cheeks flush a bright red. This makes the octopus in front of her smile. One of his tentacles reaches for her hand and plants a gentlemanly kiss on the top of it while his suction cups tease her skin. She shivers enjoyably. Another laugh escapes Cephalop.

"Where do you want to go?" Maeve desperately tries to get a grip on the situation. She's not used to flirting. "Oh shoot," she says aloud when it dawns on her that his shape might draw some attention. She clears her throat, "New Orleans is used to some strange characters, but we might attract some unwanted attention if we go out like this." Stupid! Why didn't she think of that before?

"You have magic, and I have fairy magic. I thought between us, we must be able to come up with something," he says and winks at her.

"Right," she says. Why is she so self-conscious around him? She holds one of the elemental power objects, for crying out loud. A transformation spell must be in her power. "Of course. Of course, I can."

Again, one of his tentacles caresses her arm. "Let me try one of my Fairy disguises, and hopefully, you can perfect it for this world." His alien eyes size her up.

"Let's do it," Maeve takes a step back. Just to be sure, you never know what will happen.

His tentacles start to move up and down, left to right; it looks like a complicated weave. His image begins to blur. Maeve does her best to follow the flow, but Fairy magic is different. When he's done, he looks like a more ordinary fairy. However, the wings might still be a bit much.

"You look…normal," Maeve hesitantly says. "Why don't you always look like that?"

"My Lady, this is not me. Why should I hide my true form? Don't you like it?"

"That—that's not what I meant to say. You're mesmerizing. I mean different and interesting. You're super smart. I love your tentacles and—" she snaps her mouth shut, realizing she's blabbing.

Cephalop just waits her out with a tiny smile on his lips.

Damn him for making her uncomfortable. "I'm sorry. You're absolutely right. Nobody should have to hide who they are. It's that most people want to blend in—belong. Not many are confident enough to be themselves. I included. I still can't…," Maeve says and looks at the ground.

Cephalop reaches for her and lifts her chin so she has to look him in the eye. Even though his shape is different, he still has his own eyes. "My Lady, never hide who you are from me. You might have made mistakes when you first experienced your new form. But that doesn't mean you have to hide and pay for that for the rest of your life. If you can accept who you are, embrace that power. You will be magnificent."

If she thought she was uncomfortable before, her face is now red hot.

Cephalop, taking pity on her, hooks his arm in hers. "Come on, my dear. Work your magic, and let's explore your town. I saw you eyeing my wings."

When they step out the front door, Maeve draws on the power of Air to make a deflection shield around them.

Wes is on his second Martini of the famous three twenty-five-cent martini lunch at the Commander's Palace. He is swirling the blue concoction around in his glass, anything not to look at Bridget. They are both very good-looking, a couple that attracts attention. Neither looks happy, though. Bridget is acutely aware that their previously easy-going conversations have dried up. The ritual that attuned Maeve to the Dagger had done a number on him. Magic can be fun; on the other side of the scale, it is violent and scary. It's all about the balance. One cannot exist without the other.

Wes had loved the fun part of the magic. It reflected all those whimsical TV shows—to see that come to life has been a trip. Unfortunately, some things you can't unsee, like Maeve's bloodied state while she had twirled through the air. His mind has a hard time dealing with that, which inevitably has changed how he looks at the sisters. More than ever before, he sees them as one. He doesn't think the girls realize how attuned they are to each other. It's unnerving.

Bridget has never been the caring kind. Doing and making things happen is her style. She simply doesn't know where to begin to mend their relationship.

"Wes," in those three letters, Bridget pours everything she doesn't know how to express. Her worry, her heart aches for him, and the way she misses him. The magic flowing through her has amplified this gift. It works even for ordinary people.

Slowly, Wes lifts his eyes toward hers. Does she detect a hint of fear?

"I miss you. Tell me, please. What can I do to make this right again? Did we scare you?"

For what seems like an eternity, he doesn't answer her. He just stares at her. She has the most challenging time not filling the void with endless chatter or pleading. Bridget knows in her heart how important it is to give him this time and let him work through it.

"I still love you. It's just—" he says and looks out of the window onto the patio. When he turns toward her, a hint of a smile is on his lips. "Yes, you scared the shit out of me. You two are intimidating."

"We're the same people as before," Bridget is quick to add.

"No, you're not. Not even close. The last couple of months have changed you. I feel like an outsider."

"My feelings for you have never changed. I want you. I need you. You're my rock," Bridget reaches for him. This time, he lets her touch him.

"I have no powers. I feel useless. It's not an equal relationship anymore." Sadness seeps into his eyes.

"Power is only a talent or gift, much like your ability to make art. It doesn't mean I don't value your opinion or that your support and insight don't make me more. I need you…. Probably even more than before. You're the one who can keep me grounded and sane."

Wes is still brooding. "It doesn't feel the same," he says. "You're off having adventures, and I'm in a room. Painting."

"Your adventures are different; they play in your head. You shouldn't envy us. We're not having much fun. It's more like a struggle, desperately trying to keep our heads above water. But your love and laughter can save me. Please…." Again, Bridget puts all her desperation into those words. She can't imagine life without Wes. All this witch stuff is drowning her. What would she do without him?

Wes seems to absorb her words and mull on them for a while. She can't fathom what it would be like to have no magic and see people around you use it all the time. For years, she denied her magic, but even then, she had used it unconsciously more often than she cares to admit. "I can't do anything about the magic, but I love you. I want to be with you. You're the one. The person who completes me," Bridget says and blushes; this is the most truthful she has ever been with any man. More honest than she has been to herself about their relationship. If she wants to save it now, she must show him how important he truly is to her. A bell tolls, a witch is telling the absolute truth. This, more than anything, resonates with Wes. The chandelier above their table sizzles, and the light flickers, affected by the charged air around them.

When Wes finally looks at her again, something has changed in his eyes; the spark is back. A wave of gratitude washes over Bridget and reaches Wes and engulfs him. A startled laugh escapes him. "Right. I love you too, honey."

At that moment, their bond is strengthening again. They can make this work.

The waiter clears his throat trying to get their attention. The final course has arrived.

BETWEEN SPACE AND TIME

The Maiden acknowledges the declaration of love that Bridget has just made. That girl still has a lot to learn. However, that young man is a nice balance in the family. He's a sweetheart; why not give them another chance? It's also how relationships get better, by going through experiences together and growing from there.

Sometimes, she wonders where these thoughts come from. How can she know? She has never had a relationship. Yeah, with Mother and Crone, that's not the same though. Diane had awoken something in her, something she wanted to know more about. Not the knowledge that floats in her head. She can't even remember when they came into being. Have they always existed? Did somebody create them? Desperately, the Maiden tries to stem these thoughts. Not a road that leads anywhere. Quickly, she touches the water of the pond and thinks of Diane. Instantly, she appears in the rippling water before her.

That silly woman is trying to get back with her wife. Doesn't she understand she's hers?

NEW ORLEANS

Diane and Alice are sitting on the floor in their living room. Jasmine incense fills the air, a scent they both love, which brings good memories. A pot of relaxing chamomile tea has been drunk. Diane suggested they look at some old photos, and for the last hour, they have been regaling each other with old stories and laughing at the memories. Memories that the pictures have brought back to the forefront of their minds. It feels almost blissfully normal. Diane is calmer than she has been in weeks, and the worry lines on Alice's face seem a little less deep. To laugh and talk about good times is healing. They have a long road to travel, but this is an excellent start. Slowly, they move closer and closer until their arms brush each other when they reach for the following picture. This photograph still has tape stuck to it; Diane is lying relaxed with her head on Alice's stomach on a picnic blanket under a beautiful old oak in Audubon Park. It had hung on their fridge for several months. The memory is sweet and comforting. Diane turns to Alice and brushes away one of her long strands of hair, hypersensitive to Alice's reaction. When Alice doesn't withdraw, Diane touches her face. Gently following the lines of her face as if they need to be reacquainted. Alice's expression softens, and feeling encouraged, Diane slowly moves closer and lets her lips lightly touch Alice's. A slight sigh of relief leaves her. Bolder, she moves closer and gives Alice a proper kiss. It feels familiar and safe. Comforting, like coming home, pushing aside the memory of Set or the Maiden, there's only Alice. She has been the center of her life for so many years. How she ever could have had these other feelings is unfathomable. They kiss and kiss, lying down on the floor, touching each other and whispering nonsensical endearments that only old lovers can.

When suddenly, a shiver runs down Diane's spine. Alarmed, she freezes when the unfortunately too familiar feeling of the Maiden settling inside her takes hold. Unable to stop her, Diane can only watch in horror when she kisses Alice. Not their easy kissing but a forceful, exploring, demanding kiss. Alice withdraws looking into Diane's eyes, ready to say something when she realizes someone else is there. Shocked, Alice pushes Diane away. The horror and disgust on Alice's face break Diane's heart again. Diane can feel the struggle of the Maiden, who is thinking about what to say. But with just a little satisfied smile, she leaves Diane's body. Both women are aware that the Maiden is leaving the room. After all, they're both sensitive witches. Diane jumps up and wants to comfort Alice, who tries desperately to stay away so Diane can't touch her anymore.

"Diane, stop!" Alice says, holding her hand up.

"I'm so sorry. I can't help—"

"I can't do this. It's freaky. The Maiden… It's the Maiden!" Alice can't hide her panic. The Maiden is one of the Fates. You don't want to mess with the Fates ever. If the Maiden intends to have her lover, she should give her up. Broken, she falls to the floor, tears dripping down her cheeks.

"We can make this work," Diane tries. "I don't want this either. Together, we can figure out how to please her, so she will leave us alone."

With a tear-stained face, Alice looks up at Diane. "Nobody reasons with the Fates, Diane. Not even a Madigan." The tone in her voice betrays her dislike of Diane's family.

All those years, Diane knew that she was not a fan. But the way she says their name now, it's clear her feelings about them are much stronger than she had realized.

"Please. Alice. I need you. Can we not find a way?" Diane pleads, falling to her knees. Begging Alice, grabbing her hands. "Please!"

Alice is a jumble of emotions. She wants to be with Diane more than anything in the world. The pleading, the sheer desperation of the woman in front of her. It tears down her resistance. "I don't know what we can do."

"There's always a way," Diane can't hide her relief.

BETWEEN SPACE AND TIME

The Maiden isn't proud of her actions. This is going against their code. But she cannot and will not allow Diane to be with someone else. Let them try…

ICELAND, STUDLAGIL BASALT CANYON

Freya and Luna stand on top of the Studlagil Basalt Canyon. The towering basalt columns flank a vivid blue stream of icy water. It's a majestic sight. For witches, however, it provides an enormous boost of Earth power. The geometrical blocks are formed from the rapid cooling of low-viscosity lava and are rich in Magnesium and Iron. There are some wonderful sights of these specific lava formations around the world. Iceland has multiple formations, having so much lava base. The energy still stored in these columns can hopefully give Luna's wonky powers a nudge in the right direction.

They stayed up almost all night and decided to leave in the wee hours of the morning in search of this site. Freya had gotten such a boost from the land when she arrived, it put her in a good mood, and it had been no trouble for her to stay awake. After Luna explained her problems and the curious new addition of face jewelry, they brainstormed how they could try to help her. Luna was visibly distressed, something Freya had never seen. She squashed her initial gloating, feeling sorry for her sister, and they came up with some wild ideas. One of them was a sunset ritual on basalt blocks here. There are plenty of places that qualify in Iceland, but this place wasn't supposed to be too touristy, and they hiked all the way over to the far side, hoping to avoid prying eyes. It had taken them most of the day to get there. Not a punishment for them since Iceland is magnificent, and the way the land spoke to Freya made it a pleasure to float through it. While Luna was driving, Freya cast out her witch sense and let it touch everything around them. Such delicious powers and incredible creatures. It might be on earth, but it felt like another planet. Luna played some gentle Celtic music, and it relaxed Freya; she hasn't been this serene since—she can't remember ever having felt this way. Every time she tries to go there, her thoughts seem to slide right past it.

Now, both witches are standing on this extraordinary spot, and the power of earth caresses their bodies. The stones are beyond grounding; it's like the earth is grabbing their legs and pushing its power into their bodies, and they haven't even started yet.

"Wow," Luna is searching for the right words to express herself. Rocking slightly back and forth under earth's pull. "This is unreal on multiple levels."

"Let it flow through you; drink it in," Freya encourages her.

Now, it's Luna's turn to swallow a smart remark. Of course, she knows what to do. The fact that her powers are flickering doesn't make her stupid. Quickly, she reminds herself that her sister came all this way. Quite surprisingly. Instead, she asks, "Do you know when the sun is setting?"

Freya pulls out her phone and opens an app before pointing it at the sun. Her sons insisted she keep up to date with technology. Initially, she objected, but now she couldn't imagine life without it. Yes, she could have used her witch sense, but this is easy and doesn't cost her any energy. "In thirty minutes."

"Perfect," Luna replies while she does a 360. "Let's find a spot and get ready."

The remaining tourists have left. Anyway, it's not that busy anymore now that fall has begun. The wind brushes through the canyon with a chill in the air. The icy blue water looks tempting but will undoubtedly be very cold. Water, Air, Earth, and Fire are all present. As the rock was formed from lava, the fire energy is still seeping through them, even though it has been ages since the lava cooled. After long deliberation, they had settled on a rejuvenation spell like a magical reboot.

Freya had brought her basic kit, and Luna has been able to pick up quite some exciting additions here in Iceland. There are plenty of witches around. So, if you know where to look, you can easily find powerful objects or ingredients for your witch kit.

No words are needed to fire up a protective circle once they decided to take a seat at the edge of the cliff, all the way on top of the blocks, looking down on that blue stream flirting with them. Freya seals the circle with a snap of her finger, and they both instantly feel the energy that is contained within. Luna puts down a woolly blanket to keep them warm when they sit. With intent, she's positioned her gathered objects in their proper wind direction. For Water—to the West—a cup that Tom bought for her from a local artist. For Fire—to the South—a branch from a rowan tree, gifted to her by one of the local witches from her garden. For Air—to the East—a feather from a Haförn, the White-Tailed Hawk, found on one of her hikes here. And for Earth—to the North—a rock she found on the beach.

The sun sets at last, and they can see the last sunrays peeking beneath the clouds. Freya and Luna position themselves, standing opposite each other with their arms raised straight forward, palms up, almost touching. They might not be physically touching, but their auras are forced together on that side, and it needs some effort for both of them to make it comfortable. For too long, they have irritated each other, building a natural resistance, which is not in their favor now. But as both sisters are willing, they manage to make it work. Softly chanting a little rhyme, they initiate the spell. It's in Icelandic; if you want to communicate with the land, it's advisable to do it in the native tongue.

"Kraftur minn kemur aftur til mín. Kraftur minn, fylltu mig. Máttur minn, vertu minn aftur. Skipið þitt, auðmjúka sál þína."

"Power of mine come back to me. Power of mine, fill me up. Power of mine, be mine again. Your vessel, your humble soul."

As the sun sets, they chant with more and more intensity. When the sun disappears over the horizon, they stop and sit down with their eyes closed, visualizing Luna's power flowing back into her in harmony. The flow in the circle is strong. Both women let the forces run through them and merge. All elements together are always the best to work with. No doubt that is the reason that the elemental objects are separated. To feel the powers interact without being amplified is already a joy. Freya is revitalized, and the spell wasn't even for her.

Several hours have passed when they finally open their eyes.

"Better?" Freya wants to know.

"I feel more centered. But I will only know when I start using magic. It comes and goes anyway. That's what's so frustrating about it," Luna says and shrugs.

It's now completely dark. Luna turns her hand, and instantly, a small light floats above her hand. It brings a smile to her face. It's a good sign that she can do this unconsciously; she's hopeful. She bounces it in the air. For a second, she thinks she sees movement outside their circle and whirls around. Hmm, she must have imagined it. Freya walks back their ritual circle, which releases the left-over energy, dissipating into the night. Luna swiftly gathers their supplies and directs the light in front of her to guide them to the car. Freya glances back to the canyon, "I don't know what it is about this place, but I love it here."

"That's good to hear," Lucy's familiar voice pierces the night. It sounds eerily the same as Tara's. However, this feels like stainless steel, while Tara's voice is more like velvet.

Luna drops her bag of supplies and instantly calls up a fireball with one hand and a shield with the others. Her powers sure look to be working again.

"Wow, wow, you might want to rethink that." Lucy's amused voice stops Luna. Lucy flicks her wrist, and a shimmer runs over a dome constructed over Luna and Freya, which must have covered their whole power circle. "You might blow yourself up."

"Show yourself!" Freya demands while she eyes their entrapment. Walking forward and pushing against a solid wall. "Shit."

Lucy and Mara step into the circle of light provided by Luna's light. "You ladies are way too trusting. What self-respecting witch doesn't set a ward when they do magic in a foreign place?"

"We didn't—"

Luna puts a hand on Freya's arm to stop her from sharing anything. Her hot temper might give something away they don't want the others to know.

"Not our proudest moment," Luna offers.

"Stupid," Lucy counters immediately. "It's hard to believe you set my souls free. This—" she waves her hand around, "is more like a rooky mistake."

"What do you want?" Luna demands.

"Want? I don't want anything from you. Imagine our surprise to find you here tapping into the energy. Unprotected! A perfect opportunity for some payback," Lucy gloats.

"This won't hold us," Freya states with confidence she's not feeling.

"Mara here does excellent work. She has been practicing from a very young age to escape these entrapments. Her Mother is an excellent Voodoo priestess, whom you must be familiar with; she lives in your city. You know her—right? I'm sure this will be a proper challenge." Lucy throws her arm around Mara, who hasn't said a word and stands there stiffly.

Luna steps forward and looks at her more closely. There's something about her. Something slightly different. "You escaped easily from Fairy," Luna probes.

"As I said, Mara is a gifted young witch," Lucy defends her instantly.

The Madigans notice a slight change in their body language. There's a lack of the usual comfort between the Lockwoods. Luna is not the only one who finds Mara's escape curious. Good to know.

"We know why you're here," Freya is eager to join the conversation. She might not have had many dealings with Lucy, but she's ready to show everybody she's just as much witch as all of them. Deep down, Freya has always felt side-lined by Tara, whose gentle words and understanding have been a way to soften her rejection.

Lucy smiles, which is an unnerving experience. Even though her smile lacks warmth, it's freaky to look at someone that looks exactly like your mother. "No doubt. Finding you is an unexpected bonus. I wanted to punish you for what you all did to me. Mara here persuaded me it would be better to imprison you." Patting Mara on the back like she's a good girl, she adds, "We're heading for the Cup, and there's absolutely nothing you can do about it. This dome will keep you safe and sound, tucked in here. Nothing is going in or out. It will give you oxygen, and we left you some food. We're not that barbaric."

"Oh wow! Thank you," Freya replies sarcastically. "We'll catch up with you."

"Good luck with that. Oh, did I mention there's no cell phone reception either? We must go and catch our flight. It was a pleasure." With that, Lucy and Mara disappear into the night.

Immediately, Luna and Freya probe the globe, their witch sense floating along every inch of it, hoping to find even the tiniest of cracks. That's all you need to wiggle in there and snap this thing right open. "Dammit," Luna says, frustrated. "Lucy is right; what an incredibly dumb mistake."

"You didn't think of it either," Freya falls immediately into defense mode, a bit shaken to be locked up.

"I wasn't saying that," Luna's irritation is no longer beneath the surface.

"You always seem to know everything. How do we get out of here?" Freya demands.

A big sigh escapes Luna, "I don't sense any weaknesses. The only thing I can think of is to try to make a portal to Fairy and let Ceri bring us back."

"I'm not going to Fairy!" There's a slight hint of panic in Freya's voice.

"Why not? It's the best option," her sister insists.

"I'm not going," Freya repeats, crossing her arms.

"You're just being difficult because it's my suggestion. You always refuse to do what I propose."

Freya eyes her, "It's not like that."

Luna only raises an eyebrow. For several seconds they simply stare at each other.

"Not this time. I CAN'T GO TO FAIRY. PERIOD."

It slowly dawns on Luna that something else might be the problem here. "Are you and Ceri having a fight or something?"

"What are you talking about?! Of course not."

"Why can't you go?"

For the longest time, Freya doesn't answer. It is, after all, none of Luna's business why she's afraid to go to Fairy. She can't, and she will not give the Ferrymaster another memory. The last time was extremely traumatic, and to think that Tara and Seamus had the Ferrymaster take away her memory of Ceri coming home as a baby is just too much. Her whole life, she has felt like something was missing. What if the Ferrymaster holds that key and her parents are to blame for that? Freya can feel Luna's eyes on her. She will need to give her something. "I can't run into the Ferrymaster again."

"We don't have to. We'll go to Ceri," Luna counters.

"And how do you suggest we do that? Miss almighty? We have no means to get in touch with her as Bridget is the only one with a direct link to our fairy sister. So, if we go to Fairy, the Ferrymaster will show up. He's the one that knows the millisecond someone sets foot in Fairy from another realm. I'm not taking that chance."

Luna's light flickers, a sign of her unpredictable magic.

"And your magic is still wonky," Freya turns the problem back to her.

"I feel better." Now, Luna is on the defense.

"We need to find another way—soon. Lucy said she knew where the Cup was. And it's obviously not in Iceland if they need to fly there," Freya points out the obvious.

"I don't know. I'm tired. Maybe we should get some sleep," Luna offers. "In the morning, it could look very different."

"Sleep?! On the rocky ground? Come on."

"Hey! I don't hear you making any suggestions about how to get out of here," Luna is getting pissed.

"Maybe because you never once listened to my suggestions your whole life. You're the powerful one. Your magic is fabulous. You look amazing. Luna is special," Freya lets it all out. Years of frustration with her sister's perfection. To be treated as a minor witch, even though she's the oldest—forever shoved to the side. Ignored. "Well. Look at you now. How the mighty have fallen." The air is electrifying, and little bursts of lightning disperse in the circle.

Luna is shocked and pissed at the same time; sparks start to flow from her, "That's not fair!"

"Not fair?! When have you ever been fair? You have never paid anybody any attention. You have even driven your daughter away," Freya is on a roll.

Thunder explodes in the globe; Luna is floating slightly above the ground now, "How dare you?! You've always hidden behind your 'eldest child' status.

You are forever undermining others. You never stand up and do something yourself. How do you think you can ever get any respect? It's a miracle you found a husband!"

Thunder and lightning, the witches fighting must be visible for miles in this darkness. They're too busy tearing into each other to care though

"Ha! At least I've still got mine," Freya slings back.

All the energy they had built is now wasted away with the resentment from their lifelong rivalry coming into the open.

"TIK TIK!" A loud ticking noise sounds on the globe, freezing the women.

"Do you hear that?" Freya asks, slightly calming down.

"TIK TIK!" Freya and Luna try to see where the sound is coming from. The storm inside pitters away and the darkness sets back in.

"TIK TIK!" Luna turns her hand around, but this time no light appears. Her face falls, finally realizing that her magic is still not working, and she has wasted whatever she had gained in this fight with her sister. Freya sees Luna's face, and remorse sets in for letting herself get so out of hand. Her anger is forever simmering close to the surface, but a big compassionate heart is right next to it. Quietly, Freya turns her hand around and lets her light explore the edges of the globe.

Nothing happens for several minutes, and the ticking noise keeps going on, but it's hard to pinpoint its location. Finally, the light hits on something floating above them. Both women squint to try to see who or what is up there. Is that a child?

FAIRY

Emily's face glows with happiness. This must be the best day ever. She stands in the middle of an unimaginable place. The cacophony of sounds, the sweet seductive smells, the bright colors, and the sheer number of fairies and creatures is pure sensory overload. In awe, she twirls around to drink it all in. Above and around her, fairies are buzzing around. The beating of their wings is a hum that vibrates within. For a second, her eyes lock with her mother Ceri's. The warm smile on Ceri's face lets some of the anxious feelings that welled up within her when Emily found out her mother was joining them on this adventure subside. Liam had picked her up, and it turned out most of her Fairy family was present. Uncle Maeron and Alvina flank their mother. The whole clan is dressed in matching earth tones, with not one speck of red on them.

This is the place to go to have fun. It's hard for her to figure out what exactly is going on. Liam explained that they do some form of games, and now they're in the part you could compare to an adventure park. Emily can't make heads or tails of what is what. There seem to be no waiting lines, and everything is three-dimensional. Where do they go?

Liam grabs her arm and point upward to something that looks like a giant tornado that sucks up fairies at an alarming rate. "Do you want to try that?"

Alarmed, Emily glances at her mother, who gives her an encouraging nod while scanning the crowd as if she's looking for someone. Casually, one fairy after another drops in to say hi or talk to Ceri. So strange to see her mother in that role. Until now, her mother had been a free spirit that went with the flow and was always up for something fun. A kind of seriousness has settled over her, and Emily is unsure if she likes that change.

"Come on!" Liam persuades her, "I have done it before. You'll love it!" Without waiting for an answer, he swoops her up and flings her in the air toward the beginning of the funnel.

"AAAAHHHHHHH," Emily screams, terrified. Liam is jumping up behind her. "Enjoy the RIDE!" It's the last thing she hears before the noise of the funnel reaches her, and she gets drawn into the maelstrom of air. Within the cone, it is strangely more controlled, and she's squished against the side while being twirled around, rather delicately in contrast to the noise and the violent look from the outside. It makes her laugh and laugh. Liam is managing to drift toward her, "SEE!"

"I LOVE IT!" she shouts back. For a full ten minutes, they get flung around before being spit out next to her family again. This was too weird. But super lit. "Can we go again?" she asks, emboldened by this fun experience, and strides forward toward something that looks like a watery mirror on its side. "Let's try this one!" And without any hesitation, she steps straight through the watery wall just as she hears the others scream "NOOOOOOOOOO!"

On the other side of the mirror, it's eerily quiet. When she turns back, the water wall is gone. For several seconds nothing happens, and then her insides start to hurt horribly, and a scream escapes her. This was not made for someone part human. It normally dematerializes you, flings you across the universe, and spits you out of another mirror on the other side of the park. However, Emily's body doesn't cope well with this. Not enough fairy to dematerialize but just enough fairy not to be torn apart by this. Something unexpected happens; the magic unable to perform molds itself around her and partly transforms her. Her body looks like it's made from a million twinkling stars that hold her form. More or less. Slightly transparent, like a ghost. The pain stops, but she's barely aware of what's happening to her. Again, the magic falters, and instead of swinging toward the other mirror, she gets dumped in the unlikeliest of places. Somewhere no one has ever been before, while still alive.

BETWEEN SPACE AND TIME

"What the hell?!" The crone jumps up when Emily is dumped between space and time in their core of being. Emily's ghostly sparkly image floats in the area where the clock is, and the Crone is sitting knitting. "MOTHER! MAIDEN!" the Crone's urgent voice summons the others right there.

"What have you done?" Mother immediately blames the Crone.

"I didn't do anything. She just appeared."

Curious, the Crone moves forward, and when she touches Emily, it makes her stir, and the twinkles stick to the Crone's finger for a short moment.

Emily is only vaguely conscious of what's happening but unable to move or say anything.

"She's still alive."

"How did she manage to get here?" the Maiden wonders while looking closer at Emily. "Isn't that a Madigan?"

"What?!" Mother also comes closer. "How come I'm not surprised? I think this is the daughter of that one that's part fairy. She's not scheduled to die yet."

"I think this is a sign," the Crone proclaims.

"We don't believe in signs," Mother automatically replies.

"Look at her. Made of stars. Some sort of perfect mix, human, fairy, and who knows what. These Madigans have been mingling with creatures for centuries. It's fascinating. I think we should keep her."

"Crone, I'm up for a lot," the Maiden argues, "but that is not a good idea. Nobody has been in our realm before, since—"

"Exactly. Since we came into being, I think we can use some help, and the universe is sending us this child."

Mother shakes her head. "We are Mother, Maiden, Crone. Not Mother, Maiden, Crone, and Child. We should send her to the hereafter."

"I disagree. Don't you ever wonder where we came from? Why we're doing all this?" the Crone insists.

"You two have been too busy with these Madigans; you're becoming too human. We don't have feelings. We're here to decide, Fate," Mother is getting seriously irritated now.

"I think Crone has an identity crisis," the Maiden fans the flames, keeping quiet about her own doubts.

"You're not helping," Mother shoots her a stern look.

"I think it's Fate that sent her here. Do you remember the early days? How we had far fewer people and creatures to look after. Each life was a debate. Now we just make snap decisions or watch over them without much thought. The Maiden even randomly snaps vines when she's upset." Now the Maiden gives the Crone an angry stare. "It's true. It's time for reinforcements and some new perspective."

"No," Mother stays firm. "We send her on."

"I think she should go back. She still has a life to live. It's not her time," the Maiden takes the opposite point of view.

The Crone looks from one to the other and back to Emily.

"So, what will it be? Back or forward?" Mother pointedly urges the Crone to make the final decision.

A mischievous light passes behind the Crone's eyes while she pulls a string from her knitting. Swiftly, she moves forward and weaves the string around Emily's heart.

"Stop. What are you doing?" Mother tries to pull her back.

"I've attached a string to her heart; the moment she dies, she will return to us. We—of all beings—should recognize the Universe's messages. I agree that her life is still to be lived, and when she goes back, she will remember nothing of us. A child of the stars, a mix of all beings. Until we meet again, my child," the Crone says and touches Emily's forehead, and instantly she's spit out on the other side of the mirror.

FAIRY

Emily tumbles to the ground, and her mother immediately takes her into her arms. The others have been anxiously waiting, hoping against all odds she would survive this. They are only too aware of her mixed-race, which has made this an unsuitable journey. "Emily. Emily!" Ceri weaves her hand over Emily's body, scanning for injuries. "She feels fine."

Emily coughs and opens her eyes. "What…what happened?"

Maeron has been quiet while Ceri examined her; now, he leans forward and sniffs her. "Oh, dear," is all he says.

"Oh dear, WHAT!" Ceri demands to know.

"She's been touched by Fate."

Ceri squashes her confusion when she looks into the frightened eyes of her daughter. "You'll be fine," she murmurs while she kisses her forehead. Right then, she feels that itch again, like someone is watching them. Casually, she looks around. A substantial crowd has gathered around them. No time to figure out who's putting her on edge; Emily needs her now.

NEW ORLEANS

Maeve and Cephalop sit at a table outside a small coffee place in the Bywater. This area is full of artists and has a pleasant vibe. It's devoid of the many tourists roaming the French Quarter. Steve, Maeve's Dad, and his new family live here. The magic that flows through these streets is more genuine, not as diluted with partying people. There are murals on the walls, the cheerful signature-colored houses of New Orleans, and little outside gardens, people live here. Unlike the Garden District, which is more remote with the houses behind their fences. This is life. Maeve would love to find a home here, a secret wish. Being a Siren had kept her with her grandmother, but that doesn't mean she never dreamed of a more adventurous life. Traveling, her own house, sitting here with Cephalop let her remember these things, and a small tear escapes her.

"Are you all right, dear?" Cephalop reaches out and catches the teardrop on the tip of his finger, looking at it in the sunlight before he licks it off. "A Siren tear should never be wasted." He winks.

A shiver runs down Maeve's back, setting off an alarm bell in the back of her head. Are her tears magical? What did she just give away?

Her alarm must have shown in her face. Damn, it would be wonderful if she had a little more of Bridget's confidence. Cephalop touches her arm, "Yes, your tears have a certain power to them. I apologize if you were unaware."

"What power? What did I give away?" Maeve is sitting up straight, back to her cautious self. Her easy conversation with Wes had opened her up for being friendlier with others, and with Cephalop she had instantly felt a bond, perhaps their affinity with water. They're both otherworldly in their unique way. She had let her guard down.

"As you invited me to go out, I presumed you liked me. Maybe I was mistaken." Now he looks hurt.

"No. no. I do like you. It's just—I—I—I'm not good with men," Maeve looks around for an escape.

"I'm Fairy." That is all Cephalop replies.

Maeve turns back toward him. "I know even less about fairies." Her voice sounds small now as if new tears are ready to flow.

He gets up and pulls her up into an embrace. At first, she stands there ridged while Cephalop envelops her. His tentacles might not be visible, but she can feel comforting suction cups all over her body. It's strangely relaxing. "You have to figure out who you are and fully embrace it. It's not something to be feared. This is a gift, something so special. You can't harm me; I can resist your Siren song. If you let me, I can guide you," Cephalop whispers in her ear.

A million thoughts race through Maeve's head and the one winning is out of her mouth before she knows it, "How can I trust you? I don't know you. How can I trust anyone?" Even though Bridget and Maeve's bond is strengthening and maybe even stronger than it was due to their link to an elemental object, their relationship has changed. Bridget left New Orleans several years back. Her rejection of any form of communication between them had burdened Maeve with a dose of trust issues and abandonment problems. So bad, she doesn't even trust herself.

"Trust is something that needs to grow and be earned. I'm old, by your standards, extremely old. I have all the time in the world. I'm part of your Aunt's Fairy family; that's something special. To be invited into her home has been the greatest honor of my life. I would do anything to help her human family as well."

"I don't want your help because you serve my aunt," Maeve tries to step back.

"Let me finish." These stern words make her look into those watery octopus eyes. "You are the most intriguing, powerful woman I've ever met, and you've managed to hold on to a heart of gold. You're a gem, a light that shines through my darkness; I want to know you."

This makes Maeve shudder, the words resounding within her, and confused, she steps back to look at Cephalop. Unconsciously, she has opened her witch eye and sees through his disguise. This fairy just pronounced his love for her. It's freaking her out, big time! She can't decide if she wants to fling herself around his neck or run for the hills—a whirlwind of emotions courses through her body. Seamus had drawn her as the Temperance card; it's about balance. Her heart finds the words to reply, but how can she proclaim love if she doesn't know herself?

"Cephalop, I'm beyond words. Yes. I have amazing feelings for you. However, I shouldn't give myself to anybody. It's not fair as I don't know who I am. I'm lost."

This brings a warm smile to his face. "You are perfect. I will help you if you let me. We will see what happens. I have no expectations."

"That's what everybody says. No expectations; that's impossible," Maeve immediately counters.

"Oh, Maeve," he pronounces her name like a wave crashing on a beach, "I'm not human. Never forget that. Even less than you are."

For several moments, they truly look at each other. "Thank you," Maeve whispers at last. "I would be grateful for your help." They embrace. Maeve can sense the Fates smiling down on her.

Tara sits in the study, reading a book about trees. Something light and enjoyable. It seems like ordinary people are catching on to the fact that trees talk to each other. Witches have known that since the dawn of time. Interesting, though, to read the science behind it. The flickering light of the hearth gives her comfort; it's way too hot to have a fire going, but she enjoys it and still has the air-conditioning on. Nobody needs to know. It's one of these little indulgences she has been allowing herself since Seamus passed away. The house is quiet. Bridget and Wes came back but immediately disappeared to their room. It felt like a weight had lifted. This makes Tara think back to the Three of Cups this morning. Happiness. Maeve and Cephalop hadn't returned yet, which must be a good sign.

Diane hasn't come back either, another positive. Things are indeed looking up. She hasn't heard from Luna or Freya, except that Freya had arrived safely. They're grown-ups. Tara counts on them to sort this out between them. Emily is still in Fairy. You never know how long that will take with the time sometimes running different. All in all, a good day. Satisfied, she closes her book and, with one snap of her finger, snuffs out the fire; time for bed.

Two of Pentacles

PART 3

TWO OF PENTACLES
"JUGGLING RESPONSIBILITIES"

"You can't depend on your eyes when your imagination is out of focus."

—MARK TWAIN

GREENLAND

Snowflake has trekked further inland on the ice sheet through the night. The Cup is tucked away in her backpack, and she's well dressed in modern polar clothes. No need to use up her magic to stay warm. It's already way below freezing, and although she has traveled this path many times, it feels different now. Her proximity to the Cup amplifies her senses. The Cup of Plenty represents the element of Water. Emotions, and intuition, are a few of its qualities. Except for the icy wind, there are no sounds. That doesn't mean there is no life around her. She stops and stands very still for a moment, spotting a polar beer scurrying forth on the horizon. The low rising sun casts a long shadow behind it. You better be on your guard here. This particular bear has other things on its mind, but you never want it hunting you—not even when you're a gifted witch.

A sigh of relief escapes her when she senses the tinkling of the wards surrounding this sacred space. The need to hide the Cup is pressing on her. She headed straight for this place after she came from Sedna, the Goddess of the Sea. She hadn't even gone home or brought one of her kids or siblings along this time. This is something she needs to do alone. Or maybe not entirely alone. The Berthelsen ancestors are here. This is their final resting place, much like the Madigan's tomb, yet different. As the Berthelsens had moved around a lot before settling in this area, there are no skeletons, only the spirits of the elders. Her whole family is able to pass through the wards to this spot and consult the elders. Once she has crossed the barrier, the noise of the wind instantly stops. Their ward is a complex weaving of protection and deflection. Normal humans would not be aware of this place. It looks just like the rest of the ice sheet. Snowflake takes a moment to take it in and catch her breath. Even though she's used to hiking over the ice, it's still intense. Even for her, it takes a minute to locate the icy steps leading down into their sacred space. The clear ice lets the light through, illuminating a majestic cavern in a bluish glow.

Five sculpted ice cups stand in a circle. They're about six feet tall and five feet wide, monumental works of art. They depict aspects of the lives of the spirits they hold. Roisin's cup represents the four original holders of the elements: a stormy night and a boat at sea, a volcano in Iceland, and Sedna, the Goddess of the Sea.

The spirits start to take shape. First, it looks like droplets are forming within the cups, which then morph into water, transforming into people made of flexible ice. Snowflake takes off her goggles, hat, and gloves and unbuttons her coat. It's far less cold in here, and she wants to be able to welcome the ancestors properly. However, she keeps the Cup securely on her back in her backpack. But before she even reaches the center of the circle to give her customary greeting, Roisin's crackled ice voice pierces through the cold air, "Is that the Cup?!"

The others are also drawn to it, gliding down and crowding around Snowflake.

"Ooooohhh! It's been such a long time," a short, plump ancestor tries to reach for the backpack, but another swats away her hand, "It's not yours anymore."

"Ladies, give Aputsiaq some room," Roisin orders, calling Snowflake by her real name.

"Dear ancestors, let me explain," Aputsiaq twirls around and forces them to step back. "I need your guidance and help."

Sputtering, they float back to their places. They rarely venture from there when Snowflake visits; this is all a bit unnerving. The Cup must still hold a strong pull for them, even after a long time.

"What's on your mind, child?" says her great-grandmother.

"Trouble is coming, and I need to hide the Cup. I don't think it's wise to keep it on me. Sedna tells me she's being watched. Salik has warded off a locator spell, and a strange witch is asking questions about us, claiming to want to warn us."

"We've seen the signs for some time now," Roisin says, sounding resigned. "Are you all prepared?"

"I know we have been talking about it for a while. They're coming—whoever they are—I want to bury the Cup here. Deep under the ice."

As one, the ancestors start to argue, and their crackling icy voices bounce around in the enclosed space, making it hard to make out actual words. Some speak English, some Danish or Greenlandic. Snowflake lets it all wash over her. Finally, after several minutes the noise dies down.

"Please, it would be great to have your support. This place is naturally hard to reach, well protected, and you will provide an extra layer of protection to keep it safe," Snowflake pleads.

"That's all very well, dear. Bottom line—we're just ghosts," Roisin counters.

"This is the best place," Snowflake insists.

"I wouldn't have a better suggestion," her great-grandmother supports her.

"What do you have in mind?" Roisin gives her consent.

Half an hour later, Aputsiaq, Snowflake, stands in the middle of the circle of cups, dressed in her ritual robe. The purest white with hints of blue woven through it, a testament to and in honor of the place they live, their connection to the Cup, and the purity of the ritual. A shimmering wall circling the outer rim of the cups reveals that a witch's power circle is up. The ancestors' spirits are back in the cups, in their watery form. A hum from their low chanting resounds throughout the space. With the Cup at Aputsiaq's feet and her arms raised to the sky, she begins her chant, "I call upon the element of Water; I'm your humble servant and guardian. I need your help to keep you safe. Let me hide you in your element!" With that, she kneels on both knees before the Cup and waits. The humming of the ancestor's chant presses on the air in the circle. Aputsiaq surrenders herself to the element and waits. Time passes, and finally, water starts to rise around her. Higher and higher, it quickly reaches her waist, and it takes the utmost restraint not to panic. As the guardian, she has no trouble breathing underwater, but her human instinct still freaks out when she's in her human form. She has to exert all her will not to change; she knows the importance of doing this in her true form. The water rises faster and faster until her witch circle is fully submerged. The chanting of the ancestors is now only a weird gurgling sound under the water. An element doesn't speak. It flows through you; the power of Water merges with Aputsiaq, and not since her acceptance of the guardianship has she felt its presence so strongly. No words are needed; what she knows, it knows. Elements don't have feelings or thoughts like humans do. The element does understand the threat, though, and Aputsiaq is suddenly filled with the sensation of its agreement with her request. Immediately, she lays herself flat on the ice at the bottom of the water bubble. The ice, just another form of water, starts to sing. An impossibly loud crack splits open the ice beneath her, and water rushes down to fill the void; the power of the magic keeps Aputsiaq floating above the cavity. She holds the Cup in her hand and, for a moment, everything seems to freeze—a hesitation, the last chance to change her mind. There is no doubt in her mind that this is the safest place, and she lets go of the Cup. It drifts down into the water, deep under the ice. All the water from the bubble fills up the cavity. "So mote it be!" her clear voice sounds through the void. In an instant, the water is frozen. Deep down, you can only catch a glimmer of the Cup. The energy level plummets, and the ancestors are silent.

"It's done," Snowflake turns and starts to walk back her ritual circle.

Such powerful water magic sends out a ripple throughout the oceans all over the world.

NEW ORLEANS

This significant water ripple startles Maeve and brings her witch-self back to the surface in her mind. She has been whirling in her Siren form deep down at the mouth of the Mississippi, on the edge where the river and the Gulf of Mexico meet. Vaguely aware of synapses on her tail, just barely hanging on.

After she had the heart-to-heart with Cephalop, the rest of their afternoon was fun and light as they browsed local witch shops and had a drink in the French Quarter. When darkness fell, Maeve wanted to head home, but Cephalop had something else in mind. It took some persuasion, but eventually, Maeve gave in. She took him to Crescent Park, where she could easily hide her clothes and disappear into the Mississippi unseen. At first, she was timid, Cephalop's lack of self-consciousness was disarming, and soon she managed to relax. Once they hit the water, all her doubts disappeared, and she swam down the muddy waters of the Mississippi with Cephalop right on her tail.

It was hard to imagine she had denied herself this for so long. The water is her natural habitat and with swift strokes, she moves back and forth. Although Cephalop is also a water creature, he has difficulty keeping up because of his tentacles. Hesitantly, he reaches for her, not wanting to freak her out. Maeve turns toward him, looking mesmerizing even in this mucky water. Her hair is flaming red today, moving like a giant crown around her head and body. Her tail scales shimmer, although there's no light, and when her seductive laugh reaches Cephalop, it makes him shiver. This makes Maeve laugh even more. He said he could resist her, but even this ancient fairy finds it hard and needs to do his best. What an exquisite creature! Maeve doesn't need much explanation; she has already doubled back several times to see where he is. She's tired of going slow; now she has freedom—she wants to go! Cephalop throws his tentacles around her tail, the synapses sucking tight around her, which gives her a pleasant sensation. Another sensual laugh escapes her; no longer waiting to see whether Cephalop is ready, she takes off through the Mississippi delta and out into the Gulf of Mexico, where they encounter many ocean creatures. The concept of time no longer has any importance.

Maeve has fully embraced her Siren side and forgotten about everything else until…the ripple of power hits her. It resonates with her witch-self, bringing her back to the here and now. Swiftly, she heads for the water's surface, slowing down once she senses it's there, and carefully emerges, looking to see if there's anybody around. It's quiet, and the sky is lighting up; sunrise is near. Cephalop pops up next to her.

"We need to go back," Maeve says without explanation.

"I figured," Cephalop agrees. He must have felt it too.

"Hold on."

Cephalop has just enough time to grab hold of Maeve before she takes off. This time, he's more like a backpack on her back, his tentacles all over. Something has happened to the Cup. Maeve doesn't know if they're too late to find it or what. She must get home as soon as possible.

Bridget dreams she's crying while she sits at the side of a small lake. It's an enclosed cavern, and the water is lapping at her feet. She's not entirely sure why she's so sad, but her tears keep going and going, feeding the lake. The water reacts and starts to rise rapidly. Bridget wants to get up but is stuck to her boulder. Slightly panicked, she looks around and sees no way out. A scream escapes her when a hand touches her shoulder. Unable to move from the rock, she can't turn around to see who's behind her. The hand is female, and the strange ring on one of the fingers reminds Bridget of Ceri's fairy ring. "Listen to the message," the woman whispers in her ear; she can feel her breath on her face.

Frantically, she tries to turn around, but the water is almost at her neck.

"It's time to fully embrace your responsibilities, as you hold the fate of many," the creepy whisper floats around her, mingling with the rising water. Reaching for her magic with no response, she screams.

"B?! Wake up!" Her eyes snap open and look into Wes's; his stricken face tells her she must have been screaming for real.

A little disoriented, Bridget looks around—where's the message? Willing herself to calm down, she throws out her witch sense and detects a disturbance in the power of Water. That explains it. Something happened. Hopefully, Lucy hasn't reached it yet.

"Was it a nightmare about your torture by Lucy?" Wes asks, concerned.

That makes her pause for just a moment. She was ready to rush ahead when she remembered their talk from yesterday. Breathing in and out to calm down and let the urgency subside, she turns to Wes, "No. It was a dream and a warning…I think. I don't know. Something has happened to the power of Water. Significant enough to reach another guardian," she says, keeping the strange, ominous voice to herself. The dogs are crowding her, giving her comfort. "Guys, a bit of space!" she commands. Reluctantly, they give her more room. "Do you know where my cellphone is? I need to check on Mom. Get Maeve and Gran, and let's go to the kitchen." Wes simply hands her the iPhone and slips into a pair of sweats. Bridget throws something on, and together with the dogs, they head down while she speed-dials her mother, and as they pass Tara's room, she bangs on her door. "Gran! Wake up. Something happened to Water." Not waiting for an answer, she walks on. Luna's phone goes to voicemail. Damn. "Mom, call me." She hangs up. When they enter the kitchen, it's quiet. No Maeve, no Emily, they're on their own for breakfast. Bridget throws open the French doors, so the dogs can go out and do their business. With her twin bond, she reaches for Maeve. *"Almost there"* is the response.

Tara has been awake for a while, sitting on her bench by the window with her card for the day in her hand. The Two of Pentacles, a monkey with a baby attached to her back, is juggling two pentacles. Too many things to deal with. The feeling that there is so much going on. Trying to keep all your balls in the air. What else is new lately? But Bridget's swift call reveals that their relative moment of peace is over. If Water has stirred, that means Lucy is moving for it. She knows it. Her sister never gives up.

ICELAND, STUDLAGIL BASALT CANYON

Freya and Luna are trying to discover what is floating outside their prison dome. It looks like a little girl in a frilly dress, and it's waving at them. Then with a loud, cheerful scream, she scoots down the side of the dome, like it's an amusement park ride. The sisters rush toward the edge of their containment to see what or who this is.

A cute young child, utterly adorable, grins at them. Alice in Wonderland comes to mind. She's maybe three feet tall and is wearing a pink dress.

"Who are you?" Freya asks.

"Hi, Luna. Have you missed me?" the creature smiles toothily, showing off her razor-sharp teeth.

Freya instantly steps back, which makes the little girl laugh a booming laugh.

Luna is awfully quiet; slowly, it starts to dawn on her. This must be the creature she had set free several months ago when she and Tara tried out one of the spells in Lucy's spell book. It has grown significantly, which is not a good sign.

"What do you want?" Luna wants to know.

"You know this creature?!" Freya is shocked.

"Not now," Luna cuts her off without taking her eyes off the little girl.

Freya's eyes shoot daggers, but she swallows her comments, which doesn't go unnoticed on the other side of their enclosure.

"Your sister doesn't like you. Maybe you want to trade her soul. I can let you out, you know." Her eyes glimmer mischievously.

"Enough with the soul-eating," Luna sounds firm as if she is speaking to an actual little girl. "We don't want to get out that desperately."

"Are you sure? The other two are well on their way to Greenland, and the old hag knows where the Cup is."

Luna does her utmost best to keep her expression neutral; the creature is unaware she just gave them some valuable information. She quickly glances at her sister and is surprised to see she's stone-faced, wearing her signature frown. "What's your name?" Luna asks, ignoring the bait.

"Wouldn't you like to know?" the girl says and dances around.

"Why do demons always want a soul?" Freya joins the conversation.

"It's what makes the world go around!" The girl twirls and twirls, "Our world at least. Your world as well, you know. You have them; we're only eating them. Supply and demand."

"Why are you not in the underworld? Waiting for them?"

"She set me FREEEEEEEEEE," squeaks the girl.

Freya's head whips toward Luna. "It was an accident."

"Really? Your arrogance is going to get us all killed. You set her loose and didn't bother to recapture her?" Freya sounds disgusted.

"The shit hit the fan right then. I sort of—forgot," Luna doesn't need to look at Freya to sense her displeasure.

The girl turns to Freya. "Maybe you want to trade her soul," she says, raising an eyebrow toward Luna.

"Tempting—"

Luna gasps.

"But no. She is, after all, my sister," Freya sourly smiles back.

"Suit yourself. Nice chatting. Enjoy your time here. It's a pretty good spell," she says. With that, she twirls, and a whirlwind funnel forms; then poof! And she's gone.

Luna turns toward Freya, "I know what you're going to say, but—"

"We don't have time for this. Greenland, did you hear that? All this time wasted arguing; we need to go."

Luna is flabbergasted. This is so out of character. Iceland has had a strange effect on her older sister.

FAIRY

Emily stretches herself and yawns. Wow, she can't remember sleeping this deeply. Only when she opens her eyes does she realize she's in her room at her mother's house in Fairy. Slowly, the shocking ending of their day in the Fairy entertainment park comes back to her. The others were so worried; she, however, felt strangely calm. Thinking about it, she hasn't felt so good in months. Things have been so stressful with their parents' separation, the Magical Tarot Deck stolen because of her, and her disastrous friendship with Mab. Initially, she had been thrilled that her mother was part fairy. When it turned out she didn't inherit her genes in that respect, she got so angry! Desperately wanting to be a fairy herself, she had believed Mab when she promised to help her. But Mab used her as leverage against her mother, with terrible consequences. Her cheeks flush red just at the thought. The guilt and embarrassment afterward have been weighing on her.

For a moment, she closes her eyes and tries to think back to what happened after she stepped through the portal. Pain, she remembers the pain, and calm. Some women talking, or did she make that up? Her head gets foggy when she tries to focus on that, but a sense of purpose settles in. Weird. Ah well, it doesn't matter. In an unusually cheerful mood, she hops out of bed and gets dressed while humming a tune. She finally feels special, without knowing why; it's like her heart is wrapped in a warm hug.

Yesterday proved she was at least some part fairy; things are looking up.

The hallway is quiet. Emily wants to call Alvina, but instead decides to explore the house. It has been a while. Maybe she can play with Firefly. Her initial irritation and jealousy have dissipated, and now she wants to get to know her younger half-sister!

Noises come from her mother's study when she passes. She walks on but her curiosity gets the better of her, turning back and quietly opening the door.

Ceri is sitting behind her desk, and in the room, a memory of Oberon, the King of Fairy, is playing. Several other royal-looking fairies are gathered around him, kneeling and saying something that looks like some pledge. When Ceri notices Emily, a genuinely happy smile flashes across her face, a mix of love and relief. Emily had given her quite the scare yesterday. Her daughter smiles back and things are back to normal for a brief moment.

Emily notices Ceri's eyes flickering to someone else in the room. Oops, she's not alone. Not waiting for an invitation, she steps inside and freezes when she recognizes the other person. "YOU?!" she shouts and immediately throws a lightning spell his way.

Ceri snaps her fingers and it dissolves before it can hit Cal.

"Emily!" Seamus rushes to her, full of joy to see yet another family member. She doesn't react at all and only shivers when he tries to hug her.

"She's mainly human," is all Ceri says. "Emily, this is Cal—"

"He stole the Magical Tarot Deck!" Emily is bright red again and frustrated that her mother seems so calm.

"I know. If you calm down, I can explain."

Emily whips her head toward her mother, not looking happy anymore.

"Please," Ceri motions for her to sit down.

Emily chooses the seat the furthest from Cal and sits while keeping her eyes on him the whole time.

"Emily," Ceri tries to draw her attention. But she doesn't react. "Emily!" At last, she looks at her mother. "I could tell you some things, but as you will understand, I'm a bit hesitant, to be honest."

"You can trust me," is her quick reply.

Now her mother only looks at her. Emily is no longer able to hold her stare, looking down at her hands. Is her mother right to doubt her? Probably. She would love to lash out, but unfortunately, she is to blame for certain things. Finally, she looks back up, the others patiently waiting her out. "You can. I know I've messed up. How can I prove it?"

"Good girl," Seamus says, even though she can't hear it. "Give her a chance."

All eyes are now on Ceri.

"What choice do you have?" whispers Sparkle in her ear. "She has seen the man."

When Ceri still doesn't say anything…

"Oh no!" Sparkle chastises her, "Don't you dare. You will always regret it if you bespell your child. Or worse, let the Ferrymaster take the memory. Look what that did to your sister!"

Ceri sighs, "Okay. I will include you in this secret. Prove that you can keep it, and I will let you in more family business."

"I won't let you down!" Emily jumps up and rushes over to her mother to hug her. "I promise!" With that resounding promise, the whole room gives a little shudder. A witch's promise is made—even Fairy reacts to that.

"Calm down," Ceri keeps an arm around Emily's waist to keep her next to her. "Meet Cal. Well, I guess you have met under less happy circumstances." Emily stiffens. "Cal is Lucy's grandson, and he's a friend of Seamus."

"Granddad?"

"Yes! I'm here!" Seamus twirls around in front of her.

"You can't see Seamus, but he's here and thrilled to see you. Cal and Seamus are doing something special for me. And it's paramount Mab doesn't know Cal is here. Is that clear?"

"Yes, Ma'am," Emily confirms. "I don't want to see Mab ever again."

"I know. That might not be under your control, though. And you can't tell her this under any circumstances. Ever," Ceri stresses.

"I get it, Ma!"

"I can't have an attitude with this, do you hear me?"

"Sorry, Ma'am," Emily is a bit shocked by her mother's forceful reaction. "What are they doing?" she says, trying to steer the conversation into calmer waters.

"I want to know more about history—our history and what it means for us as a family, for all our sakes. All this mixed-blood…it's coming out, and we need to be better prepared. We've been ignorant for far too long."

"Can I help?" Eager to be helpful, she's ready for some action—her confidence of this morning returning.

"Not now, maybe when you're back home. Earth home, I mean," Ceri quickly corrects herself.

This is rewarded with a full wattage smile from her daughter.

"Better," Sparkle approves.

NEW ORLEANS

Bridget has put the kettle on and is pulling stuff from the cupboards for some breakfast. The others will be here soon. The urgency she feels inside after her strange dream puts her on edge. With a snap of her fingers, cups and saucers find their way to the table, giving her pause. Half a year ago, she thought she banned all magic from her life. Now, she snaps her fingers, and things fly around. The first sun of the day shines through the French doors. Bridget stops what she's doing and walks over, right into that sunbeam, and throws her arms around herself. Although the chill that is running up her spine has nothing to do with being cold. What has happened to her? This question suddenly finds its way to her conscious mind. When Tara forced the Wand's power on her, everything changed. The warm power of the Wand quickly washed away her initial anger. It's hard to deny that rush is exhilarating! With the transition of the guardian, Tara had a hard time adjusting, and Bridget stepped into the leadership role without thinking. Everything came about at such a rapid pace, not one moment to catch her breath and think it through. After Maeve attuned to the Dagger, things only accelerated. Their bond was stronger than ever, and the need to study and keep things under control had trumped everything.

But at this moment, the weight of it all is sinking in, and it scares the shit out of her. How on earth is she going to lead the family? Nobody is taking her seriously. What about her bond with Maeve? She's not even sure they can see themselves as separate anymore. Even now, she can feel her sister coming closer and closer; it's like a constant presence in her head. Shame floods her system when she allows herself to remember she had denied Maeve any contact for years; being without her sister again is unthinkable. She would be incomplete.

The door opens, and Tara steps into the kitchen. Their eyes lock for a moment. "Everything okay?" Tara wants to know.

A thought jumps in Bridget's head; is that how Tara and Lucy feel? If that is the case—she needs to be careful with Tara. This floats through Bridget's head before answering honestly, "I don't know."

Luckily for Bridget, Wes arrives and recognizes her worried state. He walks over and kisses her lightly on the lips. "Need a hand?"

"No, Maeve is here," Bridget answers a second before the others hear Maeve and Cephalop arrive. They both wander nonchalantly into the kitchen, murmuring, "Hello," acknowledging the others. Maeve starts working with the ingredients that Bridget has left out for her, and within minutes, she slides the muffins into the oven.

Nobody has said a word; it's like you can hear a pin drop. Strange and awkward after Bridget's summoning them. Everybody is observing the other. Maeve and Cephalop seem so relaxed and happy. Wes is less stressed, his body language betraying he and Bridget patched things up. Tara drinks it all in, eager to be included again now that she feels so much better.

"Did you feel it?" Maeve asks Bridget.

"I dreamed about water. The stress—the urgency was still running through me when Wes woke me up. Something happened," Bridget confirms.

"Did Lucy find the Cup?" Tara wants to know.

"That's unclear. I tried to get a hold of Mom, but she's not picking up. Has anybody spoken to them recently?" asks Bridget.

Maeve doesn't bother answering as Bridget knows she hasn't, so they both look at Tara.

"I talked to them yesterday morning. It was an afternoon for them already, and they were heading somewhere to try to replenish Luna's powers."

"Where?!"

"I…I don't remember," Tara reluctantly admits.

"Something is off. We need to contact them," Bridget insists.

"You know how they are. Luna and Freya are both headstrong. They're probably butting heads right now," Tara tries to calm everybody down.

"I agree with B. I asked Mom to stay in touch. She knows what's at stake. Aunt Freya or not. They will try their best," Maeve sides with her twin.

"Well, if they don't answer their phones…," Tara shrugs.

"There is another way," Wes's voice sounds hoarse.

All heads turn toward him.

"Why don't you use the Magical Tarot Deck?"

Reverently, Bridget takes the Magical Tarot Deck from the Madigan's safe in the study. After some deliberation and the need for some answers, they decided it should be only her and Wes who are in the room. Maeve wants to clean up after her swim, and the girls are still trying to stay separated as much as possible. Anyway, Bridget has the most experience with the cards, and when she takes them out of the pouch and leaves through the deck, she gets hit by a wave of unexpected emotion. The pain of the torture she endured from Lucy while she was in the half state is still raw.

Lucy had used Bridget's card to call her over but managed to stall the process of coming fully through the transition of the magical card. She used Bridget as a real-life Voodoo doll in this half state. It left Bridget with a feeling of helplessness, even worse than the pain. Unable to fight back was against her nature. An experience she has not been able to process yet, and the emotions overwhelm her at unexpected moments. Tears form in Bridget's eyes, and Wes quietly moves behind her and affectionately rubs her shoulders. This brings her back to the here and now. It's over. She survived—now she has to focus on what's ahead.

Leafing through the cards, she's struck by the fantastic magical masterpiece that her grandfather had created. Such a shame it had cost them so dearly. Ah, here's Luna's card. Her mother's face is staring right at her from the Moon card. "Ready?" she asks herself, probably just as much as Wes.

"Yes, you can do it," Wes encourages her while he feels a rush of anticipation. That's what the cards do to you.

Bridget clears her mind while gently rubbing the card, calling her mother forward. The card bulges and stretches, and soon Luna stands in front of them.

"Bridget?!" Luna says that while she takes a couple of seconds to adjust to the transition; she's dressed exactly the same as on her Moon card.

"Mom! Are you and Freya okay?" Bridget jumps up and walks to stand across from her mother, a little awkward and unsure if she should hug her or not.

"Lucy and Mara trapped us in a dome. Our cellphones don't work; we've tried everything, but so far, we haven't managed to get out. I'm so glad you 'called.'" Pride shines through, that they thought of using the cards.

"This was Wes's idea," Bridget is giving credit where it's due.

Luna acknowledges him with a nod of her head.

"Where are you? Were you in a fight?" So many questions.

"We're fine," Luna reassures her. "Lucy and Mara sneaked up on us while we did the ritual to replenish my strength. Stupid of us; we were such easy targets. They must have come there for a similar reason. More importantly, they have a head start toward Greenland. They think the Cup is there."

"Is that true?" Bridget wonders.

"It's likely. With the connection to Denmark, it would make sense. Can you get us out of here?"

Bridget's mind is racing through the possible options. Going to Iceland is going to take time. The quickest way is to ask Ceri since she can make portals these days. "I'll ask Ceri."

"Freya doesn't want to go to Fairy," Luna states.

Bridget gives her a look of "I don't care."

"If there's another way—" Luna tries before Bridget cuts her off.

"—nothing quick." She's puzzled. Freya must be distraught if her mother is defending her. Usually, Luna wouldn't care about Freya's feelings. "Something happened to the Cup. But as Lucy only recently left you, someone or something else must have caused the disturbance."

"What disturbance?" Luna's interest is aroused.

"There were ripples in the power of Water. No way Lucy could have made it to Greenland for that as she was busy trapping you; that's good news. There must be some other reason why the power stirred."

"Good news?!" Luna's face reflects what she thinks of that statement. "Get us out of here as soon as you can. We must catch up to Lucy. Anything else?"

"Nope," Bridget answers. "I'm going to get in touch with Ceri. Hang in there." Without further delays, she moves her hand over the card, and Luna starts to dissolve.

"Freya is scared of the Ferrymaster; ask Ceri—" Luna doesn't get a chance to finish.

Wes breathes out, wholly fascinated by the process. Bridget had almost forgotten he was there. She was intrigued by Luna's last words. After what happened to her last time, Bridget gets it that Freya is not happy to see the Ferrymaster, especially after she discovered that her own parents had her memories removed. Who knows what else got lost? If everything goes according to plan and with Ceri's involvement, this should not happen.

FAIRY

Ceri and Seamus finally have a moment together. While Cal is reading something in her study, they're in the next room. Seamus looks positively nervous; Ceri had signaled him to follow her. She has been thinking about her upbringing and this mixed-blood thing a lot and even though she's upset with Seamus for not telling her, to have him here again is an opportunity for her to work this out and give her some closure. "Dad, can you stop spinning around, please?"

Seamus zigzags one more time through the room before he hovers in front of her, his mouth opening and closing several times before finding the words.

"I think I know what you want to talk about. I'm sorry. I know that doesn't help you. But I am sorry for not telling you. It felt like the best thing to do at the time. You always were so cheerful. And later, with Bert and the kids, it felt like you were the only one of our children who was truly happy. You felt like my own; I forgot that wasn't so. We connected in a way I didn't with the others. It's weird how those things work. The longer and further you stuff it away, the more the truth gets molded into something else," he rambles on.

Ceri, letting him sweat, waits him out. She always knew that Seamus would have told her if it weren't for Tara. He adored her.

"Who would ever think this would happen? Gosh, I never did. We had such a peaceful life. Frustrating, I'm like this. Not able to help you," he's erratically zipping around again.

Ceri takes pity on him; he's so obviously distressed. "Dad!"

Seamus quiets down and slowly hovers, now only three feet away from her.

This revelation and his reaction melt Ceri's heart. Yes, she was angry, but he's here for her and aware of his mistake. His apology sounds genuine, somehow different from the one she got from Tara. With her, you still get the feeling she would do the same if she had to go through it again. So, Ceri looks him in the eye while she says, "You are and always will be my dad."

As the words settle in, the burden falls from Seamus' shoulder, comically visible as he bounces up, as if he's lighter. "Thank you. I never expected you to forgive me. It means so much." Tears start to roll down his ghostly cheeks.

"Oh, Dad," Ceri steps forward as if they would hug, just in time to remember that it doesn't work. "It's good to have you here with me now. Make no mistake; I'm upset with you about what happened. But I'm relieved we have a chance to set this straight. I love you—always."

This hangs between them for a few more seconds before Seamus snaps back into his ghost routine of swirling around, saying, "We need to figure out this business of where we came from, how our powers come into being. I'm so excited. Cal might be a bit sulky, but he's a good kid. And ohhhhhhh, his heritage is deliciously interesting."

This makes Ceri laugh out loud. Suddenly, a tingling around her finger and a shimmer in the air warn her that Bridget is trying to reach her. For a second, she hesitates but decides it must be urgent if her niece is reaching out. When Ceri just became the Keeper of the Land, she had given one of her tattoo connections to Bridget. Unaware it's a permanent psychic bond. Both are uncomfortable with this intimate communication; they use it as little as possible.

Bridget becomes visible on the other side with a little power boost to the shimmer. Seamus is hovering immediately behind her, his curiosity piqued.

"Great, you're there," Bridget doesn't waste any time.

"Hello to you too," Ceri says and smiles.

"BRIDGET!" Seamus shouts but gets no reaction; his face falls.

Ceri is about to explain that Seamus is there, but Bridget, unaware and driven by the urgency of the Cup, keeps talking. "Here's the short version. The power of the Cup has stirred. Maeve and I both felt it. Something significant must have happened to it. We know it's not Lucy as she trapped Luna and Freya in Iceland roughly at the same time. But she does seem to know where it is. Greenland! Of all places. Anyway, a lot to catch up on, but we need to free Luna and Freya as soon as possible; they need to find Lucy. We can't let her reach the Cup first."

"Whoa, whoa whoa," Ceri tries to slow Bridget down. "Greenland? Do you know for sure? I don't know anything about that place," she states.

"We don't know anything about it either, only that the family who has the Cup most likely lives there. Can you get them out? You can make a portal, right?!"

Ceri needs to squash her growing irritation. Her niece seems to have grown in bossiness; she has plenty she needs to take care of herself.

Realizing her aunt is annoyed, Bridget pleads, "Please, Auntie?"

With a sigh, Ceri replies, "Making a portal from my home to another place is only possible if I know where I'm going. Since I've never been to Iceland, the best thing to do is use an existing one. Do you know where they are exactly?"

"Studlagil Basalt Canyon—it's in the northwestern part of Iceland."

"Okay. I will need a bit of time to make it secure. We don't want Mab to be aware that I'm going."

"Another thing is that Freya doesn't want to come to Fairy because she's terrified of running into the Ferrymaster," Bridget warns her.

"If I pick her up this way, she doesn't need to pay him. I'll make sure," Ceri assures her.

"Just be prepared for some arguing. The fact that she found out that Tara and Seamus had her memories taken as a child has literally tipped her over the edge. Not that I can blame her. Who would do that to his child?" Bridget's sincere indignation is hitting Seamus.

Ceri can sense him stop moving behind her. Another of his bad decisions is coming back to haunt him.

Bridget allows a moment of silence as she mulls over how to respond. "Is this going to work?" she then asks.

"I'm on it. After that, we need to talk. It's been intriguing on this end as well. I have two families now." These last words are spoken with a hint of reprimand. She's not at the Madigans' beck and call anymore.

"I hear you. Thank you, Aunt Ceri. I know you have a lot on your plate," Bridget changes her tone.

Ceri's features soften before she severs the connection and turns toward Seamus. "Still happy you're back?"

"Yeah, another unfortunate decision we made…." His ghostly figure sinks down to the floor.

Ceri floats through the Land of Fairy in her dematerialized state. It's hard to imagine that she had gotten so lost the first time here. Now the nurturing and support she receives in return has almost become second nature. In this state, there's an infinite amount of knowledge about Fairy and its connection to Earth. It's the easiest way for her to figure out which portal will bring her closest to her trapped sisters. Iceland has an impressive number of portals, more than most other countries. People there live more in tune with fairies, it seems. However, Greenland has just one portal, all the way down in the Southern part. She can't figure out if there's even a town nearby. It might be wise to take a broom with them. That's for later—first, get them out.

When she reaches the portal closest to her sisters, she can feel the veil is thin, almost as if she can peek through to the other side. If she leaves this place, Mab will never know where she is. She might be connected to everything as the Queen, but that limits her senses. There's only so much you can keep track of. Sparkle has taught her to make such a minor disturbance that it will go unnoticed among all the other things going on in Fairy. Gently, her body starts to materialize as if millions and millions of twinkles are drawn back together, re-forming Ceri. At the same time, she makes a thin slice in the veil. Within a split second, she steps onto the basalt rocks in Studlagil Basalt Canyon, and for a moment, she does a 360. Taking everything in before, her attention rests on the two women on the opposite side of the canyon.

Luna, becoming aware of her presence, waves enthusiastically while Freya's face falls, and she immediately turns on Luna. Ceri can see they're arguing. While it is very tempting to let Luna deal with that, unfortunately, she doesn't have much time to spare. Better get it over with. With a sigh, she realizes she should have brought a broom as well. It would have been a hop and a skip to the other side, but now she has to take the long way. She had forgotten she was a mere mortal here like the rest. How quickly you can adjust. Annoying and satisfying at the same time. It had taken a lot of effort to accept the fact that her home is now in Fairy, and being back here makes her aware that she has embraced it. Earth seems so limiting.

ICELAND, STUDLAGIL BASALT CANYON

Freya's heart sinks when she spots Ceri on the opposite side of the Canyon. So far, Luna had neglected to mention that part of the rescue. She had been so adamant that she didn't want to go to Fairy again. The time she spent with the Ferrymaster while Ceri and Ron were looking for her had been quite disturbing.

With all that had been going on, nobody had asked her exactly what happened, and she was grateful for that.

After he had whisked her away from her family, they transported to his home. The strange structure looked like endless rooms, one on top of the other. The rooms were stuffed with memory globes; unfathomable how many memories he must have taken from people. Not only people, it turns out—any creature imaginable. The Ferrymaster bounced around between his different sizes, touching the globes and replaying memories without rhyme or reason. Or that's how it seemed. It's probably a mistake to think he has no plan or doesn't know what a treasure trove of knowledge he's guarding. Some of the memories he gives to Mab. But she has neither the time nor the patience to deal with them.

The Ferrymaster was thrilled to have her as a companion and had quickly persuaded her to give him a memory, which is customary when you pass through Fairy. Of course, she can't remember which one she gave away, only that she had done it. After that, he tried to charm her into parting with additional ones. Although she resisted, she's unsure if she hadn't given him others anyway, making her frustrated and insecure. Who knows what she had lost? It took quite a while before she was finally rescued.

After, Freya learned her parents gave some of her memories to the Ferrymaster so she would never reveal the secret about how Ceri arrived in the family. She had lost it for a while. She still woke up most nights bathed in a sweat of fear about what might have been lost. It made her question many things and, most of all, her loyalty to her mother. Her family. Whom can she trust?

Not Luna, as it turns out. She could have prepared her for this. For a brief moment, Freya had felt an unexpected connection to her sister, which has now melted away. What was she thinking? They had never gotten along, and it will never happen. "You betrayed me…again," Freya accuses Luna. "I said I'm not going to Fairy."

"We tried to think of other options. Honestly," Luna pleads with her. "This is the fastest way to get there. Otherwise, it could be days. We can't afford to waste days. Who knows how far ahead Lucy is already?"

"You can go. I'll stay here," Freya says stubbornly.

"Ceri can protect you. You will be safe. You have to trust us."

Freya's eyes turn into red hot coals, and Luna takes a step back. "TRUST YOU! TRUST YOU!" Her booming voice bounces off the prison globe. "What have you ever done to deserve my trust?! Nobody takes me seriously; I'm treated like a second-rate witch. Even by my mother! They let HIM take my memories!" Desperation fills their bubble. These strong emotions stir a place inside Freya that she never tapped into before. Lightning bolts shoot from her eyes and discharge against the globe. It shudders under the sheer power of her outburst.

Luna backs up fast, coughing, choking on Freya's despair.

All Freya's frustration, fear, and anger spill out. A scream escapes her and she falls to her knees, touching the ground. The land answers; Luna can't describe it any other way. A rumble rolls out of Freya through the land, and in the far distance, it finds an outlet in one of Iceland's active volcanos.

"Calm her down!" Ceri's urgent voice reaches Luna from afar. Luna searches inside herself to find her magic but there's none. She almost tumbles into despair—the feeling of worthlessness—that she's nobody without her powers.

"Luna! Calm her down!" Ceri's voice pulls Luna back from the brink, reaching deep inside to the part that is human and not witch. Deep, deep down, she finds strength, the kind of strength she sees reflected in Bridget.

The ground rumbles again when Freya lets out another desperate cry.

"LUNA!!!" This time Ceri's urgency manages to snap her out of her stupor. The ground feels like jelly, and she wobbles back and forth as she struggles to get up. Swaying, she staggers over to Freya.

"Freya, please. Stop." There's no reaction. The sense of desperation is still choking Luna. Hesitantly, she reaches for her older sister. Does she dare to touch her? Freya is in such obvious pain. Luna's heart breaks for her, and determined she grabs Freya's shoulder and kneels behind her while she hugs her tight. Freya is rigid and steaming hot. Still, Luna holds on and starts to sing Seamus' Gaelic lullaby. It's the only thing she can think of. It had helped with Diane; let's hope it will work now.

The ground keeps rumbling, and Luna is about to give up when she feels Freya slightly relaxing. The zinging tension is leaving her. The ground is more solid, and when she looks up over her sister's shoulder, she looks straight into Ceri's emerald green. Relieved that she's not in this alone, she continues singing. With a loud snap, the dome is shattered. That didn't take Ceri very long. A sign of the tremendous power her fairy sister now wields. Ceri rushes over and kneels in front of Freya, taking her sister's face between her hands. "You are safe with me." Green eyes promise to the red-hot coals in Freya's. With that, Ceri sweeps the portal over them, and they are in her living room in Fairy. To go home is the easiest. She can always make a safe portal home from anywhere. Freya slumps down into Luna's arms, totally spent.

GREENLAND, NUUK

When Lucy steps off the plane, she's hit by the cold air. A cough escapes her, and her steps falter. Mara reaches for her. "I'm all right," Lucy brushes her off. In truth, she hadn't been all right since she lost her connection to the Dagger. The emptiness and lack of power are starting to affect her physically. She managed to push herself forward on sheer willpower for a while, but the cold weather is sapping her energy quicker than she can replenish it. In Iceland, she restored some of her magical stamina, but not enough. What she needs is a warm bath and a good night's sleep. Shaking off her weariness, she looks around her. The tiny airport is on the edge of the capital Nuuk. With only 16,000 people, it feels like a village to Americans, compared to the vastness of their country. The granite peaks are already covered in snow. Cold and harsh is her first impression. The people guarding the Cup must be a tough bunch. This will not be as easy as retrieving the Dagger.

Mara is taking it all in, not showing her thoughts. Lucy had taught her well; now, she wishes her granddaughter was a bit more transparent. Something is off with her.

"Where do you want to start?" Mara asks, ready for action.

"Let's find a hotel. There's no rush. The Madigans don't know where we are, and this is such a strange place for us. We need to figure out where it is and ensure we're prepared."

Mara nods and heads for the small luggage claim belt in the tiny airport.

NEW ORLEANS

Bridget goes upstairs to see Wes. After contacting Luna, he said he wanted to paint, and Bridget was distracted by one of her many responsibilities. Several hours later, she makes it upstairs to his atelier and finds the door locked. That is nothing out of the ordinary. Most of the time, he locks his door when he's busy. Knowing that doesn't stop Bridget from sneaking in and watching him work. Without thinking about it, she puts her hand on the lock and mumbled a simple unlocking spell, which now rolls off her tongue so easily. When she steps inside, there was no Wes but five enormous paintings, which render her speechless. They are mesmerizing, intense, and honestly, a bit frightening. It looks like they tell some sort of story. They are nothing like he has painted before and the traumatic experience of transferring the Dagger's power to Maeve has in no doubt set this off.

The first painting portrays Maeve whirling in the air, naked and with a fresh bloody wound over the length of her torso. And yes—she's literally whirling. That's what's so disturbing; these paintings are alive! Like Seamus's paintings used to be. How did that happen?! Wes has been painting with Seamus' supplies the whole time. His paintings were extremely lifelike, but they never moved.

The painting of Maeve could be horrific, but she's surrounded by light and strangely comforting images of things she has been baking. This combination turns it into something surreal. It is as if Wes tries to reconcile these different impressions he has of Maeve.

The next one makes her sad and ache inside. It's an image of herself on top of some tower; her appearance radiates power, making her cold and untouchable. At the bottom of the tower, a painted Wes runs around and around the structure, desperate to find a way in. The reality of what Wes confessed to her over lunch is barreling down and hitting her like she's been punched in the gut.

It's different when someone tells you, but nothing brings it home like this painting. Wes's desperation is palpable, and seeing herself portrayed with such remoteness will take some time to process. Is this how he sees her now? No wonder their relationship is in danger. What does she have to do to reach him again? Not having the answer to these questions, she turns to the remaining canvasses hoping for more insight.

The third one portrays magic. On the left is the frivolous kind of magic that Wes first encountered. The sparks that fly when they argue, Ceri on a broom, Diane's t-shirt flapping like a flag, they're floating around, and if you follow the progression to the right, they gradually morph into the scary stuff, flames and whirlwinds and more destruction. It's a perfect portrait of the balance of magic. If you ever needed to explain to someone what magic entails, this is an excellent example—the balance of things. There's always another side to it—Wes gets that now.

The fourth painting is not violent. However, it's no less disturbing. It's full of the three of them in all sorts of sexual fantasies. On some of them, Maeve sports a huge scar, which in real life is not there. Weird how magic works. Wes must have plenty of thoughts about the three of them. Bridget can't help but feel a pang of jealousy. This is precisely what she has been afraid of. Maybe not exactly, though. In all fairness, she's included in everything. It's like tens of erotic Unity Tarot Cards swirling together on the canvas.

The fifth and last painting is a portrait of the two sisters. Bridget sits in the garden by the fountain with her back against the overgrown wall; her legs casually spread apart. Maeve is draped against her. It's hard to determine where one sister ends and the next one begins. Maeve's wild hair floats around and merges with Bridget. It's beautiful. He has managed to portray Bridget's Fire-y powers simmering within, and you can also sense Maeve's Airy powers. They are shielded by the warmth of the garden—a safe haven, two and yet one.

Wow, this is all a lot to take in. No wonder Wes has been distant. It's now evident that he never intended her to see this. Does she stay or go? Why hadn't she spent more time with him after what happened to Maeve? It's a rhetorical question as she knows the answers and knows it was inevitable. She needs time to figure out how she's going to mend this. It triggers so many emotions within her; maybe Maeve can help. Quickly, she dismisses that idea. She shouldn't have come herself. Without waiting any longer, she takes one last look at the paintings before she exits the room and locks the door. As she stands there with her hand on the door, deep in thought about everything she has seen, she doesn't hear Wes come up the stairs.

"What are you doing?" the alarm reverberates in his words.

Bridget snaps back into her normal mode, squashes all feelings, and decides not to mention she had been inside. "Ah, there you are? I was about to go in and watch you work."

Wes inserts himself between her and the door, forcing her to step back. He looks at the ground before he looks her in the eye and says, "I would love it if you wouldn't do that for now. I would like to finish the paintings first."

Bridget struggles with the proper response, and Wes interprets that hesitation as curiosity. "I know this must make you curious. It's extremely personal."

"You can always show me. You know that—right?"

Again, Wes stares at the floor for some inspiration on how to answer that. "I know, but—the whole experience. This is a way for me to process it. Can you give me some space to do that in my own way? Maybe I will just destroy them when they're finished."

Bridget doesn't know what to say to that. She nods in acknowledgment, and for a moment, they look at each other, taking each other in, assessing their relationship. Then Bridget gives him another nod, bends forward, and places a gentle kiss on his lips. It takes a split second before he responds and kisses her back.

Without another word, she turns around and rushes down the stairs. She needs fresh air to clear her head. She has to get out of this house; the walls crowd her, and she heads for the front door while whistling for the dogs. This is crazy— how on earth is it possible that these paintings are moving? Can you transfer power to a human? Kiki, Bouncer, and Seeker meet her at the door. The others must be somewhere else. Hopefully, the ancestors will have some answers—she doesn't want to ask Tara.

FAIRY

Freya has calmed down; her eyes are back to normal. With an angry stare, she follows Ceri, pacing up and down the room. Luna sits next to her on the couch with an almost identical expression. It would be comical if only the circumstances weren't so unfortunate.

Cal came into the room with Seamus, Maeron, and Alvina. It took Ceri quite some explaining, hence Luna's expression.

"We need to go," Luna states without mentioning Greenland as Cal is still there.

Ignoring her, Ceri looks at Freya, "How are you feeling?"

Freya scans the room for the umpteenth time, just in case the Ferrymaster might show himself.

"My house is protected; only family can come here uninvited," Ceri says, catching on to her discomfort. "What happened to you when you were in Fairy?"

"I don't want to talk about it," Freya stonewalls her.

"Oh, Freya, Freya, Freya! I know it upsets you so much that you made a volcano erupt in Iceland. We need to deal with it before you can go on. Who knows what you will do next time?" Ceri points out.

"There will be no next time. I'm not coming back here, period. Do you hear me?!"

"Yes. What happened out there? You have been different ever since you came to Iceland. Have you been communicating with the land?" Luna wants to know.

Seamus is uncharacteristically quiet. Aware his two daughters who have suddenly shown up are unable to see him, he's not ready to face Freya's wrath. Even though a low profile seems like the best plan, he's intrigued by this volcano business.

Freya feels the anger bubbling up, her initial reaction, and her oh-so-familiar shield. It courses through her, but a seed of doubt had been planted in Iceland. Something changed her when she arrived. It's undeniable. It had felt so good. Like the land did recognize her, and she belonged there. It would be wonderful if she could figure out where that came from. Something inside her is missing, and as much as she doesn't want to admit it, she needs help. The memories she misses are here in Fairy. Maybe this is the place to start. Slowly, the anger ebbs away, and with a deep, ragged breath, she says, "I need help. Something is missing inside me. I'm afraid the Ferrymaster took pieces from my puzzle, and I will never be whole."

A bell tolls, the ringing sound bounces around, and the room is blanketed in shocked silence.

Seamus, Ceri, and Luna are flabbergasted with this revelation of truth. Freya never had, and that means—never, revealed her feelings. The first thing coming out is such a heartbreaking insight into her soul.

"Please," pleads Freya in a tiny voice. This snaps her sisters out of their shock, reaching for her and hugging her tight.

"We love you," Ceri says, and again a bell tolls, less loud, but it's the truth spoken again.

For several minutes, the sisters comfort her, and to everybody's surprise, Freya lets herself be held for a while before she untangles herself. "I don't know where to begin," she admits.

"Do you remember what happened when the Ferrymaster took you?" Ceri asks.

Freya tells them about his unimaginably big house with the endless rooms stacked one on top of the other, full of memories.

"We need to go there!" Seamus jumps up; he has been quiet all this time.

"We can't just show up at the Ferrymaster's door," Maeron answers him.

"Who are you talking to?" Luna looks around, as this seems to come out of the blue.

"Dad is here," Ceri sighs, waiting for the other shoe to drop, but Freya and Luna mainly look confused. "Cal still has Dad's card from the Magical Tarot Deck, and he has used it. Seamus is attached to him, and they're helping me with something."

"Something…. What?" Freya wants to know.

Ceri glances at Maeron, who shrugs. "I want to know where we came from. How our powers came into being? Why are the Madigans stronger than most witches? Stuff like that."

"Why?" Freya's happy it's not about her for a moment.

"I know it's crucial information."

"How do you know?"

"I know it here," Ceri places her hand on her heart. Gut feeling is a modus operandi for witches. Intuition is not to be ignored. "Anyway, Seamus is there," Ceri points to him. "He wants to go to the Ferrymaster, as it sounds like he has all that information."

Very slowly, Freya gets up and walks over to where Ceri had pointed. "You said he's here?" She points more or less in his direction. Seamus freezes; the look Freya throws in his general direction doesn't bode well.

"You're about two feet away from him," Ceri confirms.

"HOW DARE YOU!!!" Freya's voice resounds throughout the room. Seamus cowers under the weight of her anger. She might not be able to see him, but it hits him nonetheless. "You let him take away something from me. I have felt incomplete my whole life. Never knowing what it was or where that feeling came from. I was angry, always angry. Do you even know what that is like?"

"I'm so, so sorry—" he says. But not able to hear Seamus, Freya goes on, "I had endless amounts of therapy. Nothing. Nothing helped! And now, finally I understand. You and my MOTHER—," the way she says it is loaded with so much pain and disbelief it resonates through the room. None can stand in her presence and not feel her despair. It's new that Freya's emotions keep spilling over this way. Iceland must have awakened something in her. "What can I do?!" She says to no one in particular, "Where do I even start? Can I ever get those memories back?"

The humans and fairies around her acknowledge her pain by looking at her and letting it settle in the space. Eventually, Maeron speaks, "The Ferrymaster does make trades, but we will need to be careful with that. Mab will be in the know."

Seamus shakes himself; this anger directed at him doesn't leave him unaffected. It will take some time to absorb this and come to terms with himself; however, his problem-solving nature surfaces, and he desperately wants to help her. "It sounds like the Ferrymaster is the one to go and see anyway if he has so much knowledge."

"What is he saying?" Luna wants to know as the others in the room are looking at a space where she figures Seamus must be.

"Dad says the Ferrymaster's is the place to be for Freya's and my questions, but Mab would know, and we can't very well go there and ask. This will need additional thought and, no doubt, proper preparation. What do we know about the Ferrymaster? How loyal is he to Mab? We need to get those questions answered first."

"I don't know if I can wait any longer?" Freya whispers.

Ceri throws an arm around her, "If we want to make sure we get your memories back, we must have a solid plan. He's old, one of the old ones. We don't stand a chance if we go now."

"What do I do?" Freya's tone sounds like she's tumbling down the rabbit hole again.

"I think we should pursue our journey and try to catch up with Lucy," Luna suggests, "My magic might be iffy, but yours has become stronger since you came to Iceland. The North agrees with you. It will keep your mind off this, and we can let them sort the Ferrymaster out. We're no help here."

"Luna makes sense; it would only make you feel worse if you were confined to this house. Get your mind off things. I will drop you two off in Greenland," Ceri agrees.

"If you think so," Freya hesitates.

Ceri plants a kiss on her sister's cheek, "I do. Come on, show me some Freya."

This is rewarded with an angry stare.

Luna laughs, "I never thought I would say this, but I prefer angry Freya over despairing Freya any day."

Now, even Freya needs to laugh, another way of letting the tension out. The three sisters hug again, enjoying this renewed intimacy between them.

BETWEEN SPACE AND TIME

"Well, well, well. See how happy Seamus is now. Probably wishes he had passed over after all," the Crone cackles.

"He should have passed on," Mother can't help but always say what should be.

They both look down into the scrying pond. The tolling bell of the truth being spoken had drawn them here.

"Oh, my dear, the Universe always balances things out. You should know that by now," says the Crone with a sigh.

"Yeah, about that. What's going on with you? What the hell were you thinking to attach that girl to us?" The irritation in Mother's voice barely hides her concerns.

The Crone sizes her up, weighing her words, "I don't know. We shouldn't have a conscience, or at least not such a troubled one as humans. Recently, I'm questioning our existence—our right to decide. Even we have fallen into a routine. Every life should have value and be debated; we no longer waste one word on it. Where does our knowledge come from? Where do we come from? Who made us? Is there even a higher being? We can't just have appeared, could we? We need help, and I think we need a conscience; she can be that for us."

"You worry me," Mother states. "The Maiden worries me too. Maybe we should stop looking in this damn mirror."

"And then what? Become even more disconnected?"

Mother shrugs, not knowing what to do with all this.

GREENLAND

Snowflake enters their home, expecting to be greeted by her family and bombarded by a million questions. No doubt they felt the disturbance of the Power of Water. They might not be the guardians, but they all have an attachment to it. The hallways are empty; no Salik, not even her mother. Quickly, she glances at her watch. Ah, dinner time. One of the few strict rules they have is dinner. When you are home, you're expected to show up. No phones or other technology, an hour of food and conversation. It's a way to stay in touch and give each other some undivided attention. It strengthens the family bond, the cornerstone of their existence. You depend on each other here far north in the wild.

Her stomach growls; she has totally forgotten to eat today—magic can do that to you. A nice meal looms. Despite that, she heads to her room and decides to have a bath first—a moment to collect her thoughts and cleanse herself. You would think her trek on the ice would have given her plenty of time for that, but she was constantly on her guard and, after the toll of the ritual, it took quite some time to settle down. Her whole inside felt mangled.

The Berthelsens are hardy; their life in the Arctic has made them resilient and tough. The weather is brutal, and there's little to no margin for mistakes. Currently, seventeen family members have decided to stay in their home, and the rest of the family has settled elsewhere.

Laakki, Snowflake's mother and former guardian, gets up when she senses her daughter entering the room. The conversation falls silent. They've all been waiting for news of what happened. Laakki takes Snowflake's face between her hands and searches her eyes to ensure she's okay. Satisfied, she steps back and lets her take her seat at the head of the table.

"Mom? What happened?" Salik can no longer contain his curiosity. His hair is now snow-white; he otherwise seems to have recovered from his ordeal.

"Let her eat something first," Laakki interrupts him.

Down the table, her cousin loads a plate with meat, fish, and some vegetables. In the North, being vegan is not an option if you want to survive. Quickly, it is handed to her, and with a big sigh, she nibbles on some smoked Arctic char.

When she looks up, all eyes are on her. "My dear family, as you're aware—" she says and reaches for her son's hand and squeezes it, "We've been attacked, or at least someone is looking for us. I got three different warnings that other witches are searching for the Cup; I felt the time had come to store it in a more secure place. It's now safely hidden away in the ice in a location known only to me. Please don't ask me where. It's my responsibility, and I will not endanger you if I can avoid doing so."

Shouts of disapproval and mumblings that they're capable of taking care of things are silenced when she puts her hand up. "I want to ask all of you to help me guard this power entrusted to us so many years ago. The world is changing; we have all felt it. Not only the climate and the politics. As it turns out, the powers of the elemental objects are also stirring. We need to be on our highest alert. Magically and with our advanced technology. If there's any concern, find me. I know it won't be long before they are here."

One after the other, they all vouch their support and start to discuss what needs to be done. Snowflake sits back and silently eats from her plate while watching her family with pride. They are prepared. But are they ready?

FAIRY

It had taken all of Ceri's persuasion skills to convince Seamus that rushing off to the Ferrymaster was a bad idea. No use in wasting your time, and not a good idea to alert him, and subsequently Mab, to what they want. Grudgingly, he'd agreed.

Seamus is finally distracted. They enter the Fairy equivalent of a public library. Nobody pays any attention to them, and acting casual, they move further down. This mesmerizing structure is like a long wide winding staircase full of floating memory orbs. Minus an existing staircase. Maeron supports Cal while floating their way down. The further down, the older the memories. As they descend, the natural light dims, and twinkle lights are now guiding the way. At first, the orbs were shiny and transparent, but the older the memories—the worse the state of the spheres. Seamus tries to see if he could brush them to make them more transparent. Nope, still not able to touch anything, not even here.

"How much further down are we going?" Cal asks Maeron, feeling claustrophobic. They've been going down for quite some time, and it doesn't look like it will be easy to get out.

"The oldest memories sink to the bottom; don't worry, you will be fine," Maeron's baritone soothes him.

However, it's a strange place, and Cal is uncomfortable. The memories start to cluster together now, and the air is slightly oppressive. Maeron slows down, and they reach the bottom with a slight thump. Cal looks around to see what their arrival might have alerted, wobbling back and forth, trying to steady his feet on an uneven surface.

Seamus circles the cloudy globes, weaving past Cal's and Maeron's legs. "I think we need to start here," he says as he points to a cluster at Cal's feet.

"Why?" Cal asks as it doesn't seem to matter to him.

"I don't recognize anybody or anything in here. Fascinating," Seamus smiles enthusiastically.

"Right," Maeron bends down and touches the globe. Instantly, the space feels cramped as the light glows bright and orange all around them. Three planets or moons are visible in the distance above the horizon. Creatures scramble around, almost insect-like. The planet seems bare, and they are moving around randomly. Or are they? Seamus floats up, and when he looks down from above, the randomness turns to organized chaos.

"I don't recognize this place. I'm not sure if this is even in Fairy," Maeron sounds puzzled.

"Maybe it's another dimension," Seamus sounds eager.

The heavens slice open, and a giant hand swoops down; the creatures scatter, desperately trying to evade the hand. The images freeze and are absorbed back into the orb.

"This is more confusing than anything," Cal states.

"Yes!" Seamus proclaims enthusiastically, "which means now our search begins. Next one, Maeron."

Maeron touches the next sphere.

GREENLAND, THE MOST SOUTHERN PART

Ceri had traveled through the Land of Fairy, found the portal to Greenland, got through, and now she has made a secure portal back to her own home. Freya and Luna are waiting, and don't hesitate to step through. Ceri provided them with some warmer clothes as winter has definitely arrived here, especially if you're from New Orleans!

The three sisters stand on top of a hill, the cold wind whips around them, and they snuggle deeper into their woolen shawls. "Oh gosh, it's freezing," says Luna and turns her back toward the wind.

"I don't see a village or anything," Freya scans the horizon. "Where are we going to start?"

Luna takes out her phone, no reception. "Shoot, no reception."

Ceri says, "I managed to find out there are some smaller towns that way, but the capital Nuuk is further up the coast."

"You expect us to fly in this?" disbelief resonates in Freya's voice.

"I can only drop you off where there's a portal. I don't know anything about this place," Ceri says sounding defensive.

"I thought you were all-powerful now," the sharp tongue of the old Freya surfaces.

"Clearly not," Ceri, not bothering to hide her sarcasm. "As far as I understand, all settlements are along the coast."

"Maybe, we should fly along the coast, stop if we see something, and take it from there," Luna suggests.

"Sounds like a plan," Ceri agrees, "I have to go back, lots going on, not only with this." Now she turns to Freya, "I'm going to figure out how we can deal with the Ferrymaster." The two sisters hug before Ceri disappears through the portal, and it snaps closed behind her.

Freya and Luna look at each other, both apprehensive about what might come next.

Nine of Wands

PART 4

NINE OF WANDS "TERRITORIAL"

"It's not the wound that defines us—
it's how we rock our path afterward that's everything."

—KRISTINE GORMAN
@VISIONARYWOMANTAROT

FAIRY

The moment the portal snapped shut behind her, Ceri whirled around. She's alone in her study. Without thinking, she strides over to the window and opens the curtains. A sea of forest waves gently in a breeze as far as her eyes can see. A laugh escapes her. What was she thinking? Looking out of the window is such a human thing to do.

"What's wrong?" Sparkle wants to know.

"I could swear I'm being followed." This itching between her shoulder blades has been there for several days now. "Did you notice anything?"

"Not really, but there are not that many fairies that can track you unnoticed," Sparkle says matter-of-factly.

"That was what I'm afraid of. Mab must know I'm the one who sprang Cal out of his prison." Ceri fills in the blanks.

"She's many things, but not stupid," Sparkle agrees.

"Right. Whom do you think she has put on the job?"

"Mab has a Spymaster," he muses.

"Really?!" Ceri laughs out loud.

"That's not funny. He's very skilled and no joke."

"It's so silly. Just when I think you guys are so different, you do something out of a spy novel. A Spymaster! Don't you have something more interesting?" Ceri almost dismisses it.

"Don't take it lightly; we need to discuss this with Maeron. Did you know he was Oberon's Spymaster for some time?'

Now that piqued her interest. "He never told me." Those words are laden with accusation.

"Hey, that doesn't matter once he has sworn fealty to our house. How do you think he knows so much and is held in such respect?"

Ceri sighs; still so much to learn.

NEW ORLEANS

Tara is dressed and ready. *Ready for what?* she's wondering. Things are moving, and the only thing that seems to be left for her is to watch from the sidelines. The twins have taken over her responsibilities and even what happens in the house. Now she's feeling better; it has started to irritate her. Lucy is not sidelined. There's no reason for her to be either. It's easy to blame Bridget and Maeve, but she had dropped everything in the end. Still…they could have been more sympathetic toward her. Or at least shown her the respect she deserves. Catching a glance of herself in the mirror, she's reminded of the moment Lucy had drawn her card from the Magical Tarot Deck. Lucy looked so old. Funny how you can look at yourself and not see any change. Change, however, had come, and Tara needed to deal with it. A quick breath in and out lets her collect her composure.

She's about to leave her room when she thinks about her card of the day. At least THAT she can still do. The Two of Pentacles disappears in her deck while she shuffles.

Twos are fun, always energetic; what will today bring? Without delay, she pulls the card—Nine of Wands, not bad, a beaver has worked hard. A pile of fallen trees behind him, ready to build his fort. Something will be earned the hard way. Defending what you've achieved or your territory. The Berthelsens probably see them coming. Maybe she should warn the girls? Nah, they'll figure it out. With a sigh, she leaves the card on her altar—time to have some breakfast.

Diane and Alice have a quiet breakfast together. It's been a very long time since Diane has felt this calm. Alice does that for her. Their level of comfort together is a breath of relief. Not the searing hot attraction she felt with Set. He was in her dreams again last night; disturbing as that is, it's easier to let it go in the daylight. The Maiden hadn't stirred, so it almost felt like normal. Almost. Alice's glances toward her and the stiff set of her shoulders betray her uneasiness with having Diane back home. It will take time, Diane tells herself.

"You're working today, right?" Diane asks Alice.

"As always," her snappy reply comes immediately. Alice can't help herself. Too much had happened. She simply can't go back to how things were.

"In that case, I thought I'd head to the Hat. No doubt they can use the help. With Freya gone, it all depends on the boys. It might be a bit much."

Alice just nods as she finds it hard to say something that doesn't sound annoyed. The Madigans are not her favorite family right now. Not that they ever were....

Diane cleans the table, loads the dishwasher, and turns it on before she walks past Alice and kisses her on her cheek, ignoring Alice's stiffness. She must give Alice the time she needs for this to work.

When Diane enters Under the Witches Hat, the family bar and business seem to draw her in for a warm hug—welcoming back a long-lost friend. This makes her smile. No customers yet, but Ron stares at her from behind the bar. "You're back."

Her mysterious smile is also back as she floats toward him and sits at the bar.

"Tea?" he offers.

"Would love some. Anything urgent I need to attend to first?" she wonders aloud as if she has been on holiday.

"You're ready?" her brother wants to know while he slides her their 'Wake me up' tea.

For a moment, she hesitates, tempted to pretend nothing happened. However alluring that might be, it doesn't help her to hide it all away. There's enough she's not able to talk about. Like her soul touched Set's, a rarity between witches, a sign of a true soul mate. The Maiden who wants to claim her. Disturbing things. "I'm okay," she utters instead.

Ron doesn't say anything and lets the silence stretch.

"Okay, enough."

This apparently satisfies him, "We have some spells we need. I expect Fin any minute; he has been filling in for you and Luna. He will bring you up to speed and do the readings this morning."

"Thanks," Diane reaches over the bar and squeezes his arm affectionately. "How are you? I know this can't have been easy for you either. We all abandoned you. Leaving you to make sure we can still eat once this is all behind us. How's Selma?"

Ron looks away, trying to hide his feelings.

"Is she coming back here?"

"Selma took the kids to see her mother for a while."

Diane can almost taste his unhappiness about this. "Oh no," she says. "I'm so sorry. For how long?"

He only shrugs.

"Dear Goddess, is nobody coming out of this unharmed?" Diane says, frustrated.

Fin enters, and a glance between the siblings settles their agreement not to talk about it.

"Aunt Diane! Boy am I happy to see you," Fin, Luna's youngest, shouts. Only a year or two younger than his twin sisters, he has a laidback manner about him. His enthusiasm brings a breath of fresh air through the bar. He hugs his auntie tightly, which is uncharacteristic, as nobody is ever physical with Diane. But she'll take it. Like all of them, she needs a hug at this time.

"Come, Auntie, let me show you what I've done," Fin steers her toward the door.

A little yelp of dismay escapes Diane when she enters the back room. Her workbench is total chaos! Open bottles and pots are everywhere. A bunch of string is rolled around on the floor. Candle wax drips down from the bench, and that's only at first glance.

Fin, totally oblivious to her shock, walks over and starts to grab some finished potions from the shelves. "I made a love spell," he says as he pops the bottle open and lets Diane take a whiff. She jumps back. Fin startled by his aunt's extreme reaction, says, "Is it that bad?"

"Love potions—I can't…." Diane steps even further back; slowly, it dawns on Fin.

"Oh shit. I'm so sorry."

Diane struggles to control her composure, and says, "Don't worry about it. You—anyway, I can't be near a love potion anytime soon. So maybe you should keep making those."

Fin's cheeks are bright red, "I'm so sorry, Aunt Diane, I forgot."

"It's okay. What else did you make?"

Happy to move on, Fin opens another bottle, which he hesitantly hands to Diane, "A banishing potion."

This time, Diane takes her time sniffing and examining his work. Pretty good! "I like it. Good job." She shouldn't be surprised he has a knack for it; his Mother, Luna, is a master potion maker. "Maybe we can keep sharing the load, as I'm not back to normal yet."

"Just tell me what you want. I can give you a hand."

"One thing though—" Diane smiles.

"What?" Fin eager to help.

"We have to work on your cleaning up skills."

"What do you mean?" Fin adds teasingly, happy to see his aunt smiling.

GREENLAND

Lucy finds herself all bundled up in a small coffee shop overlooking the bay in Nuuk, the capital of Greenland. The colorful houses are in stark contrast with the somewhat depressing-looking apartment buildings. A city of opposites, as it turns out. The people are open and friendly, but the witches avoid them. Mara has been around town multiple times and is sure there are witches, but they blend into the background anytime she tries to approach them. "Do you think they're on to us?" she asks Lucy.

"It's likely. I did a tracking spell which hit home, so the family of the Cup must know we're coming," Lucy confirms Mara's suspicion.

"It's such a small community here, not sure though 'that' family is in town."

"The lightning bolt showed more up North. How are we going to get there?" Lucy wonders.

"I've talked to some locals, and they get around on powerboats. Some sort of ferry goes up the coast, and we can fly further north," Mara lays out their options.

Lucy shivers, "I hope you mean by plane. I won't survive a broom ride here."

"I figured I don't want to use a broom either; it's already freezing! No, we can get as far north as Qaanaaq by plane. Is that close enough?" Mara wants to know.

"I don't know; the map wasn't that detailed. Maybe we should book a flight and take it from there. I'm sure we can pay a local to bring us wherever we need to go." Lucy doesn't sound entirely convinced. She has never been in such remote and inhospitable surroundings in her life.

The first twenty minutes of the sisters' flight were uneventful. A tiny spark of magic kept Luna warm, and they made steady progress. Of course, they felt the cold, and it's not something you can keep up for an endless amount of time, but they hoped it would bring them to the nearest village.

In just a couple of minutes, Luna's situation has dramatically changed. Her panic is mounting; far in the distance, lights are shimmering. It's the only thing that keeps her going. Unable to reach her sister flying in front anymore, Luna doesn't know what to do. Her magic is faltering, and with that, her spark has been extinguished. The brutal cold is battering her. Unable to feel her hands any longer, she tries to shout to Freya. She needs to land. The icy wind makes it hard to breathe, let alone scream. As her magic is not responding, she's unable to reach her sister with mental communication. Tears of frustration almost freeze her eyelids together. Luna has been so confident her whole life. Her magic has made her capable of anything. But who is she without it? A scared creature, it turns out. Has she always been too reliant on her magic? Stop! She must stop thinking that way. For one, she's still in the air, so some magic is still working. Maybe she should try to go faster to catch up with Freya. That's it. Too easy to give in to despair. You don't need magic to act. Gently, she leans her weight forward and thinks about overtaking Freya; sure enough, her speed increases. Just when she's about to pass Freya, her broom sputters. Her heart flutters and in her mind she's screaming. Her mouth is now frozen shut. For several seconds, she's convinced death is imminent. Strangely enough, that calms her and gives her some control over her broom for as long as that lasts. Without hesitation, she aims for Freya in the fastest way. Leaning forward, she almost crashes into her. Freya's irritated look instantly changes when she registers Luna's terrible state. An ancient Norse spell rolls off her tongue and defrosts Luna. The sudden warmth almost makes Luna pass out. Freya steers her broom closer as she can see her sister is no longer able. With a swift move, she pulls Luna behind her on her broom. Something they had done so often as children; you never forget that. It's ingrained in your routines.

Luna slumps against Freya. But two grown women on a broom is hard. Freya looks around. The lights are their only savior. She needs to get Luna inside and warm her up properly. Magic is great but no substitute for the real thing. And on top of that, she's sure she won't be able to hold them both in the air for long. Throwing a little call for help to the Fates, she aims for their goal.

BETWEEN SPACE AND TIME

The Maiden and Crone are glued to the pond. Following Luna and Freya's predicament.

"Did you do that?" the Crone looks at the Maiden, annoyed.

"It's not her time yet," the Maiden sounds sure.

"That other one would have saved her," the Crone counters, not pleased with her.

"What is going on?!" the ever-commanding voice from Mother sounds through the clearing. The Maiden rolls her eyes at the Crone, as if saying, "Now you did it." With one glance at the image in the pond, Mother gets the gist. "I felt the call."

"Maybe we should help them," the Maiden offers. She could use a little goodwill with Mother.

"They'll make it. It's a valuable lesson for both," the Crone insists.

Mother glances at the scene. "Right. Come, I could use your help." She ushers the Maiden and Crone away from the pond. Before she dissolves the image, she sends the tiniest push toward Freya and Luna. Mother is sure the others didn't notice, but a satisfied smile plays around the Crone's mouth.

GREENLAND

That extra push of energy propels Freya forward. No time to send out gratitude; she aims for the lights. Luna is nonresponsive. It's paramount that she gets her inside as soon as possible.

Her broom feels the weight of the two sisters, and even though the lights steadily grow bigger, Freya must do her utmost to keep on course. A scared yelp escapes her when they make a violent dip. Quickly, she pulls the tip of the broom up to keep them going. Freya can make out the shapes of some houses; soon, very soon, they can touch down. Luna moans behind her back. Good, it means she's still there. Hypothermia is a dangerous thing.

Freya had always thought that you could draw endlessly from the forces around you, but this crazy ride makes her briefly wonder if that's true. It's like she can sense the bottom of her magical well. With the snow coming closer, it's a fleeting thought. Relying on her reflexes, she pulls the tip of her broom up while she has to let go with one hand to ensure her sister stays up straight behind her. Her feet are now toward the ground, almost like a plane's landing gear. Her magic slowly ventures out like a soft pillow, absorbing the forward motion, and with a quiet plop, she lands on her feet.

Dropping the broom, she turns around to see Luna's state. Icicles have formed on her sister's face. Gently, she lowers Luna to the ground. Freya's hands move up and down her sister's body, determining how much her sister is hurt and what she needs to do to help her.

"Har du brug for hjælp?"

Freya swings around and points her hand toward a middle-aged man with a white beard; his hands put up in front of him to appease her. At first glance, it looks like he doesn't mean any harm. "Who are you?"

"Ah. English—"

"American," Freya automatically replies.

"I mean you no harm. Please…." He motions toward her finger that's still pointed at him. Freya glances around; what is she going to do? Of course, they need help. They don't have much choice. However, the man in front of her is not an ordinary person; he's a witch. His power is almost like a visible glow around him. Again, she glances around. She is a stranger in a highly hostile environment. Freya is so outside her comfort zone; that she will have to trust this stranger. With a sigh, she lowers her hand. "My sister needs to warm up. She had an accident." No need to explain what happened.

"I know you have recognized one of your kind. My name is Jôrse. My home is your home. You must have many questions, as do I, but let's get inside first. Can I lift her?"

Freya steps aside. "Thank you! This is not what we're used to."

Jôrse swiftly lifts Luna, and Freya follows him toward a small wooden home. The light at the front door reveals that the house is painted light blue, much like the houses she saw in Iceland. Lace curtains frame the small windows, a small vase with fake flowers graces the windowsill, some small bones, a pentacle, and a little bottle filled with what she recognizes as a protection spell. A witch's home, all right. Comfortable, inviting but guarded.

When Freya follows Jôrse into his home, she instantly relaxes, the house has a calming atmosphere, and the warmth is welcoming. Without any problem, Jôrse carries Luna to his couch. He must be younger than she initially thought. His expert hands wander up and down Luna's aura. Under his breath, he mumbles something in what must be Greenlandic; the words sound alien. Instantly, some color returns to Luna's face, and the icicles are gone. Jôrse stares for a split second at the shell on Luna's forehead. Briskly gets up, opens a closet, and gets some blankets. He covers her, and finally, turning toward Freya. "I think she will be fine. Who are you? I gave you my name. Your presence set off one of my wards. You must be far from home."

Great, right to the point. Freya can surely appreciate that. "I'm Freya, and that's my sister Luna Madigan. We're here looking for distant relatives that we believe might be in danger."

There. That was diplomatic for her standards. Without revealing too much, she did clarify that they were looking for someone; after all, they are family. After this catastrophic start to their journey, they obviously can use all the help they can get.

NEW ORLEANS

Diane spent the morning reading cards for customers, which was interesting. With her gift, she's more accurate than her family, but the added tension of her natural disposition makes it generally strenuous for her and the querent. It beats making a love potion, so Fin has been doing that. He cleaned up to ensure she would not be upset, and the place looked spotless again.

For the afternoon, they switch, and Diane hums softly while her practiced hands find their way to the ingredients for a banishing spell. Making potions is her bliss. The magic flows through her into the spell; there's no room for anything else while she's focused. Perfect to keep her mind away from visions— or now—her stressed relationship.

A shiver down her spine makes her hand falter, a slight warning before she senses the all too familiar presence of the Maiden. This time, it's more like a joining. Diane doesn't feel wholly pushed aside like when she took over when she kissed Alice.

"What do you want?" Diane projects in her head. *"Why are you doing this to me?"*

"I'm drawn to you," the Maiden's voice cascades down her body.

I thought the Fates were not allowed to interfere, is what Diane wants to say, but her earlier experiences have made her more careful. Best not to piss off someone that has no trouble taking over your body and is in charge of your soul. *"Is there anything I can do for you to allow me to live my human life?"*

"You don't want me?"

Is that a touch of insecurity Diane is sensing? *"That's not it. There are people here that I love and would still like to explore a relationship with. This—"* Diane weaves her hand up and down *"makes that a bit hard."*

"You're mine. That should be enough," the Maiden states.

Diane starts sweating. Shit. The Maiden must be aware of that as well. For a moment, panic rushes to the surface.

"You can take the back door if you want?" Fin's voice, showing out a client, snaps her out of her state.

"You can have me after for eternity. Please let me live my life," Diane begs while turning her back toward Fin and leaning on the counter.

"That is not how it works. We live in between. You, of all people, should know that. You're always treading that line. Once you leave this world, we will help you pass on, and you will be forever lost to me!"

Oh dear, is there no escaping this?

"You are so intriguing and exceptional; I never felt this way," the Maiden goes on while she lets her hand run up and down Diane's body from the inside. It makes Diane's legs buckle.

"Aunt Diane?!" Fin says, catching her before she sags to the ground, "what's wrong?"

Don't touch me, she wants to scream, but the Maiden steps in fully, pushing her to the side with *"Who's this delightful young man?"* When she turns around and looks Fin straight in the eye, he immediately sees something isn't right.

The Maiden brushes a hand along his face, "Hmmm, delicious."

Carefully, he starts to back up. Diane tries desperately to regain control. This must stop!

The Maiden advances again on Fin, and now his back is against the wall, with no place to go. Playfully, she let her hands run up and down the collar of his shirt. Fin looks around; the Maiden grabs his face and turns it toward her. "Look at me!" His eyes grow big while his hand desperately tries to grab something. Diane tries everything on the inside, but the Maiden is simply too powerful.

"Aunt Diane!" Fin tries calling her forward.

"Dear boy, she's occupied."

"Who are you?!" he tries to keep her busy while his hands are still searching.

"You know me," Diane's seductive voice is beyond disturbing, "I know who you are. A Madigan is always gifted, one way or the other." Quickly, she sniffs along his face, "Ah, yes! You're no exception." Then the Maiden turns his face toward her. Slowly, she moves in for a kiss when a potion splashes her whole face.

A banishing spell!!! With a loud scream, she steps back. This gives Diane the opening to push her way back into her own body and take up the entire space. A banishing spell might not eliminate the Maiden altogether, but it gives her the opportunity she needs to gain control for now.

Diane doubles over and throws up.

"Diane, is that you?" Fin asks without coming closer.

"Oh Goddess," Diane heaves herself upright, "Yes, I'm in control again."

"Was that—that—"

"The Maiden. She has possessed me multiple times. I don't know what to do!"

"Dear Goddess, this was freaky," Fin rushes toward her and hugs her tight.

Tears stream down her face. "How can I live this way?" Diane's desperate plea resonates through the Hat.

Fin grabs her face between his hands, "Look at me."

But Diane can't look at him. She's too ashamed. The Maiden would have forced her to kiss her nephew; that's simply too much.

"Look at me!" Fin commands with a voice reminiscent of his mother's talent. Diane has no choice but to look at him. "There's always a way. Don't give up. We can't and will not lose you. I will help you find a way." The Hat reacts under the weight of this enormous promise.

Diane is touched. The bond of family is unique; gratitude flows through her. How come she never saw Fin's potential before? A heartfelt "Thank you," rolls off her lips.

GREENLAND

Freya stands outside, staring off into the distance. The sun is not up yet, although she can sense dawn is coming. After Luna regained consciousness, they made her comfortable, and the sisters tried to sleep. A bit awkward spending the night in a twin bed with your sister. That is not something she aspires to, but Freya is grateful for the hospitality they received. Jôrse turns out to be a chatty and amicable witch who kept them entertained and well-fed till late into the evening. However, she's worried about what he isn't saying. He never mentioned his last name, and he shared little to nothing helpful for someone who talks so much. No doubt that was his intention.

The sky is getting brighter, her whole body can feel the sun is about to pop above the horizon. Freya takes a deep breath in and out, the cool air reaching deep into her lungs. This strange, slightly hostile landscape of bare rocks and occasional green still peeking through the first snow welcomes her. Just like Iceland, the land speaks to her. Its grounding quality resonates with something inside her that she didn't know existed. Ever since she found out her parents had the Ferrymaster subtract some of her memories, her mind has been in a whirlwind. Being here makes her uncannily calm. It's like a piece of a puzzle has fallen into place. The anger, resentment, and doubts are still there, but it's more balanced. Everything seems manageable. Maybe she should have listened to Jason and traveled the world with him. Now, she's exploring it without him—finally out in the world. A wave of homesickness washes over her. She's been so lucky to have him as her husband. Hopefully, they will have plenty of opportunities to go and explore together after all the family drama is over and after she gets her memory back. It's vital for her; surprisingly, she trusts Ceri to make that happen for her. Despite Freya's endless critique of her careless lifestyle, Ceri had always been the one to help or support her. When all this is done, Freya owes her an apology. The poor woman has much more to deal with than she does. Hell, to find out you are part fairy is unimaginable.

"There you are," Luna's arm wraps around her shoulder. She'd been too distracted by her thoughts and hadn't heard her sister come out of the house.

Gently, Luna turns her toward her, grabs Freya's hands, and looks her in her eyes. "Thank you, sister. You saved me; I wouldn't be here without you. I know you find me challenging, but you are here for me in my hour of need. That's humbling—" Luna looks away for a second; this must cost her. Freya is shocked.

"—the Universe is teaching me harsh lessons right now. I can only hope to be able to return the favor one day." Right then, the first ray of sunshine of the day hits them, a positive sign. Freya doesn't know what to say. This is unprecedented. Another piece of the puzzle snaps into place. Words are insufficient; Freya pulls Luna into a hug, and they revel in this magical moment.

BETWEEN SPACE AND TIME

"Well, well, well. Now we're getting somewhere," the Crone purrs.

"We should let her have her magic back," Mother pushes Luna's case.

"Almost. Patience. Where is the Maiden?" the Crone deflects a discussion about her decision.

"That girl is trouble. She's too infatuated with that Madigan witch. You should talk to her," Mother urges.

The Crone and Mother have a moment; they've both been in that same position, you can't prevent everything. Sometimes, lessons need to be learned on your own. It appears to be a busy time in the Universe.

Mother sighs, "Okay then."

NEW ORLEANS

After waiting several hours for the others to show up, Tara abandoned the quiet kitchen for the study. She might want to get involved again, but there need to be actual people around to make that work. She has considered talking to the ancestors; maybe they can give her some tips. After all, they had passed on the power before her. For the first time, she can forgive her mother for giving up all those years ago. The loss of the Wand's power is unimaginable, and the void it leaves is hard to fill. A fresh pang of loss for her sister on that horrible day in the tomb surprises her. Is it because she had physically seen her recently? Or because Lucy would never give up, Tara could use some of that spirit right now.

Melancholy has driven her to the study, the old picture books. The Family Spellbook might have scorched Lucy's names from the chronicles, but the family pictures remain.

With a smile, she leaves through some photographs of them when they were toddlers. Just a few, it was way before picture taking was standard, let alone snapping one on your phone. Their mother had chosen to dress them alike, and you couldn't distinguish one from the other unless you knew them well. Things changed once they got older and had a say in what they could wear. Though still alike, they dressed more to express their individuality. One always supporting the other.

Tara touches a picture of them smiling in the Madigan yard on a fine day. Lucy is leaning against a tree, and Tara sits at her feet. It's likely the last picture taken with them both in it. Tara brushes her finger lightly over her sister's face. A tingle runs up her arm, and the rusty twin bond sings alive. Faint, very faint, she can sense her sister; she's cold and not too happy either. In a reflex, Tara wants to withdraw when a rush of comfort and nostalgia stops her, not knowing if this comes from Lucy or it's her own state of mind. Instead of breaking their connection, she lets it linger. Who knows what it might bring them? Valuable information could be a way back into everybody's good graces.

GREENLAND

A small red two-propeller plane touches down at the tiny airport of Qaanaaq. Lucy is dismayed when she looks out of the window of the aircraft. Snow, ice, and rocks as far as the eye can see. Around fifty houses make up the most northern village in Greenland.

"We're in trouble," Lucy says to Mara next to her, "not enough people. These tiny communities will close their ranks."

"We're here. Let's make the best of it. I'm sure we will figure something out," Mara replies with a forced positivity. They're so out of their league.

Lucy turns away when suddenly feeling their twin bond. Well, well, well, her sister is in a nostalgic mood, or is she trying to find out where she is? Anyway, it might come in handy to keep the back door open. When she senses Tara's impulse to withdraw, she floats her with feelings of longing. After several seconds, the bond remains, and a small smile plays over her lips. At least something positive.

NEW ORLEANS

After Fin finished his shift in the Hat, he went to the Madigan Family house in the Garden District. Once he steps through the gate, he feels the familiar tingling of the wards. Lights are on in the house; someone must be home. A little yelp escapes Fin when Trapper, Bridget's Border Collie, sniffs his hand. Wow, that dog had sneaked up on him. Fin drops to his knees, "Hey buddy, can you tell me who's home?" Not expecting an answer, he takes his time petting and snuggling Trapper. "Come on, boy, go to the house. I have some business to take care of." Trapper doesn't move; instead, he watches Fin walking to the back of the house through the bushes in the direction of the tomb.

Why did he promise Diane he would help her? The Maiden is one of the Fates, and in all his explorations, he rarely comes across anything about them that is useful. Maybe he offered because his aunt actually saw him today. In a witch family, the matriarch rules. Much different from traditional society, where the patriarchy still tries to be dominant. Look at Uncle Ron, a gifted witch who may not be as strong as Luna or different like Diane, but who generally gets ignored. He's good enough to keep the family business going and make sure they all have money.

Fin quickly learned the advantages of not drawing attention to himself growing up. His twin sisters had promising skills and were so headstrong that Luna's limited time for her family was always spent on them. Yes. He felt frustrated about that sometimes, but it allowed him to go his own way. Because of that, most of his family is unaware of his magical abilities and whereabouts. Which suits him just fine.

His father, a gentle soul, was even less visible. It's not that his parents didn't love each other, but his father being a regular human, simply missed out on too many things going on in his family's life.

History, his father's main study, is what brought them together. They fell in love over their shared thirst for knowledge and research. When exactly they started to grow apart, Fin can't remember. Somehow, they began to spend less and less time together, and one day his father left. For a younger woman…. It was a weird time. Bridget had just disappeared, and when his father went, Luna withdrew inside herself even more than usual. She may have tried to pretend she didn't care, but Maeve and Fin knew better. There were many nights she cried herself to sleep. That's why he vowed not to marry a regular human.

He had the occasional human girlfriend to keep the questions from his mother at bay. They never stayed long. His family didn't know that he spent many nights in Fairy. He was meeting a string of the most exciting creatures! From time to time, he got his heart broken or the other way around. The things he had learned! Like his parents, he had an insatiable desire for knowledge. It had greatly improved his witch skills, which unfortunately had come to a grinding halt when this elemental power business started, and one of his aunts turned out to be a fairy. His friends in Fairy must be wondering where he is. Or not. As time can be different, and most of them are immortal, time is not the same concept.

Fin finds himself in front of the tomb door and snaps out of his musings. Get a grip; it's never a good idea to drift off like that. Not even on the family property. Right. Aunt Diane and the possession of the Maiden. *Focus!* He urges himself while putting his hand on the fire sign, the triangle that points up. The door sweeps open. A whiff of something unfamiliar passes by him. It's eerily dark inside and oh so quiet.

"Give us a moment of peace!" Molly's muffled voice sounds irritated from her tomb. Fin snaps his fingers, and the torches light up. It takes him a moment to orientate himself. It had been a while since he has set foot inside. Every Madigan has a right to consult the Book of Shadows or the ancestors when they come of age and their magical powers fully emerge, and his mother had brought him here to introduce him.

"It's me, Fin," he answers hesitantly, not entirely sure what to say. To him, the skeletons felt still a bit freakish.

"Fin? Who's Fin?" Agnes whispers from her tomb.

A lid makes a screeching sound as it's moved. Fin unconsciously steps back a bit. Molly's skeleton sticks her head out. "The twins' brother! Of course. Young man. It's been a long time. To what do we owe the pleasure?"

Fin bows slightly, "Great-grandmother—"

"I'm Molly, your great-great-great-grandmother," Molly corrects him. Yet another lid is removed, and skeleton two emerges. "I'm Agnes, your great-great-great-great-grandmother."

"Right. Sorry. Thanks for taking the time to speak to me, great-great-great-grandmother and great-great-great-great-grandmother."

Molly bursts out laughing, "Why don't you just call us Granny Molly and Granny Agnes? We don't want you to break your tongue."

"What do you want? We were finally having a break. Even spirits get tired, you know," Agnes is impatient.

"I'm sorry, I didn't know. Tired?" Fin sounds puzzled.

"He doesn't know, dear," is all Molly says.

"So, why are you here?" Agnes sounds only slightly less impatient.

"I was hoping you could tell me something more about the Fates. There's not much information in books to find, and I was hoping there was maybe some family knowledge?" Fin tries.

"Fates? They decide our fate," Agnes' reply is curt.

"Come on, Agnes, I'm sure he knew that much," Molly steps in. "Can you maybe be more specific?"

"Did you ever hear of a Fate possessing a human? And is it possible to break that bond?"

"Are you being possessed by a Fate?!" Molly shouts, alarmed.

Quickly, he steps forward and rests his hand on the skeleton's arm, which she immediately pulls back. "It's not me who's being possessed," Fin reassures them

"Who then? I can't imagine this is a hypothetical question," Agnes bends forward, and Fin could swear she was squinting at him, even though she didn't have any eyes.

Shit. He hadn't thought this through and is unsure how willing Diane is to spread this knowledge. On the other hand, if he wants to help her, he needs to be able to share. These ladies are family. He should be able to trust them…. "The Maiden possesses Aunt Diane, and she doesn't want to leave her alone. It's not a one-time thing, it seems."

"Oh dear," Molly replies heartfelt, "she always was a child between the worlds. That's a problem."

Fin swallows a smart remark. "From what I understand, we think the Maiden is in love with her. She generally comes in, takes possession, or whatever it's called when Diane is with someone she loves."

"A jealous Fate, wonderful," Agnes is being sarcastic now.

"Glad you see the problem." This time Fin senses a raised eyebrow. "I promised I would try to help Diane find a solution. In all my studies, I've never encountered this."

Molly cackles, "In all your studies?"

"I've read most of the books in the Madigan Library," Fin says sounding irritated.

"You did?" Molly can't hide her surprise.

"He's a child of that curious one; of course he did," Agnes brushes it aside, a matter of fact.

"Do you know where I could find more information on the Fates?" he tries to focus them on the problem.

"We don't know how the Fates came into being, as it was before the time of any record-keeping," Agnes states.

"There must be something. There's always a way with magic; you must find the little crack or flaw," Fin insists.

"Who says anything about magic? The Fates are entities. They have nothing to do with magic. It's about life and death, passing through," Molly adds.

"Isn't life and death a form of energy and all energy can be magic?" he counters.

"I love him!" Molly clacks her jaws together. "An interesting young man you've turned out to be. Yes. You're right; all energy can be used as a form of magic."

"Wonderful, Molly," says Agnes. "That doesn't bring us any further. Where can he find more information on the Fates?"

It's becoming apparent that the ancestors are not the ones to help him with this particular problem.

The silence returns to the tomb for several minutes while Molly and Agnes go within. Fin sits down against the altar in the middle for a while.

Finally, Molly stirs, "I think the best place to look is in Fairy. They are better record keepers than humans. I suggest you connect with Ceri. She will be able to help you more than we can."

He gets up, "Thanks, Grannies. Fairy it is," giving them a slight bow.

FAIRY

Ceri floats through the land of Fairy. It has become second nature. The colors and the connection of everything are a delight. To be one and yet in a million pieces is something a human brain can't process. Ceri has learned to feel instead of think. As a witch, she is already attuned to her senses but being part fairy amplifies that a thousand times. Her regular duties of tending the land are something she's enjoying thoroughly. However, she has come with a different purpose today. After she had a lengthy discussion with Maeron and Sparkle, they decided she should explore her mixed blood more. Use it to her advantage. Maeron had confirmed her suspicion. He ramped up the security around her home. That doesn't necessarily mean Mab can't listen in. Time for an experiment.

Carefully, she maps out the edges of her property; it's not fenced. Every fairy is keenly aware of boundaries, even though they might not be visual. Felaern was a fairy of old. He came into being in Oberon's time when record-keeping began. His piece of Fairy is relatively large, and as the Keeper of the Land, he never had to relinquish any of it. Much like the human population, the fairies and other creatures have grown. The land has been repurposed, and cities have risen in new places.

Ceri wants to use a witch ward to alarm her if anybody is on her property. Hopefully, that won't be sensed by Mab's spies, and it would be a good test for her as to how she can integrate more of her witch magic. The amulet for Cal seems to be working, so this could be an asset.

She pulls together the four elements in her mind, invoking the fairy equivalents and setting the intention for a ward. Usually, she would recite a spell aloud, but here's what part of the test is for. In this state, she can't speak, at least not in the traditional sense of the word. So instead, she uses a visual aid to set her intention. She weaves the elements together in her mind while her feelings go out to the Gods and Goddesses to help her protect her land. She trusts that they're free of boundaries between the worlds. Counting on that her visualization will work, she pulls together an invisible dome that she attaches to the borders of her property.

Gradually, it comes together, and she reminds herself not to rush the process. It's very tempting to snap it into place. *Slow, Ceri, go slow.* She interlaces the colors from the spectrum in it as well. A tingling of worry passes through her consciousness: *What if this is too much Fairy?* Witches use colors for spells; generally, each color is for a specific purpose, while fairies are fans of the spectrum and use all colors simultaneously in their magic. Her instinct tells her to go with it. It's basically a witch spell, but she's, after all, in Fairy. There needs to be a link. And more importantly, she's both. Subsequently, she adds her connection to all things living on the land. Drawing the complex weaving together and attaching it to the roots of her tree, the heart of her home. The magic is springing to life! Ceri can feel the ward snap into place. She is the ward like she's part of the Land of Fairy.

Gently, she retreats and materializes back in her garden.

"And?" Sparkle anxiously wants to know as he can't follow her in that state.

"It's done. Can't you feel it?" Ceri is curious.

"Nope."

"Time will tell if this works. I hope it does. I got inspired while I was out there; so many possibilities!" With a spring in her step, she walks to the house.

"I'm so proud of you!" Sparkle blurts, infected by her good mood. "You've come such a long way."

Ceri smiles, and gratitude washes over Sparkle.

"You tease," he laughs.

Emily sits in the living room, her favorite spot in Ceri's Fairy home. Since her ordeal, everybody has been extremely attentive and ensured she was doing okay. Strangely enough, she's thinking about home. The Madigan house in the Garden District. Her gut tells her that the family home is her place to be, despite missing her parents and brother.

Longingly, her mind wanders to their holiday in New York City only a year ago. Hard to grasp that so much has changed in such a short time. Nothing is the same anymore in her life. For the first time since it all happened, she's strangely calm, almost serene; it's a new feeling that has settled over her since she woke up. Touched by Fate, Maeron had called it, whatever that means. Anyway, she prefers it over her anger, resentment, and despair.

When Ceri steps into the room, the usual anger that rushes to the surface is blissfully absent.

"Here you are! How are you today?" Ceri walks over and hugs her.

"Stop asking me that. I'm fine. I haven't felt this good in a while," Emily says and smiles.

"Good, good." Her mother scans the room, dragging her feet about something.

"Is there something you want to talk about?" Emily asks plainly.

Ceri sighs, "I don't want you to get upset, but I think it's best if you go back home."

"I was just thinking about that!" Emily smiles. "I think I would like to go and live with Gran, if that's okay?"

"If she agrees, I want you to be happy," Ceri simply says. "What about your father?"

"I don't think he minds," Emily says and hesitates before she adds, "The divorce is—he's still so—I think he doesn't mind."

Pain crosses Ceri's face. She never wanted to cause Bert pain, and now her daughter must deal with it. "I'm sorry," she whispers.

Emily shrugs it off. "Of course, I will miss Dad, but I want to stay with Gran."

Emily can see the lines on Ceri's face relaxing.

"Maybe you and Cephalop can do something for me there."

Emily awards Ceri with a warm hug. "Anything!"

GREENLAND

An arctic stoat races full speed over the snow; it's hard to spot the creature in all that whiteness. Snowflake has always preferred this form ever since she changed for the first time. It can be hard to keep your human identity if you learn to shapeshift. For most of them, it takes several years before they can separate animal instinct from being human. She never had that problem. It focuses and simplifies her stream of thoughts; these days, she goes out when she needs to think. Or get away from the noise of the family in their living quarters. Ordinary people might find their existence quiet, but Snowflake can find it crowded; her family is always around. All the time. Especially now. They have been milling around her since she hid the Cup in a new place. Worried and closing their ranks in an attempt to keep her safe. If they only knew safe from who?

Jôrse, her brother, had reached out to let her know two witches had landed on his doorstep. The one with the scallop shell. The women give the impression of being genuine, but how can she be sure? One way is to communicate with them through the other half of her scallop shell. It feels too risky. In all honesty, she likes looking someone in the eye. For now, she had asked Jôrse to put them on a boat to Nuuk. That will give her some time to plan. And to figure out who the older lady and young woman are that arrived in Qaanaaq. They showed up in Nuuk a day or two ago and have been on their radar ever since. Snowflake had told her family to keep their distance. But that they came this far north is worrying. It suggests they must be the ones with the locator spell. There's no other reason to go there. Luckily, they will not be able to find anybody who will bring them farther North. Very few know they are up here, and those who know will never help a stranger. Still, they're witches, so you never know what they may come up with.

Snowflake spots that polar bear again; no need to tempt it. She somersaults, turns around, and races back to their home. Her family in town is keeping an eye on them for now. That will have to do.

Mara stands at the edge of the tiny village, overlooking the vast nothingness. She tries to pull her woolen hat even further over her ears. *How on earth can people live here?* Growing up in New Orleans with its year-round warm weather, her body is simply not used to this kind of cold. It's only September! *Can you imagine the dark days of winter here?* It's making her shudder even more.

"Kind of chilly here, isn't it?" sounds the melodious voice of Mab in her ear.

The chill running through Mara is of a different kind; the Queen of Fairy is the last person she wants to see right now. Her body stiffens while Mab throws an amicable arm around her shoulder, like an old friend. Dressed in a sheer dress that reveals way too much for comfort, obviously, that statement is for the human. The cold doesn't seem to affect the Queen of Fairy.

"Where's the Cup?" Mab manages to convey much more than it suggests with this simple question. "Why is it taking you so long?"

In all honesty, Mara has been relieved that the Cup is so hard to reach. She's dreading the moment when they will be able to grab it. There's no way she can wiggle out of this deal with Mab. This fairy is too powerful and too well connected. But to have to see the disappointment of her grandmother will be devastating. It has weighed on her soul.

"It's somewhere out there," Mara waves in the northern direction.

"What are you waiting for?" Mab barely hides her impatience.

Mara glances at her while she tries to step away from Mab, but the hand on her shoulder only slightly squeezes a warning. With a sigh, Mara gives in and huddles up with her Queen.

"You're not thinking about weaseling out of our deal, are you?" Mab moves her other hand over Mara's sleeve, where the tattoo band is around her arm. A quick flash of pain rushes through her body. Mara's legs buckle; only Mab's arm around her keeps her upright.

"Of course not," she manages to say hoarsely.

"That's my girl. Now stop stalling and get to it."

When Mara looks around, Mab has vanished.

Shit. Shit. Shit. Pressure mounts on her chest. *Is this a panic attack?!* Being stuck between two powerful women will do that to you.

NEW ORLEANS

Playfully, Bridget runs her index finger down Wes' spine. They're naked in bed; their lovemaking had been steamy. It has been a while; Bridget considers it a good sign. Wes was his usual attentive self. Now he's snoozing on his belly, and she's admiring his backside. There's no rest in her mind; the Wand is an ever-growing presence, and the pull of her twin is taking up most of her other thoughts. Being with Wes brings back the vivid painting of the three of them in all sorts of erotic poses and forces her back to reality. It's great they're back to being intimate, but there are some things she should try to discuss with him. Sex is unfortunately not a cure for everything. The longer she has been thinking about it, the more confident she is that she should say something and not let this grow. If he finds out that she knows, things might get broken that can't be fixed. No more secrets, they had said.

"I have seen your paintings," she blurts out, afraid she will lose her courage.

One second, Wes was half-asleep, and the next, he stands next to the bed, looking at her in shock. The color is draining out of his face. "When?" is all he manages to say.

"Yesterday, you didn't open the door. As I used to watch you paint all the time, I didn't think it was a problem and went in. You weren't there—and you know—they were right there. It was—"

Words tumble out, and Bridget is in a rush to justify herself.

"I wasn't ready," he whispers.

"I'm sorry. I simply couldn't not look. They're—intense."

"Oh, God," Wes says while turning his back to her.

"Wes, please," Bridget begs. "We need to talk about this."

"There's nothing to talk about," he replies and darts into the bathroom.

"There's everything to talk about," Bridget shouts after him.

The toilet flushes and Wes steps out, anguish on his face, now dressed in sweats, "I can't." He makes a beeline for the door, but Bridget cuts him off before he manages to leave the room.

"We need to talk about this. Please…," she pleads with him.

He looks around in the hope of another exit.

Bridget reaches for his hands. "Look at me."

Hesitantly, Wes turns his bewildered gaze on her.

"I love you. I should have paid more attention to you when that ritual with Maeve happened. But you've been so chill with everything; I took it for granted you were okay."

The dogs start to rub along his legs. Slowly, the tension leaves him.

"My paintings are alive," he whispers.

His typical safe heaven had taken a scary turn, and the fear in his eyes betrays his dismay.

"Am I...?"

He doesn't need to finish the sentence for Bridget to know what he is afraid of.

The witchcraft had all looked so appealing to him at first, but now it truly affects him; he has second thoughts. Fear is such a human coping mechanism. It stings deep down; it makes it crystal clear for her that there is still a long road ahead to make their relationship last. It had felt so good that Wes so easily absorbed all the weird shit that happened. Everybody has a limit, and they have reached his. In all fairness, it was freakish to see her twin being cut open by the Dagger. Not hard to understand that it leaves a mark.

"I'm not sure why your paintings have started to live," Bridget answers honestly. "Magic is a fluid thing. I think every human has some form of talent or pre-disposition for it. Maybe it has been dormant in you. You've always been such a talented artist," she lets her mind wander. "As magic is about feeling and connection; it's so close to your gift. The exceptional powers released when an elemental object transitions from one guardian to the next might have enhanced that. On top of that, you've been painting with enchanted paint. Seems like a small step to me." Bridget is satisfied with her conclusion.

However, Wes looks less than thrilled. "Painting has always helped me to channel my feelings. Only this time, the feelings took on a life of their own."

Bridget hugs him fiercely. The dogs surround them, and the warm blanket of comfort doesn't fail to relax Wes. They snap out of it when a familiar voice sounds from below.

"Anybody home?" Emily's voice resounds off the walls.

"We're here!" Wes immediately replies, stepping out of Bridget's arms and into the hallway. With a quick glance at her, he rushes downstairs and envelops Emily in a bear hug. "We've missed you!"

This makes her laugh.

GREENLAND

Luna and Freya are standing on a small dock in Jôrse's village. The ferry is close, and it's time to say their goodbyes. Luna grabs Jôrse's hands and looks him in the eye when she says a heartfelt, "Thank you!" These simple words resonate with so much truth and depth that there is no need to say more between witches. He nods in acknowledgment. What he did for her was so generous. That is a debt not quickly repaid.

Freya looks around; her eye falls on a rock with a hole in the middle. Years of ice must have worn it down. It jumps out to her, and a witch needs to be attuned to these little messages from the universe. Swiftly, she scoops it up. Without thinking, she whispers an ancient spell while her finger combines the runes for protection, warrior, and relationship, as she moves it over the stone. A slight fiery glow highlights what she writes and disappears before she holds her hand toward Jôrse.

"Thank you, brother." Freya says explicitly. "Please take this as a token of our appreciation for saving us. I know there is much said already between us. There is even more not said. I know you don't trust us and must have warned your family that we're here. May this stone help keep you safe and recognize who's friend or foe. I see *you* and know we are family."

Luna's head whips toward her sister, full of questions. While Jôrse and Freya stare at each other, the boat docks. Again, nothing is said, but sometimes silence can be louder than words. Carefully, he lifts the stone out of Freya's hand. Briskly, she grabs Luna's arm and basically drags her on board. While the boat pushes off, Jôrse raises his hand in a farewell gesture, "Safe journey—sisters."

It doesn't take long before the witch is a speck on the dock. He watches them till they are out of sight completely. Luna goes to turn to Freya, only to find her gone. A quick scan of the boat reveals she's inside. Fine. Luna can use some alone time with the ocean. While the engine purrs loudly, she turns to face the front and stares at the bare hills with their fresh snow. She can feel the volume of marine life around her with her witch sense, even though not one of them shows above the water. Water has always been able to calm her and help her gather her thoughts. Her magic is present today, but she knows she's not fully healed. The backlash of the spell is almost like a bitter taste in her mouth. It has been such an ordeal. Who is she without her magic? That has been the scariest part. She felt like she was nobody without her magic. Totally and utterly useless. Standing out in the cold, connecting to the water, the shell on her head starts to sing. It brings out feelings buried deep within. Magic is only a vessel. Yes—her magic is strong. It can only manifest as it amplifies qualities within you. Human qualities. Her strength, courage, and curious intellect are what actually drive her. This revelation brings joy, and she's no longer afraid for the first time since her magic started to falter. Still looking deep inside, she's barely aware of a hand around her shoulder.

Drawn by the shell's magical singing, Freya found her sister in a deep trance and thrown her arm around her to pull her close. The broom ride had brought out her protective instinct.

While they touch, their energies mingle and seep into the deep well of Luna's Zen. It surprised Luna these last few days that she felt so close to Freya; they were at odds for so long. Were they? Her mind travels to her early childhood, and she can see herself trailing Freya wherever she goes—bugging her with endless questions, which Freya readily answered. When did that change? Luna spools forward in her memories. Picnics with Seamus, Tara, Freya, Ron, Diane, and Luna. Smiles, laughter, until—the thought hits her—it propels her back to the here and now. "Oh, my Goddess. Poor Freya!" she says before turning to her sister and hugging her tightly.

"What's going on?" Freya demands, alarmed.

Several pieces of the puzzle fall into place in Luna's mind. "Ever since you arrived in Iceland, you've been…different."

Freya grumbles.

"Please, hear me out," Luna asks her.

It's not lost on Freya that her sister is asking and not ordering. This, more than anything, makes her listen.

"When I saw you make that spell for Jôrse, something was triggered in my mind. You did it, so naturally; I have never seen you perform magic that way. Then I wondered if that was true, thinking back to our childhood. I followed you everywhere when we were young, bombarding you with a million questions."

Freya smiles, "I remember that!"

"See. We weren't always fighting. I realized you changed after Ceri came. I never registered it that way. Memories are tricky things. We don't all remember the same, and it's generally tainted, especially when you're young. The brain must be in constant motion, endlessly making new connections. What if we try to help you remember what is missing from your childhood? Maybe we can tell you. In that way, you'll know. Maybe not remember living it, but it might help you regain a part of what went missing."

"What if the memory is from when I was alone?" Freya's small voice betrays a sliver of hope.

"I don't know. But when you made that spell, you reminded me of the Goddess Freya. Seamus and Tara didn't choose our names by chance. Like my name. Luna suggests intuition but also a side that can be more shadowy. My gift to command is a dark one. Freya must be significant as well. We need to ask Tara," Luna says and starts to dig up her phone, but Freya stops her. "Not Tara." The disappointment in those words holds so much pain. "We can ask Ceri if she can ask Seamus," Freya suggests.

"That's an excellent idea. He can also explain why he chose the Tower card for you in the Magical Tarot Deck." Luna's enthusiasm brings a sparkle into Freya's eye. For the first time in forever, there is a glimmer of hope.

"Let's go inside and talk about our childhood," Luna is eager to begin and happy to have found something to help Freya. This trip is an eye-opener.

NEW ORLEANS

The buzz in the kitchen is back. Since Maeve had stopped cooking regularly, and with Emily in Fairy, it was like the heart of the house stopped beating. When Emily yelled that she was home, the Madigans scattered throughout the house are suddenly all drawn back to its center. The smell of muffins, the family signature treat, filled the air, and it's impossible not to get affected by Emily's upbeat mood. She has been talking nonstop about the delights of Fairy.

Maeve's enchanted laugh bounces off the wall while she fills the table with bread, butter, lemon curd, cheeses, cashew cream, and other delicious things. The others don't hesitate to dig in. Cephalop sits at the far end of the table, and Wes and Bridget sit opposite Emily.

Tara finally joins them. "You're back!" Seeing the family's warmth made some of her earlier irritation melt, and her genuine happiness to have Emily back shows.

Emily jumps up and hugs her grandmother. "Gran, I want to ask you something," she says.

Doubt creeps into her voice.

"Anything," smiles Tara.

"Is it okay if I come to live with you? You know. For good." The words fall out rapidly now, "I will visit Dad and Mom, but I feel this is my home now." She looks from one to the other before settling expectantly on Tara.

"This house belongs to all Madigans; you can live here as long as you choose," Tara reassures her.

"Thanks, Gran," Emily says sincerely.

The others start digging into the lunch fest. Cheerful smiles, banter, for a moment, it all feels carefree—the house relaxes.

Fin senses the joy coming from the house when he passes through the gate. For a split second, he's tempted to go in and see what created this good mood. Except he doesn't have much time. He needs to get back before the evening when his shift starts, and as it is, he's taking a risk with time running differently in Fairy. He turns away and goes for the Fairy portal in the tree in the garden. He thought about asking his sister to contact Ceri but felt it might be better to go his own way. Maybe Diane doesn't want the others involved. Anyway, this way it's easier to see his friends.

When he reaches the tree, his hand moves over the bark, and he senses the familiar tingle of a doorway running up his arm. He has missed this! Full of anticipation, he moves through.

FAIRY

With a shock, he realizes he hasn't ended up in the usual spot of the endless hallway with the gallery of doorways. Instead, he stands in a garden with a beautiful tree at its center.

"That's unexpected," a familiar voice says right behind him.

Startled, he swings around and stares straight into the emerald eyes of his fairy aunt Ceri.

"Aunt—aunt—Ceri," he stumbles.

"Surprised to see me?"

He's shocked at how much his aunt has changed since he last saw her. Fairy has definitely altered her. "Yes. No." He is not sure what to answer—his mind is racing.

"Not where you usually end up?" Ceri inquires.

Fin glances around, "No, I'm used to coming in a hallway full of doors."

"Do you think I would leave the fairy portal from our home unprotected or unguarded?" Fin feels the trap snap shut. "How often have you been to Fairy?" she casually adds.

Right. Fin might have come prepared with a memory for the Ferrymaster; however, his aunt is a different story. As witches are not the best liars, truth sounds like the best option. "I would visit Fairy regularly before—," he gestures around him.

"How did you escape the Ferrymaster?" Ceri tilts her head to the side, almost like a cat.

He finds it most unnerving as if she is looking into his soul. "I would prepare a memory."

"Prepare?"

"I would write it down and recite it until I came through and had to give him a memory. That way, I give him one that I'm willing to part with. As I have written it down, I don't remember it as such, but it's also not lost as I still know about it."

Ceri narrows her eyes her nephew surprised her. "That's very smart." She finally smiles.

Fin blushes. Relieved, he blows out a breath he didn't realize he was holding.

"Come, welcome to my home, Fin Madigan, son of Luna."

It's a strange way of inviting him—must be a fairy thing. The garden around them acknowledges him while they walk to the house. All living things seem to gravitate toward him as if they somehow want to familiarize themselves with him. Fin is mesmerized by the colorful, ever moving house of Ceri.

Once inside, her earlier playfulness is gone. "Now, young man, tell me what you're doing in Fairy."

For another split-second, Fin weighs his limited options. No escaping his aunt, and maybe she can point him in the right direction.

"Are you aware that The Maiden sometimes possesses Aunt Diane?" he wants to know.

Ceri's face doesn't show him anything. Just like the ancestors, he has no choice but to trust her.

"The Maiden doesn't want to let her go. I promised to help Diane find a way to be free of her."

"That might not be possible," Ceri quickly replies.

"I don't believe that, and I refuse to believe that. Aunt Diane is desperate and thinks her life isn't worth living this way." Anger shines through his words. "I looked on earth. I read most of the Madigan library, but I couldn't find anything on the Fates, which was helpful. I asked the ancestors, and they advised me to come here." The rest is obvious.

"More questions," Ceri replies.

"What do you mean more?"

"The Universe is spinning its web around us. I don't know what we Madigans did to deserve that. Yet, here we are. Some threads are getting woven together. The significance of that can't be ignored."

Fin looks puzzled now.

Ceri motions him to follow her. "I'll show you something I have been working on, which will help us both."

BOSTON

Tom is standing in a horse stable in Boston, staring down at a dead horse. Since he's been back, the chief put him on some strange cases that nobody else wants to work on. As it's still unclear to the police department if Bridget is ever coming back, they haven't assigned a new partner to Tom. Instead, they let him sort through cold cases or things out of the ordinary.

Well—this is out of the ordinary, and he would have dismissed it as a freak medical problem were it not for his recent experiences with the Madigans.

The horse looks dried up like someone sucked his life out. According to his owner, he was in the prime of his life and perfectly healthy when she left him yesterday. There are no signs of a break-in. They did find the door unlocked, but there was no visible damage. A lock wouldn't stop a witch; he had seen that. This reeks of evil.

Luna had explained that good and evil are not that easily separated. You didn't simply have good and evil witches. Like there are not just good or bad people. Everybody has the potential for either good or bad inside him. The experiences of someone's life, character, and talent or moral conscience come into play with which path someone chooses—the same goes for witches. The best example is Tara and Lucy. Twins with the same amount of talent and background, they ended up on very different paths.

He crouches next to the horse and unconsciously lets his left hand run up and down just above the horse. A tingling, like a slight electric discharge, runs up his arm. It startles him, and he almost falls backward. Shit, this witch shit is getting to him.

Resolute, he gets up and looks around. Time for some good old-fashioned police work. *What is he thinking?*

"Are there any cameras?" he asks the stable owner, who has been patiently waiting beside him.

"Not really," the middle-aged man replies sadly. "It has never been necessary."

Tom's reply is almost automatic, "It never is until it is."

"Wait. I installed a new doorbell, and it has a camera. I forgot all about it." He fishes his phone out of his pocket and searches for the app.

In the meantime, Tom takes a second look around the horse's stable. On the back wall, what first looked like scratches may not be random scratches at all! He snaps a picture and texts it to Luna, "Are these runes?"

"Here," the man says as he hands Tom his phone. It shows a shadowy figure moving to the gate; the timestamp is 11.48 pm. Is it a woman? He squints as she doesn't come straight for the door. "Can you e-mail that to me? It's hard to make out. I can try to have that enhanced."

His phone pings, "CALL ME!!!!!" Luna texts back almost immediately.

Oh dear, this doesn't sound good. His instincts must still be working. It is as he feared.

"Of course. This is so disturbing. I hope you find who did this," the man is distraught.

"I will take some more pictures, and then you can have the horse removed. But you can't…" Tom is searching for the right words, "dispose of it yet. I will see if we can have an autopsy done. This is too strange; maybe it will tell us something."

"Thanks. I will put it somewhere outside and cover it up. I don't want to upset my boarders more than necessary. I'm sure this will be disturbing enough as it is. I hope it won't cost me any customers."

Snapping more details around the stable, he moves outside and wants to call Luna but decides to first head for the station. Just when he goes to dial the number, his phone rings, and he accidentally picks it up.

"Tom?! Are you okay?" sounds Luna's worried voice through the phone.

"Yes, yes, I'm fine. It's from a case I'm working on."

"Which case?" Luna sounds suspicious now.

"Exactly, a witch case. What can you tell me about those runes?" Tom goes on, not willing to share more than necessary.

"Dark magic for sure. We think it has something to do with life force and energy work. And I mean energy work in a bad way."

"I got that." We? That's interesting that Luna talked it over with Freya. He hesitates, "The horse was—sucked dry. I don't know what else to call it."

He can hear Luna draw in her breath. Even over the sound of the boat's engine in the background.

"So, it's bad?" Tom stresses.

"Our rune knowledge is a bit rusty regarding dark magic. Freya's hackles went straight up when I showed her. I think you should ask Bridget. She can research for you or ask the ancestors."

"Thanks. Is everything okay with you? Do you feel strong enough to travel?" They had talked; briefly, Tom had even considered dropping everything and going to her, but Luna persuaded him to stay in Boston. It seems like the relationship between the sisters is growing. That, more than anything, made him decide to stay. After all, he was the one who suggested asking Freya to go in his place. He's glad it is panning out. "I've got to go. Talk soon. Love you." He hangs up before she even has a chance to say it back.

NEW ORLEANS

It's almost dinner when the phone rings in the Madigan family home. Tara comes out of the study and walks over. Not many people use that number anymore. Who could that be?

"Madigan residence."

"Ma?" sounds Ron's somewhat surprised voice. "Anybody around that could help me in the Hat tonight?" He doesn't beat around the bush. Tara can sense his irritation through the phone. "To add to the long line of people not showing up, Fin has failed to come in."

"I can come," it is out of her mouth before she can think about it.

"It's behind the bar," is all Ron says.

"I can still whip up a cocktail," Tara matches his irritable voice. "I might be old and a little slow, but I'm not senile."

For a moment, it's silent on the other end. "Okay. See you soon."

Tara smiles and hangs up. How could she have forgotten she still has a job? For most of her life, Under the Witches Hat had been their lifeline. Not only a good cover but a steady source of income. Before this all started, she would be there at least five times a week. The universe is smiling at her, although not as she had expected. Isn't that how it usually goes? Satisfied with this development, she rushes upstairs to get changed. It had been ages since she stood behind the bar. The nervous feeling of anticipation that runs through her is delightful. Finally, she's needed again!

Five of Pentacles

PART 5

FIVE OF PENTACLES "POVERTY"

"I feel like something is missing. I wish I knew what it was."

—UNKNOWN

NEW ORLEANS

The moment Tara steps into Under the Witches Hat, she feels better. This place! Her heart sings with joy to be back. The music and soft magical twinkle lights float around her while she makes her way to the bar. All eyes are drawn to her as if her sheer presence demands attention. Ron looks up and smiles to see his mother. It's almost like the old days; this is what she needs. Ever since she gave the Wand's power over to Bridget, she has been depressed and remote.

Tara slides behind the bar and lightly kisses her son on the cheek. For tonight, she chose to wear tight black pants and a cheerful blouse with short sleeves that come down to her elbows. Her hair is playfully tight in a knot on the back of her neck; some locks bounce around her face. A stark contrast to her usual billowy dresses—a surprising choice. Born from practicality, as a flowing dress is not handy if you have to move around a bar, it amazed her how much younger it made her look. It had boosted her confidence. Sometimes, something is missing from your life, and you don't know what it is. Maybe she should stop behaving like her life is over; she's not that old. Seventy is the new sixty, right?!

"Okay. What do you want me to do?" Tara asks Ron while she glances along the bar. There's a friendly crowd. Not too busy. Good, this will give her a bit of time to get into it.

Ron looks still a bit skeptical at his mother, "You're sure about this?"

"I'm ready," Tara proclaims.

"Things might have been moved around quite a bit since the last time you were behind the bar." He tries to be diplomatic, "Beers over here," he points at some fridges to the left. "Most hard liquor still hangs here; that hasn't changed. Soft drinks," he points at another fridge, "condiments for the cocktails, and let me know if you have any questions."

"Do you have a list of the ingredients for the cocktails?" Tara asks casually. It's been forever since she had made one, after all.

He points vaguely to a spot under the bar while he motions to a customer that his drink is coming up.

Tara rummages between the papers and fishes out a somewhat stained-looking paper with some cocktail ingredients. A quick glance tells her the basics are still the same. Just wing it—the best way to get back into it. Their cocktails are a mix of thought-out recipes and instinct. It's in a witch's nature to go with their gut, get a feel of the customer, and work from there.

"Excuse me?" A young man leans over the bar. "Could I have a 'Blackhawk'?"

"Blackhawk?" Tara replies, somewhat puzzled.

"You work here, right?" he looks around to see if he can get Ron's attention instead.

"I can help you."

"I've never seen you before. Are you new?" the young man says doubtfully.

"I'm old here," Tara's sassy answer makes the young man laugh.

"It's a beer," he winks at her.

Tara gives him a thumbs-up and looks in the beer fridge. Sure enough, it's there.

Several hours later, Tara slumps down on a barstool on the other side of the bar while the last customer leaves the Hat. She's totally exhausted physically but mentally invigorated.

Wow, what an evening! The energy of the people had spurred her forward. How could she have forgotten what it was like to work the bar? People give you a unique boost you don't get from nature. Seamus had worked the bar till the very end; at that time, she hadn't understood. As always, he was much more aware of why certain things worked. His canny insights are something irreplaceable. They were a team. A tear escapes her. Ron reaches out over the bar.

"Mom, are you okay? Why don't you go home? I will clean up and close. You've done enough."

Tara had felt his glances at her; she surprised her son tonight.

"Thanks. I must admit I'm exhausted. Do you need me tomorrow?"

"Do you know what happened to Fin?"

Tara shrugs, "I'm out of the loop." These words hold more weight than she wanted to show.

"That makes two of us," Ron says, not hiding his frustration. "He was supposed to come in in the afternoon and assist Diane with potions and readings."

"Diane is doing readings?" she sounds slightly alarmed.

"Necessity." That is all he needs to say. A look of understanding passes between them.

"I'll be there. I will cover Fin's shift as long as it's required, and then you can integrate me back into the schedule. This was—uplifting."

Ron stops his cleaning and goes over to hug his mother, "You were amazing tonight. Come, I'll get you a cab."

Mother and son walk arm in arm to the door.

The house is asleep when Tara arrives, and quietly, she makes it up to her bedroom. Barely able to stand on her legs anymore, she drags herself to the bathroom and fills the bath. Nothing like a bath to replenish some of that bodily energy before going to bed. She turns the faucet as hot as she thinks she can handle and adds sage, rosemary, and peppermint. Immediately, the aroma fills the air and helps her steady herself. While undressing, she enters her room to grab her nightgown when she spots the Nine of Wands. Eager to see the next card, she puts it back in her deck, shuffles, and pulls the card for the day; it's after midnight. The Five of Pentacles, a red-headed vulture, is staring at five pentacles floating in the air, just out of reach. Hmmm. Not what she's hoped for. Then, a smile forms on her face. It's about something missing. It can be money or simply a lack of something in your life. The card is exactly what happened tonight. "You gotta love the cards." She says out loud and glances at Seamus' painting, eager to share the night's experience with him. Only the empty painting stares back at her, making her feel the loss tonight more acutely. The initial energy she felt after the aromas reached her is gone. She makes her way back to the bathroom and slowly, very slowly, lowers herself into the bath.

FAIRY

Seamus, Cal, and Maeron are still in the old part of the library. It's like they're standing between a million stars; it's awe-inspiring. Speechless, Cal twirls around, startled when a flash of light rips open the universe like a piece of fabric and folds over them. When their vision clears from blinding light, they're surrounded by color. A hue so deep aquamarine, it's like floating in an ocean. Except it has no life or no life they recognize.

"There are more dimensions!" Seamus' voice pulls Cal back to reality. It's so easy to get sucked in by the memories; for a short while, he forgot why they were here. At first, this whole thing irritated him, the strange, dank smell down here, the creepy globes.

"Wow! Can we figure out whom this memory is from?" Maeron even sounds impressed.

It's hard not to get swept up. It's like stepping into a movie instead of watching it on screen. There's so much Cal doesn't know; who would have thought there are more dimensions? He has become keenly aware of what a tiny speck his life is in the scope of things. That he doesn't know much and this is a gift. He always wanted to be included and learn new things, sending a *thank you* up to the Fates.

BETWEEN SPACE AND TIME

Mother is alone at the scrying pond when Cal's thank you reaches them. Hmmm. Were they wrong to be irritated that Seamus had refused to pass through? It seems he still has a role to play. This young man's journey has been most unfortunate. Ever since Seamus came into his life, it had turned for the better. *Damn it!* she scolds herself. Now, even she begins to doubt herself. Are the Crone and the Maiden right to question their existence?

"Now, you start to see," the Crones sounds satisfied.

Mother shoots her a look, which makes the Crone laugh out loud.

"You know, with their little quest," she gestures toward the image of the human, ghost, and fairy in the library, "they're on to something."

Mother doesn't reply.

"Maybe we should take the time to question our behavior," the Crone cocks her head and lets the silence that follows stretch.

Mother breaks first, "We don't have time."

"You keep saying that. Shouldn't we be above the notion of time? Aren't we between space and time for exactly that reason?"

Mother squints at the Crone.

The Crone pushes her even a touch further. "We represent different generations, viewpoints, and ages, yet we all came into being at the same time, and we call ourselves sisters. What is that about?"

Mother's stare is all the conformation the Crone needs. The seed is planted. Satisfied, she turns around and moves away. "Maybe it's worth keeping an eye on them and finding out what they uncover."

FAIRY

The memory gets folded back into its globe. "That was incredible," Cal states.

"Can we take it? Or copy it or something?" Seamus eagerly asks Maeron. "This is confirmation of something huge."

"We're not allowed to take anything from the library," Maeron replies while he slides the ancient globe into his coat pocket.

"Is there a way to copy it?" Seamus says loudly, playing along.

"I wouldn't know how. Maybe the Ferrymaster would know," Maeron says and smiles.

"Another reason for a visit," Seamus muses.

"Guys! I think I found another one," Cal holds up another memory sphere.

Maeron touches it, and it springs to life. Immediately, they're surrounded by beings that look alien, even to fairies.

"Do they look like eyes?" Seamus bends forward.

"This is creepy," Cal agrees. While he looks up, a yelp escapes him. Two pairs of feet pierce through the memory and quickly become clearer. It's Ceri with Fin.

"Shit," you scared me.

"Fin!" Seamus rushes to hug his grandson, whose only response is a slight shiver.

Maeron draws the memory back into the boll for now.

Ceri makes introductions, "I come to bring you an extra pair of hands and eyes. Cal, Maeron, this is Fin. He's the son of my sister Luna."

Cal sticks his hand out, "Hey, man; glad to have you."

Fin shakes Cal's hand. "Hey. Ceri tells me you're a friend of my Granddad."

"He's lit," Cal says.

"Lit?!" Seamus looks puzzled.

"I think that means cool, Dad," Ceri answers.

"Is he here?" Fin wants to know.

Ceri points at Seamus.

"Hi, Granddad. I'm so sad I can't see or hear you. But so siked you're still around."

"I'm thrilled to see you!" Seamus cheers.

"He's happy to see you," Ceri relays. "Fin looks for a specific answer. I will let him explain. I have to go." With that, she floats up and is gone.

"I want to know when you're possessed by a Fate that doesn't want to leave if you can break that bond," he blurts.

The three men stare at him.

"It's not for me," Fin adds.

This somewhat relaxes the others.

"Aunt Ceri thinks it is related to your search for our history."

"Glad to have you," Maeron says diplomatically.

"I must say, it's great to have someone that's not as old and dusty as these two," Cal slaps Fin awkwardly on the back.

Seamus just rolls his eyes. "Come on. Next one!" he shouts enthusiastically.

"Seamus wants us to get a move on," Cal relays.

GREENLAND

Snowflake races through the water in her dolphin shape. The waiting had gotten on her nerves; not known for her patience, she decided to check out the witches in Qaanaaq herself. Her family objected, but she's the guardian and has the final say. This far north, there's no worry getting spotted by fishing boats, especially not at this time of year. She can fully enjoy her freedom, propelling herself forward with powerful strokes of her tail

Mara stands outside for the umpteenth time. What is she going to do? The visit from Mab had unnerved her, and Lucy started to get on her nerves. As if she could just conjure someone up willing to take them; they aren't even sure of where exactly. The people she talked to said it was too late in the season to go further up north. Too dangerous by water, and the growing ice not yet strong enough to take a sled. Not at least for another month. They can't wait another month! Mara doesn't even know how to get through another day. With a sigh, she wanders over to the only store, which is the heart of the town. It carries all necessities.

A bell at the door announces visitors. The young woman behind the counter glances over for a second before returning her attention to a man dressed in the best outdoor clothes you can find. Lean, bearded, with an amicable smile chatting with her as if they've known each other for years.

Mara quietly makes her way between the isles, meandering over to the coffee table, and pours herself a cup.

"We can't wait to go out there and see if the caves are accessible," the man enthusiastically proclaims. "They were very promising when we were here in July. How has the weather been in August?"

The girl's face darkens again. "Pretty warm still—"

"I know; maybe Paul can finally prove his theory about the meltwater and bring even more evidence about the amount of ice melting off every year.

"Who needs more proof?! We see the consequences every day. We are living it. Where are all those big wealthy countries now? They need to step up and do stuff!"

"I'm sorry," is all the man knows to say.

Irritated, the girl turns toward Mara, "Anything else?"

"Is that a muffin?"

The girl nods.

"One of those," Mara pays and turns to the stranger. "Hi! My name is Mara Lockwood. My grandmother and I are visiting. Are you new here?"

The man looks her up and down, which normally would piss her off to no end, but this stranger might be helpful. He sticks out his hand, "Andrew Withacker, adventurer."

"Adventurer of what?" Mara feigned interest, shaking his offered hand.

"My specialty is ice; I'm here with a buddy, a scientist. We want to explore the Moulins. Have you heard of that?" he asks, happy to have found someone interested in his quest.

Mara shakes her head and encourages him to go on.

"Moulins are ice cavities made by the melted ice water. They form melted rivers under the Greenland ice cap, all the way to the bedrock. Speeding up the melting of the ice cap from below," he explains.

Mara is intrigued, "Why didn't you explore them this summer?"

"We can't go in when the water is running; too dangerous to get swept away. We had to wait till it froze back up."

"That sounds dangerous too," Mara says flirty.

He smiles, radiating masculinity, "We returned now and hoped to go spelunking as far as the ice allows us. You're right; it's still perilous."

An idea forms in Mara's mind, "How far did you say these rivers go?"

"Nobody knows; that's the thing. Keep your fingers crossed for us; tomorrow, we'll go out on the ice to check out the moulins we found in July and see if they're stable." He gives her a friendly pat on her arm.

Mara gives him a full wattage smile and laces her voice with a touch of magic, "I would love to know more about it. Could I come along?"

Andrew hesitates, and the girl behind the counter also pays attention, attracted by Mara's voice.

Throwing in some extra poof, "I'm a decent photographer; maybe I can help document your adventures."

"Yeah. Yeah. There's always room for one more," Andrew agrees.

"Oh, Andrew," purrs Mara, while she casually touches his chest. "I can't wait to see you in action. What time?"

"We gather at eight in the morning at the airport." He's totally mesmerized.

"I won't be late." With that, she exits while she throws Andrew one last smile.

Lucy is all bundled up while she looks over the ice when Mara finds her. "I might have a lead. I'm going with some people onto the ice tomorrow. Will you be okay on your own?"

Lucy looks annoyed, "If I don't die of boredom or frostbite, I'll be fine."

Ignoring that, Mara also glances over the frozen water, "If you can get past the cold, it's kind of special, isn't it?"

"It's a powerful place," Lucy agrees.

Snowflakes made it down to Qaanaaq and is observing the two witches, together with her niece who has been keeping an eye on them. Not that you can go far in this town. Nevertheless, witches are unique. They can use other means than your regular transportation, although broom rides are not advised, as the sisters down south found out.

"Their name is," her niece peaks at her phone, "Lockwood. Grandmother and Granddaughter traveling together. Mara, the young one, claims to be an environmental student who came so far north to talk firsthand to local people about how they experience climate change."

"Very original," Snowflake says and rolls her eyes. "These must be the ones that send out the locator spell and that makes them extremely dangerous. Don't get too close. I don't want them to know who we are."

"They've tried to find transport up north, which got discouraged, of course. Nobody travels there anyway this time of year, so that was easy. What do you want me to do?" Her niece also seems ready for some action.

"Keep doing what you're doing. Keep me posted. I just wanted to get a feel for them." Snowflakes shrugs, wondering why she took the trouble of coming all this way.

NEW ORLEANS

Bridget finally managed to catch Wes alone again. He spent most of the day keeping Emily company. If that was for his or her sake, she doesn't know. Trapper, her border collie, kept an eye on them and alerted her when Wes headed upstairs.

"How?" Wes starts when he spots Bridget by the door of his atelier before he glances down and registers the dog next to him. "Traitor."

"Please. We can't let this come between us. Just when we started to do better again. Or was that—fake?" Bridget's voice gets caught on that word. That would be horrible if true.

"No. No. Of course not. It's—I'm not ready." For a moment, he looks at the door and back at Bridget. He throws his arms up and down in a resigned gesture. "Sure. Let's—figure this out."

Sounding far from convinced, he opens the door anyway.

Bridget reaches for him. "Do you think we should include Maeve? It sorts of concerns her as well."

Fear, insecurity, and a touch of anger flash over his face. "You're not going to make it any easier for me, are you? Go ahead." Wes says, defeated.

Bridget sends out a call to Maeve in her mind.

As soon as Bridget and Wes step into the room, the paintings start to move in a reaction to their presence. A slight knock announces Maeve's arrival.

"Come in," Wes says half-heartedly.

Maeve gasps when she sees the paintings, the color drains from her face, and slowly she makes her way over to them. Shocked, she looks at Wes, asking, "Did you?" as she takes it all in. She moves from one to the other; the first one is of her bloody—twirling around. That is what she must have looked like when she got attuned to the Dagger. The image is softened by the baked goods swirling around. "Did I look like that?" She sounds worried, turning to Wes for a second.

"I thought you died," he says. His strangled voice betrays all sorts of emotions.

"Oh, Wes! Why didn't you tell us?" Bridget walks to him and throws her arm around his shoulders. He remains rigid.

Maeve moves on to the one of Bridget in the tower and Wes running around it. The little Wes in the painting is still trying to find a way in. She doesn't say anything this time, and Bridget only squeezes his shoulder in comfort.

Maeve takes some time in front of the third one, representing all the witch powers, frivolous ones, and scary ones. This brings a smile to Maeve's face, "Wes, this is brilliant."

"Right?!" Bridget agrees. "It portrays magic perfectly."

Wes relaxes for only a second, no doubt anticipating Maeve's discomfort with the next one. Her smile vanishes, and quickly she moves on to the last one. The two sisters enjoying the garden. "Wow, I love this one," she says. Her voice holds much warmth.

"Me too," says Bridget as the twins mirror each other's smile.

Maeve moves a little back and without watching, points at the one with the many fantasies; her hand brushes the painting—

"Don't touch—" Bridget moves toward her, but it's too late. The painting reaches back and the images try to pull her in. Bridget grabs her sister, which only makes it worse. Wes, unsure what to do, touches both girls, and then something happens that had never happened with Seamus' paintings. His paintings reached for you, but that was it. Maeve and Bridget had ended up in Seamus' portrait when they tried to walk between the cards. This painting swallows them, and within seconds, all three of them are inside the image. They can see the studio, but somehow the picture draws them in deeper and deeper. One by one, they get whisked into the fantasies that Wes painted.

Bridget tries to stay as calm as she can while hands run up and down her body, ignoring whoever it is in the painting, and focusing on thinking. Wes is out of reach for her, and he gets swallowed by the magic, not so lucky to be able to throw up a shield. The panic in his eyes makes place for the overwhelming pleasure. Maeve doesn't cope so well. This is way out of her comfort zone, and instead of touching on her magic, it looks like the terror has her in its grip. Bridget reaches out with her mind; her sister is not responding. Instead, a wave of the rising Siren is coming her way. Quickly, Bridget imagines a brick wall in her mind; if her sister goes full Siren, she's not sure if she can withstand her. Maeve tries with all her might to get out of the painting physically. The canvas stretches and bulges but doesn't let her pop out. The Siren in her surfaces. Bridget can only watch and hope for the best for what comes next.

Maeve's hair turns bright red and moves wildly around her as if she's underwater. Hands still try to reach her from within the painting. It's like she's plastered against a transparent wall and lets out a thrilling Siren scream. It reverberates through the image, through the whole house; Goddess knows how far it goes. Within the painting, it might not have the effect she would have hoped. The images of Wes' fantasies, including the real Wes, are now focused on Maeve.

Bridget feels drawn to her sister; however, she still has her wits about her.

Her thoughts race through her mind for possible solutions. Somehow, Seamus's paint and their magic had mixed and evolved into something more frightening than the relatively harmless moving paintings that Seamus used to make. When they moved through the images, once they thought about a place in the ordinary world, they could get out. These paintings suck you in! Behaving more like the Magical Tarot Deck. Bridget is almost certain that the three of them must touch each other and focus on getting out simultaneously, if they want to escape.

This train of thought might have only taken a few seconds, but everybody inside the painting is now all over Maeve; Bridget can hardly make her out. Shit, how to find the real Wes and the real Maeve.

A door bangs open in the room and Bridget can vaguely see others coming into the room. Oh dear, Maeve's Siren song is working on more than things in the painting.

Cephalop enters the room, followed on his heels by Emily. They heard the Siren song, and it had cost Cephalop quite some power to be able to resist it. Emily is enthralled and already heading for the picture. A quick scan of the paintings, the chaos in the fantasy one spurs Cephalop into action. One of his arms twirls around Emily and pulls her away from the painting in the nick of time. Unable to pull her out of her trance, he drags her out of the room. Bridget's dogs have also shown up. They don't seem affected by the song and divide themselves. Moon and Kiki stay with Cephalop in the room, and the others stay with Emily. Cephalop is relieved; he knows the dogs will help keep her safe. He slams the door shut before she can come in again and barricades it before returning to the problem. Thankfully, there are no other humans in the house.

Carefully, he holds out one of his suckers to the painting; the painting reaches for him; in doubt if he should touch it, he stretches his other arms toward the wall and sticks his suckers firmly against it. That's when he spots Bridget, who waves her arms frantically; this must be the real Bridget. Her frantic movement and shaking her head indicate he shouldn't try it. Backing up, the painting is bulging back to normal.

Thankfully, Maeve stopped singing, and the painting humans are still searching her, but a touch less obsessive. Moon gives a couple of loud barks and draws Bridget's attention.

Bridget is glad Cephalop understood her. It's so not a good idea to get sucked in. When Moon barks, she can sense him in her head. *"Can you hear me, buddy?"* she reaches out to him.

"Yes. Where are the others?"

Bridget motions toward the pile. *"I need to find Maeve and Wes in this mess, and then I think I know how to get us out of here. You and Cephalop must make sure nobody else touches these paintings!"*

Moon turns toward Cephalop, not sure if the fairy can communicate with him, but he manages to get the message across.

Bridget starts her unpleasant task of finding the others. With her mind, she makes a tiny crack in her defense and starts to call her sister in the hope of getting through to her. In the meantime, she literary digs into the pile of humans. Once she touches the first of the fantasy Wes's, Bridgets, and Meaves, they turn some of their erotic attention on her. Trying her best to ignore the kisses, the hands in inappropriate places, she slowly but surely makes progress inside the ball of humans. First, she wasn't sure if she could separate the fakes from the real ones. Wes is an excellent painter, but he had let his imagination run wild, so the fakes are similar but not exact liking. Soon, she spots Wes. Gently, she moves forward, wedges herself into the orgy, and wiggles between Wes and the fake Bridget. Firmly, she touches her body against his back and worms an arm around him, feeling his now bare chest. It's tough to ignore her fake-self nibbling on her ear. *Focus!* she scolds herself. Going within her, she reaches for that fire magic; carefully, she pulls it to the surface and forges a bubble around her and Wes. "Wes. Wes! Can you hear me?" For an instant, nothing happens. "Wes?!" she pleads. "B—B—is that you?" a hoarse whisper escapes him.

"Oh, thank the Goddess, it's you," she says as she tries to emanate relief.

"What are we going to do?!" Fear and desperation threaten to pull him back under.

"Stay with me, stay with me," she urges. "We need to find Maeve, and then we have to get out of here together. I think it's the only way."

Dismayed, Wes tries to see beyond the sea of fantasies around them.

Several layers down, Bridget spots flaming red hair. That must be her. She motions Wes in that direction. "We can do it." Together they start working their way forward.

All the time, Bridget keeps calling her sister in her mind while she mumbles soothing things into Wes' ear to keep him with her. After what seems like an eternity, but only takes minutes, they manage to touch Maeve. Unable to hold Wes shielded so close to the force of the Siren, Bridget wedges him between her and her sister and throws everything she has magically at Maeve in a desperate attempt to pierce through her sister's Siren self. This leaves her vulnerable to the pull of the Siren, and Bridget almost gets drawn underwater. With her last breath before her conscience is overwhelmed, she pulls on that chain inside her that connects her to Maeve. A twin bond is the most essential connection they have. The chain tightens—*"Bridget?"* sounds Maeve's hesitant voice through the fog.

"Push the Siren away, Maeve! We need to stay calm, and then we can try to get out of here." Bridget pushes the message through. Bridget feels the Siren

retreating like a tidal wave subsiding. The ball of fantasy-selves is still there, but with the Siren gone, a little bit more manageable. Less frantic.

"Good," Moon's voice sounds in Bridget's head. *"Now get out of there."*

Right, no time to relax yet. "We need to focus on something outside the paintings. All three at the same thing. That worked last time Maeve and I were inside Seamus' painting. It's the only thing I can think of."

"I can't think of anything." Wes sounds scared.

"The kitchen," Maeve offers.

"Here we go," Bridget thinks of the kitchen, but nothing happens. Shit. What did Maeve tell her that time? You have to 'think' with your heart.

"It's not working?!" Wes squeaks.

"Think about those delicious muffins, the smell, and the taste of those blueberries exploding in your mouth—." One by one, they tumble out of the painting.

Without hesitation, Cephalop pulls them out of reach of the paintings with his arms.

Maeve is still recovering from her Siren state; he draws her close into an embrace of his many tentacles. Bridget moves toward Wes and hugs him tightly.

"How could this have happened?" his voice is hoarse from screaming.

"I don't know, babe. My guess is as good as yours. Somehow, the magical paint, our amplified powers, and your involvement in the ritual have amounted to this evolved state of the paintings."

"We must destroy them," Wes proclaims without hesitation.

There's banging on the door, "Open the door! What is going on?!" Emily's agitation is sensed through the closed door.

With one tentacle, Cephalop manages to open the door.

Emily looks around, "Thank the Goddess, you're all okay." Then, she rushes over to Wes and Bridget. Wes opens his arm, and she hugs him tightly. There's no doubt who her safe heaven is in this house.

Bridget lets him go and turns toward the paintings. "I'm not sure if we should simply destroy them," she thinks out loud. Cephalop and Maeve join her. "They're dangerous," Maeve says without a doubt.

"I agree with Bridget; destroying something magical always has consequences," Cephalop adds. "We should first try to figure out what makes them tick."

"If we do that, we have to secure the room," Maeve immediately stresses with a slight glance toward Emily.

"No doubt," Bridget agrees, turning to Wes, "I'm sorry, babe, no painting here for a while."

He throws up his free arm in a surrendering gesture, clearly more than okay with that!

Cephalop takes charge, "I propose you two take care of the room's security while we go down and make some food. We can all use something to eat and drink right now." Without further delays, he gently nudges Emily and Wes out of the room.

When the door falls shut behind them, Maeve turns to her sister and grabs her hands. "Bridget. B—I never—never led Wes to believe I wanted him." Her eyes plead desperately to be believed.

Bridget's first reaction will probably always be jealousy, except that through their intimate connection, she simply knows Maeve is telling the truth. Which human being would be able to resist Maeve's pull? Nobody, and after all they've been through the last half-year, Bridget herself could and should have handled her relationship better with Wes. You should never take anybody for granted! Lesson learned—check. "I know, dear; I know. You're irresistible; you don't even know how much." Maeve opens her mouth, but Bridget continues, "It's not the only thing. You are kind and have been supporting Wes while I have taken him for granted. Sucked up in my own whirlwind, I didn't notice how the magic went from being cool to frightening for him." They both stare at the painting representing all forms of magic. "I do like this one," Maeve admits. "It's such a perfect expression of the balance of magic. Good and bad, at the mercy of the one wielding it."

"Gosh! He's such a gifted artist." Bridget's passion and admiration shine through her words.

"B. You should tell him, not me," Maeve whispers.

Bridget gives a wry smile, "I know."

One last look at all the paintings before Bridget declares, "Let's lock up the room and go downstairs; I need a glass of wine."

This makes Maeve laugh, "Me too!"

Together they walk outside, lock the door the old-fashioned way before they turn toward each other, clasp hands, and connect their minds. Together they weave a web of fire and air that encapsulates the room. Nobody will be able to enter without them noticing.

Diane decided to pop home for lunch. It has been a busy morning in the Hat. To her surprise, her mother showed up, and she didn't feel like talking to Tara. Fin disappeared, which irritated Ron and put him in a foul mood. Diane wisely refrained from telling him; it was for her sake.

Her house in the Marigny always makes her smile. Its cheerful colors invite you in, and giant ferns and elephant ears grace the porch. When she finds the door unlocked, she hesitates. Instead of rushing in, happy that Alice must be home, Diane's nerves bubble to the surface. What is wrong with her? That's a rhetorical question, as she easily can explain where it comes from. Frustrated with herself and her body betraying her true feelings, she heads indoors.

"Alice, I'm home."

No reply; the house has a tense atmosphere, no longer the welcoming home and refuge. Diane desperately wants that back. Doubt has been creeping in for a while now. Even though they had a lovely quiet night, something is missing. Does she miss it because she had other experiences? Or because it's simply gone? Even with the Maiden, disturbing as that is, there's a strange adrenaline rush. Diane walks through the kitchen, and the living room, but still no Alice. When she opens the bedroom, Alice freezes, "Diane…."

A suitcase fully packed lays open on their bed. Across the room, their friend Helena looks guilty. A hefty lady, who's a power to be reckoned with. Not a witch, but nonetheless.

A pang of hurt is swiftly followed by relief, "Are you sneaking out on me?"

Alice doesn't know what to say, "I—I—I can't do this any longer. I tried…." Tears stream down her face. Helena walks over to Alice and throws an arm around her. "Diane, what you did—I know you were under a spell, but still—now the Maiden, it's too much. You have to let Alice go."

"Is that what you want?" Diane can't keep the hurt out of her voice, ignoring Helena. "I love you."

Alice looks torn.

"Sometimes, that's not enough," whispers Helena.

For the longest time, Diane and Alice look at each other. A whirlwind of emotions flow through Diane, enduring the visions all her life, taught her to let emotions pass through and hook on to only one thing. That one thing that can keep you afloat. In this case, her family, whatever happens next, they will be there for her. When she claws her way up and out of her emotional distress, Diane manages to say, "If that is what you want, stay in the house. I will move out."

Alice looks at her already packed suitcase.

"Don't worry. I will grab some things, and we can sort out all our other stuff later. I need time to…process this." Diane sounds more reasonable than she's feeling right now.

Alice is still frozen in place. Helena gently moves her out of the room, "We will give you some space."

When the door closes behind them, Diane screams while grabbing the first thing in her reach, a vase with dried flowers, and hurdles them across the room.

"That's better," resonates through her while the Maiden fills her up.

"Get out!!! GET OUT!!!" Diane screams out loud. "It's your fault!"

"Don't be so dramatic. I finally got you to myself." A satisfying feeling is flooding Diane's senses while the Maiden retreats. It had weirdly calmed her, pulled

her out of her destructive train of thought. Damn the Maiden for helping her at this moment.

Back in control, Diane opens her part of the closet and starts to take out her clothes.

GREENLAND

"Do you remember when we went to L'Anse aux Meadows National Historic Site?" Luna asks Freya. They have been talking non-stop about their youth. The long hours of their trip are gone in a blink of an eye. It's a strangely bonding experience for the estranged sisters. It turns out that when they were young, they did do a lot together.

"L'Anse—what?" This is the first time Freya can't recall what Luna is talking about.

"L'Anse aux Meadows, all the way up in Newfoundland in Canada. It was just you and me with Seamus. It was an unusual trip. We were still so young, yet Dad insisted we'd go."

"I—I don't remember at all…." The color is draining from Freya's face.

Luna reaches out to her and squeezes her arm sympathetically. "It's okay; that's why we do this," she reminds her.

"Right. Right," exhales Freya. "It still freaks me out."

"Take a deep breath," Luna encourages her. "I'll tell you what I remember. Maybe it will trigger something."

Freya gives her a wry smile.

"We were still very young; I was probably six or seven. We went by plane to New York and drove a long way. To me, it felt like we were gone for a year. I don't know; I remember a boat, a small plane, and many strange people. You know Seamus."

"He always attracted interesting characters," Freya agrees.

"He also insisted on this trip. Tara was unhappy with it and refused to take Ron and Diane up. Still, we went," Luna muses. "No. I can't remember what the purpose of the trip was. Other than it had something to do with you."

"With me? Why?" Now Luna had Freya's attention.

"I thought of it after you drew on all that power in Iceland. Something similar happened there. Seamus must have suspected something about your powers; you know he liked experimenting, research, and the unknown."

"What do you remember?!" Freya tries not to shout, unable to wait any longer.

"We have to ask Seamus to be sure—"

"WHAT DO YOU REMEMBER?" Freya shouts. The people look at them; the boat is small. "Sorry," she apologizes.

Luna tries to remember. "You touched something. I don't know what. In my mind, it was a secret; probably, we were touching something that wasn't allowed. So, I'm jumping to conclusions here that it was some rune or something. When you touched it, it was as if time froze, and the ground started rumbling."

"Magic doesn't come out until we're teenagers," Freya counters.

"Is it? I've always questioned that. We're born with magic. I agree that it finds its way during puberty, but when we grew up, Diane had visions before, or at least weird dreams. The girls did some unexplainable magical stuff when they were infants. Didn't your kids?"

Hesitantly, Freya nods in agreement.

"You did something that day. Something that Seamus wanted to be sure of. It's also a vital memory that is missing—something the Ferrymaster took away from you. Your reaction in Iceland to the land was profound. What if that's part of the bases of your magic. The crucial part between your mind and your magic is to make it work like what happens in your puberty. We become conscious of our abilities, and we learn to wield it. Before that, it's there, but pure instinct." Luna is on a roll now. "When we were in Iceland, the land talked to your subconscious; you never traveled there before, did you?"

Freya shakes her head.

"Or to Scandinavia?" Luna sounds almost victorious.

"I never wanted to travel," Freya says in a quiet voice, full of regret.

"We need to find out from Seamus what exactly happened on that trip. And maybe the more important question is: why did we go on that trip? Maybe, you don't need the actual memory back to reconnect to your magic. Clearly, there is some connection, but a key element is missing. The link to your magic and your happiness. You are so much more centered since you came."

"Since Iceland, I feel less angry," Freya admits. "It's—it's—liberating. As if I can breathe for the first time." Tears well up in her eyes. "Most of my life wasted." The tears flow freely now.

Luna takes her older sister in her arms, and the people around them discretely look away. What can she say? It's horrific to think your parents took something away from you, something vital to your happiness. Maybe they had done it with the best intentions. Unfortunately, it had cost Freya dearly. She looked back on all their fights, disagreements, and disrespect over the years. Luna gets sick to her stomach, how she had become part of feeding that anger. If only…. Yeah, that never helped anybody. "Freya. Freya! Look at me," Luna forces Freya to look at her. "I'm so sorry and apologize for feeding your anger all those years and not recognizing or realizing what was wrong. I would take it back if I could. But I can't. Hear me; I will do anything now to help you restore your soul." A bell tolls between space and time, another honest moment between the sisters.

Freya opens her witch sight and sees her sister shine with honesty and care. Luna is not to blame for what happened. "Thank you. I accept your apology. However, it's not yours to make. I'm happy to be with you now and am glad I'm not alone on this journey." They hug fiercely.

"We're approaching Nuuk," sounds over the loudspeaker.

BETWEEN SPACE AND TIME

"Awww," the Crone sounds touched. "Who would have thought?"

"Give her back her magic," Mother urges next to her.

"Oh, come on. I think this is fun."

"Don't be cruel," Mother gets ready to twirl her finger.

The Crone grabs it before she can restore Luna's magic. "Almost."

"This deserves something," the Mother insists.

"She has always been your favorite," the Crone says and winks while she restores a bit of Luna's magic. "There, that will keep them going."

"I don't have any favorites," Mother walks away.

BOSTON

Tom hesitates outside a new-age store in the center of Boston. After staring at the video for hours, he couldn't shake the feeling that he knew the person. Or rather, the woman. She looked an awful lot like Gwen, the sister of the witch who got murdered by Lucy for the Dagger of Consciousness in Boston. The case that Tom and Bridget investigated and which started all the strange magical stuff happening in his life and made him fall in love with Luna. Gwen had followed them all to New Orleans and stayed with the Madigans in the hope to get the Dagger back. Her family has been its guardian. When Maeve accidently attuned herself to the Dagger, Gwen had returned home. Not particularly happy....

He had booked a tarot reading with her on impulse; before he heads in, he touches the talisman hanging around his neck. Luna gave it to him to protect him from witches. Not entirely sure if this was a smart move, he goes inside.

"Can I help you?" a young woman asks from behind the counter.

"I've booked a tarot reading at three. Walsh," Tom replies.

The girl looks him up and down and checks her books. "Right, follow me."

The store has a cozy feel, with some sort of tranquil music in the background. Tom takes everything in while the girl takes him to the back of the store, where she peeks around a curtain, "Are you ready?"

Tom can't hear the reply but apparently satisfied, the girl shows him in.

Gwen stiffens when she recognizes him, "Tom?!"

"Hey, Gwen," he moves over to give her a quick awkward hug. "How have you been?"

"You're back," she says, stating the obvious.

"Time to get back to work," he smiles.

"Are you and…," her sentences trail, unsure if this is an appropriate question.

Tom grimaces at her, something that can be interpreted either way.

"I'm sorry," Gwen replies, presuming he and Luna are no longer together. "You were so good together." Tom looks away. It's better if she thinks they broke up.

"You're back at the police station?" she asks casually.

"Yes. It's been an adjustment. I'm still waiting for a new partner."

Gwen's face darkens with reference to Bridget before she quickly plasters a fake smile on her face again. "Sorry. Sit down."

Tom takes a seat across from her. Her reading area is colorful and comforting, with some incense burning on a little side table. The sweet smell is complimentary, not overwhelming as some scents can be. It helps him relax just a little.

"Do you need guidance? Or do you have a specific question?" Gwen wants to know while she shuffles a tarot deck. "I never pecked you for someone that would seek advice through divination. Why don't you ask Luna?" she says innocently, poking him a bit.

Instead of answering her, he smiles tensely.

"Right," Gwen assumes the wrong thing again. "Still—divination?" she insists.

"Spending time with the Madigans—it changed me. I still think it's all a bit out there—then again, there's something there. I'm stuck and thought, what the heck? It's worth a try, right?" He doesn't sound too convincing.

With a practiced hand, Gwen fans out the card over the table. "What was your question?"

He had never said, but he was sure she knew. "Am I on the right track? What can you tell me about the person who did this? Do you have any advice?" he says.

For a moment, she sizes him up; Tom does his utmost to give her a blank stare.

"Let's start with the first question: 'Am I on the right track?' Pull a card with your left hand."

Tom let his left hand hover over it like he had seen Luna do. Strangely enough, he feels drawn to pull a specific card. He hands it to Gwen.

She turns it around, "The Ace of Swords! That's a yes. Aces are about beginnings, and it governs the power of air. It signals something to do with the mind. You are on the right track!"

A chill runs up Tom's spine, and he needs to suppress the shiver. Damn.

"The next question: 'What can you tell me about the person who did this?' Why don't you pull three cards? That will give me some more depth," she suggests while fanning the cards.

Tom doesn't look at her, and his hand has the tiniest tremble when he pulls three cards.

She flicks them one by one, "The Four of Wands, the Magician, and the Devil. Hmmm."

For a moment, her piercing eyes look into his. "You know this person. He's highly skilled but has been led astray. Or is tempted or might even feel like he doesn't have another choice than to use those skills."

"For what?" Tom probes.

"That was not the question," Gwen smiles wryly.

"How do you know it's a he?"

Gwen shrugs and says, "It could be a woman, my instincts said he. What was your final question?" She swiftly moves on. Her dark gaze makes him uncomfortable. All those years of police work and interrogating suspects sure come in handy to keep his calm. "Advice."

"Ah, right. Let's pull one card, to begin with."

Tom takes his time to let his left hand choose the card; what is he supposed to look out for? When his hand tingles, he lets it fall on the card. That must be it.

Gwen pulls it and turns it around; the Seven of Swords, "Hmm, betrayal. Watch your back, buddy." The temperature in the room is dropping. "Maybe you should draw another card?" Gwen's voice barely a whisper.

Tom is feeling self-conscious; he's certain she's on to his suspicion. On that note, it might no longer be a suspicion. Should he chance to draw another card? He can't stop his hand from shaking more visibly now; witchcraft still unnerves him, not the hardened policeman anymore. He used to be rock solid. Never a doubt. Ever since Lucy has hit him with that sleep spell, he has been an emotional mess.

Nevertheless, he draws another card and turns it over himself now. The Knight of Swords—a knight charges forward on a horse. Tom looks up, and when he meets Gwen's eyes, he knows she knows. That damn horse even looks like the one that had died. He jumps up and backs up—his chair is falling over.

"Remember," drifts Gwen's icy voice toward him, "The knight goes for his goal and doesn't care about the consequences."

Tom rushes out. The girl behind the counter looks startled. "Hey, are you okay?" Tom heads for the door. "Hey! You need to pay." Quickly, he glances behind him, but Gwen hasn't followed; he fumbles for his wallet and pulls out a couple of twenties—that must be enough. Without waiting to find out, he gets out.

NEW ORLEANS

Bridget is about to slip into the shower when her cellphone rings. After all the madness with the paintings, a cleansing shower to eliminate the energy sounds like a good idea. For a second, she considers letting it go to voicemail, but these days, everything is urgent. She sighs, turns off the shower, throws a towel around her, and picks up the phone. "Madigan."

"Good, you're there," Tom sounds relieved; this piques her interest. He's generally the cool and in-control type.

"How's Boston treating you?" she opts for a light reply.

"Oh, man. You witches have gotten to me."

Bridget presumes he talks about Luna, "You should have stayed with my mom then."

"That's not the way I meant. Luna suggested I call you."

The plot thickens, and Bridget sits down on the bed. "About what?"

"They put me on a strange case, the ones that nobody wants." He lets that sink in for a minute before continuing, "As I don't have a new partner yet, they stick this to me."

"I'm sorry," Bridget automatically says, as she knows very well that's part of her fault for not being outspoken about her return. Why didn't she let them know she would never come back? It's tough for her to let her old life go completely; there's still this tiniest sliver of hope, she will return someday. "Tell me about the case."

"A horse died under the weirdest circumstances. When I saw it, I immediately understood someone less normal was involved." Tom explains.

"Less normal?" Bridget swallows a laugh.

"Well. You know…"

She lets him sweat.

"Your kind," he finally says.

"Witches?" Bridget finds it intriguing that he has still trouble saying that out loud. "What made you think that?"

"Well, it looked like the life was sucked out of the horse. He was perfectly healthy the day before. I found runes and asked Luna—"

"Luna?! Why didn't you call me?" Stupid question. "Forget it. What did she say?"

"She thinks dark magic, and as she's on a boat to Nuuk, she has no way to check and suggested to ask you, but—"

"You didn't."

"I should have. Sending you a pic of them now. If you can let me know what they're for, that would be great," he adds, trying to cover up his slip up.

"What did you do?" Bridget knows her old police partner too well.

"When I checked some video footage, the person made me think of Gwen."

"Gwen? Our Gwen?" Bridget's heart sinks. This doesn't sound good.

"Exactly. I had the brilliant idea to take a tarot reading with her to scope out what's going on."

Bridget jumps up, "OH NO! A TAROT READING?! Tom, she will understand."

"I get that now. She knows I'm on to her." He's obviously not proud of himself.

Shit. A bit stupid to think they wouldn't hear from Gwen and her family again. "Gosh, what were you thinking? You should know by now that witches can be dangerous."

"I thought I had the talisman and should be fine," Tom defends his choice.

"For some things, yes. Oh man, I can't believe you did that."

"Not my proudest moment."

"Stay away from her. I will figure out what these runes mean and get back to you," Bridget urges him.

"Thanks. I'll head back to the station."

Bridget figured he would hang up now. When he doesn't, she quietly asks, "How's Luna?"

Tom deliberately left her an opening. "Okay. She still doesn't have her powers restored, but I think Luna and Freya are bonding."

"Good." This time Bridget hangs up without saying goodbye.

GREENLAND

Mara and Lucy got claustrophobic in this small village with nothing to do. It's cold out, which they both hate. Their hotel room is bare and has no TV. The Internet is incredibly slow, but it's the only thing that keeps them from jumping back on a plane. After going around and around in circles to develop a viable plan, they decided they needed to be more specific about where the Cup was. They're huddling behind Mara's laptop.

Lucy still had the picture from her ritual on her phone, and now Mara had super-imposed it on the map of Greenland.

"A little higher," Lucy points at the screen.

Mara fiddles with the two images. "This should be it."

"Where are we exactly?" Lucy squints at the screen.

Mara points at the red dot. "Not near enough. Even though everybody denies other settlements further north, it looks like they're way up there."

"We knew we couldn't trust them to tell the truth. If they live up there, they must be ultra-private. How are we going to get there?" For the first time, Lucy starts to doubt their mission. The locals are not going to help them. Winter is coming, and the weather conditions will only worsen.

Mara senses her gran's dismay and says, "I'll check out these moulins tomorrow; who knows? There's always a way." Sounding more optimistic than she feels.

Luna and Freya walk through downtown Nuuk, a small town to American standards. Hard to believe this is the capital. It has a shopping street with a beautiful theater. Everything is modern and stark. Lots of grey high-rises, not particularly cheerful if it weren't for the occasional colorful traditional housing. Their hotel by the harbor is pleasant but basic. A member of Jôrse's family had greeted them on the docks and showed them the hotel. After that, the woman disappeared, but the sisters had no doubt they were being watched.

Luna feels the pull of water, and they stroll toward the waterfront. "Can you…" Luna motions with her hand around them. Freya immediately gets it and whispers a privacy spell. Luna does sense the spell fall into place. Is that a slight improvement? It might be wishful thinking; she's desperate for her powers to be back to normal. Instead, she says, "They're stalling us. Don't you think?"

"Yeah, no kidding. We're not even close to where we are supposed to go. Kill 'm with kindness is their tactic." Freya sounds as frustrated as she feels.

"Where do we even go from here?" Luna twirls around. This is all so unfamiliar to them.

"It's time we take matters into our own hands," Freya suggests.

"Great. But how do you propose to do that?"

"We must also find Lucy and Mara; they're here somewhere. This is such a small town; we should be able to figure out something. A tracking spell might even work," says Freya and shrugs. "And what about that." She reaches and touches the shell on Luna's forehead. Immediately, a shiver runs up her arm like a ripple in an ocean. "Oohhh, it's alive."

Luna's irritation shoots to the surface, still her first reaction.

"Wow, wow, don't tell me you haven't explored its possibilities?" Freya can't hide her disbelief.

"When should I have done that? I don't have my powers, and we've constantly been going from one emergency to the next," Luna defends herself.

"You have a magical item embedded in you! That is an emergency in itself. Evidently, it is an active thing. Shit, we shouldn't have let this slide." Freya is happy to shift the focus back on her sister. "What do you know about it?"

"I'm more emotional. I figured as it's connected to the power of Water, emotion is a given. For the rest—" she sighs. "I feel much better if there's water close." Hesitating for a moment, weighing if she should tell the rest.

Freya only lifts an eyebrow.

Her sister is correct; the time for secrets is over. Didn't she constantly blame Tara for keeping secrets? Here she does it herself. Maybe it's something that runs in her family. For a moment glancing around, despite the privacy spell in place, she goes on, "I got it from a mermaid, and I think it awakened something within me. I'm not a Siren like Maeve, but I start to think I did pass that onto her' there's something here," she gestures over her belly area down to her legs, "that constantly tingles as if it wants to transform."

Freya's eyes glister, "Maybe you should try."

"Dive in?!" Luna laughs, "It's freezing. Are you crazy?"

"You could try first in a bathtub or something."

"Right." You can't miss the skepticism in Luna's voice. "I'm going to lie in the bathtub and think about transforming?"

"Stop being so childish; think as a witch!" Freya berates her. It's like a slap in the face. "That your magic is wonky doesn't make you incapable. At a bare minimum, you should figure out what it does. Is it a communication device? Is it an amplifier? Is it magic itself or just a tool? I can't believe you didn't try to find that out. The Luna I remember would be all over this."

Luna let her sister's words wash over her. It's hard to admit, but she's right. Why didn't she do all these things? Her cheek flushes red. Damn! That had never happened before in her life either. Emotions are ruling her, it seems. Paying closer attention, she's aware it influences her constantly. Is that why she could be more empathic toward Freya? That she didn't think to examine this is not like her at all! If this had happened to one of the others, she would be the first to get to the bottom it. To have an unknown magical object on you is frightening. Startled, she looks up and into Freya's eyes. She is fighting to conceal her fear.

Freya hugs Luna, "It's normal to be afraid. You're only human."

Their bond is strengthening; this gives Luna the courage to look inside for the clearheaded strength she's known for. When Freya finally lets her go, a plan has formed.

"You're right. I will try to connect to this thing on my forehead—enough stalling. Since the boat trip, my magic feels more stable, not healed, but better. I should use it. Maybe you can see what you can find out about Mara and Lucy; they must have stood out here."

Freya smiles, "That's the spirit."

NEW ORLEANS

Bridget is surprised when she opens the front door to find Diane on the doorstep with a bunch of suitcases. She looks at her aunt's face and pulls her into a hug. You don't have to be a detective to figure out what's happening here. "I'm sorry, Diane."

A soft sob escapes Diane while gently untangling herself from the well-meant comfort. "I thought we could make it work." She turns around and tries to lift as many bags and suitcases as possible.

There's not much you can say at these moments. "Let me help you," Bridget offers and quickly grabs the remaining bags while she follows Diane to her room. The agitated look on her face is heartbreaking when she throws the door open to her old bedroom. "I don't want to be here."

"It's your home," Bridget sets down the bags.

"Nobody wants to go and live with their mother again," Diane sounds bitter.

"I understand this is your home, as much as Tara's or Emily's or my home for that matter. It's the Madigans'. It's from all of us." Bridget had finally understood that when Tara said it to Emily. It makes perfect sense, and she found it an unexpectedly reassuring thought. It doesn't seem to have the same effect on Diane.

Diane shakes off her unease, turns around, and stalks out of the room. "I'm heading back to the Hat. They must wonder where I went."

"Wait," Bridget stops her. "You're in no shape."

Diane stands straight, "It's the only thing that keeps me sane. Let me go."

Startled, Bridget backs off, and Diane rushes downstairs and out of the door.

Oh my, this is not good! Slowly Bridget closes the door to Diane's room and decides to call Ron in the Hat.

"What's wrong?" Ron's curt greeting says it all.

"Aunt Diane is on its way and I wanted to give you a heads up that she showed up with a bunch of suitcases here. I think she and Alice have called it quits."

"Shit."

"She said she needed the distraction of working right now."

This is met with silence on the other end.

"I tried to talk to her, but—"

"I know." The heaviness in Ron's words says it all. "Thanks for letting me know."

After her little distraction, Bridget is entering the tomb; runes are not her strong point, she's back at consulting the ancestors. One of them must be able to help her. Her mind sends a message out to them in their tombs, and she can't hide her surprise when Sarah is the one answering. Her great-grandmother generally doesn't involve herself in the twin's study. With a loud scraping sound, the lid moves on her tomb, gracefully, or as gracefully as skeletons can move, Sarah steps out of her casket. "What can I help you with?" A raspy, almost sensual voice asks her.

Bridget pulls out her phone and shows Sarah the picture.

A distressed clacking of her jaws confirms Bridget's thoughts about this, "Dark magic."

"That's what I thought, but can you be more specific? I'm not very good with runes, and this is one of those sigils built from multiple runes."

"Give me a second," Sarah says and bends forward to take a better look at the phone. "It's about harnessing or mining power to enable you to connect to something."

A feeling of dread starts to form like a heavy lump in Bridget's stomach; this can only mean one thing.

"Power gained this way will set you on a dark path that has no turning back from. Where did you find it?" Sarah's answer makes her worries grow.

Should she tell her? "Tom found it next to a horse. It had the life sucked out of it."

"That's it," Sarah confirms. "That's not all, is it?" She might be fragile, but she's not stupid.

Bridget takes a deep breath, "Tom thinks it was Gwen."

"GWEN…." The name resonates through the tomb while all ancestors react, immediately grasping the graveness of the situation. They all rise and start chattering at her as one.

"STOP!" Bridget tries to make them focus. "One at the time."

"She's after the Dagger," Agnes states what they all think.

"Yes, yes, that's the only explanation. More importantly, what do we do with that knowledge now we know?"

"Does she know we know?" Mary asks.

"Tom went and did a tarot reading with her," Bridget can't hide her irritation about that.

"She knows!" Agnes shouts

"Is he okay?" Sarah asks.

Bridget nods.

"That's good. These runes—she's a gifted witch. Or knowledgeable at least."

"Get Maeve," Mary orders. "We need to bolster her defenses."

Bridget doesn't wait and sends out a mental message to Maeve. The intensity with which the elders react alarms her.

"Maeve is on the way. Let me go outside and warn Tom as well."

FAIRY

Fin watches Ceri argue with Seamus, more like arguing with thin air, as he only gets one side of this conversation. After hours of sifting through old memories, they stopped for food and discussed where to go from there. Maeron, Cal, Seamus, Ceri, and Fin are gathered in the garden, as Fairy's weather is always pleasant. The heart of Ceri's home is tranquil and relaxing, and Fin takes it all in while he tries to follow what's going on.

As far as he understands, Seamus thinks it's time to scope out the Ferrymaster's place, while Ceri argues his motives. His mother and Freya had been here, which stirred things up for his grandfather. He wishes he could see him; Seamus is sorely missed in the family. Always such a rock—someone you could ask about anything. His knowledge, warmth, and especially his sense of humor left a vacuum; slowly, the Madigans as a family started to fall apart. Strange that one person can be the one holding it all together. Looking at his own family unit, he knew there was nothing that kept them connected. Even though he loves his sister and parents, Fin has been walking his own path for a long time. Tonight reminds him that it has been a touch lonely.

"Hey? Are you okay?" Cal shuffles over to Fin, the only other younger person around. He has never been a natural conversation maker, but Seamus urged him to go and connect. He said his grandson was cool.

"Yeah. Being a bit melancholy, I suppose," Fin says and turns to Cal. "Fin; we've not been properly introduced. These memory globes are a bit trippy."

Cal laughs, "No kidding. As if you're right in the middle of it all. These strange worlds—who could have thought?"

"It's been fascinating. An eye-opener, really. Unfortunately, it didn't bring me any answers."

"We can safely assume that there are more dimensions out there, whatever that means or entails," Cal says, shrugging his shoulders. "I'm not sure if I'm cut out for this stuff."

Fin takes the time to study Cal, "You're Lucy's grandson, right? Aren't you—"

"The enemy," Cal finishes for him. "I don't know. My grandmother is a scary lady. Unlike your grandfather. You're so lucky to have such a family." A flash of regret crosses Cal's face. "I don't have any siblings I grew up with. I have a half-sister who mostly ignores me. A father who doesn't want me and a terrifying grandmother." Startled, Cal looks at Fin; he never said that out loud before to anybody.

Fin instantly feels sorry for the man; that sounds infinitely worse than whatever is going on in their family. "There's something wrong with every family," he tries to console him.

"Sure," says Cal but a wry smile says it all.

"It's not a competition. I'm just jealous you get to talk to my grandfather. I miss him," Fin admits.

"I had to get used to him. At first, he drove me up the walls," Cal reveals.

This makes Fin laugh; he can see that happen.

"You seem pretty chill in Fairy. Have you been before? It's not my favorite place. I'm always afraid I will be old by the time I make it back." Cal glances around as if it would matter what the others thought.

Fin shrugs, "Don't worry, man. I used to come here all the time. If you hate it so much, how did you end up here?"

"It's a long story," Cal sighs.

Fin raises his drink, suggesting he has all the time in the world.

Seamus grins when he notices the two young men chatting; Ceri follows his gaze. "It might be good for Cal to have someone his own age around," she muses. "Fin surprised me today."

"His sisters always take the front row, but I think he prefers it that way," Seamus replies.

"We were all so busy with our lives. I must say I never paid that much attention to my nephews and nieces. It would have been useful now to be more aware of everyone's capabilities."

"Too much going on," agrees Seamus.

A tingle in the back of Ceri's neck instantly puts her on high alert. She raises her hand and dematerializes on the spot.

"Ceri!" shouts Seamus, alarming the others. "Where did she go?"

Ace of Cups

PART 6

ACE OF CUPS "DESIRE"

"You must start with desire, keeping in mind that with the magic of believing, you can obtain what you picture in your mind's eye."

—CLAUDE M. BRISTOL

FAIRY

Ceri has materialized at the edge of her property, seemingly lounging relaxed on a tree branch. Slowly, she turns her head toward a nondescript-looking fairy standing not ten feet away. Her legs sway to the ground, "Well, hello? Can I help you with anything?"

If the fairy is surprised to see her, he doesn't show it. "Hi. I'm enjoying this beautiful forest."

The tiny smile playing on his lips doesn't reach his eyes. It would be a mistake to dismiss this one; his looks might not draw any attention to him, yet that is probably on purpose. This must be Mab's spymaster. "Who are you?" he wants to know.

"Give me your name and I will give you mine," Ceri instantly replies.

His dark eyes bore into Ceri's; she gets her cellphone out and snaps a picture of him. That way, she can ask Maeron.

This makes him blink. "What are you doing?"

Now it's Ceri's turn to smile. Fairies don't know phones; it's one of the habits that Ceri has been unable to shake. Even though it's useless in Fairy, she still carries it around. You never know when you need to go to Earth; she doesn't want to be without it. And for situations like these, it has proven useful. She lets the silence stretch with no intention of enlightening him.

"I can walk here. It's not forbidden, is it?" he casually asks.

"As far as I know, you can walk anywhere that you want in Fairy. Nothing is off-limits." That is, after all the official rules. However, it's courtesy to stay off someone's private property, and this fairy knows he's right at the edge of hers.

"Of course," he says. That wry smile again. "I think I'm going back home. It was nice meeting you—"

He let that linger in the hope she will give him her name, even though Ceri has no doubt he knows who's standing opposite him. When she doesn't comply, he turns and starts walking away. Ceri waits and stares after him until he's well out of sight. Secretly delighted her ward is working! Time to go back and check with Maeron if this fairy is who she thinks he is. Always good to have a face to your enemy.

NEW ORLEANS

Tara is eager to get back to the Hat, it has proven to be an energy booster, and it distracts her from all the family drama, which is out of her hands now. Putting on a little makeup and appraising herself in the mirror, she nods to her image in satisfaction. It has been years— decades since she took the trouble of fixing herself up. Even when Seamus was alive, she didn't feel the need to do that. It's a revelation that you can do it solely for yourself. It took some digging in her closet, but she decided to explore her new look.

She snatches the Five of Pentacles from her altar when she moves through her room. Enough with that depressing card! She shuffles the cards and draws a new one. The Ace of Cups! Now, that's more promising—new possibilities for your heart's desires. The water in the cup is overflowing, signifying the abundance. The tadpoles swimming below it signal new life. Beginnings. What does she desire? It's hard to pin down. Tara still misses the warm, comforting power of the Wand. Or does she have to look more at her emotional state? Her connection with her sister? Even though her sister has been the instigator for all this trouble, seeing her. Touching her. Had brought back an old longing. Shrugging it off, she takes it as a sign of her renewed joy in working at the Hat: the people, the hustle and bustle.

With more energy than she had in forever, she goes down the stairs searching for some breakfast. Thank goodness, the smell of freshly baked goods welcomes her through the door. It's good to have Emily in the house. It's lovely that she decided to live here. The place is alive again. It seems like Maeve, Emily, and even Wes and Bridget are staying for a while. Diane, maybe for less cheerful reasons, but it's good to have her home as well. A full house again, one of the good things coming out of this mess.

When Tara opens the door, the first one she sees is Cephalop. He makes her uncomfortable, that fairy is highly perceptive, and his watery figure is frighteningly well attuned to human emotions. Tara gives him an insincere smile, grabs a muffin, and kisses Emily on the cheek. "Good morning, darling. Did you sleep well?"

"It's good to be home," Emily replies upbeat while her hands are kneading some dough.

The door opens again, and this time Bridget and Maeve come in; they look exhausted. With a big sigh, they both plop down in a chair and dig into the breakfast feast on the table.

"Another study night?" Tara casually asks.

"I'm going to bed," Bridget evades the question. "Where's Wes?"

"Still sleeping, I guess." Emily is the one answering.

"Great," Bridget gets up, and with a glance at her grandmother's appearance, she heads upstairs. No doubt she registered the change in Tara. Cephalop is not the only one with a sharp mind.

Diane shows up, and the wave of sadness following her dips the earlier upbeat kitchen vibe.

"Those are vegan," Emily points at a separate plate on the side.

Diane's eyes tear up. "That is so kind of you," she says.

"You're welcome, Aunt Diane," Emily blushes.

"Are you also doing the early shift?" Tara wants to know. "We can ride together?"

"Okay," is all that Diane replies.

Tara's eyes wander along the table, watching one of Cephalop's tentacles caress Maeve's face. It gives her shivers. Abruptly, she says, "I'm checking my herb garden; just holler when you're ready to go." Without waiting for an answer, she disappears.

GREENLAND

Luna found a Sedna statue by the water edge in the older part of town. That feels like the appropriate spot trying to find out what the scallop shell on her forehead is for. Freya is right; it's out of character that she hadn't tried before. Her wonky magic had shaken her to her core. Questioning who she truly is. So, if she's honest with herself, she never tried because she's scared. Scared that she can't control what might happen or not be strong enough to resist any temptation it might present.

For the first time since her backlash, it's like she has some control over her magic abilities, or rather it's not slipping away any further. This whole experience has been quite humbling. To find out her sister has chunks of her memory missing, to an extent it affected her state of being, is madness. At first, she felt horrible that she had always been so intolerant toward her, especially since Freya did come to her aid when she needed her. Harsh truths to deal with. Luna needs to change her attitude toward Freya, probably toward others in general. Not being so quick to judge; there's always another side to the story. Damn! Not easy to find out you've been a prick.

A cold wind snaps her out of her reverie. Enough with wallowing, you can only change things moving forward. She zips up her coat and pulls her hat further over her ears before finding a comfortable sitting spot. She bunches up her shawl to sit on, to prevent freezing her butt off. Not knowing how long this will take.

Luna faces Sedna's statue; a woman sits surrounded by a walrus, polar bear, and a seal while someone is combing her hair. The water is lapping at the statue's feet. After several deep breaths, she tries to relax and gently touches the shell on her forehead. Immediately, the rustle of the sea is washing over her, drawing her under into the ocean's vastness. Although her body still faces the statues, it's like water is all around her, the cold, cold waters of Greenland. Carefully, she explores the shell with her magic; so far, so good. The familiar tingling of her senses is promising. The shell itself is hard and ribbed. Naturally, your finger moves to the bottom, where the ribs come together and form almost an indentation. Strange, as if it's denting the wrong way. Hard to imagine how the scallop still fits inside there. With her mind, she wanders to the bottom of the ocean; there is hardly any light—sea creatures moving around her. Luna is aware of them without actually seeing them.

For a second, her magic flutters, and her eyes open. The light blinds her, in a reflex closing her eyes again, which helps her concentrate even harder on that flow of magic; she's back in the ocean. Water—the power that amplifies emotions. What does she desire? What does she want to achieve? Questions washing through her. Unfailingly, her heart desires to be able to use her magic again. However, that's not what she needs to do right now. How can she connect to the shell? What is its purpose? These are the questions she should be asking. Carefully, she focuses her mind. She is constantly checking if the flow of magic is still there. Communication is the word that bubbles up. Communication with what? Or whom? With communication in mind, she touches the shell again, and this time a strange sound, like a cry underwater, ripples through the ocean. Her magic is holding, and she tries again, a bit louder. Strangely thrilling.

Up north, Snowflake is startled when the forgotten seashell in her pocket comes to life. She can feel its vibration against her body. Warily, she takes it out and lets it sit on her hand. It's visibly moving. The woman who has the other half is calling her. In her mind, she pictures being submerge; it's no effort for her as the guardian of the Cup to let her magic float in the element. *"Who is this?"* It's been a while since she used one.

Luna almost loses her concentration when the words reach her. *Shit, there is someone on the other end. Who?* Can she trust them to tell her the truth? Her magic flutters while she quickly runs her options through her head. *NOT NOW!* She screams desperately in her mind. The magical flow is stabilizing; she needs to act quickly. Don't overthink it. *"My name is Luna Madigan; who am I speaking to?"*

Well, well, the witch finally decided to take that shell for a run. The woman that ended up half-dead on her brother's doorstep. What an idiot to fly a broom unprotected this time of year in Greenland. Snowflake faces the same dilemma as Luna. Can she be sure it's the witch on the other side, and is she willing to connect to her? This inaction has put her on edge; this is her chance to get to know them firsthand. *"This is Snowflake Berthelsen; Jôrse is my brother. I think we're distant relatives."*

Is she the Guardian? How did she get the other half of the shell? This woman must be in touch with the mermaids, as the Guardian of the Cup it does make sense. Luna is weighing her reply. There is no time to waste. Lucy and Mara are somewhere in Greenland, most likely closer to their goal than they are.

"I'm here to warn you that my mother's twin sister Lucy Lockwood is after the Cup. Our family is the Guardian of the Wand of Wisdom. We're here to help."

Help. Right. Luckily, Luna can't see Snowflake's face; it's clear what she thinks about that. *"Thank you for the warning. We'll be fine."*

Dismissed, thinks Luna. In her shoes, she would do precisely the same. *"Please. Lucy killed the Guardian of the Dagger of Consciousness; she doesn't stop at anything."* In all honesty, Luna is not sure what she and Freya are doing here, or what kind of help they can provide. They set of with a clear mission to find the family that guards the Cup. Not thinking it through, that they might not be wanted, or even qualified to help. Luna's journey with her jittery powers and reconnecting with Freya has changed her perspective. Questioning her and her family's natural superior attitude. But there's no doubt in her mind that they owe it to the other families to try to stop Lucy. When no answer follows, Luna considers what to say next. So far, they did a messed-up job of protecting the Dagger. It's hard to defend their choices now that Maeve is attuned to it.

"Please. It's a long story, can we meet? I find this—a bit disorienting."

Snowflake is still processing this news. That must be the disturbance she felt. If a Guardian is killed, it somehow affects them all. That is a scary thought. It might be crucial to know exactly what happened. It's risky. Should she let these women come up north? Jôrse thought they were sincere. He's a good judge of character. Snowflake does not doubt that the older woman she saw in Qaanaaq must be Lucy. That's almost as if your enemy is next door by Greenland standards. *"I'll arrange transport. Be ready tomorrow at first light. Dress warm; it's a long journey."* Not waiting for a reply, she severs the connection and puts the scallop back in her pocket. There's no way back now.

Luna wants to say something back, but when Snowflake has severed their connection, she snaps out of her trance and is back in her body opposite the statue. Wow! That's not what she had expected. Time to find her sister and get packing.

First light, but where? Ah well, they know where they are staying; no doubt someone will show up.

Mara is holding on tightly to Andrew on the back of the snowmobile. She's freezing and definitely not dressed appropriately. A tiny spell keeps her just warm enough as she's afraid to waste too much energy; she doesn't know how much magic she will need to use when they arrive at the moulins.

The six of them gathered at the airport—Andrew, his assistant, the scientist Paul with his assistant, and a local guide. They're all experienced on the ice, dressed in warm clothes and comfortable on the snowmobiles. Mara has never been on one before, so she ended up with Andrew.

She can almost taste their excitement. It's a lovely energy to be surrounded with. It's been forever since she has been around such positive vibes. They can't wait to find out if the moulins they selected this summer were the perfect ice caves. Mara has just as much riding on this as they do. She doesn't know what to do if this doesn't pan out. Swept away in the good energy, she decides to try at least to enjoy this day. When do you ever get a chance to go out on the ice and explore something new? It might not be on her bucket list, but she can still appreciate the special moment.

Trying to relax, she leans against Andrew's back and takes in all that whiteness. The sun is peaking through the clouds, and when it hits the snow and ice, it lights it up with a million twinkles. Pure magic. Carefully, she opens her witch sight and throws out her witch sense. The rocks are old, so old; it's like her bones ache with age. If you tune out the snoring of the snowmobiles, this heavy quiet radiates wisdom. Mara marvels at it and loses track of time and place. She is drifting in the magical currents of the place. Not many areas left on the planet feel so untouched.

She is startled out of her trance when Andrew gently shakes her to get off the snowmobile. "Where you sleeping?" he asks, amused.

"It's such a special place," she simply answers.

He looks around, "It sure is. Look, there is our first prospect." He points toward a crevice. The others already busy unloading their gear. Without further delay, he starts pulling his gear off, and joins the others.

Mara turns a 360—white snow and ice as far as the eye can see. What is she supposed to do now? Besides the idea that it might be a way to travel beneath instead of over the ice, she hadn't thought it through. How is she even going to do it? What kind of magic can she use? Snapping some pictures, she moves closer to the group to see if she can be of any help. "Can I come down with you?"

"Only Andrew goes down to assess the caves," Paul says. "He's the most experienced and able to judge if it is safe for us to go further into it."

Andrew is putting on a special harness over his clothes. He says, "We have no idea if the ice is stable. It should be frozen enough but can still crumble easily or cave in. I need to see if there's enough space left for us to move through and if it reaches far enough down for Paul to the bedrock."

Putting on a helmet, his assistant adjusts the light on top. "Ready?" he wants to know while double-checking if Andrew's harness is secure.

"Ready." Andrew can't hide his excitement. As an adventurer, this is the moment he has been waiting for. The anticipation level in the crew is spiking. With her witch sight still open, Mara can almost see them light up. They crowd around the crevice while Andrew carefully disappears into it. Turning on his lights, they divide their attention between ensuring the ropes are secure and safe and the images coming in on the iPad from Andrew's GoPro. "Can you see this?" Andrew's voice reaches them full of awe. "It looks amazing!"

They look at the image of an enormous frozen waterfall; the light from his helmet gives it an otherworldly feel. A hand comes into frame and touches the waterfall; it sets off a crumbling of icicles that fall like spears.

"Pull him up!" shouts Paul, while they drop the iPad and start pulling Andrew back up.

When he's safely back out, he rolls on his back. "Shit. Too unstable." Trying not to let the disappointment get to him, he adds. "On to the next one."

Within no time, they're on their way.

The second and the third one had pretty much the same result. One didn't go down deep enough while the other started crumbling as well.

Now, they're standing at the fourth one; this crevice is more expansive and gives a deeper view of what lies beneath. Andrew is maybe a hundred feet down, the furthest so far. "This looks promising." His voice travels up. "Looks good," he adds. His assistant agrees with what he can see on the camera's images. This time, Mara lets her witch sense travel down; together with the images, she can paint a pretty good picture of what she can expect down there. Her senses tell her this one goes all the way down and leads to an underground river. That might be frozen over now, but it eroded a cavern above it, making tunnels under the ice. This might be the way to move around. But how are they going to do that? She can't take her grandmother down one of these holes. Hell, she can't even get down properly! And how is she going to find her way? Mab's tattoo on her arm starts itching. Yeah, there's no avoiding that. Mara will need the help of the Fairy Queen to make this work. Oh, man! This has disaster written all over it—stuck between Lucy and Mab.

FAIRY

At first glance, Fin looks like a fairy. The others insisted it would be better if he blended in. He fidgets with his clothes while his aunt gives him last-minute instructions. They debated till deep into the night. The memory globes in the library were fascinating; there are other dimensions, but other than that, they didn't learn much. Seamus repeatedly stressed they needed to search the Ferrymaster's house. No doubt, looking for an opportunity to steal Freya's memories back. However, that would be far too dangerous for Cal; they couldn't chance for Mab to know where he was. That also ruled out Seamus as he couldn't be far from Cal.

In the end, they decided that Fin and Maeron would scope out the place. If Maeron got caught, he would be able to handle himself, and Fin said he would ready several memories he would be willing to trade for information or payment. After all, he had done it many times.

Ceri gives her nephew the once-over. "You look good. I asked you here because I can offer you the protection that would prevent you from paying the Ferrymaster. I didn't want to do it with the others around as it is a private matter for whoever chooses to do it."

Fin senses a catch, "What kind of protection? And what does it involve or cost me?"

This makes his aunt smile, "I like you. There's a very perceptive human being underneath all that good-natured charm. You like it if people underestimate you, don't you?"

"What does it cost me, Auntie?" Now, he's sure this will involve something he might not be willing to do.

Ceri shows Fin her hand; with her finger, she gently rubs over the little moving tattoos on her hand. "These images represent my fairy family. This mouse connects Alvina to me. This octopus is Cephalop." The image wiggles when she moves over him. "As you can see, my house is growing."

Fascinated, Fin bends forward, and asks, "What does connect them to you mean?"

"When I touch the image, I can directly communicate with them, and the other way around. I can summon them. It has some other benefits."

"Like what?" Fin takes a step back.

"It shows that you belong to my family. My inner circle as fairies interprets that. You will be protected from things like paying the Ferrymaster. Mab can't directly touch you without involving us all. In Fairy, it's a great privilege to belong to a house. It's a certain status."

Fin lets that all sink in before he finally speaks, "No offense, Aunt Ceri, but I find that a bit too much control. We're already family. Isn't that enough?"

She shakes her head.

"I appreciate the offer, but no thanks. I've always thought you were my coolest aunt, but I find this—a bit much. I'll take my chances with the Ferrymaster."

"Suit yourself," says Ceri, not offended. "You can always change your mind." With a wink, his playful Aunt is back. Seeing her in her new surroundings had broadened his view of Fairy. It had always been fun for him. Now, he sees it can be treacherous, full of intrigue, and power plays. Ceri looks at home here; strangely enough, she makes sense in this world. A puzzle piece falls into place.

Together, they walk back to the house; Maeron, Seamus, and Cal are waiting for them.

"Ready?" Maeron asks Fin while he glances at Ceri. With a tiny shake of the head, she lets him know Fin didn't accept her offer.

"Remember to look for Freya's memories as well," Seamus reminds Fin through Cal for the millionth time.

"Yes. Yes." All the things he will need to look for.

"Let's first see what the place looks like," Maeron says.

"Of course. Of course," Seamus sputters.

Ceri opens a portal to a city that Fin has never seen before. "This will bring you close, but not too close."

"Let's do it," Fin and Maeron step through.

A fairy city is an assault on the senses. It takes Fin a couple of minutes to process this sensory overload while Maeron scans their environment. Every imaginable color is moving around them, while fairies and innumerable other creatures of all shapes and sizes buzz around them three-dimensionally. The spicy smell hanging in the air makes Fin's stomach grumble, although it's never wise to eat something here. It's like you're emerged in color, sound, and smell. It's exciting and frightening at the same time. The steady hand of Maeron on his shoulder helps him to get grounded. "Thank you," he finally manages to say.

"Welcome to All Things."

"Seriously?!" This makes Fin laugh out loud.

"That's what I think it translates to in your language. It's one of the larger cities at the edge of our world. Or rather as far as we inhabit it. I'm not sure if our worlds have an edge." Maeron frowns, shaking it off, not wanting to get into that now. "We need to move. Even though Ceri did her best to put a shielding spell on us, I do not doubt that someone will sense us."

"You mean the Ferrymaster," Fin asks.

"Or worse…," Maeron is reluctant to name *her*.

Fin has no trouble understanding whom he means. "Let's go," he says. Trailing behind Maeron, he steals glances at the enticing city. He would love to come back here and explore when everything has calmed down. He thought he had seen most of Fairy—clearly not!

Their progress is slow as Maeron pulls Fin aside and shields him from prying eyes whenever he senses they draw too much attention.

"Shouldn't the Ferrymaster have felt me by now? Since we have left Aunt Ceri's home?" Fin whispers.

"I told you she shielded us," Maeron sounds doubtful.

"Wouldn't it be better if he came for me now? Otherwise, I might attract attention too close to his home."

Maeron turns toward him and sizes him up. "I am worried about that."

"Can't we bait him?" Fin says with more conviction than he feels. "I don't know how it all works. But logic applied, I should be off his radar once I gave him a memory, right?"

"Nobody knows exactly how it works, and as it doesn't affect us, nobody bothered to find that out. I must admit it makes sense."

"Let's do it. I have some memories ready," Fin insists. That must be the best way.

"Ceri won't like it," Maeron is weary.

"She's not here, and Auntie is a risk-taker; she'll understand."

The face Maeron pulls makes clear what he thinks about that.

Fin laughs, "Come on!"

The ancient fairy takes a moment to weigh their options before he nods his approval. "He shouldn't see me, in any case. Otherwise, he might get suspicious."

"Agreed," says Fin as he looks around and spots the Fairy equivalent of a bar. "There, that's a place I would visit, and he has encountered me in similar bars before. Maybe that won't attract attention, and it's easy for you to blend in." Loud music spills out from the establishment, and the brawly group of creatures outside is a colorful distraction.

"You stay outside. I'll get you a drink that is safe for you. I can hide inside and keep an eye on you. But you will be on your own with the Ferrymaster. Are you sure you want to do this?" Maeron asks still not entirely sure this is the best idea.

Fin nods firmly. Without any further discussion, Maeron walks inside while Fin finds himself a spot. He barely sits when the Ferrymaster plops down in his smaller form on the table's edge. It startles Fin. *Wow! That was quick! Focus!* He tells himself while he ruffles through his prepared memories.

"Well, well, Fionnagáin Madigan," the Ferrymaster says, pronouncing it in perfect Gaelic; it's where Fin's name is derived from. "I didn't expect you here. Evading Ceridwen while you have some fun?"

Fin looks away, not wanting his face to reveal anything. Even though he isn't as bad as Maeve in hiding the truth, witches are not the best liars.

"I see you acquired a new wardrobe. Hoping I wouldn't notice you?"

"Not much escapes you, does it?" Fin smiles.

"You know the drill." The tiny Ferrymaster's wicked smile is full of anticipation.

Fin has a memory firm in the front of his mind while he sticks his finger toward the demanding fairy.

"Wait," the Ferrymaster hops on his finger and stares him in his face, much too close for comfort.

Fin's insides turn upside down. *Shit*! Frantically, he tries to keep his memory in place. That's how the Ferrymaster gets you. He puts you out of balance and then snaps something from you that you're not willing to share. *You can do this.* He is giving himself a pep talk. After all, this is not his first encounter. *Focus.* "Do you want your memory or not?" he boldly states.

"Maybe I should rat you out to your auntie. Why do I get the feeling she would disapprove of this?" the Ferrymaster winks.

Nervous butterflies are fluttering to the surface and one lone butterfly escapes.

This makes the fairy laugh out loud. "Oh yes. What are you willing to give up, young man, to keep this between us?" The Ferrymaster has now jumped up his shoulder and almost seductively leans against Fin's face.

Fin has the most challenging time holding on to his preferred memory. His mind starts rolling with other memories.

"Yes, much better," the Ferrymaster chirps as if he senses Fin losing grip on his thoughts.

Fin stops his urge to swat off the irritating fairy from his shoulder and instead stutters, "Ccccan—ccccaan—can you give me some space?"

Within a blink of an eye, the Ferrymaster is back on the table, seemingly grown a bit. "I don't make you nervous, do I?"

Fin blushes.

Another laugh escapes the trickster. "Well! I think you should give me a memory that involves your sisters."

"I can only give you a memory that is my own," Fin tries to evade.

"You must have some childhood memory that involves you all?"

Fin's adrenaline is spiking. He hadn't prepared a memory with his sisters, and he doesn't want to give one that involves them. The Ferrymaster must have an ulterior motive. This is not good. He hasn't been this off-balance in a long time. Firmly, he tries to fix his prepared memories in his mind. "How about I give you two memories instead of one?"

"I want one with your sisters," the fairy sulks.

"According to the rules, I only have to give you one memory," Fin says as he sizes up his opponent; he's undoubtedly outwitted. This fairy must be at least as old as Maeron. Coming to Fairy this often did teach him the rules of passage. One of the things is—that he must give up the memory freely. The Ferrymaster might throw you off balance, but you have to let him in your head to really pick what he wants. As long as you pay and hold true to your thoughts, there's not much the trickster can do to you. "I was generous by offering two."

Irritated, the Ferrymaster grows a bit more. Churning this over, he finally caves, "Two it is."

Fin aligns his thoughts and sticks out his finger. The Ferrymaster touches his finger with his mouth this time, no doubt to make this as awkward as possible. Holding firm, the transfer of his preferred memories is done within seconds.

Without another word, the Ferrymaster is gone. Fin exhales; this had been scary—almost falling into the trap.

Maeron is by his side again. "Tell me what happened."

GREENLAND

When Mara enters her room, Lucy looks up from what must be her tenth cup of tea. "And?!"

"It was cold!" Mara says while she undresses, taking off some of her many layers.

"Is it going to work?" Lucy is bored stiff, and has no patience to wait until her granddaughter peeled off her outdoor clothes.

Mara sighs and plops down. "I don't know," she says honestly. "It's promising; there are underground tunnels formed by meltwater, but how far they go is totally unclear. You must go in to know where it's going. It's cold and hard to get down in the crevasses. Not sure if you would make it, Gran."

Lucy stiffens, is Mara trying to get rid of her? Ever since she was back, Lucy has noticed a change in her granddaughter—and she's wondering how loyal she still is. Maybe she's after the Cup herself?

"It will be hard for me," Mara adds, aware of Lucy's reluctance.

"We need to find another way." This is depressing. Lucy doesn't want Mara to go on her own.

"Let's not give up yet. They're going to try to go down one tomorrow. I signed up to be on the team going down." Mara doesn't sound convinced that this will be a good idea. "Is there something like a magical probe or something we could send in? You did, after all, track the Cup. Could you do that again?"

Lucy shakes her head, "That was for finding something on a map. This is completely different. We're stuck here without books or even decent Internet!" It's hard to hide her frustration. The cold is getting into her old bones. She hates it. Anger bubbles up, and she slings her teacup toward the wall. With a loud bang, it splinters into a million pieces, the tea dripping down the wall, leaving brown stains.

Very slowly, Mara gets up, gathers her things, and moves to the door. "I'm going to take a hot bath," she whispers while quietly leaving the room.

Lucy is still simmering. Absentmindedly, she scratches the sigil that Vhumut had left on her skin, which never fails to react when Lucy's temper flares. Her son's father, a fire demon, managed to lure her into a trap. He wants her soul. Her negotiation skills wiggled two more human years out of him to finish her business on earth. How long does she still have? Precious time is slipping away. She needs the Cup sooner rather than later. It's essential to her survival. The only thing that will enable her to get out of this deal with the demon. Again, she scratches it, taking a moment to examine its image. It sparks something in her mind. There might be a way…. Nah! That would be too costly.

In her room, Mara is finally warming up under a hot shower. Keenly aware of Lucy's suspicion of her. Witches are very sensitive to those things, especially ones that know each other well. Not much she can do about it. The moulins might be able to work, but she won't be able to pull it off on her own. She would never be able to track the endless number of tunnels. How is she even staying warm enough? The tunnels can be too narrow or freeze close behind her. And it all begins with finding a way to lose the research team. Letting those questions float through her mind, Mara lets her body thoroughly enjoy the shower cell's warmth. Packed with steam, it's almost like she's alone in the world. With a heavy feeling, Mara turns off the shower and quickly rubs herself dry. It might be warm in her room, but it's not that warm. While she dresses, she can't avoid looking at Mab's tattoo. No doubt the Fairy Queen would be able to help her. Liking it or not, she promised to serve her. There would be no option other than giving Mab the Cup unless she finds a way to keep it for herself. Anyway, it's obvious she needs to convince Lucy to stay behind. That would be one problem less to worry about.

She dresses and feels recharged, a plan having formed in her head. Best to make the most of her connection with Mab. Let the woman help her out. Once she reaches the Cup, she can figure out her next options. Getting there will be hard enough.

Her finger brushes the tattoo, and Mab is in her room instantly. "You rang?" the deceptively nice words are not reflected in Mab's irritated face. "What do you want? I'm busy."

Mara takes a step back, but there's nowhere to go in the little room. "I—I—I think I know how to reach the Cup."

This seems to mellow Mab ever so slightly.

"I need your help. Under the ice are tunnels formed by meltwater that might reach up north where the Cup is hidden. However, I need help mapping, staying warm, and I might be too big to go certain ways. Can you make me smaller? Give me wings or something?"

The Queen cocks her head while she mulls this over. "Interesting."

"It's the only way to get us up north unnoticed, as we don't exactly know where we're going."

Mab moves her index finger with a razor-sharp nail through the air. She is slicing open a tiny portal to Fairy. A pocket-size fairy steps through and sits patiently on her hand. "You remember Petal?"

Mara nods: he was her teacher to tell her what was expected of her as a servant of Mab. A sleazy, underhanded, loyal subject of the Queen. Not someone she would have picked. With Mab, it rarely is what you hope for. She likes you off balance; you're easier to control that way. "Of course; welcome, Petal."

"He should be able to help you. I have to go." Petal jumps out of her hand as Mab disappears.

Curiously, he flutters around her room. Warily, Mara follows his every move.

"Why don't you fill me in?" His high-pitched voice reverberates through the room.

It takes every ounce of self-control not to roll her eyes or make a snappy comment. Years of tip-toeing around Lucy come in handy now. Mara sits down and starts to explain her plan for tomorrow.

BOSTON

Gwen walks through Allandale Woods at night. A faint glow from the light ball hovering above her hand leads the way deeper and deeper into the forest. It reminds her so much of her older sister Alana; the memories of the many times they came here for a ritual are like a knife into her heart. A reminder of why she's doing this.

For several days, she questioned her quest for revenge on the Madigans and her play to get the Dagger back for her family. At first, when she came back, her family comforted her and they discussed the options open to them. None were very appealing. The loss of Alana took the fire out of them, and the loss of the Power of Air had a rippling effect on the family. After many bottles of wine and endless nights of discussion, they decided it had cost them enough. Let the Madigans have it and deal with this power struggle if they want it so much. Gwen had reluctantly agreed, but for her, the Madigans are like a ring of fire constantly twirling in front of her eyes. No way could she let this go.

For weeks, she searched through the occult books in the rare book room of the Boston Public Library. Their selection is extraordinary. At last, she found something that would boost her powers and help her connect to a powerful object. There was a catch—it's dark magic. It would lead her down a path that she couldn't return from. Her family would not understand.

It took her several other weeks before she had the courage to try something. Something small. Her first experiment was on a rat. Nobody would care if she killed one of those. People killed rats all the time. Even such a slight energy elevation was thrilling. Sure enough, Gwen craved more. She moved on to a stray cat. Helpful to get off the streets, she justified in her mind. At first, she had been keenly aware that every kill was a little black smudge on her soul, constantly questioning herself, almost like she was two people for a while.

The horse was a choice of convenience. A friend has a horse at that stable, and after visiting her, that particular horse tried to bite her. It sparked something in her. It was appealing to her dark side. That night, without overthinking it, she had done the ritual. It provided her with such a boost; it had given her several seconds of euphoria, after which she got violently sick of herself and barfed up her guts. It had shaken her badly. *She never thought herself capable of that.*

And then, Tom, that policeman, showed up. Renewing her doubts, she'd gone too far. The dark battling with the light inside her. The hunger for more growing—is she even able to stop?

The whirlwind in her mind keeps going. A branch snaps under her feet, jolting her out of her train of thought. Her rituals demand life force from bigger and bigger prey. Gwen doesn't think she can go through with it anymore. Yet, that wheel of fire grows in her brain, feeding the anger—the injustice of losing her sister. The pain of the memories she experiences walking under the trees is a conformation that she can't give up—for Alana.

Thinking outside the box, she wants to try something different tonight; trees are living things. Witches are acutely aware of that. A good forest bathing can be a boost to the soul.

Not able to kill a friend, she walks to a part of the forest that is less familiar to her. Majestic oaks rise up tall, their leaves already changing color. They will soon withdraw within themselves to be reborn in the spring—no time to waste. Looking around for a perfect tree, her eye falls on an old Maple, its branches a welcoming crown. The leaves are a bright red and yellow. A mother tree, as forest herders would call her. For a split second, Gwen hesitates; Alana, the Madigans flash through her mind. Taking a deep breath, she walks to the tree's bark and puts her bag down. Resolute, she carves the fatal runes into its bark. In her mind, she can sense the shock of the tree. *You're a witch! Shouldn't you mind the forest? Help!* Pulling up a shield, she tunes out the begging. When she's finished, she turns around, sits down with her back against the tree's bark, and starts her chant. The forest, already quiet at night, seems to have stopped breathing.

Gwen closes her eyes when the life force of the maple starts to flow into her; it's like a warm bath—it makes her skin tingle all over. Greedily, she draws in more and more of that power.

When she resurfaces, Gwen is exhilarated. What a perfect idea—far less traumatic—and the earth magic pulsating through her is exquisite. Not long now before she's strong enough to make a move.

Packing up quickly, she no longer needs a light. All that power sets her aglow. Only when she walks away does she realize that all life has left the forest within a fifty-foot radius around the tree. Shit, she hadn't intended to do that. It must be true then that the trees are connected. Shrugging it off, she makes her way home.

NEW ORLEANS

Bridget has to use all her persuasion to get Wes out of bed and out of the house. The episode with the paintings has hurdled him back into a depression. Not wanting to ask her sister for advice, the only thing she can think of is to take him to the French Quarter. Wandering along the shops, some music, and good food generally lifts anybody's mood.

Bridget wears a cheerful summer dress, and Wes simply has shorts with a t-shirt. It might be fall, but it will take until November before it seriously cools down. They chat about the state of the world and the art they encounter, avoiding talking about anything magic or family-related. The paintings on Jackson Square make them smile; it's made to draw in tourists. But it is hard not to enjoy the vibrant colors and curious characters selling it. Bridget even buys a small piece for their house in Boston. A fake kind of normalcy that they both need desperately. Craving a beignet, they make their way to Café du Monde; the line is so long that they ditch that idea. Weaving in and out of shops, they suddenly find themselves in front of Under the Witches Hat. The colossal hat is gently swaying in the breeze.

Wes sees Bridget's hesitation. "We can go in." He laughs and kisses Bridget gently on her cheek, adding, "Thanks. I needed this." His mood has improved considerably.

"Me too," she whispers. "I think it's good to touch base here. Poor Ron has to deal with keeping us going while, one by one, we abandon our duties."

"I fancy one of his cocktails," Wes winks.

Bridget is so happy to see a smile on his face. Having a relationship is so much more complex than she had envisioned. Nobody tells you it's constant work. It's not like in the movies; you fall in love and live happily ever after. Wes is so worth it—what a good guy.

"Come on," he snaps her out of her musings.

She draws him in for a thorough kiss before heading inside.

It takes them a second to adjust to the dim light of the floating orbs. To her surprise, it's not Ron but Tara behind the bar. Her change of appearance unnerves Bridget, as she resembles Lucy this way. Her grandmother looks ten years younger working behind the bar. This warms Bridget's heart, glad Tara found renewed purpose. What to do with the emptiness that the Wand had left behind in Gran has been much debated between Maeve, the ancestors, and herself.

Tara welcomes them with a warm smile. "What can I get you?"

Wes slides onto a barstool. "Can you make me that cocktail with the bourbon and the honey?"

Tara winks and turns to Bridget, "And for you?"

"A Fairy cocktail for me. Is Ron here?" Bridget scans the bar one more time.

"He's in the back with Diane," Tara answers while her hands are already busy with the cocktail ingredients.

Bridget squeezes Wes's arm; he nods that she should go ahead. "I'm fine."

Giving him a quick kiss, "I'll only be a second."

Wes laughs, "Famous last words. Seriously, don't worry."

Bridget disappears through the door leading to the back room. Softly, she closes the door behind her, taking in the scene in front of her. Diane is humming and floating around the room while Ron is swaying to the rhythm and pouring ingredients into a potion. A blissfully normal image, for witches, that is. Bridget pulls her phone from her pocket and snaps a picture. Unfortunately, it's not on silent, and Diane drops to the ground while both of them turn toward her. "Oh, it's you." Diane's gentle voice sounds relieved.

"Where have you been?" Ron's irritation immediately shows.

It's a question they all know the answer to, so Bridget doesn't bother to reply. "How are you holding up?"

Ron opens his mouth to give her an ear full, and instead closes it and takes a breath. "We're managing," he says. "It's great that Tara is back, and now Diane is here. With Freya's boys, we can just about keep the Hat going."

"Maeve and I are doing better, so if you need a hand with readings, we should be able to fill in."

Diane turns toward her and caresses her face. "That's so sweet of you. But you won't have time for that. The wheels are turning again." The room contract and expand in response to the truth being spoken. A chill runs up Bridget's spine. *Shit! Trouble is coming.*

Ron's expression mirrors Bridget's. It's always unnerving when Diane speaks a truth; as a gifted seer, you know there's no escaping whatever is coming your way.

Not sure how to react to that, Bridget says, "I—I—be heading back to Wes. We're having a cocktail at the bar." Making her way out of there.

Ron gives her a sympathetic smile; all earlier animosity is gone.

FAIRY

Fin follows Maeron through a forest-like area. Once they had left the city, the growth had been thickening, and it takes magic and physical effort to plow through it. It is like they have been walking for hours. So hard to keep track of time in Fairy. The light, the sun, or rather the suns, work the same and yet are very different. Not to mention that the sunlight hardly penetrates down here. The surrounding doesn't have a particular friendly feel. The forest is alive, and not only the trees. Fin constantly scans around; strange noises follow them. "It's like the trees are suffocating me."

"Don't worry; we're protected." Maeron sounds confident.

"Are we getting there?" Fin asks, hopeful.

"You humans and your worry about time."

"Easy for you to say; you don't die as easily as we do."

Maeron glances back at him, "Point taken. I don't know. This area is moving."

"What do you mean?! Moving?" Fin can't hide the alarm in his voice.

"As I explained earlier, this is the edge of things. Fairy is a living thing. Unlike Earth, our dimensions can shrink and expand. What you sense is the restless energy of growing. The Ferrymaster has chosen his home well."

This triggers Fin's interest. "What do you mean by that?"

"As this place is always changing, his home is never in the same spot. It will take considerable skill to track and find it. Sort of a natural way of protection," Maeron approves.

"I guess you possess the skills needed," is Fin's smart-ass reply.

Maeron doesn't bother answering him. The look he throws over his shoulder says enough.

Suddenly, his arm shoots out and holds Fin in his place. With his other arm, he weaves in front of them. Gently, he pulls them backward. They're relying on Maeron's Fairy magic as Fin can't possibly use witch magic. Mab would be upon them in seconds. It's not allowed unless you have a special status like Ceri or Mara.

"There's some sort of safety barrier here," Maeron says as he points toward the invisible, whatever it is.

"Can you disable it?" Fin leans forward to try to see if he can spot it.

"I don't want to disable it. I want to pass it unseen. If we simply snuff it out, it will have the same effect as triggering it."

"Good point."

Without further explanation, Maeron makes himself comfortable in front of the barrier and zones into it.

With nothing else to do, Fin does a 360; if he must wait, he might try to learn as much of this place as possible. He doubts he will ever revisit this specific spot. Nothing appealing about it. Beautiful—yes, but it has a foul atmosphere. With a sigh, he sits next to Maeron, making himself comfortable. He suspects this is going to take a while. His mind wanders to his childhood. The Ferrymaster was after a memory of him and his sisters. Maybe he should prepare one, just in case. He is trying to shift through his memories from the perspective of the Ferrymaster. Weighing what he could learn from each particular memory. With this new perspective, even the most straightforward memory appears to reveal something. If it is not of him, or his sisters, it tells something about Luna. To minimize the damage, he should choose a memory with his dad. It's like they hardly ever had been alone with Steve. There's only a handful he can think of. In his earlier memories, his sisters are in their early teens, which is probably a good time.

Maeve and Bridget would sit opposite each other in the garden, not saying a word, letting flowers swirl around them, making him laugh. Hmmm, not a good one, thinking about his sisters' strong connection now. That has always been there, even before their magic fully came online. Not one to share.

This one, maybe. In his mind, he sees a cute street of a small town in upstate New York; he was too young to remember its name. Steve was holding his hand. His father was always in his study, buried in books. Fin can vividly recall the joy he felt that morning. So happy that his father is taking them to the bakery, he doesn't even mind that he's holding Fin's hand. The twins are striding along in front of them—their long hair swaying in the wind.

That is perfect! This only explains that their father didn't do much with them. There's no harm in that. He starts to recall the memory repeatedly, ensuring that if needed, he can call it up instantly.

GREENLAND

Freya and Luna find themselves back on the water. They're on a private power-boat this time, moving swiftly up the coast with other members of the Berthelsen family. They made sure to outweigh them, four mature witches aged from the early twenties to probably their age. The boat is not made to carry this many, so they're cramped together in the hut. Too cold to stay outside for too long. The uncomfortable silence stretches, with the droning noise of the two powerful motors roaring on the back of the boat. A lanky middle-aged witch with cropped dark hair confidently navigates the boat through the waters. As boats are the main transportation, every Greenlandic person learns to be at home on the water. The group informed them that they would hop from town to town until... unwilling to reveal their final destination.

This is going to be a long trip. Freya tries to find something else to look at than the Berthelsen's. Unable to keep her conversation going with Luna, she is alone with her thoughts in her head. Not something she currently aspires. It would be rude to use a spell against eavesdropping, and she didn't want to take the chance to use mental communication, as some witches are deeply attuned to it. Not knowing what the gifts of this group are, she doesn't doubt they have been chosen for specific skills.

Freya's thoughts are tumbling through her head. These last weeks, she has been swaying between feelings of belonging; the sense of calm that came over her when she first arrived in Iceland is hard to fathom now. It's overpowered by the revelation of finding a memory that is gone. It's terrific that Luna is helping her. This trip unearthed many emotions and, more importantly, restored something between them. At last, Freya found a reason behind her rage; it makes it easier to bear. Regrettably, the rage still gets fed by the anger toward Tara and Seamus for having allowed the Ferrymaster to take her memories at such a young age and to herself for volunteering to go with the Ferrymaster—so stupid!

Obviously, she was not the right person for that job. She has always seen herself as decisive—resilient. Oh, she learned quite the lesson from the Universe—a confronting, humiliating, and humbling experience. What are the odds she will ever be able to retrieve the memories?

Talking with Luna about their past has been remarkable. Imagining their home life, the journeys, when you relive them, it jogs the brain. The memory of the trip to the Viking village still eludes her, but it helped to hear about it. To store it. Like a piece of a puzzle. For the first time, the puzzle is growing again instead of losing pieces. Freya might not live the memory, but to know it is unquestionably beneficial. Would she even need her memory back to become whole? By coming up north, it is as if part of her soul is restored. Is that enough? So many questions need answering, and this boat trip makes her restless. She can't shake the feeling that they're wasting precious time. Not sure what else they should be doing, but not this.

Grilling Seamus is high on her list. Ceri dropped them off, declining to leave them with the means to get in touch with her. Luna tried to persuade Bridget to ask Ceri, but she was reluctant. Apparently, Ceri had given her a hard time when she asked her to rescue them. Her younger—*NO*—Freya corrects herself; her older sister has become a scarily powerful being. Not sure what to call her anymore. Fairy changed her so dramatically; does she even still know her? Unable to quiet her mind, Freya gets up and squeezes herself between everybody's legs to the door. "I'm heading out for a minute," she mumbles while she whispers a tiny keep warm spell. The cool air hits her face, instantly invigorating her.

BOSTON

Tom stands in Allandale Woods in the ruined circle of trees. He has no doubt this is Gwen's work. He found the same runes carved in the bark at the circle's center. Luna taught him that witchcraft is about energy flows, connecting to living things around us. Seeing the horse was sickening. This, however, makes him profoundly sad. This tree must have been standing here for decades, maybe centuries, protecting those around her. All gone. For what?

That's a hypothetical question, as he knows very well what Gwen wants. He pulls his phone from his pocket, ready to dial Luna when he changes his mind, and calls Bridget.

"Any news?" sounds her anxious voice through the phone. She's picking up his bad habits.

"Gwen did another ritual. This time, she killed a bunch of trees. I found the same runes etched in a tree at the center." Falling back into their old routine of police partners.

"So soon?"

Tom knows that's not a question he needs to answer. It worries her that Gwen is speeding up.

"Don't go near her, Tom; I mean it," Bridget urges him to be careful.

"You know I can't do that. It's my job. And I still wear the amulet that Luna gave me," he adds, not that confident himself.

"That will only help you so far."

He can almost hear her think through the phone.

"We're stretched thin here as it is. I don't have anybody I can send to help you." Bridget's frustration is palpable.

"Can you send me another protection spell or something?" Tom suggests.

"If it was only that simple. We're not sure what she's becoming. I can't send Maeve, as she must be after the Dagger. We can barely keep the Hat open with our family left here. Fin has also disappeared on some sort of a mission for Diane."

"I must do something. What if she hurts a person next?" Tom voices the worst-case scenario.

"Let me talk to the others. I'll get back to you."

"I give you twenty-four hours," Tom says and hangs up.

Not comfortable with that, he would prefer to get Gwen behind bars as soon as possible. However, he very well knows that will not work for a witch.

Going after her alone makes him nervous. Tom has not forgotten what happened with Lucy. The whole thing was very traumatic; luckily, some good came out of it. Luna! She's in his mind all the time these days. He can't wait for her to come back home. Home…. He hopes she was serious when she said she's considering Boston. Who would have thought he would fall so hard in love at his age? As welcome as this distraction is right now, he focuses back on the problem in front of him.

NEW ORLEANS

Cephalop, in his human disguise, Emily, and Maeve walk through the French Quarter. Emily shakes off the remaining powdered sugar from her beignet. "I have missed this!"

"Nothing as comforting as a beignet." Maeve is pleased that her cousin is happier than she has seen her in a long time. The poor girl had much to deal with lately. Since Emily returned from Fairy, it's like she has grown up, more at ease with herself.

They're on their way to the Bywater; Ceri put Emily on a mission to discover as much as possible about the history of witches and 'other' people. Ferociously, Emily went through the books in the Madigan library in record time, declaring that it was interesting but not what they'd been looking for. Maeve suggested visiting an old acquaintance, the ever so curious 'Whiskey' Dan. His name might sound more like a bar than someone minding the oldest books in New Orleans. His knowledge and library are exceptional and he's an excellent source for the occult community. Nobody knows his age, but his looks have been wrinkled and leathery for as long as Maeve can remember. Tara took her to his home as a kid, and it had left a lasting impression. The smell of old books, this tawny strange man, and the dark, dusty rooms are not something you would ever forget. Maeve has been back many times and learned 'Whiskey' Dan is a mellow man with a photographic memory.

"Couldn't we have taken the car?" Emily complains.

"Stop whining—it's good to get some fresh air. It's such a beautiful day," Maeve proclaims.

Cephalop stays out of this conversation. Maeve notices he remains close to her without losing sight of Emily and constantly scanning his surroundings for possible dangers. Fairies are natural multitaskers. He touches her as often as possible without it being too obvious. A hand on her back to move her forward in the line at Café du Monde. He is pulling her out of the way of traffic and throwing an arm around her shoulder to point something out to her with his other hand. It makes her smile. She likes him. She likes him a lot! It warms her heart that he takes the time to make her comfortable with him; after his declaration of love, she felt ill at ease. Her affection for him is growing, no doubt his intention. Maeve gives him a warm smile.

Once they cross Esplanade the number of tourists wanes. It's a lovely avenue, of which the two opposite lanes are divided by a park-like walk, a nice place to shelter from the sun in the summer. By the time they reach the far end of the Bywater, they stop in front of a curious-looking building. It's two stories tall, with high round windows, and the bottom ones have their shutters closed.

"Once upon a time, this house was used as a temple for some sort of masonic order," Maeve tells Emily, while she puts her hand up. "You can still sense the energy." She lets her hand wander along with the building's aura. Emily mirrors her cousin, doing her best to reign in her bubbly energy. "I can feel it!" she chirps.

Cephalop smiles. No doubt, he got a vibe from the building. It still resonates peculiarly.

Maeve doesn't need to knock; the door opens and reveals 'Whiskey' Dan. His dark rail-thin skin hangs like a too-big suit along his bones—impossible to guess his age. Luna told her once he already looked like that when she was young. Whatever he is, he's not sharing. "Well, well, little Ms. Maeve has grown up at last." He appraises her from top to bottom. "Not only grown in size, I see." His hand with long curious fingers moves toward her when Cephalop's hand shoots forward to stop Dan. Maeve, however, is even quicker, stopping him and giving him the tiniest shake of her head. Nothing goes unnoticed by Dan. He smiles and turns toward the fairy, "Hello, master fairy. What brings you here?"

Emily's mouth drops open. How did he know?

Cephalop doesn't answer; he just gives him one of his non-committal smiles. This man needs to be handled with care. Definitely not human.

"And who is this lovely young lady?" Dan asks while he peeks around the others.

Maeve steps aside, "This is Emily, my cousin." It's best to give as little information as possible.

Emily hesitantly shakes the hand offered to her. Dan pulls her a bit closer and stares into her eyes. "Hmm, interesting." With that, he lets her go and turns back to Maeve. "What can I do for you?"

"We would love to search your oldest records about the dawn of time, the beginning of things."

"How can I refuse such a gorgeous lady with such an interesting entourage?" He steps aside and welcomes her in with a sweeping bow. "Welcome, welcome." The smell of old parchment is flowing toward them. It takes a few seconds for their eyes to adjust when they're in the front room. Its darkness keeps the books as safe as possible, and the temperature in the room is cold but dry, perfect for the preservation of the documents.

Emily and Cephalop start to wander through the room. They are reading some titles out loud while they pass them by.

"You know the way. Put everything back as you find it. I'll be behind my desk if you have questions."

"Thank you, Dan." Maeve slightly tilts her head to convey her gratitude. To browse and handle these kinds of documents without supervision is a rare gift. The Madigans and Dan have a long understanding. Tara and Seamus brought back many precious scrolls for Dan while they traveled the globe searching for Tara's herbs.

"I've always liked you. Good to see you're growing into your own," Dan says before withdrawing.

Maeve swallows her questions; it is sometimes better to leave things alone. Bridget would not have been able to resist. She has always been the inquisitive one. It makes Maeve smile to think her twin felt she chose a profession as far away from witchcraft as she could think of. Nothing is further from the truth. Witches are great at sniffing out lies, which must be an excellent advantage for B. Focusing back on the scrolls and books, she tries to locate the oldest section.

"Here!" Emily and Cephalop must have already found it.

GREENLAND

Luna has escaped the crowded cabin of the boat this time, staring over the waves produced by the two powerful motors on the back. Its roaring is strangely soothing, and the white foamy spray is always fascinating—almost meditative. Even the cold is calming; the awkward conversation inside is exhausting.

"Penny for your thought?" A high-pitched voice shouts in her ear over the noise of the motors.

Luna stumbles backward.

Next to her, the creature appeared that stopped by when she and Freya were trapped. This time, she's dressed in a complete modern black outfit.

"Do you like it?" the creature asks while she twirls to show her new clothes.

"What do you want?" Luna demands while reaching for her magic, which is frustratingly elusive in moments like this. Cursing in her head, Luna tries to radiate calm on the outside.

"You could be nicer to me, you know," the creature says with a pout.

"What do you want?" Luna insists.

"Is it so hard to believe I like you and just fancy a chat?" Her smile shows her unnerving row of razor-sharp teeth.

"Why are you hanging around? There are so few people here. Not a lot of easy soul snatching, I would think. I thought you would be off to New York or some other crowded place," Luna casually inquires.

The creature drapes herself over the two motors—it looks weird and uncomfortable. "Are you kidding me? Miss this?!" Her small arm swings around as if the fast ocean and the white snowy granite mountains hold some sway for her.

This time, Luna doesn't reply, and within a blink of an eye, the creature stands face to face, hovering in the air so their faces are on the same level. She is grabbing Luna's face between her tiny hands and squeezing it painfully. Luna goes very still.

"Something is going down very soon. I will be there. Whoever's soul will be up for grabs will be exceptional. It will be worth the wait."

Now, Luna is shaking, not from the cold, but from the chill these words give her. Before she manages to shake loose, the creature vanishes. Breathing hard, the outside no longer feels relaxing. Quickly, she heads back inside.

The ice in the water is closing fast so far up north, and it gets harder and harder for the powerboat to evade the icebergs. It's pitch black when the boat finds its way back to the shore. It's a mystery to Luna how they navigate. They must know these waters so well. As far as she can determine, there's nothing. The young man helps them ashore, and when Luna scans around, there's no life. No houses or anything, only whiteness as far as she can judge with the faint glow of light there. "What now? Is this your home?"

"Not yet. But this is how far the boat is getting you. There's no other way than to fly from here," replies the woman who steered the boat. Her arms are full of some form of clothing. Luna stiffens, her broom ride still fresh in her memory. No way she's going to do that again.

"Don't worry," the woman smiles sympathetically. "Here! Put on one of the suits, and you will fly with Stene. He will make sure you stay warm." She hands Luna a padded onesie.

Luna turns it around; it's some sort of artic suit that fits over your clothes and has a hood. Grateful, she starts to put it on.

"We count on you being able to keep yourself warm," the woman says as she addresses Freya while she hands her a suit as well. "You fly with Pilu, and she will have no additional strength to do that. Will you be okay?"

"Yes. Thank you," Freya simply answers, wasting no time getting dressed.

"We will turn back. Otherwise, the boat will get stuck in the ice." Without so much as a goodbye, the woman hops back on the boat and takes off—leaving them all alone in the dark. It's a strangely eerie feeling. As if you're stranded on an alien planet. The only sound is the lapping of the waves on the rocks, the screeching of the ice rubbing together and the wind rushing over the icy landscape. The two Greenlandic witches have suited up in record time and produced brooms and are now waiting for Luna and Freya to be ready. Once they're done, Pilu double-checks if they have closed it correctly and hands them goggles. "To protect your eyes."

"Thank you." Luna is glad they have thought about everything. They have undoubtedly learned over the years when your house is this hard to reach. Luna and Freya would have never found it on their own.

"How long is the flight?" Freya wants to know.

"It's several hours. You might want to make your heat just a small spark. These suits will keep you warm. It's a big improvement over the stories my Gran tells me about how they had to keep warm in the old days."

"Shall we go?" the muffled voice from Stene urges them to get going.

He and Luna have an awkward moment when they get on the broom. Luna feels slightly humiliated that a young man must ensure she's warm. This would have been unthinkable for her when her magic was working. It upsets her to no end. Stene is equally mortified about taking care of her. It's obviously out of his comfort zone. These Greenlandic people are a curious mix of hospitable and reserved. After several uncomfortable seconds, they finally settle on the broom. A bit bouncy, Stene gets off the ground. Luna has no other option than to grab him around the waist to avoid falling off. She must have made him nervous—poor kid. In the air, he quickly takes control, and Luna gently leans against him, leaving her arms secured around his waist.

They move into the nothingness. The suit is warm and toasty, and she cannot see anything except the stars—she almost dozes off. Stene shouts something, and when she opens her eyes, she's treated to the magical lights of the Aurora Borealis, better known as Northern Light. Its colorful glow surrounds them. The energy it emanates is a wonderful wave of power. Luna has never seen it before and is awestruck. So much beauty! The light bounces back up from the ice, and there are no words to describe this wonder that would do it justice. What a gift!

Luna looks to the side and sees Freya on the back of the broom, balancing with her arms wide. The Northern light is drawn to her like a magnet. It's as if she's aglow with it like it welcomes her home. Even though Luna can't see her sister, there's no doubt this is an exceptional experience for her. It warms Luna's heart to see her sister happy. Following an impulse, she sends out a huge thank you to the Fates.

BETWEEN SPACE AND TIME

The Crone has been following Luna and Freya's journey. A satisfied smile forms on her face when Luna's heartfelt gratitude reaches her. Now, we're getting somewhere. Genuinely happy for someone else without wanting something in return. With a little twirl of her index finger, she restores another little bit of Luna's magic—holding back just before giving her back that complete control. The Crone knows to trust her instincts; one more step must be made. Almost.

Three of Swords

PART 7

THREE OF SWORDS "HEARTBROKEN"

"The worst feeling in the world is knowing you did the best you could, and it still wasn't good enough."

—UNKNOWN

NEW ORLEANS

Diane instantly knows she's not alone when she opens her eyes. It's still dark. Only the faintest light betrays that dawn will come soon. Physically and emotionally exhausted, she had fallen into an uncommon deep sleep, undisturbed—until now.

The Maiden is exploring her body from the inside out. The movement inside her must have woken her up. "There you are," a sensuous whisper floats around her, tingling her skin. Diane, no longer in control of her own body, can feel her hands brushing her nipples and teasing her skin. Shit, this is disturbing on so many levels. Her body betrays her, being aroused by the Maiden's exploration, while her mind is franticly thinking of ways to get rid of her as soon as possible.

"I never felt a human body like this," the Maiden says fascinated. "We don't have these senses or urges. We have been missing out." Diane's hands are traveling down, brushing between her legs. "Ohhhh!" the maiden shouts out in delight.

This merging of their bodies is the weirdest thing ever. It's like they are one, and yet they have two consciousness. The Maiden has all the sensations and reactions Diane is feeling. It's like they're together and pleasuring themselves at the same time. Diane tries to ignore the sexual delights and find a way to push the Maiden out—while the Maiden full-on follows this new experience with ferociousness, which is unsettling. With an orgasm building, it becomes increasingly difficult for Diane to focus, but something is happening, which didn't happen before. The Maiden has never experienced this; the waves of pleasure grow and consume the Maiden's awareness. She is fully embracing the joy. Once the orgasm hits, she shatters, all her defenses are down, and Diane has the upper hand in this union. Knowing the feeling and riding the orgasm instead of being consumed by it, she catches a glimpse into the Maiden herself.

For a split second, Diane recognizes that they're nothing like humans. They're some kind of celestial beings that don't even know what it means to be human. They only mirror the image that humans think they look like. Through their interactions with mortals over the hundreds of years, they have constructed ideas of themselves that would be understandable to us.

The Maiden comes back into herself, and the door slams shut. "This is incredible. I'm getting it at last. How often do you do this?"

An idea forms in Diane's head. If she could repeat this, maybe she could look inside the Maiden with more purpose and find a way to expel her. "Do you want to do it again?"

"Yes!" she says without hesitation.

"Let's take a shower, and I will show you another way," Diane suggests.

No words need to pass between them. Diane gets out of bed and heads for her dresser, grabbing a dildo to up the pleasure. Getting rid of the Maiden is her top priority, whatever it takes. Turning the shower to a steaming hot temperature, they step in. The maiden has stepped back a bit to give Diane some control. Diane takes the time to soap herself and enjoys the hot water cascading along her skin, allowing herself time to fix her goal in her mind. Aware of the Maiden's hyper-focus on this newfound joy. Time to up her game. Turning on the vibrator on a gentle, low buzz, she starts to massage herself, bringing her body back into the mood. A warm sensation is building in the bottom of her belly.

"Oh, you can do it again so soon?"

"You can do it as often as you like," Diane answers.

"It's a miracle you find the time to do anything else. That people don't get consumed."

Getting impatient, the Maiden steps back into complete control and pushes Diane's hand back down. Soon enough, the orgasm starts building again. Diane readies herself to snap out of the feeling and is all set to explore the Maiden's mind—"Shit," the Maiden sounds beyond irritated, "the others need me." And she's gone. Leaving Diane on edge, with the Maiden gone, she doesn't want to finish and bursts into tears instead. All that build-up energy needs to go some-where. Disillusioned, she slides down to the ground and sits under the shower for a long time. Hopefully, Fin finds something soon. She can't sustain this for much longer.

Tara is waking up in a good mood in the room across the hall. The morning sun rays hit her. She always sleeps with the curtains open, preferring to gently wake her body with natural light. Instead of fighting her ever-growing list of aches and pains, she's going with the flow. Something within her is changing as if she's liberated. Having the burden of the Wand, the responsibility for the well-being of her family must have weighed her down all these years. No lon-ger—she's free! Free—to explore the things she wants to do without any attach-ments. She is enjoying herself working behind the bar. Try out different clothes, maybe travel a bit. If the others don't want to include her anymore, they can have it!

Getting up, she smiles at the Ace of Cups; right on, she thinks. The birth of her newfound desires. Let's see what comes next. Shuffling the cards, she decisively draws the next one. The Three of Swords; her heart skips a beat, not what she hoped for. A swan sits in the middle of the water, left with only a ghostly image of her partner. Three swords pierce down while a line in the water separates them. Swans mate for life. Heartache is not what she wants. Unable to put the card back, she lays it face down on her altar. Determined not to let this terrible card influence her good mood, she rummages through her closet and pulls out a red dress shirt. Perfect. Put some color in the day.

GREENLAND

Mara is back on the snowmobile behind Andrew. This time, she's better dressed. Yesterday, she went to the local store and got a snowsuit. Even though she's nice and warm now, she's still uncomfortable. Acutely aware of Petal stuffed away in her inside pocket, she knows he's constantly twisting and turning. As her arms are securely around Andrew's waist, she hopes he doesn't feel the restless fairy. Nerves course through her veins; Mara has no plan beyond getting into the moulins. How will they shake the rest of the expedition?

The bright red marker they left at the crevice is rapidly coming closer. In an attempt to calm herself, she hums a childhood song, which used to help her focus when her mother had locked her up in one of her magical cages to test her abilities.

With a sweeping move, Andrew parks his snowmobile next to the marker. Within seconds, he's unloading his equipment, good to go in record time, anxious to climb down. This is the moment he has been waiting for—he's not about to waste any time. Mara steps out of the way and lets the team do their job. To keep up appearances, she snaps a couple of pictures.

Only Andrew and Paul are supposed to go down. Geared up, they do the last check on their helmet cameras and a final one to assure their harnesses are secure.

"We're good!" shouts Andrew's assistant.

"Let's do it!" Andrew's enthusiasm is contagious.

Mara looks down into the crevice while Petal wiggles out from under her suit and peers over the edge of her collar. "Shall I follow them?" he whispers.

"Wait. I want to go down myself and will need your help with these two," Mara murmurs.

"Okay. Okay," Petal doesn't sound happy.

First, Andrew and then Paul disappear into the hole.

"How are we doing?" Andrew's assistant keeps in contact. "It looks the same as yesterday. Still good."

"It's amazing down here," Paul replies. He reaches the bottom of this moulin and is doing a full turn. "Can you see that?!" Paul shows them the icicles and different forms made by the melted and refrozen ice. It's a mesmerizing array of textures. Some water looks like it has frozen in an instant and is transparent, while others are more crystal-like or clouded—an infinite number of different icicles.

"It all looks solid, and I think it will be safe to explore further in," Andrew confirms.

"Great. Here we go, guys. The moment we've been working for." Paul's eagerness is palpable.

Both assistants are hyper-focused on their jobs to keep Paul and Andrew safe and to ensure the data are recorded. Mara unzips her suit a little and lets out Petal. With a head nod, she tells Petal to sedate the assistants. After an extensive discussion, they decided that a bit of Fairy dust was the best to distract them. They wouldn't remember Mara climbing down, but it would not endanger their mission. Petal wanted to take them out completely. However, Mara wasn't willing to sacrifice these people. What had they ever done to her? They had done nothing other than helping her and being kind. Mara is accumulating enough bad karma as it is. She might not be a goody-two-shoes; murder is a line she's not willing to cross.

Petal flies around the assistant like a buzzing insect while he dusts them in a good dose of fairy magic. "Now!" Petal's voice is surprisingly loud coming from such a tiny body. Mara pulls a stick from the snowmobile. She had brought a broom disguised as a walking stick. No way she was climbing down ropes;

better to maneuver down on a broom. Quickly, she mumbles a spell and hops on. Petal lands on her shoulder. Together, they disappear down the hole. The assistant's none the wiser.

Paul hadn't exaggerated—it is gorgeous down here. Mara calls up a little light boll to illuminate the way. A faint glow shows from one of the tunnels when they touch down. Turning around, there are multiple ways to go. "Which way is north?" Mara quietly asks.

Petal points to the opposite way the others went.

Mara doesn't question him; there's much riding on this for both of them. "We can do it."

She encourages herself.

"What? Anybody there?" comes from further down.

Shit! That was too loud. Quickly, they disappear down the other tunnel. It's hard to focus and not get distracted by the strange, enchanting surroundings. The ice glows in the soft light of her witchy source, and there are so many different shades of white and blue—it's magical.

A loud crack makes her jump. Behind her, the tunnel caves. "NOOOOOOO!!!!!" Panic rushes through her body. She's trapped. It feels like she can't breathe, and she starts hyperventilating. The beautiful-looking walls turn hostile and are closing in on her now. Petal hovers before her face and slaps her right on the cheek. "Snap out of it!" He hits her again and again until sanity returns to her eyes. "Ow," she says while feeling her cheek, which is burning red hot.

"We're trapped!" Mara twirls around and around.

"I did that on purpose," the smug little fairy says.

"You did what?!" In a reflex, Mara grabs the tiny fairy and squeezes. That little prick!

"Ssssstop," he rasps.

Disgusted, she throws him down the tunnel.

Effortlessly, he twirls and gains control over his wings. "Now they can't follow us. We're never trapped. You're connected to Mab; she can snatch you and me for that matter from anywhere."

He's right, of course. That doesn't make her any happier about this situation. Without another option, she turns and keeps going. Petal quietly follows her.

On the other side of the cave-in, Andrew and Paul look dismayed. They rushed back when they heard the sound. "I didn't see that coming," Andrew says, sounding disappointed.

"We better head back up." Paul says. "We can't chance it."

"Wait," Andrew points at Mara's broom. "Is that Mara's walking stick?"

"Boys! Is Mara up there?"

Some incoherent shouting back and forth follows before one of them answers, "She's nowhere up here, and the snowmobiles are all accounted for."

"Is it possible?" Paul doesn't need to finish his thought.

Andrew had crouched down and is pointing at some footsteps in the crunchy ice leading toward the cave-in. "MARA!MARA! CAN YOU HEAR US?"

Nothing, a deafening silence. Andrew tries to move the ice, but it's not budging.

"Oh my God!" Paul sounds horrified.

"MARA!!!! MARA!!!" Nothing....

After several more tries, Andrew's shoulders slump, "Let's get up before more of the cave is coming down."

Efficiently, they climb up and stare into the worried faces of their assistants. "What happened? We never saw her go down." One of the assistants quickly adds. "We were so focused on you."

Silence follows, in which nobody knows what to do or say.

"We need to go back. Maybe one of the locals can help us," Andrew suggests.

The assistants start to gather their equipment.

"Leave it! Every second counts."

He hops on his snowmobile, starts, and races back to the village.

FAIRY

Fin took a nap and recited the memory over and over again. He recorded it in his phone, in case he needed to part with it, and had been staring at Maeron for several hours now. At long last, the fairy blinks. Several minutes later, he's moving. "It's quite complicated," he murmurs.

"Can you do it?" Fin is eager to get moving again.

"Yes. Yes. You have to be as close to me as you can. We must move as one."

"What are you proposing?" Fin wants to know, a little less eager now.

"I thought if you cling to my back, much like a tortoiseshell. That way I can use my hands. It should work," Maeron says and motions him to jump on his back.

"Right," Fin's eyeing the fairies back. What the heck? It needs to be done. Don't overthink it. "Ready?" Fin wants to know.

Maeron spreads his arms and Fin jumps on, feeling like a little kid again.

"Hold on tight! I won't be able to support you. I will need both my hands to get us through this.

Fin locks his arms around Maeron's neck without strangling him. His legs do the same around his waist.

"Sit still," Maeron commands. He takes a deep breath, and his arms move in a strange harmony. Fin imagines it must be some sort of symbol. Unlike witch magic, which he would be able to follow, he's like an outsider. This must be what witch's spells look like for ordinary people. Instead of trying to see what Maeron is doing, Fin tries to feel it. Both kinds of magic are based on natural flows; it's worth a try. Although he senses something, the fairy magic is still out of reach.

"Sit. Still," Maeron urges between clenched teeth. This must take quite some strength from the ancient fairy. It is for the first time that Fin notices he's tense.

It takes longer than expected, and Fin's muscles start to burn in an effort to stay still. Maeron's arms move faster and faster.

"I can't hold it much longer," Fin whispers—his arms are screaming in pain.

Fin can't even see the movement any longer. Maeron's arms are like a blur. It's getting too much for him. His arms—right then, Maeron moves. It takes the utmost willpower for Fin not to let go. He's not able to use magic to boost his strength; maybe he should go to the gym more often.

Agonizingly slowly, Maeron moves through. Until, after what seems an eternity, "You can let go now."

Instantly, Fin drops to the ground, his muscles completely cramped up.

Although Maeron doesn't react as dramatically, Fin can see this was a challenge.

"Come on. He will sense us at one point. This was a clever boundary," Maeron says and sets a brisk pace through the woods again. Fin rushes to keep up. The old fairy has long legs. After a while, they reach a lake; on the other side, they can make out a curious-looking construction. "There it is," Maeron scans their surroundings wearily.

Too far away to see what it looks like exactly, Fin squints. "Whatever it is, it looks massive."

"Hurry," says Maeron who doesn't waste any more words and resumes their track toward the house, along the lake's shoreline. He's keeping one eye on the forest and the other on the water. Fin spins around every now and again to ensure they're not followed.

It's strangely quiet here; the lake is flat as a mirror, with no animal noises of any kind. Not since they crossed the barrier, Fin realizes. Why would the Ferrymaster want to keep out everything? He must collect memories from other creatures as well. Typically human to think you're the only one; naturally, he takes memories from everybody except fairies. Immediately, it conjures up all sorts of fantasies in Fin's mind. The possibility of seeing some thoughts of the crazy creatures he had encountered in Fairy is tempting. The treasure trove!

Soon enough, they're closing in on the house, and Maeron stops to assess the situation. The house is the strangest thing you have ever seen. You can barely recognize the structure of room upon room because the collected memories burst out of the building, forming a mountain of memories globes. Fin's heart sinks. How on earth are they ever going to find a specific memory in here?! It's impossible! "This is not going to work," he hoarsely whispers.

"It looks somewhat unorganized," Maeron agrees.

"Understatement of the century." Fin's quick comeback can't hide his irritation.

"Am I right to presume you have memories prepared to bargain?" Maeron turns toward him.

"I have—you don't—"

"I think it's the only way. This is much worse than we anticipated, and we will need the Ferrymaster to trade us some memories if we want to start somewhere. We did not come this far for nothing. If we go in, I bet he's waiting for us anyway."

"What are you going to trade? You can't betray Ceri," Fin defends his aunt.

"She's my family!"

Fin steps back, overwhelmed by Maeron's intense stare.

"We're not like humans. We don't betray our family!"

Fin holds his hands up in surrender. Wow! Note to self, don't piss off an ancient fairy.

"Maybe I should be worried about you. If that's the first thing you think of," Maeron counters.

Now, it's Fin's turn to be pissed, "I would never betray mine."

"It's going to be hard not to give him more information than we want to. Stay focused and only give him a memory you want to part with. I will help you as much as possible, but this will also take all my skills. The Ferrymaster and I go way back. It's his gift to wiggle information out of everybody and everything." Worry lines show on the fairy's face.

"How old is he?" Fin wonders.

"We're from the same beginnings."

That's a strange way of saying you're the same age. Fin would like to ask questions but files it away for another time. Now it's game time. *Focus!* He tells himself. "Anything I need to know?"

"He's loyal to Mab. On the other hand, he is not family. You can compare his status to the one Ceri, and the other Keepers have. Short to the point answers. Take your time before you reply," Maeron says and nods to him; that's it.

The closer they come to the Ferrymaster's home, the more disorienting it is. The images in the piled-up globes are always moving. It's confusing. It gives Fin the sensation of being seasick.

"Don't look at it," Maeron puts a steady hand on Fin's shoulder.

"Ha! They're everywhere; you can't 'not look' at it!"

Between the chaos of the moving globes is an arch that must be the entrance.

Fin nods to Maeron to lead the way. Without hesitation, the fairy steps inside. Fin does his utmost to ignore the moving images, following into a winding hallway that opens up into a surprising airy room. The bolls are pushed to the outer rim of the spacious room and in the middle lounges the Ferrymaster on a sofa in a familiar way. This time, he's the same size as they are. A hand full of globes is twirling around him, much like a constellation.

"Gentleman!" That is all he says as a welcome while he gestures for them to sit down on the only two other chairs in the room. "Brother, why didn't you knock? Now I have to presume you're up to something," he says, addressing Maeron first.

Maeron doesn't reply, bows his head in a greeting, and sits down graciously.

"And you, young man, to let me believe your aunt doesn't know you're here…. Tut, tut."

Fin shrugs and also sits down—almost toppling off, as the chair wobbles like it's filled with water. It takes him a minute to find his balance.

That makes the Ferrymaster smile. "Takes some getting used to." He winks. "Give me one good reason why I shouldn't ask our Queen to join us?"

Fin opens his mouth and closes it again, remembering Maeron's advice. The fairy is most likely better equipped to deal with this situation.

"Why bother her? She must be so busy. Surely, this little incident is something you're capable enough to handle on your own?" Maeron smoothly answers.

"I have missed that silky tongue of yours. It has been quite some time since we shared bread together," the Ferrymaster says with a smile.

"Some centuries at least. So hard to pin you down. I can see you have been extremely busy." Maeron points at the memories.

"What about you? How are you? All those years, many wars, you managed to stay neutral, and now you have a new family." The Ferrymaster swiftly changes position, sitting up straight and looking intently at Maeron. "I guess congratulations are in order. Ceri is an interesting choice. That creature hasn't unlocked her full potential yet."

"Thank you," Maeron says, staying true to his own advice.

"You were always a sucker for a damsel in distress." The Ferrymaster smiles while he plucks one of the globes circling him from the air. With a faint touch, it springs to life, and if Fin thought Maeron sat still before, it's like he's now frozen in place. Plainly unhappy with what is about to be shown.

They're in Mab's Hall of Entertainment. It's filled with colorful fairies and other creatures. Maeron arrives with a stunning female fairy on his arm. From their body language, it's clear they're in love. From across the hall, Mab sees them coming in. The resentment flashing across her face betrays that she's not approving.

With a twist of his wrist, the Ferrymaster speeds the memory forward—slowing it down again when the lady and Mab are arguing. Maeron tries to step in, but two guards cut him off and hold him in place. The argument gets more and more heated. Maeron shouts something, which the female fairy ignores. Panic crosses his face when Mab transforms into her scary true form. The lady's face falls, realizing too late that this is what Mab had wanted to happen. Her claws grab the fairy and simply rip her apart, shouting a spell, and the woman turns into a million twinkle stars, being absorbed by Fairy itself. Mab throws her head back and laughs! Everybody in the hall is dead silent except for the soul-piercing cry of Maeron.

With a snap of the Ferrymaster's finger, the memory is gone. The raw pain visible on Maeron's face is almost too much to bear. It brings tears to Fin's eyes. He's always been a compassionate soul.

"I see you haven't forgotten our fair Maurelle." The Ferrymaster sweetly pushes harder on the sore spot.

"Stop! Why are you doing this?" Fin can't help himself. This is cruel!

The Ferrymaster turns to him in a blink of an eye. "What are you doing here? What do you want?"

Fin's mind is racing; this is a game he's not used to playing. He came for Diane, but the others have another agenda, Aunt Freya and the origins of species. Juggling what he should ask first, he opts for Freya's memories. It would make sense and wouldn't betray any of their other purposes. "We were hoping to retrieve some of my Aunt Freya's memories. She's not well since the last time she stayed with you." There, that should give him enough to justify them being here. "Is it possible we get some of her memories back? You took something away from her that—how can I say that? Something that makes her tick."

A twinkle in the Ferrymaster's eye betrays that he has something special from her. "Why would I give that to you—coming here uninvited, like thieves in the night? No. I think I will hand you over the Mab. Let her have some fun with you."

"Maybe I have something you want more than handing us off for entertainment. I'm willing to trade," Fin tries.

"Those Madigan's are a crafty bunch, aren't they?" He turns to Maeron as if he's telling an inside joke.

"Leave him alone," Maeron says gruff. "He's no match for you."

"Neither are you, it seems," the Ferrymaster says, playfully. "Let me have my fun. And I might forget you trespassed."

Fin's slightest head nod convinces Maeron to give him a chance.

The Ferrymaster focuses back on Fin, "What memory do you want?"

"If she knew which one she had lost, it would be easy, right? She doesn't remember. That's the whole problem," Fin explains.

"Don't be coy with me, young man. Something tells me you know exactly what you're after."

Shit, should he simply ask? Fin ruffles through his options. He decides to go for the truth. "I would like to get back the memory you took from her as a child. When Tara and Seamus asked you to erase a certain memory."

The Ferrymaster plucks the next memory from the air, saying, "This one?"

Fin leans forward and recognizes a young Tara and Seamus and what must be a baby Ceri. Fin reaches for it. The Ferrymaster pulls it back and throws it back up where it's twirling in between the other memories again. "Not so fast, young man. What are you willing to trade for that?"

"How about a memory of my sisters?" Fin shrewdly replies.

"Ha! A fast learner," the Ferrymaster applauds him. "But young man, I would never trade that one. It's special. But I tell you what. If you give me that memory, I won't betray your visit to Mab."

Fin starts to sweat, ferociously flipping through possible comebacks. He's always been sharp. Quick to have the fitting reply ready. However, never anything as serious as this been riding on it. Click—the right answer pops in his mind. "Send us to Mab. I'm sure she would love to know that you valued a memory over telling her that Seamus and Tara were in Fairy, and she could have had her revenge right then. Probably, she could have had Ceri back. Things would be different now."

The anger crossing the Ferrymaster's face says it all. Maeron is behind Fin instantly; he hadn't even seen him move. "We should be able to come to an agreement and don't bother our magnificent Queen," Maeron suggests.

"I'm not giving back that memory," says the Ferrymaster with a sulk. "Ask another one. None of Freya's."

A firm hand of Maeron on his shoulder reminds him to take his time. Think this through. If he can't have any memories of Freya, he could ask about the dawn of time, but it's probably not wise to alert the Ferrymaster to that quest. He's way too perceptive. Fin should ask about the Fates for Diane. It's, after all, what he came to do here.

"Come on. We haven't got all day. I'm a busy man," the irritated fairy in front of him pushes.

"Do you have a memory of the Fates? One that explains how you can get rid of a possession by one of them?"

The Ferrymaster, taken off guard by this change of direction, leans back and sizes him up. "And why would you want to have that one?" Always inquisitive.

"Do you want to trade or not?" Maeron says before Fin even gets a chance to answer.

"I have what you seek," he states.

"Are you ready?" Maeron wants to know if Fin has his memory prepared.

"I'm ready," Fin says and scoots forward, eager to get this over with. "Where's the memory?"

The Ferrymaster snaps his fingers—a loud rumble sounds from the depths of the house, and a slight tremor betrays the globes are moving. It takes several minutes before a sphere finally floats into the room. "This is the one you seek. It's an old one." The Ferrymaster spins it around and around on his finger. "A curious choice."

"Let's do this," Fin sticks out his finger.

"Maeron, please step back. I don't want to get one accidentally from you." The Ferrymaster feigns sincerity. "Come sit with me?" he pets the spot next to him on the sofa.

Fin resists looking at Maeron. It's not a good idea to let the trickster touch you. What choice does he have? If he can get away with this memory, that would be a small victory. Reluctantly, he gets up.

"Don't be shy," the Ferrymaster says as he seductively smiles.

Oh, dear. He desperately tries to hold on to his prepared memory. Don't get distracted. With no other options, he sits. The fairy sticks out his hand and follows the lines of Fin's face, the curve of his neck, and down his chest. "You're in good shape," he murmurs.

"Take the memory," Maeron snaps.

"Tut, tut. You can't deny me all my fun. Or do you have a prior claim?" he says without taking his eyes off Fin. "I've had many encounters with this one, but somehow I feel I've missed out." Fairies are sensual creatures; they're not prudent like most humans or seem to prefer one specific sex. "He has such nice muscles."

Fin, much less confident, starts to lose his grip on the memory he intended to give. He is distracted by the delicate hands of the Ferrymaster, which are exploring his chest. No doubt, on purpose teasing his nipples through the fabric. "Were your sisters always close?" he casually asks.

Involuntarily, Fin's mind calls up the memory in which his sisters sat opposite each other and made things twirl around them at a young age without using any words. "Thank you." The fairy draws it out of Fin's mind, and albeit he tries to grab it, it's being sucked into one of the globes.

"Noooooo," shouts Fin.

"It's too late now," the Ferrymaster smiles, satisfied.

"Give us the memory you promised, and we will be on our way," Maeron gruffly says.

"My pleasure," he plucks it from the air and hands it to Fin. "Good luck with that. Now. Go! And don't try to sneak into my house ever again! You won't like it."

They take it for the warning it is. A portal opens next to them.

"This will drop you close to Ceri's property."

Maeron and Fin step through, the portal snaps shut, and both men breathe out heavily.

GREENLAND

Luna lost track of time after so many hours in the dark. True to their word, the suits kept her warm, and Stene did an excellent job giving her that necessary spark. The Northern Lights was such a treat. To experience flying through that is something that she will never forget. No doubt a once in a lifetime experience. Truly magical!

The sky is lighting up, a sign that it must be somewhere in the morning. Stene and Pilu are heading down toward a specific spot. A person slowly comes into focus; at first, her white clothes blended in with the vast whiteness of the landscape. The white is just as disorienting as the dark. Luna misses her sunglasses; it might have tempered the overwhelming feeling a little. Not before long, they touch down in front of the witch. It's hard to guess her age; maybe she's slightly younger than they are. Once they've peeled down their protection, the woman greets Freya, "Welcome. My name is Snowflake. I think we've chatted over the scallop?" Then she frowns, realizing there's no shell on Freya's forehead.

"Hi. I'm Freya. You've talked to my sister Luna," Freya says as she points in her direction.

"Hi! So nice to meet you," Luna says as she offers her hand.

Snowflake hesitates slightly before shaking it. "Why don't you come in?"

Without further niceties, they follow her into the Berthelsen's home. Freya and Luna are impressed by the huge sculptured icy hallways.

"Wow!" Freya says in awe when she spots the whales carved out on the ceiling.

"What a work of art," Luna agrees.

"A labor of love in honor of the sea creatures in this area," Snowflake explains.

Unbeknownst to Luna and Freya, the rest of the family agreed to stay out of view, not willing to betray too much about their numbers or powers. Snowflake leads them into the kitchen, where a steaming pot of tea with some bread is waiting for them. "You must be hungry and thirsty after your trip. Especially if you're not used to it."

"We flew through the Northern Lights—it was magnificent," Freya elaborates.

Luna smiles: her sister is changing. To make small talk is a new and welcome shift in her personality.

"It is special," Snowflake agrees. "We're so used to it. You make me realize we shouldn't take it for granted. Sit."

As soon as Luna and Freya are seated, and she gives them something to eat, the seriousness in the lines of her face returns. "Talk. Convince me why I should trust you," Snowflake gets to the heart of the matter.

Luna can appreciate that. Freya agreed that the only option was to tell them the whole story. As a family that guards another elemental object, they have a right to know. "It's a long story."

Snowflake gestures for her to begin.

Further down south, there's a knock on Lucy's door. Eager to find out if Mara was successful she throws the door open, "It's about time!" And snaps her mouth shut when she sees it's Andrew.

"Who are you?"

"Are you Mrs. Lockwood? Mara's grandmother?" The dread on Andrew's face doesn't bode well.

Cautiously, Lucy takes a step back. "Yes, I'm Lucy Lockwood. Where's Mara?"

"I—I—I—there's been an accident. A cave-in. She wasn't supposed to be down there."

"What are you saying?" Lucy demands.

"We think Mara got trapped in the moulins under the ice. We went back with local help and tried to dig her out. It—it didn't work. I'm so sorry." Andrew reaches for Lucy's hand, but she swiftly steps back and puts more distance between them.

"You're saying that she's probably still alive but unable to come out?" Lucy's eyes narrow. Is it possible her granddaughter had done this on purpose? She would know if she was dead; Lucy is convinced she would have felt it.

A tear escapes Andrew's eye, "Yes, or buried under the ice. It's horrible. I don't know what else we can do for her." His desperation is heartbreaking, however, totally lost on Lucy.

"She's not dead," Lucy says out loud.

"How do you know?!"

"I would have felt it. I'll take it from here." Lucy starts closing the door, leaving a shocked Andrew on the other side. This is not how he expected this conversation to go.

Andrew knocks on the door again, "Mrs. Lockwood? Are you okay?"

Lucy ignores him and paces up and down in her little room. She knew Mara was up to something. She must be going after the Cup herself. She highly doubts this was a genuine accident; her granddaughter is smart. That's a perfect way to ensure nobody can follow her. For several seconds, doubt creeps in, but her gut tells her Mara has struck out on her own. Lucy didn't get this far without trusting her instincts; it has been her friend for a very long time.

What now? Trying to get down in the moulin herself doesn't make sense; it would most likely kill her. She doesn't have many options, if any. They tried everything to go up north by boat or other means, but the locals were not going to help them. Could she hire a plane or a helicopter? She doesn't even know exactly where she's going. Damn. Lucy is fuming now. Unconsciously, she scratches the sigil on her arm. It always acts up when she gets heated. The itch snaps her out of her spiral of no options. Baring the sigil, an opportunity comes back to her, one she hadn't wanted to consider before. It could work. It will cost her, but if it means she can lay her hands on the Cup, it is worth it!

Mara is struggling to move forward in the ice caves. If it weren't for her magic, she would be hypodermal by now. It's freezing down here, and the air is thin. The moulins go from wide and spacious to tiny tunnels she has to crawl through. Thankfully she's not alone. Although Petal is unpleasant at best, it's better than being alone. His tiny body can scout if the moulin essentially goes somewhere, and he has a keen sense of direction—guiding them steadily north.

A couple of times, Mara completely lost it—panic taking over, Petal slapping her in the face until she would snap out of it again. She's never been claustrophobic, and even though she knows she can always reach out to Mab—there's no guarantee that Mab will, in fact, help her and not leave her behind to die. When you disappoint the Queen, you never know what she might do.

Mara's mind is stuck in an endless loop of worry. This plan is looking more ludicrous by the minute. They don't even know exactly where they're going. They have no idea how long the road is. Petal might not need much food, but Mara's energy bars are running thin. What was she thinking? She's using just enough energy to stay warm, as she has no idea how much magic she will need once they reach the Cup—if they reach the Cup at all! *Don't despair. Don't despair.* She encourages herself.

A rush of cold air brushes her face. For a moment, her dark mood is lifted. A crevice! She's inhaling the fresh air deeply. *See, there is an escape if necessary.* Occasionally, they pass an opening, as the meltwaters that caused the moulins are endlessly connecting under the ice. Finding a way to the ocean. "I don't think we're moving fast enough," Mara voices one of her concerns out loud. "At this rate, it will take us weeks to get there. I will be dead by then."

Petal whirls around her head. "Can't you fly?" he wonders.

"My broom was still on the other side of the cave-in," she says, swallowing the rest of what she wanted to say. No need to piss him off needlessly.

Petal rummages around in his pockets. "I might have enough fairy dust." He blows some in Mara's face.

She coughs while she senses her feet no longer touch the ground. *Wow! Why didn't you tell me this sooner!* Her head screams. "Thank you." That is all she squeezes out. The fairy will never help her out unless asked for or ordered.

"Ready?!" Petal zooms around her. "Let's use it while it lasts."

Mara leans forward as if she's riding a broom; this particular part of the moulin is pretty wide. With a little whisper, she enlarges her light, and they speed up. Perfect! So much better. Making serious headway now, they zoom through the moulins.

Snowflake has been awfully quiet while the Madigans tell their story. Her mind is in overdrive. With only an additional question here and there, her focus has been on their auras. One of her personal witch gifts is to see and be able to read someone else's aura. It took her quite some time as a child to realize that not everybody saw it and even longer to master the skill to use her sight to her advantage. Now, she's even able to ignore it if she wants as it can be terribly distracting. It's a comfort to think the rest of her family is probably cramped into their control room and following every word on their monitors.

Luna, the witch telling the story, has been telling the truth. As far as the truth goes with witches, no doubt she had left plenty of details out. This woman's aura is fractured; black lines are all around her like a cracked egg. The lines are healing, and some are very faint. This must be the reason she almost froze to death. She did mention a backlash from a spell. Is this what it looks like? Her sister has been mainly quiet, which is interesting as her aura is a whirlwind of raw power. You wouldn't expect such a powerful witch to take a back seat. Looking closer, Snowflake spotted patches of brown blobs scattered throughout. A sign of insecurity, the spots seem to be receding, but they're still there.

"So, here we are. We wanted to warn you that Lucy is extremely dangerous and not to be underestimated," Luna concludes her story.

"That is quite the tale. You could have told me that from home and didn't have to bother to come all this way," Snowflake says and smiles mildly.

"We see it as our responsibility to help catch or contain Lucy. She's our mother's twin, after all. We should right this wrong," says Freya, who has always had a strong sense of duty.

"You didn't do a very good job so far. To attune one of you to the Dagger is—concerning." A slightly hostile tone creeps into Snowflake's voice. These women might be genuine, but so far, they messed up big time. It might not be their personal doing, but still—

"I will not allow you to stay. I appreciate you coming all this way. This warning is taken to heart. Tomorrow morning first light, they will bring you back."

"Please—" Luna tries.

"This is non-negotiable. I have no doubt Lucy will show up. I can't have you here, wondering if you will try to get your hands on the Cup yourself. We can take care of ourselves."

Freya gets up, "I would probably do the same in your position. However, that's exactly what we thought. Together we are stronger. You're making a mistake."

The two women stare at each other for several minutes; nobody is budging. Till finally, Luna gets up and puts an arm on Freya's shoulder. "You know where to find us if you change your mind. When this is all behind us, we should get together and talk. Is there a place we can get cleaned up?"

The tension breaks.

"Follow me," Snowflake gestures.

Luna and Freya are arguing in their guest room. A hot shower and clean clothes are a welcome gift. The clothes are warm and comfortable, much better soothed for the weather. Although this home is inside the ice, it's comfortable; it is only a touch cooler than a traditional home.

"She's not going to change her mind," Luna says for the tenth time.

This time, Freya sighs deeply and says, "I know. It's so frustrating."

"We would do the same, and it's hard to imagine how awful Lucy truly is."

"How are you feeling?" Freya abruptly changes the subject.

Luna knows what she means, looks at her hands, turns them over, and lets a small glow escape. "I feel better, not like myself yet, but better."

"That's at least something." Uncharacteristically, Freya gives her a quick kiss on the cheek, "Come on, let's meet the rest of this family, and eat! I'm starving."

Further south, Lucy is lying down on her bed in the small room. Finally, Andrew gave up his banging and pleas, Lucy refusing to open her door again. He was so distraught. She shakes off her anger; what she's about to do requires her complete focus. In her mind, she goes through all her options one last time. Except for giving up, which of course is not in her disposition, this is the only way. Her room is cozy and warm, the blinds are down, and she makes sure to lie down as comfortably as she possibly can. You never know how long this will take! While she's on the Astral Plane, her body will be here, unguarded. It's risky. Hopefully, the spell she put on the door will keep her safe from prying eyes.

Scooting from left to right, she wonders if there's a comfortable position left at her age. *"Get on with it!"* she scolds herself, knowing full well she's stalling.

Closing her eyes, Lucy's breath is slowing down. In—one, two, three, four, five. Out—two, three, four, five. Her mind quiets, and slowly, she envisions her entry point onto the planes. Like most witches, she created a forest-y area, the smell of fresh green, the chirping of birds, sun filtering through the leaves. Behind her eyes, she senses the warmth of the sun. When Lucy opens her eyes, she's standing in the middle of her familiar spot.

A quick scan of her surroundings confirms she's still alone. Not for long, though; no doubt Vhumut has felt her arrival. Should she wait or should she try to find him? There isn't much time.

"Well, well! I didn't expect you back so soon. I thought you would try to weasel your way out of our deal," Vhumut's red hot voice resonates behind her.

Lucy spins around and stares into Vhumut's true form. Backing up from the sheer heat he radiates. A booming laugh escapes him, and he transforms in a blink of an eye into the young man she had met that faithful night. But not before he gives her skin a slight burn. A touch of suffering. However, Lucy pretends not to feel it, refusing to give him any satisfaction from it.

"I'm here for a favor," Lucy comes straight to the point.

"Hahaha! Girl—you ran out of favors long ago. Please don't waste my time. As you're here, you can come with me now," Vhumut says and turns around as if he thinks she will follow him.

"A deal is a deal. I have almost two years left," Lucy counters.

While he turns around, a sly smile crosses his face. "Always so feisty; you know I'm willing to trade. What do you need?"

"Do you know where the Cup of Plenty is?" She needs to hurry if she wants to beat Mara there.

"Powerful objects emanate a unique energy," Vhumut cocks his head.

"I thought so. Can you get me there?"

Amicable, he throws his arm around her shoulder, "Darling, now we are getting somewhere. It's going to cost you the remaining of your two years, though."

"Then I might as well skip it. What use is it to me?"

Vhumut only shrugs.

"I gave you a son!" she tries.

"Wow, what an asset he turned out to be." Sarcasm literally dripping from his lips. Some strange red hot drops sizzle when they hit the ground. Lucy does her utmost not to get distracted by this. "I can give you half a year."

Vhumut throws his head back, and for a split second, his demon face is back—flames sprout from his mouth. If the Astral Plane was quiet, it's dead silence now.

"Nine months…." Lucy whispers, unable to keep her discomfort hidden.

Vhumut, perfectly human-looking again, turns toward her with a smile, "One year. No more, no less."

Lucy takes a moment to think this through; the mounting pressure has a strangely calming effect on her. Sharpening her mind. If this doesn't work out as planned, she has less than one year of her life left before Vhumut will come for her soul. Not forgetting she has to come up with a second soul as well. Her only chance to get out of this mess entirely is an elemental object. "Deal."

They shake hands.

"How does this work? Are you pulling me through the Astral Plane?" Lucy is eager to get going.

"My Darling," Vhumut kisses her hand and pulls her close, his lips very close to hers. She can smell the sulfur. "I can't pull a human body through the planes. You know the rules. I can get you where you want, but you will be—how do you call it? Ghost-like."

"What?!" Lucy pushes him away. "That's no use!"

"Maybe, you should have thought of that first. Your body will stay in your room; there's nothing I can do about that."

Lucy explodes; spit flies from her mouth while she throws every curse she can think of at him. However, magic doesn't affect him in the regular sense. To be careful, he did come prepared—shielding for these kinds of attacks. Instead, he grows and seems to enjoy it thoroughly.

"Darling, darling, calm down." He irks her.

"CALM DOWN! I can't believe I let you trick me!!!"

"Although I like the show, you shouldn't waste your energy. You didn't let me finish."

Lucy narrows her eyes and sucks in the last bit of her anger.

"Your body will be in your room. But it will be like when you're on the Astral Plane. You can touch everything and can perform your magic. Nevertheless, you will look translucent, and whatever happens to you there will happen to your natural body."

"Fine. What's the worst that can happen?"

"My thoughts exactly. You would be mine," he says, satisfied.

"It's a matter of speech," Lucy mumbles.

"Once you join me, you will brighten up my day. You're so delicious."

"Focus," Lucy urges. "Let's do this."

Vhumut takes her by her hand, "One last thing. It's because I really like you," he holds his other hand up, blows over it, and Lucy is glowing up. A rush of power courses through her veins. He has replenished her powers.

"Thank you," she whispers, surprised.

Before he lets her go, he cups her face and gently kisses her.

Far down below the ice, Mara senses an energy shift. No witch can come close to an elemental object and not be drawn to its power. "Slow down," she orders Petal.

They lost all sense of time, hours or days could have passed, but they've arrived. "We're close," states Mara.

"Shall I summon the Queen?" Petal is eager to please his mistress.

"Wait!" Mara still would like to get her hands on the object herself. "Let's first see if I'm right and where it is exactly." Opening her witch sight, the tunnels appear to pulsate with energy, like light flickering. Carefully, she moves toward the gravity of the power. The element of water is a strange mix of warm and cold. Water and ice are not particularly warm, but it rules the emotions that are warming the heart. Desire rushes through her, a mix of power, craving, and even sexual pleasure. To be able to wield this power must be magnificent. The pull in her core grows and grows; it becomes almost unbearable, the desire to possess this. When all of a sudden the sensation wanes. Confused, she turns around. That's strange. She didn't see the Cup. Where is it? Moving back to the center of the pull, she is now more aware instead of being overwhelmed. Walking back and forth, she finds the exact point where the force is the strongest.

"What are you doing?" Petal demands.

"Shhh," she urges him to be silent. First, she looks around, white walls of ice and snow, nothing new. It's been like that when she came down the ice shaft. Where is it? Slowly, she looks up. The ice is crystal clear; far above her it looks like a glimmer of something. Her hand reaches up, and as soon as she touches the ice—

Alarm bells go off in Snowflake's head. The family is having dinner with Luna and Freya, and it's been a surprisingly pleasant evening. Icy chills run down her back, and her connection to the Cup tightens. This can only mean one thing—"Someone is at the Cup!" she says and jumps up.

Her family is confused and rapidly fires questions. Snowflake doesn't wait—rushing out while she shouts, "The ancestors!" and she's gone.

For a short moment, the room falls quiet before erupting in a chaotic exodus of the rest of the family. Freya and Luna don't hesitate and follow the others.

Snowflake is already outside and on her broom. She is going as fast as humanly possible. Within several minutes, she reaches the ancestral spot. So different from tracking over the ice. Unfortunately, she used up some of her powers to stay warm at that speed. Jumping off her broom, she rushes past their wards and into the circle where the ancestors are supposed to be.

A fireball nearly hits her in the face; she barely puts up her shield in time. *Someone is already in here?! Why didn't the wards go off?* She's not able to follow that train of thought as the next fireball is leaving the hand of a ghost-like figure on the other end of their sacred space. Snowflake pulls up a dome around her from ice and water to protect herself. She needs a second to assess the situation. Quickly, she scans around and notices with horror that all the cups that hold the ancestral spirits are melted and deformed clumps on the floor. Again, she wonders how the woman—yes, she can see it's a woman—came in here. This must be Lucy.

In between bombarding her with fireballs, Lucy puts her hand on the ice and mutters a defrosting spell; slowly, the ice starts to melt. Vhumut had put

Lucy right in the middle of the Berthelsen's sacred space. To set off the wards, you must cross them.

Snowflake utters a counter spell, and the water freezes again. This is her element; anger flares through her. The rest of her family is arriving. Vaguely, she registers screams of horror and others running to surround Lucy. The older woman calls up a ring of fire around her, making it unable for the others to grab her. However, it also prevents her from doing much harm to them at this point, but the heat does start to melt the water again.

Snowflake lowers her shield. What is that? Deep down, she can sense the water melting as well. Shit, is someone below the Cup?

Down below, Mara has also started to melt the water; a simple spell took care of that.

"We should get the Queen," Petal urges her.

"Wait till we have it in our possession," Mara says as she dismisses him—sensing that the shit hit the fan above her.

Petal nervously twirls around her.

"Just a little bit longer," she can almost taste the power.

Snowflake can feel the threat from below and looks around and spots her mother. "Laakki, keep her contained!" she yells. "There are others." Pointing down, Snowflake hopes her mother gets the message. Luna and Freya are part of the circle that tries to keep Lucy contained.

Within the circle, Lucy ignores the witches around her and concentrates on the melting water. She only needs to keep them away until she reaches the Cup. The extra fire boost that Vhumut had provided her comes in very handy.

Snowflake's mind is racing, figuring out the best way to stop the person below. Should she keep the Cup frozen, or should she let the water melt and summon the Cup? After all, she's its guardian, and it is connected to her. She can use the power to stave them off. Yes. That's the way to go. Reversing her freezing spell into rapidly melting the ice. The cave begins to fill with water, hampering Lucy and the others. Not all can breathe underwater as easily as she can.

Down below, Mara is struggling with the amount of water coming down. The tunnels are unable to drain the water as quickly as it's building. Petal is no longer buzzing around her; maybe the water washed him away. The water is already at her chest. Riffling through her mind, she now tries to find a spell that will help her to stay alive underwater. Her mind is blank. Mara panics—the water reaching her chin. "Help!" she shouts, knowing very well there's no one there to help her. Taking one last breath, Mara disappears underwater. *Oh, my Goddess, I'm going to drown!* Her lungs are burning; how long can she hold it? She considered herself capable under pressure; here she is, dying alone under the ice. If she could cry, she would; it overpowers her mind.

BETWEEN SPACE AND TIME

The Maiden, Mother, and Crone are glued to the pond. The Universe is putting up quite the show, bringing this all together. Not even the Fates are unmoved by the clash of power. They can only watch how this is going to unfold.

GREENLAND

Mara can feel a hand on her shoulder, and suddenly, she can breathe. "You should have called me sooner." A familiar voice is whispering in her ear. "We will discuss this later."

Tons of water is being drained through a portal. Mab, in all her glory, is standing behind her, looking up. Her eyes twinkle when she recognizes the glimmer on the Cup. "Hello, beautiful." With a snap, her wings fold, disappearing out of sight. Water and wings are not a good combination.

On top, Snowflake is alarmed by a new entity arriving; unable to see what happens below—she can sense the Queen of Fairy's power. Again, she's forced to make a choice, trying to help the others or going down. Some of her family members are struggling to survive the water and have to leave the cave. Less of them down here to keep Lucy at bay. Vaguely, she registers that Luna and Freya are still there.

Snowflake takes one last look before heading for the Cup. For a moment, she freezes, horrified by a mouth full of razor-sharp teeth coming for her. The mouth looks enormous! That moment of hesitation will cost her—someone pushes her aside. She tumbles and disappears underwater, out of the way of the hurtling mouth. Luna screams at the top of her lungs when the demon girl bites her full in the chest. Amid all the chaos, she'd spotted the young girl going for Snowflake, and Luna had sprung into action. She fought her way through the water and flung herself before Snowflake in the nick of time, her magic still spotty. Pain shoots through her like a hand reaching inside her, searching for her heart. With the pain, something else comes to life, her magic! Her familiar confidence is instantly restored, keeping her calm in this terrifying moment.

Ignoring the searing pain and the creature digging a hole in her chest with her mouth, Luna finds the spell inside her mind to banish and bind a demon. No longer able to stand, she disappears underwater while shouting the words. Even though the water mangles them, they're just as effective. The creature goes rigid while the shell on her forehead sings. Expecting to lose consciousness soon, she's eager to secure the creature. Resisting the urge to go up and breathe, she pushes her hands together as if trying to squeeze the little girl. For a moment, nothing happens, and then the demon screams and starts to shrink, and shrink until—she winks out of existence. Luna is losing consciousness, floating underwater, but grateful to have her magic back.

BETWEEN SPACE AND TIME

Mother looks at the Crone, saying, "Wow, you really cut that close."

"Lessons are learned on the edge of things. She showed sacrifice. Good girl."

Mother only rolls her eyes before the three of them focus back on the fight.

GREENLAND

Snowflake swims down to the Cup while she's calling out to it, all too aware someone is trying to reach it from the bottom. She is frustrated not to be able to use her dolphin form, as she needs to be ready to perform magic at will.

Lucy is getting agitated, the water is now at her chest and the ring of fire is withering. Water and Fire are opposites. The water thinned out her opponents, but the guardian disappeared underwater. Time to follow her, but how is she keeping the people up here occupied? She touches the sigil on her arm and sends a plea to the demon. It's her only hope.

The cave's roof is torn open, which hasn't happened since the ways were shut between the dimensions. Vhumuts demonic form stares down and a huge hand sweep through the water. His red hot hand and the cold water instantly create steam, like a sauna. The Berthelsens scream. Lucy blows him a kiss, touches one of her talismans across her neck, and dives underwater. Knowing that getting to the Cup must involve water, she'd come prepared.

Some of the Berthelsens throw fireballs at Vhumut, which he simply absorbs. Freya is mesmerized, never having seen something like this. Screams and fireballs are snapping her out of her inaction. Gathering her magic, awakening the connection she made when she first set foot in Iceland—Nordic power flows through her veins. Something inside her clicks in place, a door opens; her mind is flooded with images. Her hands automatically draw a complicated rune in the air. Energy from the granite flows through her, and a simmering light highlights the symbol. Too late; Vhumut becomes aware and spews fire at her. The tear in the fabric snaps shut again, not preventing Freya from being scorched. Immediately, she falls forward and lets the ice-cold water take away most of the pain. Hands pull her back up while they try to reach higher ground.

Underwater, Snowflake calls the Cup to her, expecting it to shoot to her hand. But nothing happens. Instead, something is pulling at it.

Mab raises her hands down below; vine-like tentacles sprout from her fingers and weave their way up, encapsulating the Cup. A little yelp escapes her when she gets dragged along when the Cup tries to reach its guardian.

In the meantime, Lucy is sneaking up on Snowflake. She might be older and not as comfortable in the water as Snowflake and Mab, but she's spent much time preparing. Also, her desire and desperate urge to get her hands on one of the power objects is giving her the necessary extra boost. Lucy positions herself just behind Snowflake who's too occupied with the Cup.

The Cup starts to shine, reacting to all that energy swirling around it. The element of water is bursting at its seams. The water begins to funnel, the ice cracks, and the steam above swirls around. The three different forms of water emerge and intertwine, making it hard for anybody to see anything.

Snowflake is suspended in the swirl while the Cup does its utmost to reach her; as the guardian, the funnel doesn't affect her.

Lucy is not so lucky—she can feel her skin getting battered by the ice and steam. Ignoring the pain, she only vaguely registers that her body will pay for this at some point. She can hardly see anything and has no choice but to try to stay as close as she can to Snowflake.

Mab gives up trying to see and uses her senses instead. Retracting the vines and getting slowly pulled closer and closer to the Cup. The ice shards in the funnel cut her skin. But the Queen of Fairy has endured much worse than this; after all, this is only one of her forms.

Snowflake calls up a protection spell and readies an icicle to shoot at whoever tries for the Cup. As it's near impossible to see anything, she wants to ensure she's set for whatever comes for her. The Cup is near; she can feel its power warming her insides. When she peers through the mess, she can see that the glow of the Cup is coming closer and closer. Something is grabbing it. Not waiting for the Cup to truly reach her, she shoots an icicle blindly passed the Cup.

Mab senses something and screams when the icicle cuts a long gash into her arm before it hurtles further down. Her fairy blood drips from her arm into the ice funnel, forming dark red crystals that shimmer in the glow from the Cup. This only infuriates her. Unfortunately, both her hands are stuck to the vines, and she can't sling something back at Snowflake.

Lucy is biding her time. Let these two hash it out; it will make it easier for her to grab the Cup as long as she survives the onslaught of the water mix.

Snowflake fires another of her icicles; this time, Mab is better prepared, heightened by her awareness, and manages to dodge this bullet.

Soon, the two women are facing each other. Snowflake reaches for the Cup, trying to rip the vines away, while Mab retracts the vines knowing she will need her hands to grab the Cup. That's the moment Lucy chooses to make a push for it herself. Initially, she is shocked to recognize Mab; up till now, she presumed it was Mara. Her granddaughter had sold her soul, it turned out.

As soon as Snowflake's hand manages to get hold of the rim of the Cup, she gets filled up with the power of Water. However, at precisely the same time, Lucy gets hold of the edge as well and blasts her with a powerful force of sheer energy. Right when Mab also gets hold of the brim and does something similar with her fairy powers. The three enormous forces collide; for a brief moment, the world is suspended, frozen in place, followed by a loud bang! The Cup simply can't sustain itself in the face of so much pure force and it breaks into three pieces. Its power shatters and mixes between the three who hold a piece of the Cup. All three of them get hurdled backward by the power they created.

Lucy gets slung back onto the Astral plane, her body wholly battered and she barely breathing but clinging to her piece of the Cup. The watery power that came with her is all that sustains her life force.

Mab gets flung back into Fairy. Breathing hard, she too holds her piece of the Cup. This strange watery energy she's added to her mix of powers makes her laugh. Although her body took a beating, now she's back in Fairy, and it will be no problem for her to restore herself. Like Ceri, she lives in symbioses with Fairy. As the Queen, she has even more sources to draw from.

Snowflake finds herself back in the cave of the ancestors and clinging to her piece of the Cup. As the guardian, she has been shielded from most of the onslaught, but inside, she is shattered. Part of the watery power has been ripped out of her. Although some of it still flows through her veins, she is broken, like the Cup itself.

The cave is unrecognizable! Her ancestors are destroyed by Lucy, the pain and emptiness not yet registering. Part of her family is huddled together on the far end. Luna and Freya are between them. Snowflake lets out the most heartbreaking cry, echoing all around them.

The following day, Snowflake wakes up in her room. She has no idea how she got home and cleaned up. Desperation and grief are all there is for her right now. Her heart is broken, for as long as the power of the Cup is fragmented, there will be no hope for her. Bursting into tears again, she rolls up into a fetal position, curling up with the remains of the Cup.

Laakki whispers a little healing spell while gently caressing her hand along her daughter's back. She stays with her, feeling Snowflake's despair. They need to find the broken pieces if she wants her daughter to survive this. Laakki hoists herself up with a sigh, dims the lights, and leaves the room.

In the kitchen, the rest of the family is quietly having breakfast. They all look at the matriarch when she comes in. "No change." That is all she says as her voice breaks.

Luna gets up, still sore from her fight with the daemon. One of the family had dragged her to higher ground while she floated unconsciously in the water. The Berthelsens are excellent healers, and her chest feels much better. She envelops Laakki in a warm hug. This comfort of a stranger breaks Laakki, and for a short while, tears flow freely. Finally, she works herself free of the embrace. She takes Luna's face between her hands and looks her in the eye when she says, "We are family." This resonates through the house.

"We will do whatever we can to help you restore the Cup," Luna promises, only just healed from her last broken promise. The kitchen groans under the weight of that promise.

Freya nods to her sister in agreement. Still a little red from her ordeal, she too has healed. With all the devastating things that had happened, Freya is reluctant to say that she's well. Better than well! For the first time since she can remember, she's whole. Somehow, this trip, this fight, restored her being, reconnecting those missing dots. No longer worried about her lost memories; she doesn't need them. This is who she is, who she is meant to be.

After they returned to the Berthelsens home and healed everybody, the sisters finally had some alone time. Luna confessed that despite the wound, her powers were back.

They've updated their own family; there's not much they can do at this time. They are staying on high alert. No doubt the fragment of the Cup will boost Lucy and Mab's powers. Maybe, it is a blessing that the girls hold the Dagger and The Wand; their twin bond is a special connection, which might be the additional advantage they need if they hope to heal the Cup.

Lucy is in agonizing pain in her body in her hotel room. Nobody around to heal her, she lays there holding onto her piece of the Cup. Her body is mangled and bloody, parts are burned, and other parts have frostbite. She will need to drink and eat soon if she doesn't want to die like this. None of it matters; the power of the Cup, even though shattered, gives her a familiar warm feeling.

BETWEEN SPACE AND TIME

The Maiden is nowhere to be seen while the Crone and Mother are back at their daily chores of deciding fate. "We didn't see this coming," the Crone states while she snaps a vine.

"I'm glad you gave Luna her full powers back. What a mess!" is all Mother says.

"She immediately made a new promise. I wonder if she did learn her lesson."

"It was the right thing to do," Mother still defends her.

This makes the Crone smile. No doubt, she needled her on purpose. "This is far from over."

"I must admit you even got me interested in this mess," Mother reluctantly admits.

"Told you so!"

FAIRY

Diane is restlessly shifting back and forth opposite Ceri in her study in Fairy. "So, this is it?" Doubt is audible in her voice.

Fin puts an arm on his aunt's shoulder, "It's better to know," he reassures her.

It's just the three of them—to keep this as private as possible; too many are already aware of the problem.

"That's easy for you to say," Diane snaps, unlike herself, but instantly regretting her short fuse. Her nephew had gone out of his way to help her. "Sorry. I know," she says and gets up. "How does this work?"

Ceri picks up the globe from her desk. "I open it for you, and the memory will play itself in the room. We will be able to see, hear, and even smell it. We haven't watched it yet; we wanted you to be the first to see it."

"You are staying, right?!" Diane sounds alarmed.

"We both are," Ceri says. Fin reassures her, "We are here for you."

"Okay." A firm nod of her head is hiding the turmoil she feels inside.

Ceri touches the globe, and it springs to life.

Diane catches her breath.

Tall trees waver in the wind, their leaves are big, birds are singing, and the sun barely filters through. The smell is intoxicating; its moist, sweet scent has something tropical. This must be an ancient forest; a small woman is making her way toward a fairy. Her face looks vaguely familiar. Maybe this is a fairy forest. The striking fairy has a regal posture, the forest bending to his will. The trees almost lean to the woman, as if welcoming her.

"Eztli, I've missed you," his baritone voice resonates through the forest. He reaches for her hand, which holds a ring much like the one Ceri wears, though a touch different. "Why don't you stay with me? I want you; you want me."

Gently, they kiss, "I love you," she whispers against his lips. That's when something changes behind her eyes—she stiffens. The fairy lets out a curse, "Go away, Crone; she's mine."

Eztli, now possessed by the Crone, throws her head back and laughs. "I want her! You can't have her."

"What can I offer to you to set her free?" the fairy tries to bargain.

"Nothing you have is as delicious as being one with this woman," the Crone crows.

"I love her," he proclaims; for a moment, the Crone falters before laughing in his face again.

"Good—loving each other is the first step, but not enough to get rid of me."

"What else is there than love?" he asks. Fairies are not known for giving up a bargain. "There must be something."

The Crone sizes him up, not sure to tell him, but overconfidently, she goes on, "Love is the first step, but to be free of any possession, me or others, your souls much touch. A rare gift from the Universe. As you have known each other for a long time, I guess that hadn't happened yet, so you're out of luck." She turns away from him.

The fairy is not ready to give up; he grabs her arm, turns her to him, and says, "Eztli, come back to me!" He kisses her, truly kisses her. He throws all his passion, love, and longing for her into that kiss. It startles the Crone, giving an opening to Eztli to answer his kiss. Together, they explode, standing at the abyss and looking at each other's souls. They see each other's essence. The good and the bad, and still love each other. Neither is aware of time; the Crone is gone when they hit their bodies. "Oberon," Eztli gasps. That one word holds everything.

The memory folding back into the globe stunned everybody in the room.

Diane bursts into tears, "I'm doomed." While she's sobbing uncontrollably, Fin can barely keep her upright.

"My soul has already touched another, and it didn't work!"

Ceri rushes to her sister, "Diane, Alice might have left you for the moment, but if she's the one—"

"It's not her!" wails Diane.

Ceri and Fin exchange confused glances when the truth hits them at last.

"You mean—you mean your soul touched with Lucy's son?" Ceri whispers.

Diane doesn't need to answer.

"Shit," Fin sums it up. His mind is racing; this can't be it. Quickly flipping through the memory again, something dawns on him. "Aunt Diane—" he says and turns her toward him. "The love potion, you didn't make a conscious choice to love him. But now you can."

"But I don't love him," she whispers.

"There's hope," he insists.

"There is no hope," says Diane, sounding frighteningly fragile.

"Aunt Diane. Look at me!"

Very slowly, her tears-streaking face looks up. "There's always hope. At least we know who has touched your soul. Imagine you still need to find that person. That would be impossible. You must go and see him. Find out how you truly feel about each other."

"I can't," she says, passing out in his arms.

"Thank you for reading. If you enjoyed this book, please consider leaving an honest review on your favorite store." —Marieke.

LIST OF CHARACTERS:

Agnes Madigan: The second Madigan to guard the Wand of Wisdom

Alana Jansson: The guardian of the Dagger of Consciousness

Alexandra Birdwing: A fairy of the House of Aelfdene, Keeper of the Sky

Alice: Diane Madigan's wife

Alvina: Servant of the House of Finvarra

Ann Neumann: The first guardian of the Pentacle of Growth

Aputsiaq "Snowflake" Berthelsen: Guardian of the Cup of Plenty. Her name means Snowflake

Bert: Ceri Madigan's husband

Berthelsen: Former Giordano and the second husband of the first guardian of the Cup and the name of one of four families that guard an elemental power object; they protect the Cup of Plenty

Bouncer: Bridget's black Labrador

Brian Madigan: Freya and Jason's oldest son

Bridget Madigan: Maeve's twin sister; daughter of Luna and Steve

Cal Lockwood: Lucy's grandson; son of Set and Helen

Cephalop: An octopus fairy

Cephina: An octopus fairy; Cephalop's sister

Ceri(dwen) Madigan: Oldest daughter of Tara Madigan and Felaern Finvarra

Colel: Ancient ancestor of the Madigan Family. Her name means "Mother of Bees" in Mayan

Diane Madigan: Tara and Seamus' third child

Dylan Madigan: Freya and Jason's youngest son

Emily: Ceri and Bert's daughter

Eztli: Ancient ancestor of the Madigan Family. Her name means 'Blood' in Mayan

Felaern Finvarra: A fairy, the Keeper of the Land of Fairy; Ceri's father

Ferrymaster: A fairy that guards the realm of Fairy; he will let you pass in exchange for a memory

Fin Madigan: Luna and Steve's son

Freya Madigan: Tara and Seamus' oldest daughter

Giordano Family: One of four families that guard an elemental power object; they protect the Cup of Plenty

Gwen Jansson: Alana's sister

Jansson Family: One of four families that guard an elemental power object; they protect the Dagger of Consciousness

Jason: Freya Madigan's husband

Jax: Steve and Lilian's son

Jôrse: Aputsiaq's "Snowflake" brother

Kiki: Bridget's Chihuahua

Laakki: Mother of "Snowflake" Aputsiaq and former guardian of the Cup of Plenty

Liam: Ceri and Bert's son

Lilian Neumann: Steve's new wife

Lisa: Ron and Selma's daughter

Lucy Lockwood: Tara Madigan's twin; banned from the family and forced to take another name

Luna Madigan: Tara and Seamus' second child; mother of Bridget, Maeve, and Fin

Mab: The Queen of Fairy

Madigan Family: One of four families that guard an elemental power object; they protect the Wand of Wisdom

Maeron: A fairy, one of Felaern's oldest friends

Maeve Madigan: Bridget's twin; daughter of Luna and Steve

Mara Lockwood: Lucy's granddaughter; daughter of Set and a Voodoo priestess from New Orleans and Cal's half-sister

Mary Madigan: The first Madigan to guard the Wand of Wisdom

Megan Madigan: The fourth Madigan to guard the Wand of Wisdom

Mike: Ron and Selma's son

Molly Madigan: The third Madigan to guard the Wand of Wisdom

Moon: Bridget's Rottweiler

Neumann Family: One of four families that guard an elemental power object; they protect the Pentacle of Growth

Obelow: A fairy, the Keeper of Water

O'Seachnasaigh: The family name of the four sisters who originally took the elemental objects and pledged to never use them

Petal: A fairy and loyal servant of Mab

Rhiannon Firefly Madigan of the house of Finvarra: Daughter of Ceri, and a fairy

Roisin Giordano/Berthelsen: The first guardian of the Cup of Plenty

Ron Madigan: Tara and Seamus' only son and fourth child. His full name is Oberon. He runs the family business Under the Witches Hat

Salik Berthelsen: Son of Aputsiaq, the guardian of the Cup of Plenty. His name means "one who follows the spiritual path"

Sarah Madigan: Tara and Lucy's mother, the fifth Madigan to guard the Wand of Wisdom

Seamus: Tara's husband, a powerful witch and artist; the creator of the Magical Tarot Deck

Sedna: The Goddess of the Sea and marine animals, also known as Sassuma Arnaa, Arnakuagsak, Arnaqquassaaq, and other names

Selma: Ron Madigan's wife

Set Lockwood: Lucy's son, her only child

Sparkle: Ceri's fairy guide

Steve: Luna Madigan's ex-husband

Sunbeam: A fairy, the Keeper of the Light

Tara Madigan: The matriarch of the Madigan family and Lucy's twin

Tom Walsh: Bridget's police partner

Vhumut: Fire Demon, and Set's father

Wes: Bridget's boyfriend and an artist

'Whiskey' Dan: A collector of manuscripts in New Orleans with an extensive library

Wisteria: A fairy, the daughter of Aloé, Faelern's sister

GLOSSARY:

Astral Plane: A parallel dimension that witches can visit. It has similarities with earth but is inhabited by dangerous creatures. Only your spirit travels there, but any injuries you receive while there are reflected on your body on earth

Book of Shadows: A witch's book full of spells and occult wisdom, passed down in the family. Constantly updated with new knowledge, it also chronicles the family's history

Cup of Plenty: One of the four elemental power objects denoting the element of Water

Dagger of Consciousness: One of the four elemental power objects denoting the element of Air

Elements: Air, Fire, Water, and Earth

Fairy: A magical world where fairies and other creatures live. You can enter the Fairy world through portals

Fates: Maiden, Mother, and Crone—three mythological goddesses who decide the destinies of humans

Fountain in ~ nacinniúna: Fountain in the Lap of the Gods

Magical Tarot Deck: A tarot deck of 22 major arcana cards that depict the three generations of the Madigan Family: grandparents; children and spouses; and grandchildren. When used, the images on the cards come to life, and the person comes out of the card. That person will disappear from their current life until the querent's question is answered

Pentacle of Growth: One of the four elemental power objects denoting the element of Earth

Portal: A doorway into another world

Querent: Term for a person asking a question during a tarot reading

Ti'tsa-pa: Native American name for the Great Salt Lake; it means 'Bad Water'

Tsé Bit'a í: Navajo territory in New Mexico; the American name is 'Winged Rock'

Under the Witches Hat: The Madigan family business. It's a cocktail bar and witch store

Wand of Wisdom: One of the four elemental power objects denoting the element of Fire

AUTHOR

Marieke Lexmond reads tarot cards, loves food, photography, and travel. She has three sassy little dogs that she likes to take everywhere and even have their own Instagram account @urbandogsquad. Her background in filmmaking enabled her to travel and live around the globe. Storytelling is in her blood, from saving her allowance from a very young age to buy books to her master's degree from the Dutch Film Academy. Fantasy and science fiction are her favorite genres. She prefers to write fun and mystical stories. Her attraction to nature and places with a magical history brought her to New Orleans and the West Coast of Ireland. As a pagan, she felt an instant connection to the land; it feeds her imagination and has become the inspiration for the Madigan Chronicles.

ILLUSTRATOR

Nicole Ruijgrok has been drawing ever since she could hold a pencil. Her inquisitive mind likes to explore any kind of creative outlet. After her communication and multimedia design study, she took over her father's body shop, not one for the conventional routes.

She loves art, music, reading, museums, and motorcycle riding. There are just not enough hours in a day! Her current favorite pastime is designing jewelry. She has a goldsmith degree from the only school in the Netherlands where you can get such a degree, in the historic "silver" town of Schoonhoven.

Nicole and Marieke have been besties since they were six years old. Growing up, you would rarely see one without the other. They always made-up fantasy worlds and built fairytale castles of hay on the Lexmond family farm.

Even though they have pursued many different things in life, they've always remained close. The Madigan Chronicles was the perfect project to collaborate on!